the hours of you

ALSO BY FIONA COLLINS

Spring, Summer, Autumn, Us
Summer in the City
You, Me and the Movies
The Sister Swap
Four Bridesmaids and a White Wedding
Cloudy with a Chance of Love
A Year of Being Single

the
hours
of
you

FIONA COLLINS

LAKE UNION
PUBLISHING

Text copyright © 2024 by Fiona Collins
All rights reserved.

Published by Lake Union Publishing, Seattle

www.apub.com

Amazon, the Amazon logo, and Lake Union Publishing are trademarks of Amazon.com, Inc., or its affiliates.

ISBN-13: 9781662507267
eISBN: 9781662507243

Cover design by Emma Rogers
Cover image: © EgudinKa © Pranch © Javvani © fstop Images
© GreenBelka © Mamont / Shutterstock

Printed in the United States of America

the
hours
of
you

Prologue

When they were in love, it seemed the sun shone on them every day. When they were in love, when day became night, dark skies blanketed them in a velvet warmth and drew them closer together. Every hour they knew was succulent and miraculous. Every moment they shared was a kind of paradise.

Sometimes she caught him looking at her, entwined in sloping grass on a seasidey summer's day, or in the pearly milk of a winter's morning as they lay plaited and half-awake in bed. She drank in the trace of his lopsided smile and his green eyes steady and true and full of love for her – for her! – and almost believed it could be forever, this love. That they would always be this way, lying in each other's arms and summoning their combined future to be both certain and endless.

Maggie and Ed. Ed and Maggie. How could it be any other way? When they were young and in love it appeared they had a lifetime, but they were wrong. Lifetimes were long enough roads to see them stumble, or lose their way, or take each other far from reach. They were roads that led where she least expected: a wintry pier on a blustery December afternoon where an icy wind, whipped from a grey sea, did nothing to dry her bitter tears.

That day, she had cried until she felt her heart was all wrung out, like a useless rag. She had just lost him forever and he had not even said goodbye – that word was hers – and she knew she would not see him again. There was no road that might lead her back to him now. No rising and falling sea that would carry her his way again.

He was lost, and so was she.

Chapter One

The sun was too bright, the sea was too blue, but the hand of the young man waiting to help Maggie Martin step off the rocking wooden fishing boat into the azure shallows, bathwater warm on her calves, was reassuringly steady.

'Welcome to Mémoire,' the young man said. 'I will be escorting you to your accommodation. I am Amine.'

'Thank you, Amine,' Maggie said. She didn't expect Amine welcomed many lone female travellers – aged sixty-one, in shorts and a *Hotel California* vest top, with a camera slung around their neck and a boat boy's Man United bucket hat – to Mémoire Island. She clung on to Amine's hand like she never wanted to let it go.

'Where is your luggage?' he asked her.

'Here!' called out Salou from the boat, the mischievous barefoot boy who had pelted her with unanswerable questions about Premiership football all the way from Le Digue and had laughingly plonked his hat on her head as the boat first loped into the miraculously clear waters of the port there.

'Don't burn your head, my lady!' he had exclaimed before coiling up the mooring rope, and she had laughed too, but she was more worried about getting her fingers burnt here on the island.

Salou reached over the idling and silent driver at the boat's stern, hooked up her orange rucksack by his thumb – the rucksack that made her feel like an overgrown, over-aged backpacker, but had been a practical choice – and swung it to Amine.

'Travelling light,' Amine commented with a smile, as he caught it.

'Hardly,' muttered Maggie. She felt the baggage of her past permanently slacking off her like a deflated lifebelt.

'See you tomorrow, my lady!' Salou shouted. Maggie took off his hat and threw it back to him, squinting now behind the sunglasses she had bought at London City airport. They were not dark enough for the dazzling butter-yellow sun glancing off the turquoise Indian Ocean. They didn't provide enough protection. She wanted to get back on the boat. Then the other boat. The ferry to Praslin. The smaller aeroplane. The big aeroplane. She wanted to be back in London, in her neat little flat with its heavy furniture, its worn brown leather sofa with the folded green blanket at one end, her record collection and her books; the rain drumming on the dirty window that looked blankly down on the street below.

Instead, still holding Amine's hand, Maggie scooped through the water to the shore, her espadrilles in her hand and the undulating sand cool and silky beneath her toes.

'Bungalow Marguerite is over there,' said Amine, as they emerged from the gentle surf and her toes became buried now in the dry sand, almost pearlescent pink, of a never-ending beach. 'See?' Amine released his hand from hers and pointed along the verdant slip of palm trees and vegetation flanking the beach. She could just make out, at the furthest point, a jutting elbow lipped by golden sand and scattered with pale cottages.

'Wonderful,' she said, repeating what Simone, her editor at *Supernova* magazine, had said after uncharacteristically booking Maggie's accommodation herself, so intrigued had her friend been by the tiny island of Mémoire.

'Quaintly beautiful, my dear, if a little basic,' Simone had added as she handed Maggie a printout with a photo of a crumbling yellow cube of a bungalow, topped with a pitched thatched roof and fronted by a veranda hitched together by bamboo canes. 'And from what I read online, you'll probably be the only tourist, apart from *you know who*. Whoever would have thought,' the younger woman had concluded, shaking her silky black bob prettily at Maggie before gliding back to her office, 'you'd wind up on a remote desert island like Mémoire for your last ever job?'

An island like Mémoire . . . It certainly was remote. It had taken Maggie twenty hours to get here. And it was definitely beautiful. Maggie was in a picture postcard scene: the sea, the sand, the palm trees, the sun . . . and the heat was miraculous to her for January, when in London she'd be shivering her socks off. But her last Where Are They Now? profile for *Supernova* was going to be memorable for all sorts of reasons, and the remote and beautiful setting would be the least of them.

Amine set off up the beach, Maggie's limp rucksack slung over his shoulder. Maggie followed, squinting. The sand was deep and scalding hot. She wanted to put her espadrilles back on, but Amine was striding ahead. He and the rucksack disappeared into the pretty mesh of palm trees and tropical foliage, and she had to trot inelegantly to catch up with him on the canopied scrubby path. It wound between the scaly trunks of palm trees and the smoothly viscous tangle of roots.

'Mind yourself, Miss Marty,' said Amine, as, espadrilles back on, she navigated a low-hanging branch camouflaged by palm leaves the size of small cars.

It was too late for that, she thought. She was already here. She wanted to get on and off Mémoire as quickly as possible. She wanted to get what she had come for and run.

They walked. They avoided low-hanging branches. Finally, the dense grove of giant green leaves and dappled, sandy earth opened out and the path morphed into something more pedestrian – and recently and resolutely brushed. There was a rusty sprinkler keeping idle and near-silent time on a spiky teardrop of grass. Five rough-hewn bungalows nestled in a cluster. On the veranda of one leant an old bicycle. In the doorway of another, a small girl was poised on one foot, like a crane, in a faded red sundress.

'These homes belong to islanders,' said Amine, 'but Pa Zayan is happy to move out of his to accommodate the occasional visitor . . .' He led her past the first two bungalows and to the third, whose veranda looked like it had just been doused with water.

'Welcome,' he said, as he stepped on to the veranda and opened the door for her. 'I hope you like Bungalow Marguerite.'

'Oh, it's lovely,' Maggie exclaimed, and she immediately felt bad for Pa Zayan, who she hoped had temporarily moved in with a kindly daughter not too far away. The bungalow was cute. There was a small bed with pale blue bedding, tepee-d by a gauzy mosquito net. A bamboo bedside table with an upside-down book on the top (*fiction?* she wondered. She didn't read fiction any more. She'd devoured slim volumes of Fran Leibowitz and Joan Didion essays on the plane). A table and two wooden chairs tucked into each other on a swept terracotta floor. And to the rear was a white bathroom, simply tiled.

'Only cold water,' said Amine apologetically, showing it to her. 'But it's very warm on the island so . . .'

'Cold water is fine,' said Maggie.

Amine placed her rucksack carefully in the corner of the room. She could imagine the letter at the bottom, nestling under her make-up bag whose edge was bulging against the canvas. She was strangely reminded of being pregnant with Eloise: a foot jutting from under a rib, an elbow attempting to stretch out of what had once been her waist. That letter at the bottom of her rucksack was a message in a bottle she had been asked to deliver – if the hours and the man allowed.

'Thank you, Amine,' Maggie said. Amine looked surprised and delighted to be tipped. As he turned to leave, she asked him, 'Do you happen to know where I might find a man called Ed Cavanagh on the island? At this hour?' she added, amused at sounding like a stilted Jane Austen character in an Eagles vest top.

'*Mr Ed?* Sure.' Amine grinned. 'He'll be down on the beach, west of where your boat came in,' he said.

'West, as in, to the right?' she clarified. *Mr Ed?*

'To the right, yes. He'll be there with his boat. Just past the little jetty. Blue boat, yellow mast.'

'He has a *boat?*'

'Yes. Goes out in it every morning.' Amine nodded his head. 'Enjoy your stay, Miss Marty.'

She still didn't bother to correct him. 'Thank you, Amine.'

Once Amine had gone, Maggie showered in cold water, unrolled a raspberry batik maxi dress and retrieved flat leather flip flops from her rucksack, then made herself up to look decent but not as though she had made a great effort. She headed out of the bungalow, walked back through the shaded grove and down to the beach, where the sun was low in the sky but still fiercely hot.

Setting off to the right, she slipped off her flipflops to walk barefoot in the cooler-now sand. Soft waves were breaking lacka-daisically on the shore. A gull, swooping on the horizon, took off towards the sun, and lone clouds drifted with no particular place to be. She passed a small jetty, two young boys at the end, fishing lines and dangling bare legs in the water. There was a boat, in the distance, bobbing on the turquoise water. It looked like a blue boat with a yellow mast.

Maggie stood and watched it for a while, her heart an anxious prisoner behind her ribs, her nerves a jailor's jangle of keys. Finally, she saw him, a figure who came to stand at the mast. *Was* it him? Her missing person? She raised an arm, wondering if he could even spot this stick figure on the beach, waving hello.

They were so far apart, she thought. She was sixty-one, worn around the edges, voluntarily detached from life. A woman who needed to work on both her posture and her regrets. He was *Ed Cavanagh*, and likely to turn the boat around and sail away once he saw her.

They had known each other for so long, but now didn't know each other at all. They had first met a stone's throw from another coastline, one that couldn't be more different, where the sea was a grey-green sludge flanked by a pebble beach and a host of glaring seaside attractions, and where nothing much ever happened – not to her, anyway – until the hot August afternoon when she finally spoke to Edward Neville Craddock.

Chapter Two

5 P.M., 11 AUGUST 1971

Maggie sat on the wall. It was an afternoon very much like every August afternoon in the school holidays on Charlotte Road. She was bored, she was hot. She was idle, something her mother didn't like, but what was there to do? She was fed up of plomping on the furry sofa reading *Nancy Drew* mysteries, or lying on the itchy carpet, chin on her hands, watching *The Adventures of Robinson Crusoe*, wondering why the hypnotic music on the opening credits always made her want to cry. She had reluctantly made corn dollies and attempted botched macrame. She had lain in the garden on a towel, resisting a tan (*thanks, Irish ancestry!*) and overhearing the neighbours mowing their lawns or shouting from parallel strips of garden through open windows to wives or husbands or kids inside terraced houses.

Maggie had come out to the wall for some peace, but it wasn't totally serene out here; there was the odd car beetling or whizzing up the road, the occasional slammed front door. The woman in the house four doors up with the geraniums in the windows, who marched down the street with her handbag every morning on her way to the shops, aggressively twitched the lilac net curtains of her closed bay window. Maybe she didn't like fourteen-year-old girls sitting on walls, cluttering up the street.

Still, it was better than being inside. Mum was cooking the tea – liver and bacon – and wheeling herself around the kitchen between cupboard and fridge and oven in a sleeveless denim dress and a bit of a hot huff. Dad would be home soon from the factory. Coming in the back way and throwing his lunchbox on the kitchen table in great joy, then bending down for a kiss with Mum and a wink from under his Beatles haircut before thundering upstairs, desperate to strip off his factory overalls. Her brother Stevie would be lolling on his bed with his top off, above the carpet of Rizla tins and coagulated cereal bowls, being luxuriantly on the dole. Doling out sarcastic comments, if he ever came downstairs. Maggie was at the eye-rolling stage of the holidays with all of them. She missed Janey. Janey was her best friend, but she had betrayed her by going on holiday with her cousins to Pleasurewood Hills in Great Yarmouth. She was probably traitorously screaming her head off on a rollercoaster at this very moment.

Maggie swung her legs, liking how her heels, in red leather sandals, struck the wall and dislodged a shrapnel of brick dust each time. She liked the warm, muggy air and the sounds of the street in summer. She liked to sit here and watch the people of Charlotte Road and wonder where they were going, or where they'd been. She would strike up conversations with old people on their way back from the shops. She would stare across to the windows opposite and try to see what people were doing inside.

She heard voices and turned her head, dipping it quickly at the sight of them. Of *him*. Four older boys were walking down the street. Seventeen-year-olds. Almost adults. There was swagger. There was laughter. There was already a discernible symphony of *Brut 33*. The boys were wearing flares, and t-shirts that were a little too tight, with rainbows or stripes on. The lowering sun was behind them like a golden halo. They could have been a young rock band on an album cover. Indeed, one of them had a radio up on his shoulder crackling out T-Rex, and they were unselfconsciously walking in time to it. Ed Craddock was in the middle. He was laughing the loudest and, as she dared raise her head to look at him, she saw he had a stick in his hand – picked up from who knew where – that he was trailing along the pavement, over the bumps and cracks. She hadn't spotted him for a while. He was the best-looking boy she'd ever seen. She liked his legs in those flares. And the rainbow on his t-shirt. And the way his dark brown dishevelled curls bounced as he walked to 'Get It On'.

They were getting closer. The stick was now trailing past Geranium Woman's house, tapping over the bricks of her low front wall, one by one. They would ignore Maggie, these boys, because she was fourteen and ginger – her hair like Crystal Tipps – and they were handsome and cocky and on their way to the pub. Maggie only knew Ed Craddock's name because he had been getting in the back of a car once at his end of the street, while she had been getting into a car with Mum and Dad at her end. Mum had remarked that the Craddocks looked smart, and that 'Edward was growing up into a nice young man'. Maggie had wondered where they were going and if it was to Cliffs Pavilion to see the panto, like they were. Maggie hadn't seen him there, despite looking for him. But she *had* seen him walk down this road, this summer, with his mates, on Wednesday half-day closing, like today.

'Oh hell, sorry.' Ed Craddock's stick had scraped Maggie's left leg. He hadn't been looking. 'Are you alright?'

'Yeah,' she said. 'It's okay.'

'You've got a scratch,' he said. He had stopped. His mates had carried on. One turned back with a hop and shouted to him.

'Come on, Ed! The *pub*!'

'Hold on a minute,' Ed called out. 'Here,' he said to Maggie, and he pulled a folded hanky from his back pocket. 'My mum always sends me out with one,' he added with a lopsided grin. 'And I let her,' he laughed, 'you know, easy life and all that. Give it a wipe.'

Maggie looked down at her leg. She had a thin zip of a graze, tiny beads of blood studding the inch of it. She took the hanky.

'Thanks,' she said. She didn't wipe her leg. She was staring at Ed's face. She liked how his curls fell into his eyes; she imagined if she tugged on one it would spring right back. *Her* curls weren't shiny like his; they were frizzy. She had pale blue eyes with even paler lashes; his were the colour of Christmas trees and fringed with sweeps of sooty pine needles. He had a nice mouth, too, his bottom lip fuller than the top. Above it there was the shadowy trace of a moustache. Maggie blushed. She'd never felt more like a little kid. But she looked at Ed's eyes and considered what she could see there.

She knew something else about Ed Craddock, apart from his name and how his curls fell into his eyes. She knew that on Valentine's night, earlier this year, his dad had walked out of the house at the other end of Charlotte Road and not come back.

'Are you going to wipe it?' Ed asked. A bead of blood hesitated at the bottom of the graze on Maggie's leg and slid slowly down her milky shin. Maggie nudged it with a corner of the hanky and watched as red encroached on white. Ed was already walking away. He trotted to catch up with his friends. She watched without blinking as they rounded the corner and disappeared.

Talk was rife about Neville Craddock, mainly of an affair. Word on the street – *their* street – was that he had 'buggered off', and speculation about a 'fancy piece' was bandied around with the glee of people totally unaffected by him going missing. But there was no evidence of this. Neville Craddock had not popped up anywhere else in a new life. He had not been spotted around Southend, hanging off some *fancy piece*'s arm. He had simply disappeared.

Maggie stared at the corner of the street where Ed Craddock had just been but now was not. She would have to carry the image of his face in her head until she saw him again. Well, that was easy. She had committed to memory every inch of it. And she *would* see him again, maybe next Wednesday, or maybe at the weekend, from her wall. And she would definitely spend the rest of the summer hoping he would speak to her again because, although she'd decided she was never going to fall in love, if she did, it would be with someone exactly like Ed Craddock.

Chapter Three

Maggie watched and waited as Ed's blue boat with the yellow mast slowly made its way towards her, bowing and dipping on the clear, calm sea. Ed was still standing at the mast, and, as the boat ebbed closer, he came slowly into focus.

The first thing Maggie noticed was that his shorts were the exact same colour as the boat – a cornflower blue – low on his hips, as though they were a little too big for him. The second, his sixty-four-year-old curls, last seen by her on *The Graham Norton Show* in October, when he had been sparky and acerbic and funny, with no indication – none at all – that he was going to flee from Hollywood a week later. They were pure silver and a little wild in the sea breeze. Lastly, she realised Ed looked *athletic* in his shorts and red t-shirt, with visible muscles in his tanned arms and legs.

He'll be able to see me now, Maggie thought, as the boat propelled closer still, but his expression, as he held on to the mast with a brown arm, could not be determined.

'Hello?' Ed called out to her, and she was as planted here on the sand as he was on his boat, swooshing towards her, and there was no escaping it now that she had come to find him. There was no running away, for her, to the quiet and comfort of her single life in London – the green blanket, the rain on the window, the wry essay anthologies on the coffee table. She had found him.

Maggie took a hesitant step forward. Ed's boat was rocking hypnotically now as it approached the shallows. The horizon suddenly seemed to be unfixed, too. Fragments of every hour she had ever spent with Ed broke on to her memory like indistinct waves on the shore and she was no longer planted. The reason she was here – why she had travelled twenty hours, why she was on this beach, trying to make out the contours of his face and the exact shade of green of his eyes, after all this time – was shifting beneath her feet. The sand beneath her toes could no longer be relied on, like every decision she had ever made, every instinct she had ever had; everything that had brought her to this day.

Maggie Martin was on Mémoire to interview Ed Cavanagh, escaped Hollywood actor and stalwart of the silver and the small screen. Ed Cavanagh, who she had met as a teenager. Ed Cavanagh, who had broken her heart, and she his. She had twenty-four hours in which to interview him. Salou and the boat would be back at 5 p.m. tomorrow. Twenty-four hours was as much as she could bear.

'*Maggie?*' Ed called.

She raised a hand in assent and, as the boat lazed towards her, the engine at its stern put-putting, slow waves slapping at its edges, she noticed things. A transistor radio inside the boat at the stern. Wooden slats bleached white by the sun. A small rolled-up towel. A grey round tin with a lid – bait? A plastic water flask. A pole. A shallow pail full of silver-grey fishes with curling tails flanking and overlapping each other. And now Ed was switching off the engine and hopping off the boat into the water, and he was pushing the boat on to the sand, wedging it still with a heave and a short grunt, and he was walking towards her, pushing his curly hair back with his hand and letting it shake down again, coarse and silver.

'What are you doing here?' he asked her. For an actor, his voice was devoid of emotion. She couldn't tell if he was surprised, accusatory, angry or completely unaffected. His face didn't provide any answers either, so, terrified, she looked down at his legs and the rivulets of sea water running down them from the bottom of his shorts.

'That's not a very nice greeting,' she said to his left leg, flippant to the point of shaking to death. 'I wasn't expecting a slow-mo movie run and then a loving embrace or anything, but that seems somewhat . . . lacking.'

'I'm all out of slow-mo runs.'

She dared glance back up at him. There was a halo of sunlight over his right shoulder, backlighting his curls. There were his eyes, so known to her, Christmas-tree green. Eyes that had last left her face fifteen years ago, at the end of a breezy pier under dove skies and in a howling wind.

'You found me then.' It was so strange, hearing his voice again after so long. His eyes were narrowed at her.

'Oh,' she replied. 'Your boat. I think it's drifting back to sea.'

'Fuck,' said Ed, and he loped towards it and shunted the boat further up the sand until it was held fast. 'That should do it,' he said brusquely. He grabbed the shallow pail of curly fish and the pole lying in the bottom of the boat and started busying himself with taking each fish, one by one, and hanging them from the pole, mouths gaped on to waiting hooks. He planted the pole in the sand like Neil Armstrong setting his flag on the moon. He gathered in the small net slopping in the water at the back of the boat, concertinaing it under his arm. Now, he was folding the sail, which looked like it had been patched together from potato sacks.

He threw the folded sail on to the sand, then unscrewed the mast and dropped it down next to it. 'You can help me carry that,' he said.

'Okay.'

Ed heaved the pole with the fish on it over one shoulder, hoicked the sail up under his other arm and picked up the front end of the mast.

'Take the other end,' he said. 'And fetch the bait tin,' he added, nodding down to the silver cannister.

'You've grown very bossy in your old age,' she commented. 'I'm not sure being a fisherman suits you.'

A smile hesitated at the corner of his mouth but then disappeared.

'I'm doing my bit,' he said, 'providing fish suppers for the folks at Olly's Bar.'

She smiled internally at 'folks'. One of Ed's best-loved characters, Tim O'Shea the astronaut's son, from *Echo Beach* and then *Echo Drive,* had said 'folks' a lot. 'Well, good for you. I'm sure "Olly" is very grateful.'

He shook his head at her, stared a little too long, those green eyes glinting at her in the sun. She looked away.

'Come on then,' he said. 'We'll drop the gear at my shack and then take the fish to Olly's.'

Maggie picked up the other end of the mast. It wasn't too heavy. She bent down to retrieve the tin. Ed started walking, heading left, with her behind at the end of the mast. The sea, to their right, lapped at the shore. The sun beamed down, pinkish and gold. A sea bird swooped overhead. Ed didn't turn his head as he spoke.

'Why are you here?' he asked, and his voice was so quiet, or so caught in the tropical breeze lulling off the sea, maybe, that she almost asked him to repeat what he'd said.

She swallowed. 'I've been sent by my magazine to do an interview with you.'

'Ah, *Supernova,* I presume,' said the back of Ed's head. His feet carried on walking. The pole continued to bounce on his shoulder.

There was a long pause before he spoke again. 'An interview about why I'm here?'

'Yes.'

'Well, there's no story there, I'm afraid,' he said, his voice louder now. 'I just needed a break, that's all. I was tired. Sorry to disappoint. You may as well just turn around and go back. Well, not *right* now. You can help me drop this stuff off first.'

'Oh,' said Maggie. 'Well, I can't do that. Go back. There's no boat for me until tomorrow afternoon. That's when I'm being picked up.'

'*I* have a boat,' said Ed.

She didn't answer. She fixed her eyes on his feet. The soft sand kicking up from his tanned heels.

'This way,' he said, turning her and the mast in the direction of the bank of palm trees edging the beach. 'My shack's up here.'

Chapter Four

6 P.M., 26 AUGUST 1971

Ed Craddock was walking along Charlotte Road on his own. There was no entourage. No album cover. He had his hands in his pockets and a t-shirt with a sun on it and he stopped when he got to Maggie, sitting on the wall. It was two weeks after he had scraped her with his stick and given her the hanky, and today she had watched him from the moment he'd left his front gate.

'Your mum works on the pier, doesn't she?' Ed said.

'Yes,' Maggie replied. She had been sitting out here for about an hour. 'How do you know that?'

'My mate told me. He knows your dad, from the working men's club.'

'Oh, right.' *Which mate?* she wondered. Maggie was aware she was squinting at him. The sun was still bright, despite the hour, and it was hot, too. She was wearing her jeans shorts with the *Partridge Family* badge on the back pocket, and a white t-shirt with red trim at the collar and the sleeves. Thank goodness she had a bra now that Mum had agreed to buy her one. She hoped Ed noticed the strap that had slipped an inch down her shoulder.

'Someone said they saw my dad down that way.' He frowned, staring at the pavement and dabbing the toe of his trainer against a lower brick in the wall. 'The night he went missing. Did you hear about that? My dad?' He looked up at her, and his eyes were earnest and clear, with a little sorrow behind them, and she nearly fell off her perch.

'Yeah,' Maggie said. 'I think everyone knows about it. Sorry,' she added, as she felt she should. She had pondered quite a lot on what people had said about Neville Craddock, Ed's dad. How he could just disappear like that. The theories. He could be anywhere, she thought.

'Some woman from the council,' continued Ed. 'Who was down at the pier, coming out of Top Deck bowling. She said she'd been to your mum's kiosk and bought some chips. I was wondering if you could ask her if she'd seen anything.'

'Won't the police do that?' asked Maggie.

'The police aren't doing anything now,' Ed said. 'But still,' he added. 'I wonder if she saw anything. Your mum. Did she ever used to see him? He used to go out walking in the evenings a lot, down to the pier. Did she ever see him there?'

'She doesn't work in the evenings. She finishes at six.'

'Oh.' He looked a bit cross.

'But I can ask her when I go in,' said Maggie, desperate to be helpful. 'Just in case.' He looked at her with the disdain she deserved. He put his hands back in his pockets. He was about to walk away from her.

'You could go and look for clues,' she said suddenly. 'Or *we* could, down there?'

'What kind of clues?' Ed turned. One hand came out of a pocket and hesitated in the air. 'They've already looked. My dad had a chain with his initials on it. It fell off a lot as it had a dodgy thingy – *clasp*. They've searched for that.'

'Well, there might be other clues,' said Maggie. 'Did he smoke?' Maggie liked clues. And mysteries. She took out Agatha Christies from Southend Library every couple of weeks and immersed herself in them. Last summer she'd ordered a detective set from the back of the *Beano* comic – a magnifying glass and a notebook, plus a plastic moustache for a disguise. 'What're you gonna do with all that?' her dad had asked, laughing under his mop hair. 'Skulk around the neighbourhood solving crimes?' He said she had a 'natural and exhausting curiosity', which she took as a huge compliment.

'Yes.' Ed nodded. 'My dad smokes.'

'We could look for cigarette butts, if they're a particular kind. They might still be there.'

'Might they?' said Ed. 'He smokes Rothmans. They have a gold band round them, and he never smokes them right to the end.'

'There you are then,' she said. 'That's what we could look for.' They were both being ridiculous, she knew that. They both had their reasons.

She had already jumped off the wall and started walking with him. She feared she'd never see him again once the holidays came to an end next week. She wouldn't be allowed out on to the wall once she had homework to do, and the nights started drawing in. The thought of the autumn made her feel sad. Locked in the house with Mum and Dad and Stevie. Dark nights around the gas fire. Casseroles and scratchy jumpers.

They crossed the road to turn left down Davis Street, and headed for the seafront. They cut through the huge car park where TOTS (Talk of the South) nightclub was and came down the side road to cross the esplanade. They hadn't spoken since they'd left Charlotte Road. Maggie hadn't dared. But when they had the sea to their left, green-grey and sludgy under the disappearing sun, she turned to him and said, 'What do you think happened to him? Your dad?'

'I don't know,' said Ed. He looked morose. He kicked a bottle top, sending it scurrying into the gutter.

'Maybe he's become a homeless person?' Maggie offered. Perhaps they would find him tonight, slumped in front of the Palace Hotel, she considered, in a grubby sleeping bag, asking for change.

'He wouldn't become a homeless person,' sniffed Ed and she knew he was close to saying 'Don't be so stupid' but had been brought up to be polite, even to idiots. 'Sometimes people just go off,' he said gruffly. 'It's not the first time it's happened in my family.'

'Oh?' Maggie was intrigued.

'My grandmother's brother did a bunk.'

'A bunk?' She didn't know what that meant.

'Yeah. He walked off after work one day with his life savings, and caught a boat to New York.'

'New York, wow!' Maggie had never been anywhere. Well, she'd been to Kent once, on a yawn-inducing family holiday. Never abroad. She knew someone in the year above who had gone to Disneyland, and this was astounding to her. Dreamlike. She lived vicariously through Janey and her annual trip to Great Yarmouth, envying the rides and amusements as though they were something exotic just because they weren't *here*.

'And he didn't come back?'

'Nope. He sent a telegram when he got there, saying he had arrived safely, but that was it, and he never came back. So maybe it runs in the family.'

'You think your dad's got on a boat to New York?'

'Nah, he doesn't like big cities, but maybe a tropical island somewhere, like on *Robinson Crusoe*. A desert island.'

'I watch that,' she said, remembering its sorrowful sweeping music that sounded like waves crashing on to the shore.

'Me too.' He looked at her, tilting his head slightly, then looked away. 'Dad likes the sea,' said Ed, and he stared out across the water. There were a couple of dilapidated boats, two dirty buoys. Some stragglers on the beach. A fallen-down windbreaker. 'And the beach – but not the pebble and shingle we have here. He always talks about white sand, palm trees, coconuts. He has dreams,' he added, 'dreams beyond Southend. He has dreams of going places, doing things. Maybe that's where he is, somewhere beyond this shithole, doing those things.'

Maggie blushed at the swear word. She'd never heard that particular one before, only the 'bugger' and 'sod' of her mother's occasional frustrations. She wasn't sure Southend *was* a 'shithole'. Yes, it was dull and overfamiliar, but it was a decent place to live, wasn't it? That's what her parents always said.

'He has a book called *Islands of the Indian Ocean*. There's one – Mémoire Island – which is his favourite. It has giant tortoises and a blue lagoon and apparently the oldest man in the world lives there. Dad's always looking at that book.'

Maggie stared down at the beach. Across the murky water. At sunken barges. Industrial schooners. She stared all the way to the power station, wondering if Neville Craddock had caught a little boat out there – the first leg of a long trip away from his family. Perhaps if he was a secretive person, he could have done it. Left them with no idea and ran away to that desert island. *Mémoire*. Maggie considered herself a secretive person, actually. She sometimes kept her feelings hidden. She had a mum who often asked her if she felt guilty and she always said no.

'Yes,' she agreed. 'Maybe he's off doing something wonderful on a desert island and then he'll be back.'

'Maybe,' said Ed, shoving his hands in his pockets again. 'Maybe.'

They were walking past the life-size moving waxwork in the glass box – one of the seafront's most fabled piratey attractions, in front of the replica of the *Golden Hind*: the cowered man in brown rags who lowered his head just in time, before the pirate looming over him swung a recurring scythe at him. Normally, Maggie would stand and stare at this for minutes, captivated. Tonight, she was indifferent to its terror.

'Well, we can look,' Maggie said, 'for the cigarette butts.'

Windmills from still-open stalls twirled in the breeze. Shrieks issued from Peter Pan's Playground; an arm outstretched from the top of the Ferris wheel grabbed at fun. Ed and Maggie were at her mum's fish and chip kiosk now. It was all shut up for the night, the white shutters dragged down, the sign saying, 'Fresh fish caught every day!' packed away. Mum's section of the counter inside would have that red tea towel draped over it. Maggie could still see a triangle of the beach from here, pebbly and grey. A lone man was sitting on an egg-yolk yellow towel, in the triangle, white legs stretched out in front of him.

'Here,' said Ed. He had a cigarette butt in his hand. It had a gold band.

'Good,' said Maggie. 'Good. See if you can find another one.'

She walked back and forward in a five-metre radius, but she couldn't see anything except for pavement and a wooden lolly stick and a Black Jack sweet wrapper. She expanded her circle. She wanted to please him, this boy with the sad eyes. She wanted to find the Hansel and Gretel trail of cigarette ends that would lead him to his dad.

Ed picked up another butt, but he threw it back to the ground, disappointed. *Wrong brand.* Maggie wondered how long they would be doing this for, when it was clearly hopeless, but she didn't mind the time at all, as she was spending it with him. Just him and her. She felt like he'd *chosen* her when of course he hadn't. She'd suggested the whole silly thing. But still, this felt special to her. This felt like *something*.

'Let's try over this way,' he said, and she followed him to the concrete steps down to the beach. The man on the yellow towel was lying flat out now, soaking up the overcast evening, his feet pointed outwards like a ballerina's. Ed plonked himself down on the grey pebbles and crossed his legs, frowning out over the blank sea. Maggie sat tentatively beside him, the stones crunchy and uncomfortable. *Does he really think Neville clambered aboard a dinghy and set sail to new horizons from Southend beach?* she wondered. Was Neville now stretched out on golden sand on Mémoire, his arms crossed behind his head, blissfully unaware his son back in Southend was scouring the street for the remains of cigarettes? Wasn't it more likely he was shacked up with some woman in Hadleigh, eating beans on toast from under an unwashed eiderdown and avoiding standing near windows, until he came to his senses and went home?

'Here's one!' declared Ed, reaching out in front of him and extracting a cigarette butt from between two pebbles. 'Ah, no, wrong kind.' He threw the butt to the ground in disgust. Maggie stared at her legs. Her red open-toed sandals, the ones her mum had bought her last summer, and which were slightly too small for her, looked so childish. Her toenails looked grubby. She curled her toes into the footbed of the sandals, trying to tuck them out of sight.

Ed gazed at the horizon, his eyebrows knotted. An escaping curl fell into his eye and he brushed it impatiently away. Sitting silently next to him, staring at his beautiful profile and trying not to communicate that she was absolutely in awe of him, Maggie knew she must hang on to this moment. She was sure this was all she would have of him, as a gloomy sky sat over a Southend horizon and the waves slumped on to the disconsolate shore. This one-off, strange and wonderful evening.

'My dad and I go fishing off the end of the pier,' Ed said. 'On Saturday mornings.'

'That's nice.'

Ed looked displeased. 'Not for a while, though,' he grunted. They both fell silent for a few moments. 'It's hardly *From Here to Eternity* is it, this beach?' he muttered eventually.

'What's that?'

'It's a movie. Deborah Kerr and Burt Lancaster.'

Maggie looked blank.

'Frank Sinatra's in it.'

'Oh,' she said. 'Yes. *Frank Sinatra.*'

'It's a good film,' said Ed, 'you should watch it sometime. There's a scene on an amazing beach in Hawaii. Not like this beach. Sandy, you know. White sand. *Paradise.* It's . . . well, it's romantic. That scene.' He looked embarrassed. Fancy saying 'romantic' to some ginger kid with too-small sandals on. 'Do you like Burt Lancaster?' he asked.

'I don't know,' she said truthfully. There were a few actors muddled up in her mind: Robert Mitcham, Kirk Douglas, Charlton Heston.

'Have you seen *The Swimmer?*'

'No,' she said, 'what's it about?' She baulked at her own foolishness, scuffing at a dirty great pebble with the end of her sandal, her toes still curled in.

'It's about a man who swims through all the backyard swimming pools in his neighbourhood, to get home,' he said. 'But when he gets home, his home is gone. It's great. I like movies.' He shrugged. 'Even all the old ones. Musicals and stuff, you know. I don't tell my mates that, though,' he said, flashing her what she assumed was a warning look.

'Well, *I* won't tell them,' she said. 'You can rely on me.'

Old movies, eh? she thought. The last film she had seen was *The Return of the Pink Panther* and she didn't remember much about it. There was a long silence now, both of them staring out over the water.

'I'm sorry,' she said finally, 'about your dad. You must be really upset.'

'Well,' he said, turning to face her, his lovely eyes green and wide in his face. He looked *surprised*, as though no one had suggested this to him. 'Yes,' he said. 'Yes, I *am* pretty upset.' She waited. 'I keep expecting him to walk in the door and chuck his keys on the kitchen table and for Mum to tut and put them in the drawer. It's so weird, he isn't here. That he's just *gone*. You know, I'm sure . . .' He hesitated.

'Go on,' she said, and she had never felt more grown up.

'Well, if he was dead, actually dead, then I reckon I'd know. I *really* think I would know.' He sighed. 'But I don't know. I wake up every morning and I simply have no idea where he is . . .' He laughed bitterly. 'God, I can't believe I'm saying all this to a kid!'

Maggie was crushed, but at the same time she was smiling inside, which was awful, because he was sad, but she felt he'd shown a secret part of himself to her, and that thrilled her.

'I'm sure he's okay,' she said feebly, because it wasn't a fact, was it, and she liked facts. 'I'm sure he hasn't gone far,' she added, as though Ed's father was an escaped dog from a back garden, bounding under a hedge after a neighbouring cat. And then she remembered that saying he hadn't 'gone far' disputed the narrative about Neville Craddock escaping to a lovely desert island, and then she didn't know what to say.

'Let's go back now,' Ed said. Maggie felt her heart sink. They would walk home, and he would never talk to her again. He would not acknowledge this evening to his mates – that he had walked down to the seafront with that fourteen-year-old girl who sat on the wall, to look for his father. He would be careful when he was trailing a tree branch along the garden walls of Charlotte Road, making sure it didn't touch her.

They walked home in silence; Maggie scuffing her feet, Ed moving quickly. A van beeped at them as they crossed the road to the car park and Ed nudged her out of the way by tapping her gently at the elbow. She smiled deludedly at this touch. Him shielding her. But at the corner of Charlotte Road, he grunted, 'See you then.'

'See you,' she replied, and she knew she was in huge trouble when she got in as all three of them were there in the living room. Mum with her legs out on the pouffe. Their cat, Marmalade, an orange sphinx on her thighs. Dad with his silly pipe and in his after-work summer uniform of t-shirt and dry navy swimming trunks. Stevie lounging like a topless David Bowie on the carpet, flicking through the local paper, the *Southend Gazette*, pretending to look for jobs.

'Where on earth have you been?' asked Dad, with an air of casual concern. Malcolm was a terrible liar; he could never conceal his emotions like Maggie could. He had an open, expressive face, round eyes that crinkled in delight or surprise, a mouth that relaxed easily into a big grin. Maggie didn't think he had 'dreams' like Neville Craddock had, or any desire to leave 'this shithole', or *them*. Dad hated his job, but he always said he got through the days because he enjoyed the evenings and the weekends so much. He liked a drink and a song. He laughed at things on the telly. He lived for his wife and his children, that's what he always told people. She had once heard her nanna, her mum's mum, say he was 'useless', but Maggie was sure that wasn't true.

'Just out walking,' she said.

'Out walking where?' She hadn't realised she might have worried anyone. That Dad might have been worried. He had

28

a crease between his eyebrows that only appeared rarely, and it was there now.

'Down to the seafront.'

'Doing what?'

'Just walking.'

'Okay. Well, don't go down there on your own again, Maggie. You never know who's about.'

'Sorry, Dad.' Teen embarrassment meant she wasn't going to tell them she'd been walking with Ed Craddock.

'We were worried, love,' said Mum. Marmalade's tail twitched on her thigh. 'I looked out to the wall, and you weren't there.'

'Sorry, Mum.'

Sandra was a kind mother, with fair hair and pale blue eyes, who swore sometimes when she thought no one was in earshot. She liked a song, too – an occasional singalong to Neil Diamond or Elton John – Dad's favourite – around the gas fire, correcting Dad as he didn't know all the words like she did, her fingers tapping on the arm of her chair. She liked lemonade and a good cup of tea.

'Probably chasing stupid lads,' commented Stevie dryly. He'd taken on an affected Jagger-esque drawl recently. He pulled on a scraggy bit of hair at the nape of his neck. 'I've seen her on that wall, mooning after the likes of Ed Craddock and his mates.'

'Shut up, Stevie,' muttered Maggie.

'Now, now,' said Dad, 'let's not start a row. We're just glad you're home.'

'Yes, she's home now,' said Mum, and she smiled at Dad and the crease between his eyebrows disappeared.

'Get upstairs, then,' he concluded, 'and no wandering off in future. Don't forget there's a man on this street who's disappeared. Southend doesn't need another missing person.'

'He's on a desert island,' Maggie whispered as she walked up the stairs, and her heart swelled for Ed Craddock and his missing dad. For how upset Ed was, but he had only told *her* just how much. How it had been an evening that, if anyone were to ask her about it, she might be tempted to tell the truth of her heart and answer, 'It was brilliant.'

'Night, love,' Dad called up to her.

'Night, pet,' called Mum.

'Na-night.' Maggie opened her bedroom door and hoped she would dream of sitting on the beach tonight, and looking for cigarette butts, and Ed touching her softly on the elbow as they crossed the road, and thinking, maybe, that she was okay, for a ratty little ginger kid.

Chapter Five

Ed's shack was in a brushy clearing. It was a grey shed of faded, hatched-together planks threatening to concertina in on themselves, a roof of tattered and fraying palm fronds, one tumble-down slatted front window, and a door only identified as such by its crusty doorknob. The whole thing looked like it was leaning slightly to the left.

'Not exactly Bel Air,' Ed commented dryly. He leant his pole of fish against the front of the shack, took the mast from Maggie and propped it beside the pole. Maggie set down the metal container and watched as Ed opened the door and let it swing open. 'Home sweet home,' he said.

Maggie looked around her. The inside of the shack was simply furnished. There was a single bed with a white pillow and sheet, a striped cotton blanket folded at its end, a scrubbed table and a chair with a rattan seat, a small Calor gas stove in the corner. A tiny fridge. One tall cupboard.

'So, do you like what I've done with the place?' Ed brought in the mast and the sail and the bait tin, leaving the pole of hanging fish propped up on the outside wall. He laid everything on the simple wooden floor.

'It's very nice,' she said, trying to keep calm in his presence. Trying not to let any feelings rise up and out of her. 'Although definitely not what you're used to.' Ed had lived for years in an enormous mock Tudor villa in Beverly Hills, set in three acres with a heart-shaped swimming pool and a pool house five times the size of this shack. 'No bathroom?'

'There's a fenced-off area out back,' he said. 'A cold-water pipe, open air – good for the soul. I cook on that thing.' He motioned to the gas stove in the corner. 'Just rice and beans, mostly. Simple stuff.'

'Very Robinson Crusoe,' she commented, peering through the shack's only window and the competing blades of fern knocking at it.

'It has suited me.' Ed shrugged. 'It has suited me very well.' And those green eyes turned almost steel grey, like they sometimes did. Was he angry? Angry she was here? 'Do you want to sit down?' he asked, pulling out the rattan chair, and she had the impression he might continue to pull it, from under her, as she went to sit down. 'You must be tired. How long did it take you to get here?'

'About a million years,' she said, feeling awkward on that lone chair in the middle of Ed's shack.

There was the trace of a smile on his face. 'I need to get this fish to Olly's. I suppose you want to come?'

'Well, sure, okay.'

'Right, well, I'm going to have a quick shower first. Can I fix you a drink?'

'Thank you.'

'What would you like?'

'What have you got?'

He opened his one tall cupboard. It was divided into two. In the left half were two shelves: folded clothes on the bottom, a few plates and cups and two glass bottles of dark liquid on the top.

In the right-hand half were shirts hanging from what looked like handmade wire hangers, an intriguing glimpse of polished, honey-coloured wood between them.

'Rum and Coke?' Ed asked. 'No ice. Plastic mug. Sorry.'

'Perfect.'

Ed mixed her a drink and handed it to her. She watched as he grabbed a folded-up t-shirt and a pair of shorts from the bottom shelf of his cupboard and was surprised to recognise the t-shirt, a coral pink one with a palm tree on the front. He had worn it in Venice Beach, that awful time, fifteen years ago.

He tucked the clothes under his arm. 'Would you like to sit outside? While you wait?'

'Yes, that would be nice.'

Maggie rose from the chair and Ed took it out to the front of the shack.

'You're looking good, Maggie May,' he said to her as she sat down, his eyes lingering on her for a moment, almost in surprise.

'Old now,' she said with a short smile, glancing away from him.

'Never *old*,' said Ed, and she looked up to see him flashing her that famous Ed Cavanagh smile which audiences adored. That delicious blend of cheeky mischief, a promise of a little danger and the seductive hint of vulnerability. 'Right,' he said, tapping at the clothes under his arm. 'Shower.'

He disappeared round the back of the shack. Maggie exhaled, relieved she could be alone for a moment, to adjust to being here with him. She crossed her legs and sipped her drink, taking in the view of the sea, latticed beautifully by the nodding leaves of a gigantic palm. She watched a yellow-breasted bird hop from branch to branch in an olive tree. She could hear the distant rumbling of a boat engine and the soft rain of the water pipe of Ed's outdoor bathroom. She knew he would like the feel of the cold water on his body. The blast of freezing water on sunburnt skin. But she shouldn't be thinking about things like that. How they both used to be. She had a job to do and the quicker these twenty-four hours were over, the better.

How will I start the profile? she wondered, sitting outside Ed's dilapidated wooden shack, drink in hand. Ed on his boat, sailing towards her as she waited alone on the beach, the blue sky above her? Ed pottering in his little shack, fetching her a drink from his cupboard of basic provisions? Or Ed in other places on the island, yet undiscovered by her. She wondered when she would give Ed the letter at the bottom of her rucksack. In which of these twenty-four hours she might have the courage.

Ed emerged from the doorway, his curls wet. He rubbed at his hair with a thin bath towel. He was wearing the beige shorts and the coral palm tree t-shirt. He leant against the rough planks of the shack.

'Are you ready?' he asked her.

'Yes,' she said, but she didn't know if she was. For his curls and his green eyes and his tanned skin. For him. For any of it in the next few hours.

'You still take all your own photos?' he asked her, after they had stepped outside and Ed had closed the door. He gestured to the Minolta camera on its leather strap around her neck.

'Yes,' she replied. She had done for years.

'Want to take one of me outside the old abode?'

'Why not?'

And Ed Cavanagh, movie star, stood in front of his little home on this remote island and smiled, and she snapped a few photos of him.

'Let's go,' he said, after she was done, and Ed touched her on the elbow and steered her into the warm evening.

Chapter Six

7 P.M., 28 JUNE 1975

The day eighteen-year-old Maggie met Ed Craddock again had not started with any hint, or any promise, of how it would end. There was no indication that a day which began by pushing Mum down to the bank on the high street ('My left wheel's playing up. You're not doing much today, are you, pet? Would you mind coming with me?') would be brought to a miraculous close with Maggie being asked out by Ed Craddock.

Her A-levels over, Maggie had planned to spend a lazy Saturday reading in her room, popping to the library in the afternoon and watching Lindsay Wagner in *The Bionic Woman* in the evening. The theme music to that programme made her cry in a strangely satisfying way, but it may have been because Jaime Sommers had missing parts of herself replaced with better ones, when it didn't work like that in real life.

'Do you want to pop into Boots as well?' Maggie had asked after the bank, whilst pushing Mum along Swan Street.

'Yes, please, love. Let's have a look at the make-up.'

Maggie stopped at the double doors of Boots and propped one of them open with her foot. A man in a suit held the other one for them.

'Thanks,' said Maggie and Mum in unison as they went in, and the man smiled condescendingly at them.

Sandra had been in a wheelchair from two weeks after Maggie was born, her daughter's birth triggering an immune disorder that had left her paralysed from the waist down, and from the moment Maggie was old enough to understand, Sandra had made her daughter promise she would never ever feel guilty about it. She repeated this entreaty at intervals – summer days, winter evenings, at Christmas, always on Maggie's birthday in March – her pale eyes brimming with love and tears. But Maggie *did*. She felt guilty about it every day. Sandra Walsh had been a dancer, a Tiller Girl in the 1950s, when everything had been black and white (not brown and orange like it was now), according to the pictures in her photo album. She had come over to London from Cork to seek her fortune, confident and pretty and talented, and danced in a line-up of girls all the same height and weight, like identical dolls, with their arms linked so they didn't fall over. She had danced frequently on *Sunday Night at the London Palladium*. She had danced at the *Royal Variety Performance* in front of the Queen. And one night she had met Maggie's dad, who had gone up to London for the evening from Southend with his mum. He had won a ticket on the back of a Cornflakes packet to go to *Sunday Night at the London Palladium*, including a backstage pass, and Malcolm had been very good-looking and very good-natured, and appealingly silly and full of fun, and Malcolm and Sandra had fallen in love.

'And it was just like a fairy tale,' Mum always said, 'and it still is, because I've got Stevie and I've got you, and you are worth ten million performances at the London Palladium and ten billion dances. You both are.'

Maggie wasn't sure she was worth ten billion dances. She wasn't sure she was worth Mum being in a wheelchair, but she found everything so much easier if she told Mum she didn't feel guilty at all at being the cause of it, and swallowed her feelings without ever giving voice to them. She bet *Stevie* thought he was worth ten billion dances, though.

'Nothing lasts forever,' Sandra often summarised, when talking about her Tiller days, but Maggie thought life wasn't fair, and that some things should have lasted a lot longer than they had.

After Boots, Maggie and Sandra went home. It was quite a long way, the walk to the bank. There was a bus that did the route, but buses didn't take wheelchairs. Some eighteen-year-olds might have been embarrassed pushing their mum along the street in a wheelchair, but Maggie wasn't. She owed it to her mum to be cheerful and non-embarrassed, wherever they were.

Janey had telephoned after lunch and said there was a band playing at The White Horse, tonight, where her boss's dad, Trevor, was the landlord, and they should go. She told Maggie Trevor needed someone to do some glam rock face-painting and 'tattoos', for ten bob each, if Maggie was up for it.

'Where do we get the stuff from?' Maggie had asked Janey. She was sitting on the bottom stair in the hall, winding the curly phone cord around her thumb. 'For the face-painting and the tattoos?'

'We'll get them from the stationery shop on Church Road,' said Janey. 'Trevor will pay us back for everything. You never know,' she added, 'we might meet some great boys there tonight. God knows I've depleted the stock at the office.'

Janey worked in accounts at a small printing firm. She had indeed gone out with anyone under the age of thirty there. She was playing the field and the field was long and wide and ready to run amok on as far as she was concerned. Janey was fun. Janey was a warm riot. Janey and Maggie had the best nights out, and tonight was bound to be another of them.

'Decent boys would be nice,' Maggie had commented. 'For you, I have to add.'

'Yeah. You've got the interminable Glen,' Janey had replied. 'Now, there's a long word! Is that right, *interminable*? You're the brainbox. You're the one who did English Lit A-level.'

'That's exactly right,' Maggie had said. She had enjoyed studying English Literature, Sociology and History at Sixth Form. Poring over *The Great Gatsby* and *Wuthering Heights*, the history of the Tudors and the intricacies of social mobility. Now all she needed were her results. And Janey was right, too, about Glen, but that was okay, for now.

◆ ◆ ◆

The pub garden was packed and most people in it were already sozzled, as they'd probably been here since after work, and everyone seemed up for it and happy in the warmth that remained in the still air. It was the kind of midsummer's evening where the leaves on the trees suck up every last drop of light and heat from the vestiges of the day. Where midges circle above people's heads, and bushes smell mulchy and sweet and a bit like weed. Where drinks warm quickly in glasses and everyone is delighted not to have to put a jumper on when the sun goes down.

Maggie and Janey moved through the laughing, jostling people to the makeshift bar at the rear of the garden. They were carrying a Tupperware box each: Janey's containing face paints in different colours and little pots of glitter, Maggie's paper transfers with peel-off backs – stars and flashes and diamonds she would administer with a sponge to make temporary tattoos.

Janey tucked the Tupperware box under her arm and dug her purse out of the back pocket of her flares.

'I'm so fat,' she complained. 'I'm one great big heifer.'

'No, you're not,' said Maggie, tucking her own box under her arm and retrieving her miniscule snap-clasp purse from her bag. 'You're lovely.' Janey's special and exasperating talent was putting herself down. Constantly.

'I *am*. I look a state.'

'You look *fine*.' They were both wearing flared jeans and suedette gypsy tops. Tiny, impractical tasselled bags hung at their hips from double shoestring straps. 'Stop self-deprecating.'

'That sounds like something unsavoury. You and your big words, Maggie Martin.'

'Big words make my world go round,' said Maggie, shrugging, as Janey grinned at her.

'At least *Glenda* didn't come,' said Janey. She looked around her, winking at a boy over by the back fence. He grinned at her then turned back to his mates.

'Not really Glen's scene,' admitted Maggie. 'Glam rock.' She glanced over to the 'stage' to the right of them, constructed from palettes from the local soft drinks factory. There were speakers and sound boxes and wires scattered over it.

'God, no, can you imagine?' Janey laughed. 'He'd pass out as soon as look at a sequinned cape!'

Maggie giggled. Glen had just finished Sixth Form, too, and had got a job as a welder. He had a gruff voice and a tall, reedy physique, but he was funny and a fairly good kisser so she continued to go out with him.

'Has he ever kissed you and you thought you would *die*?' asked Janey.

'Well, no,' said Maggie. She had gone round to Glen's house after Sixth Form most evenings for the past four months, and now in the holidays after her summer job at the local newsagent's. They sat on his floor in his bedroom, leaning against his bed, listening to Burt Bacharach records and kissing perfectly satisfactorily, with his mum knocking on the door and bustling in at intervals, brandishing a basket of washing or details about when Glen's dinner was – as though each time she was halting a catastrophic teenage pregnancy.

There was no danger of that. The kissing was fun, but Maggie didn't want to have *sex* with Glen. He was just someone to pass some pleasant time with until she fell in love, which she wanted to now she wasn't fourteen any more.

'Shame.' Janey rolled her eyes with glee. 'Kissing is *everything*.' She fiddled with her hair. 'What about your brother? He likes glam rock, doesn't he? Is he coming tonight?'

Janey fancied Stevie. She'd never made a secret of it. If he was in the kitchen when Janey was round, she hung around in the doorway, a silly look on her face, blinking her eyes like trapped flies and trying to look beguiling, while Maggie stuck a tongue out at her and Stevie completely ignored the whole scene.

'No,' replied Maggie happily. 'We don't want *him* here. Shall we do a kitty?' she asked, pulling a note from her purse.

'Yep. What time's the band on again?'

'Ten past. What time are we required at our stations?'

'After they come off. Wired Tomb,' said Janey. 'It's a funny name for a band. Where're they from?'

'Fairly local, I've heard,' said Maggie. 'The lead singer's from Benfleet.'

'Bet they're crap.'

'Hope so.' Maggie grinned. 'More fun that way.'

Fifteen minutes later, a skinny bloke shuffled on to the stage – drainpipe jeans, greasy hair – and arranged himself behind the drum kit. A mocking cheer immediately went up from the waiting crowd. Three other band members ran out from the passage to the toilets at the back of the pub and on to the stage. There was a stocky guy with a cape ('I knew it!' said Janey) who stood behind the microphone, and two guitarists – one with a blond mullet, another with curls dado-railed by a velvet headband, low-slung trousers and a shirt unbuttoned to his waist. The velvet headband boy looked shy. He exhaled, puffing his cheeks out so a curtain of curls rose and then fell back into his eyes. He risked a small sheepish smile at the crowd.

'*Ed Craddock*,' whispered Maggie.

'Who?' Janey asked. They were about halfway back, on the grass.

'A boy I used to know. An old neighbour. He moved away.'

'Well, thank god he's back!' exclaimed Janey. 'He's bloody gorgeous!'

He *was* gorgeous. Ed Craddock seemed taller than before, his hair was darker, longer. He had the shape of muscles under the sleeves of his shirt. He was wearing black eyeliner. Ed glanced nervously back to the drummer, who started to thump out a beat – one two, one two three. Ed lowered his eyes to his guitar and started to plonk out some notes. The other guitarist set to his, too, frowning in painful concentration. The lead singer, chunky in his cape, pulled the mic towards him with his little finger and began to sing, his voice surprisingly high-pitched. They were making a fist of a song no one had ever heard before – a rocky, largely incomprehensible ditty that seemed to be about horses on a beach, or nothing at all. It was terrible. A wailing dirge with malfunctioning guitars and out-of-time drums. Yet, after a few seconds, something happened to the second guitarist, and it may have been Maggie who noticed it first, as she hadn't taken her eyes off him.

Ed came alive. Suddenly – though the *sounds* coming from the guitar-playing were still terrible – he adopted the mannerisms, the swagger, the *feel* of a rock guitarist. He bit on his bottom lip and nodded his head. He bent his back leg and jutted out his hip. He *looked* the part; he had a moochy flourish, a bold theatricality. He played a bum note and brazened it out, shrugging and giving an adorable grin. He blew up his curly fringe again, but this time as the curls fell, he looked doe-eyed from under them and winked insouciantly at the crowd. A thrilled ripple went through it – an appreciation of this spellbinding performance.

He's really got something, thought Maggie. As a band they were all atrocious, and the song was clearly nonsense, but Ed had people believing in him, willing him on, *investing*.

'He's lovely,' said Janey dreamily. 'Your *Ed Craddock*. Just lovely.'

'He's not mine,' said Maggie. She was transfixed. An impromptu crush evolved in front of the stage; Janey pushed them both into it. They were close now to the front of the stage. And Maggie could really *see* Ed, as the appalling music and the wailing about wet horses washed over her, and she remembered everything about him from Charlotte Road – how he strode down it with his mates, how she had sat on the wall, watching him. The evening they'd walked down to the seafront. His eyes when he had spoken about his dad. She wondered if he still searched the horizon for traces of his father or looked for those particular cigarette butts. She wondered if he still thought Neville Craddock was on that desert island. *Mémoire*, she remembered, aptly. And the local paper hadn't forgotten Neville. The *Southend Gazette* still printed small articles about him, asking for information.

The song crashed to an end. Wired Tomb bashed out another, then another. The audience was dancing, furiously and frenetically, loving every second of this warm night and this crazy band. Maggie didn't take her eyes off Ed; she was in the very front row now, the grass tickling her ankles. At the end of song four, called 'Love in Ruins!', according to the shout of the chunky blond lead singer, Ed crescendoed with a reverberating twang of the guitar and a slap of his palm on its shiny body, then he looked straight into her eyes.

'What's your name?' he called out huskily, and she turned behind her to see who he was *really* looking at, to be met by two cheerful blokes in denim.

'He's talking to *you*, kid,' one of them deadpanned.

She turned back.

'Yes, *you*,' Ed said.

'Maggie,' she answered, her voice sounding loud and stupid in her ears.

Ed's face broke into a grin. He winked at her and walked over to the lead singer, to whisper something in his ear. The singer went over and communicated something to the drummer, before taking Ed's spot on the stage. And Ed walked up to the mic, and Wired Tomb launched into a rocky cover version of 'Maggie May' with Ed strumming badly at his guitar and singing every word to the Maggie in the audience.

Maggie blushed furiously. Ed's voice was not bad – it was tuneful and sweet – but he had the perfect combination of cheek and charisma. He brought the song alive with a wink and a grin. The crowd loved it, continually glancing at Maggie to enjoy her discomfort and her red face, while Janey nudged her in the ribs. *Janey's* face told Maggie she thought this was the very best thing to ever happen to either of them.

'He fancies you,' she mouthed ecstatically to Maggie, and Maggie just shook her head and squeezed her lips together to stop herself smiling.

At the end of 'Maggie May', when the music trailed to nothing, Ed still didn't take his eyes from the Maggie in the crowd, and then he was gone from the stage, loping off in a slow 'rock god' run, like he was leaving the stage at Wembley.

Janey grabbed her arm. 'What the hell? Maggie! Fancy having a whole song sung to you like that, you lucky cow!'

Maggie face was purple now, she was sure. She was thrilled and exhilarated. She had been momentarily adored. This was a novel feeling to her – Glen said she was 'pretty', but adored football and steak and kidney pie, not her. She rotated this feeling inside of her, left and right, and she liked its pleasing angles and its shiny facets. This was a feeling she would like to have again.

'Oh, god,' she said. 'Oh, god. I need a drink.'

'You can't yet,' said Janey. 'You have to do tattoos.'

◆ ◆ ◆

Maggie was on her third star and her second lightning flash. She wasn't too great at this tattoo business. Some girl had been disgruntled at a missing point of the star on her shoulder, and she'd forgotten to peel the backing off one of the flashes before pressing it down on a hairy arm, and in the end its drunk owner in leathers had told her not to bother and had stomped off.

'There you go,' she said, smiling now at a girl in a green dress, a fresh star on her fleshy forearm amongst a forest of pale hairs.

'Thanks.'

Maggie squeezed the sponge into the dish. Janey was the other side of the beer garden, liberally slapping paint and glitter on people's faces. Maggie waved to her, and Janey grinned and waved back. Then Janey started pointing at something ahead of Maggie. Making the thumbs-up gesture. When Maggie turned, Ed Craddock was standing there – eyeliner, lopsided grin, one foot tucked behind the other.

'Hi,' he said.

'Hi.'

'Can I have a tattoo?'

44

'Of course,' she said, trying not to blush. 'Take a seat. What would you like, lightning flash or star?'

'Star, please.' His smile was pure cheek. The eyeliner made the green of his eyes almost toxically gorgeous.

'Alright. Star coming up.'

He sat on the tiny chair opposite her. She cut awkwardly around another star on the card – she was left-handed, and the scissors were not – and carefully peeled off the backing, not looking at him.

'Where would you like it?' she asked him, risking a quick glance. *Oh, he is beautiful.*

He held out his wrist. Pulled up the sleeve of his shirt.

'Here, *Maggie*.'

Blushing, she placed the star upside down on Ed's wrist. She could smell a trace of aftershave. Something woody and sedating. She wetted the sponge and pressed it lightly on to the transfer.

'You survived the mosh pit, then?' Ed asked.

'Yes, just about. It's a great band.' She tried to sneak a quick look at Janey, for moral support, a grin of solidarity, but she couldn't see her now; the drinking crowd was too dense.

'I think we both know that's not true.' Ed grinned. 'But thank you. We enjoy ourselves, and our five songs. And we look the part, at least. I mean, I can't see us being on *Top of the Pops* any time soon, you know, but fifty bob is fifty bob.'

'Maybe you could spend the money on guitar lessons,' Maggie suggested.

He roared with laughter, and she loved that she had made him laugh. His green eyes settled back on hers, steady and sweet and sexy. 'I was acting the whole way through,' he admitted. 'Acting the part of a guitarist in a better band. I gave myself a name, before I went on. *Rick Hastings*.'

'Rick Hastings?'

'Yeah,' he said shyly. 'Rick Hastings, top guitarist for made-up band Electric Nights. Actually – and this is pretty funny, unbeliev-able really.' His face was alight with astonishment and delight. He leant towards her. 'When I came off stage I was asked to be in *a play*.' He laughed, his eyelinered eyes sparkling. 'By some bloke in the crowd. A theatre director or something. Just for a local produc-tion, you know, pretty small fry. But he said I had the right look.' Ed shrugged. '*A play!*' he repeated incredulously.

'What play is it?' Maggie asked, thrilled to be taken into his confidence, the recipient of his delighted smile.

'I can't remember. It's something about a waiter. He wants me to play a bloke called Gus.'

'*The Dumb Waiter?*'

'That's it.'

'Are you going to do it?'

Ed shrugged again. 'Yeah, probably. How hard can it be?' He mussed at his hair with a hand that had an opal ring on it, second finger. *Rick Hastings*. 'Guess what my real job is,' he said.

'Make-up artist?'

Ed roared again. 'My mum will have a fit when she sees this eyeliner,' he laughed. 'Particularly as I stole it from her make-up bag. She still hasn't got over the time I tried to dye my hair black with boot polish. She said I looked like I had the neighbour's cat on my head.'

It was Maggie's turn to laugh. 'I remember that cat,' she said carefully, 'so I agree it didn't really work for you.'

He tilted his head at her quizzically. 'You know my old neigh-bour's *cat*?' he asked.

'You don't remember me, do you?' she asked shyly.

'No . . .' He searched her face while she drank in his.

'I used to sit on the wall.'

'Which wall?'

'The wall on Charlotte Road. Outside my house.'

Her peered at her closely and his mouth broke into a wide smile. 'You're that scrappy kid on the *wall*?'

'That's me,' Maggie replied, 'ginger and scrappy.' Except she wasn't, not any more. She had 'filled out', as the saying went. The milk-white stick legs had become long and quite shapely, if she did say so herself. She had boobs, and apples in her cheeks.

'Well, blow me down! I scraped you with a stick, once, didn't I? Sorry about that. You've changed so much! "Redheaded and glorious" these days, more like.'

'Thank you.' She blushed. She wondered about mentioning the evening they had walked down to the entrance of the pier together, feeling strangely embarrassed about it, like she had witnessed a part of him she wasn't supposed to have seen. Like she had trailed along the sea front behind his open heart.

'Blimey,' he said, shaking his head at her.

'I've seen *The Swimmer* now,' she ventured shyly, wondering if he would remember. 'The Burt Lancaster film.'

He looked at her in a way that told her he did. Her and him. Sitting on the beach. Talking about movies like *From Here to Eternity*. She'd seen that, too. The scene he had mentioned, Deborah Kerr and Burt Lancaster lying on the sand, kissing, as waves crashed over them, had made her blush. 'What did you think of it?'

'Great,' she said. 'Allegorical.'

'*Allegorical* . . .' he said, rolling the word over his tongue. 'You need to press a bit harder,' he added, and she realised she was not pressing down on his wrist, but her hand was simply lying there, fingers almost curled around it. She pressed her fingers more firmly against his wrist. Felt the warmth of him through the soggy paper. 'So, your real job . . .?' she asked.

'I work in a women's shoe shop,' he said. 'Down on Arch Road.' He pulled a face. 'Embarrassing, isn't it?' he said. 'Shoes, tights, protector spray . . .'

'It's a *job*,' she commented.

'Yeah, it's still embarrassing,' said Ed. 'I mean, I don't want to make a career out of it or anything. I'd rather do something else.'

'What else do you want to do?'

'I don't know.' He fixed his green eyes on hers and all the people around them, standing, drinking, talking, laughing, faded to nothing. 'I'm hoping it will come to me, at some point. I know I don't want to work there forever.'

'Maybe it's being in plays,' she offered.

He laughed. 'Yeah. Right.' And he still didn't take his eyes from hers.

'I think it's done now,' she said, glancing at the transfer. The people came back, the laughers and the drinkers. The garden full of happy faces.

She carefully peeled off the sodden paper from his wrist to reveal the gold star, one of its points refusing to lie flat so she had to gently nudge it on to his skin with her fingertip.

'What time do you get off?' he asked her. 'From the tattoo table?'

'Oh, in ten minutes, I think.'

'I'll hang around for you.'

'Okay.' A warm feeling spread upwards from her toes and engulfed her whole body. She liked it. She hadn't experienced a feeling like this before, especially not with Glen and his bedroom-floor kisses.

'*Ed!*' shouted a voice. They both turned round. The blond lead singer was striding towards them, cape flapping. 'We've got another gig,' he said, stopping at Maggie's table. 'Now. Tonight. At The Nag's Head. We need to load up our gear.'

'Now?' Ed questioned.

'Yeah, Trevor got a telephone call. It's forty notes. Get up, man!'

Ed reluctantly stood up and grinned at Maggie. 'That's me, then. Bye, Maggie.' He turned to go but then he turned back again. 'Actually, would you like to come and see me in the play? It's at the old Ritzy, next Thursday. I can leave a ticket for you on the door.'

'Next Thursday? That's quick.'

Ed shrugged again. 'How hard can it be?' he repeated. 'Will you come?'

'Yes,' she said, 'I'll come.'

'Great!' And he was walking away from her, and she watched him go, until a girl in a blue velvet dress coughed loudly and said, 'Excuse me, are you doing these transfers, or what?' and in a part of the garden crowd she could see Janey grinning at her from her face-painting table, and she was grinning, too, and feeling that new and delicious feeling from her head to her toes.

Chapter Seven

The bar was noisy. It wasn't just the rumble of the enormous generator, somewhere behind Olly's Bar, chuntering away. It wasn't only the loud reggae music that was pumping out of speakers on the walls – Bob Marley's 'Three Little Birds'. No, when Maggie and Ed had reached Olly's Bar, in its shaded spot at the top of the beach – basic but colourful, a red and yellow slatted wooden hexagon with a thatched roof – they'd been met by both a rotund man in a dirty apron who had seized Ed's pole of fish from him with a '*Merci*, my friend, *merci*,' and the high-decibel chatter of the locals. Crowds gathered here on a Friday night where, as Ed told Maggie, the drinks were dirt cheap and there was fried fish for six francs.

'Fishermen, farm hands and furniture-makers,' Ed had said, summing up the men and women down-timing here, in cross-hatched chairs or high stools, the soles of their bare feet cocked on the sandy boards, their heels slipping free of dangling flip-flops. 'Mémoire's economy survives on the export of coir rope, cinnamon, sweet potatoes and rattan footstools.'

Maggie looked around her. Took in the curious faces and the smell of woodsmoke and spices, the relaxed Friday-night vibe of the sweet-potato farmers and the footstool makers meeting up for fresh fish and conversation. She liked Olly's, she decided. Her Friday nights were usually spent in the company of the television and a dinner you pricked with a fork and nuked for four minutes.

'Do you always sit in the same seat?' Maggie asked Ed as they sat, on high stools up at the bar, with their drinks. A large fan whirring like a slow helicopter cooled their faces from the end of the bar. A candle in a ceramic holder flickered lazily in front of them. Behind the bar, a beauty Maggie guessed to be in her early thirties, with a mass of dark curly hair tethered into a wooden barrette at the back of her neck, glanced at Maggie so often she wondered if Ed was sleeping with her.

'Yes,' he replied. Apart from his precis of the local economy, Ed had been as reticent as a plank of wood since they had left his shack. Never mind the interview, she didn't think she would get more than three words of anything out of him while she was here. She studied him in profile, sipping on his rum and Coke. She needed a sense of him, at least, to write any sort of article. She needed some brushstrokes. Like his heels planted on the bottom rung of his stool. One elbow propped up on the bar. The beer mat he had peeled from edge to centre, like a square orange. His crumpled pack of cigarettes. That one curl sticking obstinately to his forehead.

'Quite the fixture.' She noted the crease at the corner of his mouth, which hadn't been there the last time they met, radiated white from the sun. *That could go in.* She would have to paint Ed Cavanagh in words as she had no idea how to read him in person right now. 'You never used to like rum,' she said.

'People change.'

'Do they?'

He stared wordlessly at the tin signs latched behind the bar: ads for kerosene and coconut shampoo and soap.

Eventually she asked, 'Why are you – and now me, briefly – the only tourist here? Why is Mémoire so undiscovered?'

'Few roads,' replied Ed. 'Tracks, really. No Wi-Fi. No mobile phone signal.' Maggie had sussed that back at the bungalow. 'No infrastructure for tourism. Too many boats to get here. Give it time,' he added, flashing her a wry smile. 'Nothing goes undiscovered forever.'

Not even you? Maggie nearly asked, but she kept her mouth almost as closed as his.

'Who's this, Ed?' asked the woman behind the bar, approaching them to give an already clean patch of it a wipe, and clearly no longer able to contain her curiosity about this sixty-year-old woman in the batik dress sitting in Olly's with Ed. Maybe she thought Maggie was his spinster sister, or his agent.

'This is Maggie,' said Ed. 'And this is Delphine,' Ed told Maggie.

'Pleased to meet you,' said Delphine, and Maggie was sure Delphine's eyes would have been flashing with jealousy if Maggie hadn't been so old. Maggie wondered if the people on Mémoire knew Ed was famous, but they must do, as everyone in the whole world knew who Ed Cavanagh was. 'How long are you here for?' Delphine was examining Maggie – every wrinkle, probably, that couldn't be erased by her expensive face cream.

'Twenty-four hours.'

'Oh, not long,' said the woman, French accent. Relief.

Don't worry, thought Maggie, *you'll have your Mr Ed back soon enough.* And she was jealous suddenly, not only of Delphine but of Ed's island life: of going out in a little blue fishing boat and padding barefoot around his rustic shack and his soul-cleansing outdoor bathroom, when all that awaited Maggie was a blank retirement and her little flat in London, grey skies and emptiness. She had *found* so many people, in her career, she thought, that wasn't it ironic she had ended up almost completely alone?

'Why have you come here?' Delphine asked directly. 'To Mémoire to see your friend, Ed?'

He'd never said they were friends . . . 'I need to interview him,' said Maggie. That was all, she thought. Just a little exposé between people who weren't friends any more. *All those hours gone to waste,* she mused, that they had once spent together, resulting only in a cold twenty-four hours on this hot island. Hours now far from reach but, at the same time, sometimes so acute and so vivid they could be plucked from the air and lived over and over, sweet and bitter and tart and painfully lovely. 'For a magazine,' she added. 'If he lets me.' She smiled at Ed, but he didn't return it. 'That's why I'm here.'

Delphine nodded, looking satisfied with Maggie's response, and moved away to serve another customer.

'Are you sleeping with her?' Maggie asked.

'Does it matter?'

'Not at all.'

'Well, then.' His face was inscrutable. 'Who are *you* sleeping with?' he asked. 'Graham, I suppose.'

'How do you know about Graham?'

'You mentioned him in one of your profiles. Something about waiting for him to pick you up from The Dorchester at the end of an interview. You put far too much personal detail into your pieces, Maggie.'

'My editor likes it. She likes . . . stories. You read one of my profiles in *Supernova*?'

'I *do* read the occasional magazine, Maggie . . .'

'Right. Well, Graham's no longer on the scene,' she said. 'It fizzled out a year ago. Wasn't going anywhere.'

'That's sad,' said Ed, no empathy in his voice.

'Nothing lasts forever,' she said. *They* should know, she thought. The two of them sitting up at this bar, half-talking. Graham had never really been a contender for her heart, anyway. Nobody had for a long time.

'No, it doesn't. How's Eloise?' asked Ed.

'She's great, thanks,' said Maggie, brightening at the thought of her daughter. She'd phoned her before she'd left, telling her she was going abroad for a story. To the Seychelles, she said, for some old actor. Eloise had said, 'Lucky you, Mum! Have fun!' Maggie hadn't told Eloise about Ed Cavanagh. Not ever. 'She's a scientist. She's getting married next year.'

The next question on her lips was, 'How's Michael?' but she didn't dare ask Ed about his son. Not yet. She had to get the interview first. Her *cautionary tale* in the can. So the unasked question hung in the air, like a quivering cartoon arrow, no way for it wobble its way from her parapet over to his.

'Your parents,' asked Ed. 'Are they still . . . ?'

'Mum's gone,' said Maggie. 'Ten years ago. Dad's nearly ninety. In a nursing home. Parkinson's.'

'I'm sorry to hear that,' said Ed.

'Your mum . . .?'

'Seven years ago.'

'I'm sorry.' Neither of them brought up Neville Craddock.

'How's Stevie?'

Maggie smiled. 'Very successful, big house in Hadleigh, five children . . .'

'Good for him,' Ed said. 'Why are you only here for twenty-four hours?'

'I planned to get in and out. I've a life to get back to. A retirement.'

'You're retiring?'

'Yes.'

'No more writing? No more profiles?'

'Nope. I'm hanging up my notebook.'

'That's a shame. You love that job.'

'Nothing lasts forever,' she repeated. They were both saying nothing, meaning nothing. At one time their words would have ebbed and flowed like the sea.

'No, it doesn't,' he said, his own echo. 'No more missing people, then,' he added, and the barb of that stung, like he had probably meant it to. He looked away from her and fixed his eyes on a tin ad for mango soap and she remembered the last time she'd seen him. She knew the time, the day, the season, the weather, and what they were both wearing. She knew every word she had said to him, and him to her. She could still remember the smell of the sea and of candyfloss and chips, and the sound of seagulls and the train rumbling up the pier. She wondered if *he* did. 'You *do* look good, Mags,' he said, turning to her again. A dagger and now a rose; she had no idea what he was offering her.

'No, I don't,' she said, touching her unruly charcoal and silver hair. She was becoming Janey, always putting herself down. Dear sweet Janey who had died thirteen years ago of pancreatic cancer. 'Life,' she sighed. 'We knew it was going to happen, but we never quite believed it, did we?'

'Nope,' said Ed. 'Ageing is not for the fainthearted, that's for sure.' She hadn't quite meant that; she'd meant that when they were young and in love time had stood still, that it had tricked them into thinking nothing could ever tear them apart.

Ed ran his finger along the length of a beer mat peel. Re-crumpled his crumpled pack of cigarettes. 'There's a band later,' he said.

'Really? You were in a band once,' she couldn't resist saying and she could swear he almost laughed, that he wrestled to keep his face straight.

'Indeed, I was,' he said carefully. 'Do you remember that night?'

'Of course,' she said lightly. 'The band you were in was memorably awful, so why wouldn't I have done?'

'What was the name of it?'

She scoured her memory and frowned in concentration. '"Wired" something . . .' she pondered. '. . . *Wired Tomb!*'

'Wired Tomb . . .' Ed shook his head and allowed himself that laugh. 'What a bunch of pretentious idiots! I mean, what does that even mean?' He looked animated suddenly. His face, she thought. It was as she had always remembered it, its contours and its expressions.

'It led to great things, though,' she said instead. 'Wired Tomb.'

'Yes,' said Ed, and his voice was soft, but also cold, like an arctic wind was gusting all the way through it. 'Look what it led to.'

Chapter Eight

8 P.M., 3 JULY 1975

When Maggie had turned up to the former Ritz cinema on Curzon Road, which was now the Top Rank Bingo Club, she'd entered the swirly carpeted lobby in the giggling slipstream of a gaggle of high-spirited women, loudly celebrating their escape from marital homes, before they'd disappeared behind double doors to the bingo. Maggie had made her way to reception, where a woman was disdainfully thumbing through a knitting magazine.

'Hello,' Maggie said. 'I'm picking up a ticket for *The Dumb Waiter.*'

'The play? It's in the Old Bar,' the woman lazily replied, sliding open a drawer under her desk with the long red talon of her little finger. 'First on the right. *Good luck,*' she whispered, handing Maggie the ticket. 'I'd take a book if I were you.'

Maggie patted the bag on her hip as though she already had one. She followed the migraine-inducing carpet to a propped-open door with a chalkboard sign outside it, bearing the apology, 'Pinter's *The Dumb Waiter*. Only £1, if you fancy it!' Next to it was a round ashtray on a tall metal stand, cradling an ambivalent cigarette, still smoking; on the other side, an optimistic empty plastic tub with a single note in it.

Three sets of eyes landed on Maggie when she entered the room – a darkish space with a small stage at one end. Another dozen chairs remained empty. Maggie sat down but felt she was too close to the stage, so she moved back two rows. Three more people shuffled in: a couple in matching denim jackets and a scruffy man by himself, who slouched in his seat and immediately lit up a pipe.

'Come to see someone in the play, have you?' asked the woman nearest to Maggie. She had huge coiffed hair and wrinkled stockings under the flap of her pea green housecoat. 'My son Freddie is "Ben",' she said proudly.

'I know the person who's playing Gus,' Maggie said, feeling awkward, as she didn't really know him at all and she was nervous being here. What if Ed looked out from the stage and was disappointed at the sight of her? What if he had only promised her the ticket on a whim, had left it in politeness, and had met someone else since the pub on Saturday? Someone he liked better than her?

'Oh, right. Girlfriend, are you?'

'No,' said Maggie quickly.

'Recent stand-in, I'm told,' said the woman, looking displeased. 'Still, my Freddie can always carry him, if he's not very good.'

'Thank goodness for Freddie,' muttered Maggie, but the woman had already turned back in her seat and was rustling in a large bag of humbugs.

There was some banging from backstage. A hammering sound, then a big thump. The plum polyester curtain wobbled a little. A man wandered on to the stage: biscuit-blond hair, severe side parting, rail-thin, turned-out feet, a thin khaki-coloured suit hanging off him like a flag. If he looked unhappy at the turnout, he didn't show it.

'Ladies and gentlemen,' he said with a strong Essex accent and a big smile, over-egging the rather sad assembled pudding, 'welcome to the Rupert Robertson Esquire production of *The Dumb Waiter*. I'm Rupert Robertson and tonight I'm introducing two new talents, Fred Duffy and Edward Craddock. Tell all your friends,' he added earnestly, 'if you enjoy the performance, as we have three more shows, and it would be nice to have a few more backsides on seats. *Tell all your friends*,' he repeated. Then he bowed with a self-conscious flourish and cantered sideways off the stage.

There was silence, followed by a coughing fit from the man with the stinky pipe, which caught along the front row, causing lots of spluttering into tissues, then the curtain started to tremble open, but one side got stuck and a teenage girl in a Buzzcocks t-shirt had to come out and manually pull it back. A yellow light illuminated two beds – a stocky lad with short dark hair lying on one, reading a newspaper; Ed Craddock sitting on the other untying his shoelaces. Both of them were dressed in black suit trousers, white shirts and braces, their faces expressionless.

Maggie felt conspicuous. She felt she was being too keen, turning up here like this, even though Ed had left a ticket for her. She felt exposed, even though Ed was the one who was on stage, waiting to deliver his first line.

It took a while until that happened. 'Gus' continued to fiddle with his shoelaces. He stood up, awkwardly pulled a flattened box of matches from one shoe, then a flattened cigarette packet from the other, and put them both in his pocket. He attempted to re-tie his shoelaces, immediately getting a laugh from the audience as he tried and failed to do it, over and over again. It was funny. Then he shuffled off to the 'bathroom', and Maggie was ashamed to note his bum looked really nice in his black trousers.

There was silence again. 'Ben' spoke first, something about an old man and a lorry, a story from the newspaper. Of course, Maggie knew the play. She had studied it for O-level English. She knew Ed's first line was, 'What?' But, right from the start, Ed was mesmerising. Vulnerable, confused, terrified, hilarious. 'Ben' seemed to be just saying the lines – he was stodgy, he was inauthentic. Ed inhabited his role – he was fluid, playful and convincing. Maggie couldn't take her eyes off him: Ed had the exact presence he'd had as Rick Hastings, rock guitarist. He was handsome in his white shirt and braces, he was beguiling; he had *curls*. Maggie reckoned he was the sexiest 'Gus' *The Dumb Waiter* had ever known.

Even the audible hails from the vast bingo hall next door didn't daunt him. Freddie was flustered by them – they made him lose his momentum or fluff his lines; Ed incorporated them into his act. He rolled his eyes at the interrupting audacity of 'Top of the shot, ninety!' – getting a laugh – or looked crossly bemused at 'All the sevens, seventy-seven', which made the sparse audience laugh even more, and when there was an exuberant shout of '*House!*' from next door, he stopped in his tracks, mid-sentence, taking an unscripted existential pause, and the 'crowd' was transfixed.

By the time that familiar *Dumb Waiter* motif came around – the envelope under the door – the seven of them in the audience were completely in Ed's hands. Maggie turned quickly to look at Rupert, at the back of the room, who was operating the lights, and he also looked in complete raptures at Ed's performance.

At the end of the play, in the dramatic tableau when Ben pulls his gun on Gus, the moment was almost ruined by a gusty cry of 'Legs eleven!' from next door, followed by a loud and enthusiastic chorus of whistles and 'Whit woo!'s. The audience froze, then collapsed into nervous giggles, but Ed held his terrified stance, unfazed, then finally relaxed, breaking into a smile and winking shyly at the crowd before giving a cute little bow, while Freddie, who had already come out of character and simply looked horrified, placed the gun on the floor and backed away from it, outsmarted.

Ed stayed in the spotlight, staring out at his auditorium, his eyes shining. There was a fire in them, an acknowledgement he was talented at this, that he really had something. *And he's right*, Maggie thought. Rupert ran from the back of the room, retrieved Freddie from the wings and dragged him out so the two players could take a bow together, but all of the applause, except that of Freddie's mum, was for Ed.

'Tell all your friends,' Rupert had implored again, his arm around Ed. 'Make sure to tell all your friends!'

Maggie had hung around. There didn't appear to be a 'back-stage', so she'd loitered by the side, her bag over her shoulder, until she was the only one left in the room. Ed finally materialised from behind the curtain in jeans and t-shirt, looking impossibly hand-some and glowing with the surprise of his success.

'What did you think?' he asked, hopping off the stage to stand next to her.

'Fantastic,' she replied. 'You were really brilliant. Did you enjoy it?'

'I *loved* it,' he said, and his broad smile was in no danger of leaving his face. 'I loved it so much,' he continued excitedly, thrust-ing his hands in his pockets. 'I almost chickened out, just before. I thought what the hell am I doing here? I should be down the pub, or watching *Top of the Pops* or something – but didn't that get me here in the first place, watching *Top of the Pops* and imagining myself as some sort of pop star?'

'I guess it did,' Maggie said, returning his smile. 'You were very, very good,' she added.

'Thanks,' grinned Ed. 'Thanks for coming.' God, he was gor-geous, she thought. Lit from within. 'Do you want to go to the pub?' he asked. 'It's only eight o'clock. We could go to The Crown on Pedlar Street.'

'That would be nice.'

The foyer was empty but for a couple of women at arcade machines at the far end. One of them had been in the audience of *The Dumb Waiter* – by the fire exit, red skirt. She was cranking her handle with gusto and waving at them with her free hand.

'Well done, Ed!' she hollered over. 'Why didn't your mum come?'

'She had to work!' hollered back Ed. 'She's coming tomorrow!'

'My mum's friend, Renee,' Ed explained to Maggie in a stage whisper. 'We'd better go over.'

'Ah, good,' said Renee, once they got to the fruit machine. 'She'll love it. I mean it's a bit *dull* – not a lot happens, does it? But you're so *funny* in it,' she added warmly, and then looked all sad and touched Ed heavily on the arm. 'You know, I thought word might have got out and your dad might have shown his face,' she said, pouting a heavily lipsticked bottom lip. 'You being in a famous play and all that.'

'No,' said Ed, and his face remained largely the same, but Maggie could see sadness clouding his forest-green eyes.

'*Shame*,' said the woman, as though she were saying it about the weather, or there being no Battenbergs left on the shelf in Safeway. 'Ah, well,' she added cheerfully, 'maybe tomorrow night.'

'Yes, maybe tomorrow night. Thanks, Renee.' Ed steered Maggie away. 'Bloody woman,' he muttered to Maggie, and she could only pull a sympathetic face – the forthrightness of the earnest fourteen-year-old on Southend seafront, asking him questions about his dad, now tempered – and they walked through the foyer and past the bingo hall where one of the double doors was open and whoops and cheers were coming from inside. Someone had just won 'House'. Ed turned to Maggie, the sadness in his eyes gone and a playful look on his face instead. 'Shall we have a game of bingo? Do you fancy it? It's a bit of a laugh.'

Maggie peered into the hall. She'd never been to the bingo before – Mum said there was no wheelchair access. Well, hardly any places had it, to be honest.

'Alright,' she said, amused. It *did* look a laugh, and she was with Ed and happy to do anything with him. 'I've never played before, but why not?'

'You haven't lived!' he said, and he took her arm and they walked in, to be hit by a wall of sound – of excitement and laughter and a man shouting a list of numbers into a microphone so a winning ticket could be checked. And colour, too – shiny red plastic seats, the multicoloured ball machine, competing hues of blouses and handbags, and a blue and yellow carpet of a thousand hallucinogenic whorls.

Ed bought two books of bingo tickets and a Top Deck shandy for them both. They squeezed on to two side-by-side red plastic seats screwed into the floor at the only free melamine table, right at the back.

'I haven't got a pen on me,' said Maggie.

Ed employed his charisma and scored a couple of marker pens off a tiny lady on the table behind. He folded the front cover of the bingo book over for her and explained how the game worked.

'Keep your wits about you!' he warned, with a wink. 'My mum's an absolute demon at this, but you need sharp reflexes.'

'I'll try,' answered Maggie. 'How hard can it be?'

The next round began. The bingo caller had a very nasal voice, arched bushy eyebrows and a bald head. Maggie's eyes darted over her card, searching for the numbers as the caller announced them. Ed kept a close eye on her numbers, too, and nudged her if one of hers came up.

'Sixty-six,' he'd say, 'you've got that,' and watched while she ringed it.

'Number three, there you are,' he'd whisper, pointing at the number on her ticket.

They played three games. Every time a number was called there was an 'Ooh!' or a chorus of muttered 'Got that!'s from the crowd. As the tickets filled up, with more and more numbers ringed, these rumblings increased, accompanied by an air of mounting excitement, to the crescendo of a 'Line!', someone would shout, or 'Yes!' or 'Here!'

Shouts of 'House!' were the loudest and immediately met with collective giant sighs of surprise and disappointment, players at the tables throwing their pens down or shaking their heads in congenial resignation. Maggie was really enjoying it. It was great fun. And as the games went on, she realised their thighs were gradually moving closer to each other's until Ed's leg was almost pressed against Maggie's and she really liked it. He touched her forearm occasionally, when pointing out a number to her, and she liked that too.

'You look really pretty tonight,' he said, as another player's numbers were checked for a line.

'Thank you, so do you.'

Ed laughed. He was still illuminated from his success. His face bright and engaged. His curls a marvel. 'You really are far from a scrappy kid now,' he said, and she blushed with pleasure. 'What do you do for a job?'

'I've just finished Sixth Form.'

'What are you going to do next?'

'I want to get a job on the *Gazette*.'

'You want to be a journalist?'

'Yes. I need to get my A-level results first, though.'

'Wow. Good for you. You're ambitious,' he said.

'I guess I am.' She shrugged. 'What about you? What are *you* going to do?'

'What do you mean?'

'Well, you're not going to stay at the women's shoe shop, are you, not now you realise you have all this talent?'

'Well, I don't know,' said Ed, but he looked extremely pleased.

'You know you need to pursue this, don't you?' Her fourteen-year-old forthrightness was back. She wasn't nervous now, being with him. She felt excited and curious.

'Yes, I think I do.' He looked serious now.

'Good,' said Maggie. 'Good.'

'You really believe in me!' laughed Ed, and he looked surprised.

'Hasn't anyone ever believed in you before?' Maggie asked quietly.

Ed looked at her. His eyes were soft. 'My dad did,' he said. 'He said I had more in me than being a factory worker or a shop assistant, but I had to find out what it was. He said I was going places – I just didn't know where yet.'

'And now do you know where?'

'Maybe,' Ed said, his eyes gleaming. 'Maybe.'

'And *all* the twos, twenty-two!' The bingo caller's voice burst across them. 'Yes, that's a *House*, ladies and gentlemen! And now we're going to take our half an hour interval. Drinks and snacks at the bar!'

The caller stood up and quickly slugged the remainder of his pint, then lit a cigarette. The decibels went up in the room. Ed smiled at Maggie.

'Another shandy?' he asked her.

'Yes, please.'

He came back from the bar with another can of Top Deck each and a packet of Chipsticks. Ed opened the packet all the way out on their table so they could share them. He looked at Maggie, appraising her.

'I remember the night we went down to the seafront really well,' he said. 'Do you?'

'Yes, I do,' she answered softly.

'Thanks for humouring me,' he said, looking pained. 'Those stupid cigarette butts.'

'It was my stupid idea,' replied Maggie. 'And it was a long time ago.' But she could tell it wasn't for him. From how he had looked when Renee had mentioned his dad. From how he looked now. 'You've never had any word from him? Your dad?' she asked.

'No,' said Ed. 'Nothing at all.'

'Do you still think he's on a desert island?'

'No! God, how ridiculous!' exclaimed Ed, laughing sadly. 'That I even thought that. No, I don't think so. I have no idea where he is.'

'I'm sorry,' said Maggie.

'I know. You were sorry then, too.' He looked at her tenderly. He wound one of the curls flopping from his forehead around his forefinger. 'I hope you don't mind me saying this, but I get the feeling you'd be someone who'd always show up for me,' he said. 'Is that mad?'

'Well, it depends how long "always" is,' she replied. 'We might not know each other very long.'

'I think we might,' said Ed. 'At least I hope so.' He flashed her a dazzling, lopsided grin. 'Sorry,' he added, 'does that sound arrogant, me talking about you showing up for me? I didn't mean it to. I think I mean you seem like a really nice person.'

'I'm not *bad*,' she joked. 'I have my moments.'

'I like most of your moments so far,' he said, staring at her. 'You know, I really liked not being *me*,' he said thoughtfully, 'in the play.'

She was surprised. 'Is it not good, being you?'

'Not always.'

'Because of your dad?'

'Ooh, that's direct.' He mock-grimaced, then smiled at her. Sighed. Popped a Chipstick in his mouth. 'You don't want to hear all this.' He shook his head.

'Try me.'

He looked at her. 'What is it about you that makes me come out with all this stuff?' He smiled. 'On the prom, and now in a bingo hall of all places! You must just have a way of getting things out of people. You'd make a *good* journalist.' He laughed. 'Or a secret agent.'

She grinned. 'I'll go for journalist, if you don't mind.' She really liked the way he was looking at her.

'Okay,' he said, bending his head nearer to hers, over the bag of Chipsticks. 'I'm going to tell you something I've never told anyone. I think a crowded bingo hall is *exactly* the right setting.' He smiled a half-smile, picked up another Chipstick, then set it down again. 'The papers reported that we were a happy family, you know, when my dad went missing. "A normal, happy family", I think they said, but I don't know if we were. There was a lot of . . . silence,' he said. 'Pinter would have really got off on it.' Maggie smiled. 'My mum . . . she's very domestic, very particular, almost obsessive about the house – how clean it is, how tidy. She's got worse with every passing year, starting from when I was a kid. She would clean the same thing – the cooker top, the back step – over and over. She would scrub something endlessly, or wipe over a surface a hundred times. When Dad was still with us . . . I know he just wanted to escape. He'd go out walking a lot in the evenings. And there were days when he looked so unhappy, and then he would cheer up a bit and he would want to arm wrestle with me again and he would put his arm round Mum when she was cooking and say, "What are we having tonight, then?" and everything would be alright. But it wouldn't last. So, actually, sometimes I *do* think he's on that desert island, that he's escaped somewhere. Because I think he wanted to. And sometimes . . . it's hard, now it's just Mum and me. In a different house, but with the same *absence* all around us. And sometimes I want to escape, too.'

'I'm sorry,' Maggie said. 'I'm sorry for before, and for after. And for now, especially.'

'Thank you. Nobody else knows all this stuff,' repeated Ed, shaking his head again. 'I haven't told anybody any of it, just you. You're a really good listener, Maggie May.'

'Why, thank you,' she joked, but she was lost in his eyes. His eyes were amazing.

'But it's not just that,' he continued. 'You're curious about the world. You want to *know*.'

'I suppose I do.'

'I like that.' Ed grinned, and she grinned too.

'And we're back!' called the caller, returned to the stage. 'Eyes down, everybody, for a *line*.' Their eyes went down, and the room played six more games, and Maggie and Ed laughed and joked and smiled shyly and not so shyly at each other. They checked each other's numbers. Ed larked around, doodling on the edges of his card: little houses, stars, hearts.

'I like you,' Ed whispered to her, as the fourth winner went up for their cash prize. 'I like your face.'

'I like yours, too.' Maggie felt all giddy inside. She wanted to doodle a great big heart down the side of her card and write Ed's name in it.

'If I get a line, well, I'd really love to kiss you.'

'Would you?' Maggie asked, her insides tumbling and rumbling as fast as the bingo balls inside the caller's giant machine.

'Yeah. To celebrate.' Confidence, not arrogance, that's what he possessed. 'Would that be okay? Would you mind?'

'Not at all,' she said, and she was nervous and pink in the face as they played. Ed had two numbers to get – seventy-seven and thirty-three.

'All the threes, thirty-three!' cried the caller. Ed ringed the number on his potential line with his pink pen. He winked at her, and her stomach flipped.

'One and six, sixteen!'

Ed pulled a really disappointed face, tilting his head to one side. She laughed as he pressed hard, ringing the unhappy number on the wrong ticket with disgruntlement.

'On its own, number two.'

Ed pretended to throw his pen down in a 'darn it!' fashion. He didn't even bother circling the number on the other ticket.

'All the sevens, seventy-seven!'

Ed raised his eyebrows, grinning mischievously, and slowly, very slowly, ringed the number. Then he leant towards Maggie and kissed her very softly on the lips. He tasted of shandy and Chipsticks. A woman on the next table whistled the 'legs eleven' whistle at them and a few other people joined in, to a smattering of applause. They eventually pulled away from each other, laughing.

'*Line!*' shouted Ed. And he beamed, not taking his eyes off Maggie until the woman came round to their table and checked his card. 'Let's get out of here,' he said, once he had been given his five-pound cash. He took Maggie's hand and they scurried from the hall and across the lobby and out into the warm night. It was dark now, almost eleven o'clock, and the wind had picked up a little. The moon was large and bulbous in the sky. They stopped by the willow tree in the car park, where the branches wept silently and shimmered in the breeze of the night.

'Would you come and meet me after the play again tomorrow?' Ed asked. 'And I promise we really *will* go to the pub.'

'Okay.'

'Great.'

'But I need to get home now,' she added. 'I've got Sixth Form in the morning.'

'You're so conscientious.'

'I try. And you've got the shoe shop,' she teased. 'For now.'

'Can I kiss you again?'

'Yes.'

'Shall we imagine one of us has got a full house?'

'That's a big prize.'

'It's a very big prize.' He was bringing his lovely face towards hers. He kissed her again, and it started like the kiss in the bingo hall, but it continued into something she had never known before. His lips were warm and delicious, and she was surprised, after a few seconds, by his tongue, too, exploring hers, and it brought with it a passion and *naughtiness* she hadn't experienced with Glen of the Upper Sixth, and she smiled into that kiss, as it was amazing. When she opened her eyes, his were closed, as though he were totally absorbed, lost in it, and that made her stomach flip somersaults like a circus performer. She closed her own and when she opened them again, at the end of the kiss, he was staring at her and smiling at her with that cheeky smile she imagined would remain boyish for the rest of his life.

'Can I kiss you forever?' he asked, his green eyes glinting and his arms still around her.

'Nothing lasts forever,' she wanted to say, those three little words her mum was so fond of, but something stopped her, as maybe she was already wondering what a *forever* with Ed Craddock might look like. So, instead, she burrowed her face shyly into his shoulder and whispered, 'Maybe. Let's see how things go.'

Chapter Nine

9 P.M., ON THE ISLAND

'Would you like to eat something?' asked Delphine. She was behind the bar, cleavage primed, brightest smile on. 'Sardines are a special tonight.'

Ed and Maggie looked at each other. Two virtual strangers, sitting on high stools in Olly's, wondering how to be with each other again after all this time.

'Yes, please,' said Maggie. 'I'm starving, actually. I haven't eaten since one of the planes.'

'Two plates of sardines,' Ed said gruffly to Delphine. 'Is it on your expenses?' he asked Maggie and, as he wasn't smiling, Maggie wasn't sure if he was joking or not.

'Why, can't you afford to treat me?'

At last count, Ed was worth 85 million dollars – Maggie had read it in a Sunday paper. Although his superlative box office pinnacles were behind him, he had invested wisely, maintained his wealth. At one time, they both would have laughed at this exchange. Now, Ed pulled a face and made an infuriating 'humph' noise, then returned to his rum and Coke. He made her want to run away. She imagined herself on Ed's stolen boat, in the dark, paddling ferociously from this island . . . She looked at her watch. Nine o'clock. Twenty hours left on the island with Ed Cavanagh and the small matter of an interview he didn't seem to want to do.

The fish arrived swiftly, grilled sardines with sea salt and coconut shards. Ed ate hungrily, nodding over his food like he always did, slotting in forkfuls of fresh sardines and asking her, 'Good?' and she was reminded of all the times they had sat in restaurants together, eating and drinking and laughing. When they had dawdled over huge glasses of red wine and idled over rich pasta dishes and it had been fun, so much fun. All those hours that had slipped by and were gone.

'Do you want to see the cocktail list?' Ed asked, when the sardines had all disappeared. 'Well, there isn't an actual list. There's only two cocktails, and they both involve rum.'

Maggie plumped for an Island Dream – rum and milk and coconut. Ed ordered another rum and Coke, and she wondered if he was in here every night, propping up the bar, enjoying his self-imposed exile and the postponement of real life, far from Hollywood. She wondered if he was haunted by the ghosts of his past and whether her face was amongst them.

'Here's to . . . well, I don't know what,' said Ed, when the drinks arrived, and they clinked their glasses reluctantly together.

'No, I don't know either,' she agreed. She had no idea how this time together would pan out, whether she would get the interview or not. How she would get through it all, these hours with him.

'*My friend?*'

A mountain of a man was standing behind them. Late fifties, early sixties, he was wearing a white suit, like a US Navy passing out uniform – stiff epaulettes but grubby at the lapels and the trousers creased at the bottom and a little too short. His shoes – black, lace-up, round-toed leather – were scuffed, and he was holding a smart white cap with worn gold edging.

'Hello, Baptiste,' said Ed warmly. The two men shook hands and Ed clapped Baptiste on the back.

'You're having a date?' asked Baptiste. He had steady brown eyes, close-cropped hair the colour of mercury and a small mouth below a huge Omar Sharif moustache, which parted in a shy smile to reveal a giant's causeway of crooked teeth.

'No,' said Maggie and Ed in dry unison.

'This is Maggie,' said Ed. 'An old friend. A still very beautiful friend,' he clarified, and Maggie was wide-eyed, unless this was simply a dose of Hollywood charm for Baptiste's benefit.

'Hello, Maggie,' said Baptiste. 'Welcome to Mémoire. Will you be taking the tour?'

'Sorry, he asks everyone that,' said Ed. 'It's his opening gambit.' Baptiste did a practised little bow, circling his military cap. 'Baptiste does very occasional tours of the island. He can take you to some wonderful places here.'

'We have giant tortoises,' said Baptiste, 'and a lagoon so blue it is like a painting. And the old plantation house,' he said to Ed, and Ed nodded.

'Wonderful,' echoed Maggie, 'but I'm not sure I'll have the time . . .'

'We can start early,' said Baptiste. 'In the morning?'

'Maybe we *should* take the tour,' said Ed, looking at her. 'It might be fun.'

'And a great way to avoid the interview . . .' Maggie raised an eyebrow at him.

'Maybe you'll get something great out of me over the back of a giant tortoise. Though I wouldn't count on it.'

'You've just been "tired".'

'That's it.'

Ed wasn't tired. He had recently lost out on a big role, which, after *The Swimmer*, he assumed would be his, the press reported.

It was the role of the 'old man' in a remake of *The Old Man and the Sea*, the Hemingway classic. Ed had lost it to George Clooney. That was why he was here, the world knew. That was why he had flounced from Hollywood and come to Mémoire, resulting in headlines almost every week that shouted, 'Where is Ed Cavanagh?', 'Hollywood Legend Now Missing for Three Months!' and 'Who Can Explain Disappearance of Veteran Hollywood Star?'

Maggie shook her head at him and turned back to Baptiste, who was beaming at her, the row of gold signet rings on the hand holding his *An Officer and a Gentleman* cap glinting in the candlelight.

'Are you also an actress?' Baptiste asked curiously. 'Like our famous Mr Ed? Man, I love his show, *Echo Drive*. Are you in it? Are you that woman who works in that store?' He narrowed his eyes and peered at her face.

Maggie laughed. 'No,' she said. 'I'm not an actress. I'm a writer.'

'A writer? Well, that's *almost* as exciting!' proclaimed Baptiste cheerfully.

'Almost.' She smiled.

Baptiste now looked at Maggie quizzically, then at Ed, then back to Maggie again.

'You two have history?' he asked.

'No,' said Maggie.

'Yes,' said Ed.

Maggie looked at Ed and he raised his hands in a shrug. 'Don't we?'

'Yes, but it's better if we don't talk about it.'

Ed gave her a strange look. 'Thank you, Baptiste, we'll do the tour,' he said. 'Much appreciated.'

'Great,' said Maggie half-heartedly. The interview was slipping from her grasp.

'Well, I'll leave you to your drinks.' Baptiste smiled warmly at them. 'See you later, my friend.' He strode off, tall and broad and serene, like a white pillar candle.

'He's quite a character,' she noted. 'I like the suit.'

'Yes, I keep thinking there must be some story to it,' mused Ed. 'He told me he got it in the Seychelles, on Mahé. He wears it every day.'

'There are no tourists on this island. Apart from you, and now me. How does he make a living as a tour guide?'

'He doesn't. He's a handy man – a *concierge*, as he likes to call himself. He delivers, he runs errands, he fixes things for people. He used to be a mechanic, over on La Digue. He commuted there by boat as a young man, as it was the only island nearby to have cars and he was always fascinated by them. Baptiste owns the only car on Mémoire, what little use it gets. He loves that old wreck – legend has it his cousin dismantled some old jalopy and sent it over to Baptiste bit by bit on a boat to rebuild it here.' Ed grinned. '*Rumour* has it he's still on its first tank of petrol.'

Maggie laughed. 'Did you take his tour when you first got here?'

'Yes. He was the second person I met, actually, fresh off the boat. I met him here in Olly's. He took me on the tour, then set me up with the skiff and all the fishing equipment. We just get on well.' Ed shrugged. 'He's a good sort, is Baptiste. Enigmatic, you know, but solid.'

'And you're not worried he'll go to the press and tell them you're here, make himself some extra cash?'

'*Maggie,*' chided Ed. 'You're dashing my happy tableaus. Me and Baptiste, out fishing together. Sitting in this bar, putting the world to rights. Brothers in arms . . . No. Well, he hasn't done it yet, and neither has anyone else. The islanders here are private and loyal. No one has betrayed me. They're just not that kind of people.'

Was that an arrow meant for her? Maggie let it pass through her and hit a tin advertising sign on its way out. 'You haven't told Rupert where you are?' she asked. 'Or Alexia?' She didn't mention Michael. 'How could you not tell them where you are . . . ?' They both knew what she was getting at. His dad's disappearance. The hurt and confusion it had left behind. *How could he do the same to his friend, his wife or his son?*

'They know I'm alive,' he said brusquely.

She nodded. It had been in the press that Ed had phoned his wife Alexia from LAX, from a payphone, while he was running away, so there would be no criminal investigation, no police search. He had told her he was getting on a plane and not to worry about him. He had been seen at the airport, too, making that call, by several bystanders. He'd even given a couple of autographs before he disappeared.

'How come no one spotted you on the way here?' Maggie asked. 'In the Qatar Airways departure lounge. It *was* Qatar Airways, wasn't it?'

'Always the detective,' grimaced Ed.

She let that arrow thud dully against her. 'Or saw you on the plane to Doha? Or the one to the Seychelles?'

One of the sillier headlines about Ed's disappearance, from a less-than-serious American publication, was 'Has AWOL Star Gone to a "Desert Island" Like Father?' Ed had been quoted from an interview he'd done many years before, during which he'd spoken about his missing father, Neville Craddock, saying he'd once had this ridiculous notion his father had gone to 'find himself' on a remote island somewhere. Maggie had read that article, like she had everything on Ed's flit from Hollywood, and had dismissed it – along with the rest of the world.

'After the phone call,' he said, 'which I made in a very public place, on purpose, I went to the restroom' – she noted his

Americanism – 'and put on a disguise. Oh, don't look so thrilled, it was just a jumper, a pulled-down hat and a silk scarf wrapped around my face. I didn't dress up as a clown, or anything . . . After I'd got here, the flight records couldn't be checked,' he shrugged, 'as everyone knew I was alright. I'd signalled my departure. No police. No FBI. It was nothing like it is in the movies.'

'*The escaped man . . .*' She waited to see if he would mention the postcard he had sent her, but he was down off his seat and excusing himself to go to the restroom. 'Be right back,' he said, and she watched him go.

Ten days ago, twelve weeks after reports of Ed Cavanagh absconding from LA appeared in the papers, a postcard had arrived at Maggie's London flat. It was a postcard of the clocktower in Victoria, the capital of the Seychelles, on Mahé. The postmark, also the Seychelles. Maggie had turned it over in her hands as she stood in the doorway of her little kitchen, snow softly falling at the window and blanketing London in a white shroud. There was nothing on the back of the postcard, just her address, written in Ed's utterly recognisable handwriting, the white space next to it empty. No airmail sticker. She had taken the postcard, her morning cup of coffee and her dappled memory of all their past conversations to the laptop, and a quick Google search told her that Qatar Airways flew from LAX to the Seychelles twice a day, via Doha in the Persian Gulf. A second search of possible routes told her that a ferry called the *Petit Coco De Mer* left every Monday afternoon at 4 p.m. from Praslin Island in the Seychelles, to an island called Le Calme and that it was sometimes possible to get a small boat from there to Mémoire Island.

The postcard then idled on her sideboard, and she eventually slipped it between the pages of a Nora Ephron hardback there, until Simone, her editor, had picked up the book and flicked through it after a drunken dinner party *à deux*, extracting the postcard and slurring, 'The Seychelles? Who's this from?' and Maggie had made the mistake of sleepily answering, from her prone position on the sofa, 'Ed Cavanagh.'

Three and a half hours earlier, Simone had turned up already half-pissed, her normally sleek raven bob in dire need of the hairbrush she always kept in her handbag, her ears poking through it like coins. She'd tottered in on stack heels, cigarette pants and a white shirt, like Uma Thurman in *Pulp Fiction*, lighting up before she was even through the door ('Thank fuck! Your flat is only one of two indoor spaces I can smoke in. The other is the loo at the Culvington Club') and stuttering, 'It's all gone tits up.'

'What has?' Maggie had asked. She was stirring a Béarnaise sauce and setting out two glasses.

'*Supernova.*' Simone took a drag of her ubiquitous Marlborough Light. 'We're being forced to go digital.'

'Well, that's not a bad thing, is it?' Maggie had taken the bottle of Bombay Sapphire from Simone's slender hand and poured her a glass from it, adding tonic and ice. She and Simone had been fierce friends for nearly thirty years, from when they had first worked together and had clattered from bar to bar, arm in arm and drink to drink.

'Well, no,' Simone said, grabbing the bottle back and swigging from its neck, 'but it's not what I know and the pressure's on. We have to launch with a big splash and I'm fresh out of ideas.'

'Right,' said Maggie. She wasn't sure what to say next. The truth was she was planning to retire and had been wondering how to tell Simone for months. She would do it tonight, maybe, after a couple more gins and the full low-down on plans for the magazine.

'*Ed Cavanagh!*' Simone had exclaimed, standing at Maggie's sideboard and peering with boozy eyes at the date on the postcard's postmark. She knew all about Maggie and Ed, all their history. She had spent many a time, pointed chin on pale folded fingers, delighting in the edited stories and the second-hand glamour of it all. 'Mahé – well, that's interesting . . . Is that where he is?' She peeled a Post-it note from the clocktower. 'Mémoire? What does that mean? Is that a place?'

'Mémoire's the name of an island,' muttered Maggie from the sofa, remembering the note she had scribbled. 'In the Indian Ocean.'

'And that's where you think he is?'

'Yes,' Maggie admitted miserably, too drunk to save herself from what was coming.

'Well, you have to go there!' cried Simone. 'Go and find Ed! Get the scoop on what he's doing there! Why he left! This could launch us in digital, Maggie!'

'No. No.' Maggie shook her head. 'I was going to retire.'

'*Retire?* When? Why?'

'Next month. The month after. I just thought it was time.'

'It's not *time*! You've got loads more good work in you, Maggie! And a profile on Ed Cavanagh could be *great*! I know he's not *huge* now, not like back in his glory days, but the remake of *The Swimmer* has put him back on the map. Piqued the public's interest. Especially *our* readership. This could be the kind of big profile that could really blow up. *Where Is He Now . . . ?* This is what you *do*!'

Maggie sighed. She had been writing Where Are They Now? features for over forty years, in one form or another – from poignant and nostalgic pieces in the *Southend Gazette*, back in the day, to profiles of once-feted soap opera cast members in hugely popular *Actually!* magazine in the nineties, to studied and in-depth features on lost and faded stars in *Supernova* magazine. She thought she'd had enough. She never thought she'd be asked to profile *Ed Cavanagh*.

'No, no, I'm not going to go and find him,' she muttered, sitting up and rubbing her head. 'I can't. Besides, everyone knows why he's there. It's a Hollywood flounce, when he didn't get *The Old Man and the Sea*.'

'Yes, I read that,' said Simone. 'Well, maybe you can come up with a different angle.'

'Maybe.'

'One last job!' Simone had pleaded. 'Like in heist movies. Book your flights and anything else you need. I'll do it for you myself, if you like. And go as soon as you can, in case he does another flit. I know you'll write a *brilliant* profile. And you never know, you might get "closure" on him.' She had done that awful bunny-ears finger gesture.

'I don't think I'll ever get closure on Ed Cavanagh,' Maggie had laughed bitterly. 'He's not that sort of man.'

'*Find* him!' Simone had insisted. 'If you pull this off and we launch with a big enough splash, maybe I'll be able to keep *Supernova* alive and everyone on the payroll.'

'Is digital that important?'

Simone had pulled a resigned face. Maggie knew that it was.

'I don't know,' she had replied, shaking her head, but somewhere inside her something was stirring. A desire to hunt down a missing person. A latent anger she maybe could finally exorcise if she wrote about Ed and what he had become, compared to what he had been, in their past.

◆ ◆ ◆

Ed returned from the restroom, hoisted himself back on to his stool and took another slug of rum. Maggie studied him in profile. His chin. His straight, handsome nose. The slant of his tanned forehead.

'How long are you planning to be here for?' she asked him.

He turned to look at her. 'Honestly, I don't know. No current plans.'

'I suppose at some point you'll just decide to go back,' she said. 'And you'll slot into your old life.'

'I guess so.'

'But for now, you're here. Because of all the *tiredness*,' she said.

'Exactly.' He picked up his cigarette packet, crunched the lid open and shut.

Maggie had found her angle. She had come to Mémoire to do a piece on Ed Cavanagh about what fame can do to a person. She was going to write about who Ed used to be and who he was now. How he had become the sort of person to do a Hollywood 'flounce'. She thought readers would like to know.

Ed glanced at her, then looked away. The candle in front of them finally dripped on to the bar. He dipped his finger into the warm candle wax and rubbed it against his thumb until it became a ball.

'There was a little Italian restaurant once,' he said, without looking up. 'Every time I've been to a fancy restaurant in Hollywood I've thought of that place.' Immediately conjured up for Maggie were images of checked tablecloths and red candles in wine bottles, their wax dripping on to the table. Franco's. 'And the table in the corner.' Maggie wasn't sure if Ed sounded nostalgic or bitter. Memory lane was certainly no tree-dappled avenue for either of them. It was lined with barbed wire and littered with landmines. Franco's . . . She hadn't thought about that place in years. 'The band will be on soon. Would you like another drink? I'm having one.'

He looked up at her. She could leave right now and go back to her bungalow. She didn't know if she'd find it in the dark, but she could risk it. There was a torch on her phone, until the battery ran out. But Maggie needed to get this interview. She needed to warm Ed up. Dip into those memories. And leave with her profile, after these hours.

'Okay,' she said. 'Yes, I'll have another.'

Chapter Ten

9 p.m., 17 September 1975

Maggie had worked late. There was something delicious about that phrase, she'd thought as she'd walked through the town, where the leaves on the trees were beginning to turn brown and a pre-autumn breeze was gearing up to switch a scuffle of them down the pavement. *Working late* – it meant you did something important, that you were needed. That maybe you were going places.

Eighteen-year-old Maggie Martin, who had received three As in her A-levels, had been working at the *Southend Gazette*, selling advertising space, for three weeks and four days. She sat in a smoke-filled office next door to Accounts and across the corridor from the newsroom. She had to telephone both previous clients and untapped businesses and sell them space in the newspaper – quarter pages, half pages or full pages. She had to fill out order forms and send them off to Graphics. She was already one of 'the girls' – the girls of Advertising, Accounts and the typing pool – who, it seemed, right from her first morning at the *Gazette*, were required to wear short skirts, high heels and pretty blouses, go for lunch together at the local café (as the pub was reserved for the men), know all the showbiz tittle-tattle of the hour (including which film star was in which film) and be constantly boiling the kettle.

Maggie liked Advertising, but considered it a start only, as it was across the corridor in the newsroom where she really wanted to be, but they hadn't been hiring when Maggie had been looking. Her phone calls to the *Gazette*, citing her A-Level grades, asking to be a junior, a dogsbody, anything in the newsroom, had not been fruitful, but Advertising *had* been hiring, and Maggie could wait. She was in the building. She could *see* where she wanted to be, when the doors to Advertising and the newsroom were both open at the same time, and she could spy across the corridor through the brown fug of smoke of both offices to the journalists. And two of them were women! Both wearing trousers! Either dashing around with bits of paper or frowning in concentration at their desks. There were the copy-editors, scowling over mugs of coffee and A4 notepads and scratching their heads with pencils. The editor, occasionally yanking open the stiff brown door of his office in the corner and beckoning someone inside. All the purposeful, clever people, she thought, doing exciting things – reporting facts, solving mysteries, investigating the world – while she sat at her desk in her pretty blouse and punched out the numbers of boring local businesses on her thick beige telephone.

Tonight, on this September evening, three weeks into Maggie's new job, one of the female journalists had been working late, too. While Maggie had been negotiating a rate for Glitz Nightclub, down by the gasworks – the fog-horn-voiced owner having said he was only able to speak on the telephone after 7.30 p.m. – the doors to Advertising and the newsroom were both open and she could see the woman, at her journalist's desk, also on the phone, a rapt and earnest expression on her face as she scribbled on a notepad. The female journalist tapped the back of the phone with her forefinger as she listened to the person on the other end. She crossed and uncrossed her legs under the desk – navy trousers, brown lace-up shoes. She had cried a little at one point, wiping away fierce tears with the bent knuckle of her thumb, then she had scribbled furiously on her notepad some more before breaking into a gratified smile.

Soon, Maggie had thought, offering a further half-page discount to the booming nightclub owner, as the journalist caught her eye across the offices and the corridor and nodded curtly in her direction. *Soon*.

◆ ◆ ◆

Ed sometimes waited for Maggie, as he had tonight, in a little Italian restaurant up from the seafront. Franco's was halfway up a set of steep steps – the slopes, they were often called, the terraced gardens and grassy interludes that rose from Southend's promenade and scaled up the hill. Sometimes Ed and Maggie had a picnic on the slopes. Sometimes they walked all the way to the top and kissed on one of the benches near the shaped flower beds. They had been going out with each other for three months. The play and the bingo had turned into a night at the pub, which had turned into more pubs and nights at the Kursaal, on the penny arcades and bowling, and a few more nights at a few more pubs until one of the pubs became 'their pub' and they were 'going steady'. Ed had met Maggie's mum and dad, and Stevie, who grunted 'Wotcha' to them as they sat at the kitchen table drinking mugs of tea. Maggie had met Ed's mum, who served them coffee in dainty cups and fairy cakes on paper doilies in the clinically pristine 'front parlour', where one of the velour sofas still had its cellophane wrapper on.

Maggie and Ed had kissed *a lot*. Outside pubs and on benches and whilst walking along the street. In her bedroom, in his bedroom. Under a magical tent of overlapping tablecloths at the end of a barbecue at his cousin's house in Hadleigh this summer, as, around them, in the dark, paper plates were folded around leftover chicken drumsticks and shoved in bin liners. They had even kissed at a stage door, coming out from a play – and the people waiting there for Ed to sign their little autograph books cheered and Maggie blushed, and Ed had kissed her again.

Tonight, as she'd walked over to the secluded table in the corner of Franco's, she'd wondered if they would do that thing where they would outstay everyone else in the restaurant and remain talking long after the candles in bottles had burnt down to stubs, the staff clearing up loudly around them and trying to get them out. Because that was one of their *things*.

'Hi, you,' Ed had said. He had an almost prohibitively sexy black shirt on, with three unbuttoned buttons. His hair was tousled and inviting her to tousle it some more. She had to will herself not to ruffle his curls before she sat down.

'Hi, *you*. How did rehearsals go?' she asked. He had a script resting on the table, and she had a blue cardboard file she was able to place proudly on the empty seat next to her.

'Great thanks. I think the company's coming together really well on this one now.'

'Oh, the *company*,' she teased, settling back in her seat and noticing how lovely his green eyes looked by candlelight. 'Things *have* become swanky!'

After *The Dumb Waiter*, there had been a small write-up in the *Gazette*, suggesting Ed Craddock was both a 'wunderkind' and an 'emerging talent'. Ed had brought the newspaper to their second date, The Ship and Anchor on Cook Street, and had read it out to her at the bar. When they next met, Ed told her Rupert Robinson had telephoned him after work and said he wanted to be his agent, and Ed hadn't been sure exactly what that meant, and Rupert had said it meant he had someone looking out for him, who would help him get jobs. He told Ed that yes, he was an untrained actor, yes, he had only been in one play, but there was a casting for an Agatha Christie production coming up at the Cliff's Pavilion – and he would eat his hat if Ed tried out for it and didn't get it.

Ed went for the audition, as young Ralph Paton in *The Murder of Roger Ackroyd*, and he got the part, announced by Rupert the next morning, who pretended to tuck into his dad's old flat cap with a knife and fork at a greasy spoon down on the seafront before tossing it to the floor and giving Ed the good news. That had recently finished, and Rupert had just sent Ed up for Arthur Kipps in *Half a Sixpence* at the Regent Theatre in Ipswich, and Ed got that part, despite never having sung or danced before but apparently he could do that, too. He told the women's shoe shop on Arch Road he wouldn't be working there any more, sold his last pair of tights, and the script for *Half a Sixpence* lay on the checked tablecloth, next to the candle in the bottle.

'I'm so happy for you,' Maggie said, shrugging off her navy-blue blazer on to the back of her chair. And she was. Reviews for *Roger Ackroyd* had been fantastic. The *Gazette* had called Ed 'highly charismatic', 'a name to watch', said, 'there's something about this kid', 'born to be a star'. ('Born to be a star!' she had exclaimed on reading that one in a pub on Rose Street. 'Bloody hell!') 'How's learning the banjo going?' she asked him, as he filled her waiting wine glass with Chianti. Arthur Kipps plays a banjo in *Half a Sixpence*.

'Not bad,' said Ed. 'I'm beginning to master it slightly better than I did the guitar.' They both laughed. 'I'm enjoying it, actually. I'll soon be an aficionado of all the string instruments. Maybe it'll be the ukulele next. How was the *Gazette* today?'

'I've had to come straight from there,' she said. 'Hence the office blouse and the short skirt,' she said, attempting to yank the skirt down her thighs.

'I've no complaints about the skirt,' said Ed, with a little wink.

'I didn't think you would.' She smiled, blushing. 'I had to wait to talk to the boss of Glitz. I sold him a full page. I also sold a half page to the butchers on Quince Road and another to the dress shop above the Kursaal today.'

'Fantastic,' said Ed. 'They must be really pleased with you.'

'I think so.'

'But it's not what you want to do?'

She shook her head. 'No. I might go and see the editor next week. Ask him if there's an inroad for me. I'm nervous, though. The other female journalists are much older than me. They look . . . serious.'

'*You're* serious,' said Ed. 'Go for it. You can do this. You're an excellent writer.' She had shown Ed some pieces she'd written: little film reviews and write-ups about local events, like the summer carnival. 'You're going to become a world-famous journalist, you know, Maggie.'

'Thank you,' she said, but that wasn't what she wanted. She didn't want to be a *world-famous* anything. She didn't want glory or her name in lights – things she was sure *he* was on an ascending path to, his steps assured, one after the other, a spotlight sparking up at each one he took. She just wanted to *work*. To find out stuff and write about it. And to be good at that. 'I'll take in samples of my writing, see what he says.'

'You'll do great, just you wait and see. And you'll make a *very* sexy reporter,' he said, placing a hand on her thigh.

'I don't really think that's the point.'

'No, but I like it.' Ed leant forward and she leant in to meet him and he kissed her, softly and seductively. 'Let's order,' he whispered.

They ordered garlic mushrooms and bruschetta with tomatoes and olives for starters, and *arrabiata* pasta dishes for mains. They ordered another bottle of red wine. They didn't take their eyes off each other, apart from to speak to a new, sharp-nosed waiter.

She wasn't close enough to Ed, Maggie thought. She subtly shunted her chair towards his. Ed reached across the table for the wine, and when he sat back, he shifted his chair nearer hers, too. The wick of their wine bottle candle flickered. Ed caught a bead of melted semi-cooled wax on the tip of his finger and rolled it into a ball with his thumb.

Kiss me again, thought Maggie. There was something about him tonight. How he looked. How his curls fell in his eyes. How his eyes danced in the candlelight, and he looked so happy and so confident and so full of excitement for the future. She wanted to be in that future, she thought. She wanted more hours like this with him. More days, more months, more years. She wanted all of it, with him.

Kiss me again.

'You look really beautiful tonight,' he said.

'Thank you, so do you.'

'All I want to do is kiss you.'

'You've still got all that pasta to get through.'

'I'm not sure I want it.' He looked at his watch. She looked at hers. It had just gone nine.

'Everything alright with your meals?' The waiter was at their table, peering disapprovingly down his sharp nose at their unfinished plates.

'Yes, thank you,' they said in unison.

'Will you be wanting any more drinks?'

'*No, thank you.*'

The waiter tutted and stalked off. Ed set down his fork. 'Would you like to have dessert down on the beach?' he asked.

She tilted her head at him. 'What do you mean?'

'I mean, would you like to have dessert on the beach,' he repeated. 'Yes?'

'Yes,' she replied.

Ed fished in his wallet for some cash and flung it on the table. Maggie hurried into her jacket. Hand in hand, Ed led her down the steep steps to the promenade, and across the road to the other side, past one of those Victorian shelters where old ladies sat in the winter. They were running and kissing. Laughing. Delighting at how lucky they were, to feel like this. To be laughing and kissing and running in the moonlight. Ed led Maggie down to the beach and a blanket, laid out on a shallow well of pebbles in front of the low sea wall.

'Is this for us?' she asked. The blanket was striped and edged with fronds of tassels lifting in the night breeze.

'It is. I'm glad it's still here,' he laughed.

'It's a nice blanket. Where's our dessert?'

She watched as he lunged towards the wall and retrieved two Walnut Whips, in their clear wrappers, from a mousehole at the bottom.

'Here you are,' he said, holding one out to her. 'But first I need to kiss you. Properly.'

He fell to a heap on the rug and pulled her, giggling, beside him. Clutching their Walnut Whips, they entwined their yearning bodies, kissing and kissing and kissing, their hands in each other's hair and holding each other closer, closer, until the Walnut Whips lay discarded amongst the pebbles. The blanket was cool against Maggie's back, the pebbles moulding themselves to her. The sea beyond them was black and endless, melodic on the night shore; the moon a perfect half of itself, hanging in the sky like a folded paper plate. It was their hour; it was their night. It belonged to them. Maggie felt she had known Ed forever but also that he was brand new. That this moment was as fleeting as it was everlasting.

'Maggie,' Ed whispered finally, his arms tight around her waist. 'I need to tell you something.'

'What is it?' she whispered, their mouths barely an inch apart, their breathing heavy in the night air.

'I want to tell you that I'm in love with you.'

'Are you?' Her voice was barely audible. She spoke into the side of his neck, the softness and heat of it.

'Yes. I love you, Maggie. Do you love me?'

How could he not know? she thought. How could he not feel her heart beating through her chest, or witness how her eyes drank him in, or understand how her lips wanted to press on his, and how her body longed to adhere to him? Hadn't the floodgates already been unlocked? Her heart, prised open to be exposed and beating only for him, since he first sang 'Maggie May' to her?

'I love you, too,' she said, and she felt great joy in its admission. A great release, a giant soaring freedom. She'd been ready for him, she thought. Ready for love. For *life*. And she kissed him, again and again, hungry, as they smiled into their kisses and she knew, like the sea knows the shore, over and over again, that this love was once in a lifetime. 'Mum and Dad are out,' she added eventually, breathing hard. 'They've gone to my auntie's for the week. And Stevie's stopping the night at his mate's.' Her open heart was thunderously loud in her ear.

'The house is empty?' whispered Ed, his pupils large.

'Yeah.'

'What are you suggesting, Miss Martin?'

She swallowed. 'I'm suggesting we go back to mine.'

'Right . . . well, okay. We can do that, if you're *sure*?'

'I'm sure, *Mr Craddock*,' she whispered. 'Roll up the blanket and retrieve the Walnut Whips.'

This time she took his hand and pulled *him* through the streets of Southend, their feet echoing on the pavements, and lights from upstairs windows glancing down on them. As they neared Charlotte Road and her house, Marmalade was meowing at the front door, and she had to feed him in the kitchen, with Ed waiting – leaning against a kitchen worktop, a soft smile on his face as he never took his eyes off her.

'There you go, boy,' Maggie said, stroking the soft fur on Marmalade's head. Then she took Ed's hand again and led him upstairs to her bedroom. Once there, she sat on the bed, suddenly shy, slipping off her work shoes and letting them tumble to the floor.

'Have you done this before?' she asked Ed.

He nodded, silhouetted in the doorway.

'Thank god,' she said. 'At least one of us knows what we're doing. Would you like some music on?' She was shaking. She tucked her hands under her thighs, under the thin material of her skirt.

He came and sat on the bed beside her. 'What have you got?'

She leant over to her desk under the window and flicked through her record box. 'The Carpenters?'

'Go on, then,' Ed said, with a grin. '"Superstar", please.'

'Really?' She smiled at him. 'It's the second to last song,' she said. 'You'll have to wait.'

'I can wait.'

They sat and kissed through 'Rainy Days and Mondays', then a song called 'Saturday' – jaunty, only a minute long, a little incongruous. In 'Let Me Be the One', Ed started unbuttoning Maggie's pretty blouse, popping the buttons carefully, one by one, and smiling gently at her between kisses. During '(A Place to) Hideaway', he carefully moved his hand up Maggie's thighs, to the zip at the side of her skirt, and she began to slowly, slowly unbutton his jeans. Through 'For All We Know', and to the accompaniment of Karen Carpenter's clear, true voice, they gradually unpeeled each other from their clothes and – tenderly, tenderly – by the opening bars of 'Superstar', they were both naked and lying on the bed facing each other, and Maggie had soft tears in her eyes.

'It'll be you one day,' she whispered, as the drum beat steady as a metronome and the oboe blended with the melancholic harpsichord of the intro. 'A superstar. And I'll be the one at home wondering if you remember you once told me you loved me.'

'That's never going to happen,' whispered Ed, reaching for her, but Maggie worried, even as he began to touch her, making her gasp, that it was in his reach – being a superstar. It was both on the horizon and written in the stars, whichever he got to first.

Chapter Eleven

10 P.M., ON THE ISLAND

The singer's voice was high and melodious. She was wearing a loose red t-shirt dress, almost down to the sandy floor, her hair pulled into a bun. With eyes closed, she swayed in time to the music, and what was left of the audience at Olly's were enraptured by the band – the singer, a bongo player and a backing track from a tiny tape deck – who had pitched up, nailed nine really nice pop songs, and were currently making a lovely job of 'Say a Little Prayer', as marginally cooler air drifted in from the beach through the bar's open windows.

The two people up at the bar had nothing much to say to each other now, let alone a prayer. After Maggie had mistakenly agreed to another drink, Delphine had served them both and then engaged Ed in a long and funny story one of the fishermen had told her, something about a sea turtle and a bread roll. Ed had found the story very amusing, and his laughter had been loud and robust, his back turned to Maggie.

Maggie had found herself staring at the melting candle on the bar, resisting then succumbing to splinters of memories of Franco's and her single bed, and how, after they had made love for the very first time, they had lain there on their backs in the dark, listening to the sounds of the street at night – a car door slamming, someone putting the bins out, Mrs Sullivan calling for her dog to come in from the back garden – or were these things she only imagined she remembered? Holding hands and whispering to each other for an hour or so, until Ed had said he'd better go, 'work in the morning', or words to that effect. She remembered how he had kissed her at the back door, how he had said he wanted to see her the next night and the next night and the next.

'And when he turned around, the turtle had gone!'

Maggie had shaken her head free of fragmented memories as Delphine had finished her funny story about the bread roll, to Ed's laughter, and the band had set up and started playing.

'Say a Little Prayer' ended to warm applause. A man in a *Hawaii Five-0* t-shirt wolf-whistled and a table of four got up and made their way to the door. The Friday night crowd was beginning to dwindle now, slowly peeling off and heading for bed.

'Would you like dessert?' asked Ed, finally turning to face her. They had listened to the band, lost in themselves, not talking. 'There are only two on offer. Coconut ice cream or rum baba.'

'Rum baba, please,' said Maggie. She still liked a dessert.

Ed nodded. He called Delphine back over and ordered two. Maggie looked at her watch, shiny on her wrist. Ten past ten. Eighteen hours left on the island. When she looked up, Baptiste was at the bar again.

'How is everything here?' he asked Ed and Maggie, as though he were a solicitous waiter.

'Great, thanks,' said Ed.

'You like Olly's?' Baptiste asked Maggie, his steady eyes not moving from her face. 'You like our island so far?'

'So far,' assented Maggie, non-committedly.

'Ed is very good company, no? He tell you all his Hollywood stories?' Baptiste's mouth curled into a shy, snaggled smile.

'I know most of them,' she said. The women, the drinking, the dreadful relationship Ed had with his son. How he had turned up at his son's wedding to singer Leoni James six months ago but had been turned away . . . It had been in the papers.

'Of course, if you two have history. You are very happy to see each other again?'

Maggie pulled a face. She didn't dare look at Ed's. Baptiste narrowed his eyes and smiled enigmatically at Maggie.

'Well,' he said, 'I will see you tomorrow for the tour. It will start at 7 a.m.'

'Oh, that's early.'

'There is lots to see,' said Baptiste, 'including a morning swim in the lagoon. Pack your swimming costume.'

'I'll be fishing until 6 a.m.,' Ed told her. 'I'll knock for you just before seven.'

'That's really early,' repeated Maggie. In London she didn't rise until eight o'clock and needed at least three coffees before she got in the shower. 'Although I suppose it gives us plenty of time. I leave the island at five,' she told Baptiste. And before that she had to get everything she needed for her piece.

'Tomorrow? You leave tomorrow? But *mon dieu*!' Baptiste exclaimed. 'So soon?' He glanced at the big metal clock behind the bar.

'Sadly, Maggie is only here for business,' said Ed, his face unreadable. 'Tour at seven, then interview about two o'clock?'

She hoped that would be long enough to do what she needed to do.

'We will make it the best tour ever!' declared Baptiste. 'See you tomorrow.' He looked at them both curiously for a few seconds, gave another little bow, then walked away.

'See you, my friend,' Ed called after him.

'*Sadly?*' Maggie queried. 'Very sarcastic. Very gruff. I see you haven't left your infamous Hollywood exterior behind, then.'

Ed shrugged. 'Travels with me everywhere I go.'

The band announced their next song. 'Tequila Sunrise', the Eagles hit. They sat in silence for a while, but during the second chorus, Ed asked her, 'Who was your last Where Are They Now? on?'

'Dilly Baxter,' said Maggie. Dilly had been a child star, had acted in a *very* famous Christmas movie and now lived in the Outer Hebrides on an alpaca farm.

'What was she like?'

'Charming, funny, irreverent. Gave me a tour of her wardrobe.'

'Nice.'

'But a sad character, too. Ruined by all her good fortune, she said.'

'How so?'

'She had too much, spent too much, gave too little value to anything and ended up with nothing.'

'Well, fame's a funny thing,' he mused, nursing his glass. 'It gives you everything, but it takes so much away.'

'Or, in your case, it just gives you everything . . .' she retorted, although she knew that wasn't true, and then, as she couldn't resist, added, 'I'd never seen you more delighted than when you said the only person more famous than you was the Queen.'

'It was *you* who said that.' She smiled; he didn't. 'Fame and money is just a game.'

'In which there are always losers.'

'And don't we both know that!' retorted Ed, and they both fell silent again. That dormant anger, so much of it between them when they had last met, fifteen years ago, swilled like the dregs of a warm rum in a glass tumbler. She was a little drunk now, she realised, four drinks in. She didn't trust what she might say. 'How's Michael?' he asked abruptly.

Oh, we're here already, she thought.

'I don't know,' she replied.

'You haven't seen him?'

'No.' She thought of the letter burning a hole in her rucksack, back in the bungalow. 'When did *you* last see him?'

'His wedding day.' Ed looked rueful. 'I turned up uninvited. I knew I shouldn't have done, but I found out where the reception was, and I turned up. I wanted to show how happy I was for him. I wanted to offer my congratulations. But he sent me away.'

'I heard,' she said.

'Leoni was kind, though. Or she tried to be. I think she felt sorry for me. The poor old boy, the spectre at the feast . . . I shouldn't have gone.'

Maggie nodded. There had been about six photos of the event in the *Daily Mirror*, noteworthy because of the photographs of Ed being ushered from a simple but pretty outside reception by an angry-looking Michael Gray-Cavanagh. One had shown Leoni's hand on Ed's arm, a plaintive look on her face.

Ed and Michael had always been doubles of each other. Same curls, same green eyes. 'Two peas in a pod,' Ed had once proudly referred to himself and his son. And now they couldn't be further apart.

The letter in Maggie's rucksack had been sent to her in the post by Michael three weeks ago. It was in a sealed white manilla envelope inside a larger brown one and he had included a note.

If anyone can find Dad, you can. Can you get this to him?

Maggie had no idea of the contents. Was it a cease and desist? A written notice to finally sever the father and son connection? Another returned cheque? She knew there had been many, over the years, from Michael back to Ed; she'd read that in the papers, too. Maggie had an interview to get through. She couldn't risk giving the letter to Ed yet. A big upset could scupper her plan.

Ed took a mighty shuck of his rum and Coke. Their rum babas arrived but they did not touch them. 'Let's change the subject,' he said. 'I shouldn't have brought up Michael, I'm sorry. It still gets me, *fathers and sons*.' He sighed, then smiled. Fixed his eyes on hers. 'It *is* nice to see you, Maggie. Is it nice to see me?'

'Are you joking?'

'Maybe.'

'Then I honestly don't know.'

'But you had to come.'

'To do the interview, yes.'

'Nothing about coming was to see *me*, Detective Martin?'

'I *am* seeing you.' She tilted her head at him. 'I'm looking at you right now.'

Ed laughed. 'Okay, we can play this game, too, if you like. We've got all day.'

'Twenty-four little hours.'

'Exactly. All the time in the world. And here we are again, not making it work.'

'Because we never could.' Maggie tapped at the stem of her glass. Condensation had created a pool of water around its base. 'I don't know what you're getting at.'

'No, neither do I. If I don't give you the interview, what will you do?'

'I'll go home without it.'

'Will you be happy with that?'

'Nope.'

'Course you won't. Maggie Martin always gets her man. Well, you better be nice to me then.'

It was her turn to laugh. 'Being nice to each other never seemed to be enough.'

'True. We tried, though, didn't we, Maggie? Didn't we try? And wasn't a lot of that trying a whole lot of fun, especially in the early days?'

'Shush,' she said, putting her finger to her lips as the band struck up another song. 'I like this one. And I really don't know what you're getting at.'

Chapter Twelve

10 P.M., 12 OCTOBER 1976

Ed and Maggie were *Ed and Maggie*. A couple. An entity. A collection of over a year of memories: cosy autumn evenings at Franco's, shrugging on jackets to venture home, arms around each other. Cold fingers delving into newspaper cones of hot chips at the end of the pier in winter. Walks along the seafront on deceptively sunny spring days when the wind sliced through them like a pirate's cutlass. Balmy nights when Maggie waited at the stage door for Ed to come out, his eyes and his talent shining. And endless hours tumbling in Maggie's single bed, and sometimes his, in all four seasons, before they had got a little place to rent together.

55 Brook Street. The house with the red door. It was very modern to be living 'over the brush', shacking up, whatever people liked to call it, but Ed was earning, and Maggie was earning, and they wanted to be together and there was no time to get married when so much exciting stuff was happening, and marriage could wait, couldn't it? They didn't care what anyone thought. Marriage to them seemed staid, old-fashioned. It was what other people did but they weren't like other people and wasn't that wonderful?

It was October again, and their favourite kind of Friday night – when Ed was not on set but at home, and Maggie was not working late at the *Gazette*. Ed had cooked spaghetti bolognaise and had it waiting for her when she had got back from work at half seven. They had cleared up, Ed washing and Maggie drying. Now it was ten o'clock and they were reading, in happy communion, Maggie's legs across Ed's on the sofa. Maggie was halfway through *Valley of the Dolls*; Ed was scrutinising the latest script for *Trent Hill Comprehensive,* a TV drama he was shooting the second series for – three episodes of the first had been shown on television so far, where he played a just-qualified teacher at a London secondary school.

And they were listening to *One of These Nights*, the Eagles album they both loved and played over and over.

'Do you want another cup of tea?' Ed asked Maggie.

'In a minute.'

They had a tiny sitting room with a big bay window, and a small kitchen with a two-ring electric hob. Upstairs, if they stood on tiptoe at the bathroom window, they could see the sea. There had been power cuts several evenings this week. On Tuesday they had spent the night by candlelight, eating cold Heinz minestrone soup out of the tin. On Wednesday, they had eaten cheese sandwiches, brushed their teeth by the light of a torch and gone to bed early. Last night, Ed had played the guitar he stored leaning up against the door of the boiler cupboard, in a painful serenade to her – his skills had not improved, despite his best efforts. Tonight, the power had mercifully been back for spaghetti bolognaise and episode three of *Trent Hill Comprehensive,* at 7.40 p.m., where rookie teacher Phil Hume had dealt creatively with a group of Third Year bullies and asked Miss Hill, the Biology teacher, out on a date.

'You're wonderful in this,' Maggie had said, as they'd balanced their dinner plates on their laps. 'Everyone's going to completely fall in love with young Mr Hume, the cheeky but vulnerable Physics teacher.'

'Thanks,' Ed had said delightedly, not taking his eyes off the screen, as though he couldn't believe it was him.

'Can you help me with my lines?' he said now, looking up from his script.

Maggie set down her book. 'Of course.' She removed her legs from his lap. Ed got up to turn down the record player and handed Maggie the pages. 'What's the scene about?'

'It's in the staff room. I'm about to have a row with another teacher who helped some kid cheat on his exams.'

'Okay.' She sat up straight. 'So, I'm Mr Gillick?'

'That's right.'

'I just read his lines and you'll read yours?'

'Yup.'

They did a few lines. Ed was very funny, very convincing, very nuanced; *she* sounded like a robot. 'No wonder I never got picked as Mary,' she laughed.

'In the nativity?'

'Yeah. The back half of a donkey was the limit to my thespian talent.'

He grinned, and she loved the way he grinned at her like she had said the funniest thing on earth. She knew how this grin – in this poky living room, with the suspect brown carpet and the electric fire and the floral orange curtains that didn't quite close – looked on the small screen, and how those watching would melt when they saw it. What did the *Daily Mail* write-up say? That viewers must feel dissatisfied they either *weren't* him, or weren't *with* him? That his smile, 'encapsulating mischief, danger and a hint of vulnerability' – temporarily hers alone, in this hour – was making him a star.

They tried it again, the same scene, and Maggie ended up reading Mr Gillick's part in a silly voice and they both collapsed into giggles.

'You're a lovely distraction,' he said, grabbing his script off her. 'But you're not really helping. I'm going to make us both a brew.' He doffed her gently on the top of the head with the rolled-up script and walked into the kitchen. 'What are you working on at the *Gazette*?' he called from the kettle.

'Oh, it's boring compared to your stuff,' she called back. '*Hunky Mr Hume* . . .'

'Come on, I want to know! What's your current Where Are They Now?'

Maggie was no longer selling advertising space for the *Gazette*. Just under a year ago, she had knocked on the brown door and gone in to see Damian Figgins, the editor. He had been on the telephone and had signalled to her to wait. She had stood in the doorway of his office for a long time, feeling utterly self-conscious, with any confidence she had mustered rapidly leaving her. Eventually, Damian had said, 'Thanks, mate, see you in court,' into the telephone and slammed it down with a grimace.

He'd gestured for her to come in. He was the king of the gesture, she knew, from what she'd spied of him across the corridor: the nod, the beckon, the rolled eyeball, the jolted sideways thumb to signal someone should get out of his sight. The slice of a finger across the throat to say something was dead in the water.

'What can I do you for?' Damian had said, once Maggie had approached his desk and said she worked across the corridor, in Advertising. 'I've seen you,' he added, and he looked her up and down. From the high heels to the skirt to the pretty blouse. He had lascivious, bulbous eyes.

'Well,' she'd said, and she'd twittered on (when she wasn't *usually* a twitterer) about wanting to become a reporter – the slow and measured voice she had planned and rehearsed going out of the window and landing with a thump on the concrete of the car park outside – and how she had been praised for her essay-writing skills both at school and at college. That her typing was fifty-five words per minute, that she had an A-Level in English Literature and another in Sociology and another in History – all A grades. That she had an eager and enquiring mind, which did seem like the right thing to say, she'd thought, as he'd nodded sagely at that one, and that she was willing to learn on the job, and she was a fast learner and could she be transferred from Advertising, please, if there was a vacancy?

Damian had looked at her for a good half a minute following her speech, taking in her earnest red face, then rubbed his fingers together as though contemplating money, or crumbling an OXO cube. 'Alright,' he'd said. 'I do have something I need someone for. Follow me.'

He hitched himself up from his chair, swayed his rump over to a metal filing cabinet in the corner of his office – the grey fabric of his trousers stretched so tight he reminded her of a hippo – and pulled open the first drawer with a flourish, rattling it out on its runners. It was full of cardboard files, blue and beige, hanging from metal struts like bats.

'We're doing a new feature called Where Are They Now?' he said. 'I need someone to be in charge of it.'

'Alright,' she said efficiently. 'What needs to be done?'

He thumbed through the hanging files like they were bar chimes.

'We've got photos in here. Events we've covered in the last decade or so. Long service dinners, golf functions, parties at the mayor's office, gardening club presentations, Follies nights, that kind of thing. I need half of page fifteen filled every week, using one of these photos and the tagline, "Where Are They Now?". We want people to write in, you see, if they recognise themselves – well, if they don't, we're bloody stuck – but I'm sure they will, as who wouldn't be delighted to see themselves in the paper? Or if *they* don't, someone else will know the buggers. We'll put a phone number under the photo – that'll be *your* phone number, if you're game.' Here he gave a great big donkey laugh. 'Once we get going, we'll print the photo from the previous week – smaller, underneath the big one – with a few words, something chintzy like,' and he put on a silly, high voice that Maggie worried was supposed to be her, '*We heard from the lovely Marge Anderson, second on the left, in magenta taffeta, who remembers her colleagues at Braithwaite's Pies with much affection and says they served a lovely melon cocktail at the annual Pie Fanciers cocktail evening in December 1972.* Do you get it?' he buffed at Maggie, his coffee and cigarette breath wafting displeasingly up her nose.

'Yes, I think so,' she said. 'We print a photo and hope readers supply us with a few lines of copy for the following week.'

'*Walla!*' said Damian, clicking a fat finger triumphantly against a fat thumb. Did he mean *voilà*? 'Lazy journalism at its finest, my girl! You'll soon learn.'

'Got it,' said Maggie. 'And you'll transfer me, from Advertising to the newsroom?' she asked. 'Tomorrow?' she added hopefully.

'Sure thing,' replied Damian, sounding bizarrely American. 'You can start on the Where Are They Now?s in the morning, nine o'clock *sharp*, and do any other dogsbody running around for the journalists. Whatever's needed.' He gave her a jaunty thumbs-up.

But wasn't she going to *be* a journalist? Maggie had thought, on her way out of Damian's office. Never mind, she was *in*; she'd made it to the *newsroom*. And the next morning, she walked through its door wearing a pair of trousers and a plain button-up shirt, in flat shoes, and she'd felt a million dollars.

'Good morning,' the female journalist whose eye she'd caught across the corridor had said, looking up from her desk.

'Good morning,' Maggie had proudly replied.

The first Where Are They Now? that went to print featured a photo from the filing cabinet of four people in the mayor's office, toasting each other with large whiskeys and grinning toothily at the camera. Maggie's new newsroom phone number was printed beneath it, with her compelling (she thought) entreaty to get in touch and, two days later, she got three phone calls.

'How funny to see myself!' The callers had all said exactly the same thing; three of the four toothy people said hadn't it been a great day when they met the mayor, after winning a local business award for excellence in their processed meat business and wasn't it sad about 'Bob Noakes, who is no longer with us'. Maggie wrote her three lines of copy, making it nostalgic and a little humorous, and Damian had declared it 'just the ticket'. She was off and running.

By the third Where Are They Now?, the calls had begun to take a different direction. A woman called and said she recognised Jean Wright on the far left of a photo at a work's canteen Christmas party, and wondered where she had got to, as they had lost touch, and wasn't it a shame no one knew where she had gone. Maggie had ended up promising she would do some digging, just a little, to see if she could find her, and she made a few phone calls and ended up talking to Jean, who had moved to Saffron Walden in North Essex and ran a little jam-making business there. Maggie was able to write as such under the smaller photo the next week, under the new photograph of three men in the RAF enjoying a drink at the Naval and Military Club. When *that* photo went out, a man called Jim called and said he'd love to know what had happened to the other two men, Francis and Bert. And she eventually found them, too, although one of them had sadly died in an industrial accident, but his widow was so thrilled to be in touch with his two old RAF mates that Maggie had felt she'd done a public service. She had felt thrilled, too, even allowing a single tear to come down her face – wiped away by a secretly pilfered man-size tissue from Damian's desk.

'I'm currently working on finding a brother and sister from a photo taken at the Kursaal,' Maggie replied to Ed's question cheerfully, as he returned from the kitchen with their teas. 'I've become a bit of a detective and I've probably got a bit too involved in everyone's stories, but isn't that what journalism is?' She took her mug from him. 'I don't want to be all cold and objective. I want to be at the heart of things.'

'Getting to the heart of things is what makes a good journalist, I'd say.' Ed turned the record player back on and sat down. 'But what would I know? I just pretend to be other people for a living.'

They sat and read again to the sound of The Eagles. Ed regarded Maggie over the top of his script. 'You look very beautiful tonight. Shall we go upstairs?'

'Upstairs? Whatever for, *Mr Hume*?' Maggie asked, all wide-eyed.

'You know what for.'

They were halfway up the stairs, hand in hand and already pulling playfully at each other's clothes when there was a knock at the door.

'Damn!'

'Who on earth's that?'

'Shall we just not answer it?'

They crouched together on the stairs, shushing each other with forefingers pressed to lips. There was silence, so they continued to rush up the stairs, flung themselves on the bed, and Ed had already got one leg of his trousers off when the knock came again. Insistent this time.

'We'd better get it,' said Maggie, with a big, disappointed sigh. 'It might be my dad – he said he might drop round tonight – or your mum.'

'I suppose it might be an emergency,' said Ed reluctantly. He had admitted to her recently that he still expected a knock on the door about his dad sometimes. Just sometimes.

'I'll go,' she said. 'You put your trousers back on.'

'Unless it's a false alarm,' he said with a grin, 'or some past-their-bedtime Scouts knocking on the door for Bob a Job week.'

'Be back in a sec,' said Maggie. '*Put them on!*'

She trotted down the stairs and opened the front door to a rush of energy, a cascade of girlish voices and gasps and giggles, and a lot of scarves.

'Hello,' said a girl in a red coat and a stripey scarf, three other girls behind her equally well-wrapped. They looked in their mid- to late teens.

'Hello,' said Maggie.

'Is Ed Cavanagh here?' asked the first girl, her eyes glittering with nerves.

'Well . . . yes,' said Maggie. They had changed Ed's name when he'd got a part in a *Play for Today*. Someone up the televisual chain had decided that 'Craddock' wasn't going to cut it, that it was a name for a fishmonger, not a hero of the small screen, and *Ed Cavanagh* was born.

The girls all took a step forward, excited.

'He's here? He's in?'

'Yes, he's here.' Maggie was bemused.

'Oh my god, we've found him!' exclaimed one of the other girls, from under a long fringe and above an even longer Doctor

Who scarf, wrapped twice round her neck and trailing all the way to the ground. Maggie realised they all had photographs of Ed in their hands – A4 black and white headshots of him as Phil Hume in *Trent High*.

'Is he really here?' questioned another girl. She was a pixie of a thing, bundled into a huge coat and wearing silver tights and platform shoes. Her scarf was bright purple.

'Well, yes,' said Maggie hesitantly.

'Can you go and get him? Can he come to the door?'

'I'll just go and see,' said Maggie, half-amused, half-wishing she'd said he was out or that she'd never heard of him. She softly closed the door on them, wincing at her perceived rudeness, but worried they might storm through into the living room, all coats and scarves and chilly night air or, worse, bundle straight up the stairs.

She walked upstairs and entered the bedroom. Ed was on the bed in his underpants, a saucy look on his face. '*Please* put your trousers back on,' she said calmly. 'It appears some fans of yours are outside.'

'*Fans?*'

'Yes, four of them – girls. They're on the doorstep wanting to see you.'

'Really?'

'I could tell them you've gone out.'

'No, I'll come down.' Ed leapt up from the bed and hauled his trousers back on. He resurrected his curls with a quick brush of his hand and Maggie followed him as he clattered downstairs to the door. When he opened it, there was an audible, collective gasp, then a four-prong surge, bringing in cold air.

'Oh my god, Ed, *Ed!*'

'Can you sign my photo, please?'

'Oh my goodness, you're even more good-looking in the flesh!'

'Oh, I can't believe it, I can't believe it!'

'Mr *Hume!*'

The girls swarmed round him in the tiny hall. They pawed at his arms. They thrust his own face – the headshots – under his nose. They knocked askew a Constable print Maggie and Ed had both felt very grown-up for hanging on the wall. The girls were adoring, overwhelmed, revved to the point of hysteria.

Maggie stepped back, eventually finding herself in the doorway to the kitchen, while Ed and his fans swelled in the hall, their faces tilted up to his, needing a little piece of him to take home with them.

Maggie retreated further into the kitchen, steadying herself against the oven. She waited. Eventually, the chattering and squealing stopped, there were cantering footsteps down the path, and she heard Ed close the door.

'Well,' he said, coming into the kitchen.

'Well,' she replied.

'Fancy that! That was a turn up for the books!'

'Was it?' she said, smiling. 'I think it was thoroughly expected, don't you?'

He laughed, loud and utterly thrilled. 'You don't mind?'

'Mind? Why should I? I think I'd better get used to it.'

'Maybe,' he said.

'Definitely,' she replied.

'None of them were as pretty as you.'

'I know.' She shrugged. Sulking was not her thing. Sulking was *not* pretty. And she let him step towards her and fold her into his arms, and he smoothed her hair and she clung to him. And then the power went out and they were in darkness.

'Shit,' said Ed.

'Sexy,' said Maggie, coming back to herself, in the dark, with him. 'I can't find you . . . where are your lips?'

'They're here.' He wrapped his arms more tightly around her.

'So they are.' She brought her hands up to the back of his neck, held them there, let him kiss her – softly, slowly – and then they felt their way upstairs.

Chapter Thirteen

11 P.M., ON THE ISLAND

Maggie went to the ladies' room, noticing a single, avocado-coloured telephone on the wall in the tiny corridor outside, and wondering if that was the only means of communication on the island. When she returned to the bar, the band at Olly's was on their final song and Ed looked deep in thought.

'Did you request this?' she asked Ed as she slipped into her seat. A few lone punters were up dancing. There was a little jiving to 'One of These Nights' by The Eagles. The band had been through quite an eclectic medley of songs, from Neil Diamond to The Black Eyed Peas. She'd liked the ones that had no connection to her and Ed.

'I might have done,' Ed replied.

'You hate me that much? Are you winding me up?'

'I like this song.'

'Are you drunk? I hope you're not nostalgic.' There were too many shards of memory skittering her way. Single beds. Fans at the door. An autumn evening with a power cut.

'Sometimes I am,' said Ed, an odd look on his face. 'Are you?'

'The past is a stranger.' Maggie didn't want to be lost in memories. She didn't want to dredge up the past, drag a net along the bottom of a lake, to bring up silt and not gold, for their golden moments had all gone, ruined by both of them and washed up far away on other lands. She wanted to be safe in her London flat, after all, with her books and her radio, the window closed against the loneliness of the outside world and all her regrets.

'But *I'm* not,' said Ed. 'I'm not a stranger.'

'Aren't you?'

'We haven't seen each other for over a decade but we know each other well, don't we? We haven't forgotten.'

Maggie hadn't forgotten. All the reasons they couldn't be together. 'We *did* know each other well,' she said. 'Once upon a time . . . How's Veronica Gray?' she asked him. Veronica Gray was Michael's mother and an actress, too. Ed, Veronica and Michael were quite the dysfunctional acting dynasty.

'In a sanatorium somewhere,' said Ed. 'I'm surprised Michael's not keeping you up to speed. In his emails.'

'He hasn't emailed me recently.' *Only sent me a letter*, she thought.

'Well, she's not good. Being dumped from the *Montgomery Blue* franchise has sent her into a spiral.'

'Chewed up and spat out.'

'Is that still your take, Mags?' And she winced at the sound of this former endearment. 'That Hollywood is the root of all evil?'

'I've seen what fame does to people, in time,' she said.

'From all your missing people.'

'Yes.'

'And what do you think it's done to me?'

She didn't answer. She would save such a question for the interview.

'I'm living in a shack on a beach, Maggie,' Ed said. 'This has where fame has brought me.' He held his palms out in a shrug.

'Because you flounced off.'

'*Flounced off?*' He laughed. 'You think I flounced off?'

'That's what they're saying back in Hollywood.'

'Oh, really? Interesting.' Ed stroked his chin. 'Because of *The Old Man and the Sea* and Clooney? That's rather a long flounce . . .'

'And it's not true, is it? Because you're "tired".'

'Time will tell,' Ed said absently, staring at her. 'Man, I love this song . . . How about a temporary ceasefire? We've had a few of those, over the years. Would you like a ceasefire?'

'No, I don't think so.' She wanted to go back to the bungalow now. Sleep until morning. Do the tour, do the interview and then go home.

'Would you like to dance?' He stood up and held his hand out to her.

'Don't be so stupid!'

'Why not?'

'You're a little drunk and we hate each other.'

'We can hate each other on the dancefloor.' He grinned at her, his green eyes like rock pools. He had already placed his hand on her forearm and the feeling of his fingers was so familiar to her, the firmness and the strength and the warmth, that she was instantly flooded with the soft-sharp reminder of a long-ago happiness, and she didn't want it. 'Ceasefire,' he said. 'Come on!'

She didn't know what he was doing, and she didn't know what she was doing either, but she got down off her stool and followed him to the tiny, sandy dancefloor where an old farmer in a faded Hawaiian shirt was softly jiving with a woman half his age, and a lone man with sad eyes turned in a slow circle. She briefly wondered about the man's story and if someone, somewhere, had ever missed him, but then Ed and Maggie were dancing, too, to 'One of These Nights', and she was taken back, way back, to how they had started and how sweet and true it was. How wonderful it had been when it was right, and how bloody awful it had been when it had all fallen apart.

Ed went to place his hand at the small of her back.

'I don't think so,' she said.

'Don't trust yourself?'

Maggie burst out laughing and so did he, and she remembered all the things she had ever loved about him, but they had never been enough, all those things – not enough for them to last. As she laughed, Maggie saw Baptiste at the side of the room, watching them, a soft, shy smile on his face and his steady eyes unblinking. He doffed his officer's hat to her, and she did a silly salute back.

'Oh, Maggie,' Ed sighed, as she turned back to him. 'It's been a long time.'

'It has,' she whispered, forgetting herself, and when he went to place his hand at the small of her back again, she let him. Her pulled her in close to him and his eyes were kind and his smile warm, and she was drunk enough, too, to smile back at him, and sway with him to The Eagles.

'Do you remember us like this?' he asked.

She didn't answer. The last time they had danced had been in London in the nineties. The last memory she'd had of them was at the end of the blustery pier in Southend fifteen years ago, when he had been so cold. Now he was warm, so warm, and she swayed with him, until the hours and the days and the months and the years slipped away, and they were just Maggie and Ed again.

But the song, which on the album fades gradually into a sweet nothing, ended with the female singer doing a giant whoop and the man in the Hawaiian shirt crying, '*Oui!*', and the spell was broken.

'I need to get some sleep,' she said, stepping back from Ed and smoothing down her dress. 'I need to go back to the bungalow now.'

'Now?' asked Ed. His face was blank, his hands in his pockets.

'Now, please.'

'Let me settle the bill, and I'll walk you.'

'No, it's okay. I'll find it.'

Ed shook his head. 'You may be the thinking woman's answer to Scooby-Doo, but even *you* won't be able to find your bungalow, not in the dark,' he said. 'I'll walk you.'

Maggie stood by as he pulled a note from his wallet. As they stepped outside into the still, hot night, Ed dropped back slightly to let her go on ahead, brushing his arm against hers, and Maggie flinched.

'It's alright,' he said. 'I'm not going to touch you again.'

Chapter Fourteen

11 p.m., 13 November 1978

Ed held on to Maggie's arm, his warm hand giving it a squeeze through her gossamer sleeve.

'Alright?' he said. Around them swirled the hubbub of the green room, the chink of champagne glasses, the excited chatter of the London showbiz world.

'I'm at the London Palladium.' Maggie placed her hand on top of his. 'I'm more than alright.'

Maggie had only been to London four times before, despite the capital being just thirty minutes on the train from Southend. Once, accompanying Janey to a schools' careers fair at Earl's Court, where they had wandered miserably around accountancy stalls before giving up and escaping to the nearest Angus Steakhouse. Secondly, to go Christmas shopping with her mum, by coach – with Sandra's wheelchair stowed underneath in the luggage hold – to a lit-up and crowded Oxford Street. A third time, on a riotous Fifth Year trip to see *Coriolanus*. Tonight, she was in the West End with Ed – and Mum – at the London Palladium for The Royal Variety Performance.

It had been a *very* glamorous evening so far, and Maggie and Sandra had spent a lot of it open-mouthed. It had started with a black limousine pulling up outside the house in Charlotte Road and a driver in a peaked cap hopping out to help them, picking Mum up and placing her gently inside, before folding her wheelchair and popping it in the back. Maggie had been helped in with a gloved hand and a small, cordial bow. They had both giggled. As they had driven away, a few of the neighbours had seen them off from their windows. Denise Sullivan at number forty-seven, with the lilac net curtains. The old couple with the caravan on the drive at number twenty-eight. The kids at number thirty-three, all grinning madly. And at the window of twenty-two Charlotte Road was a beaming Dad and an eye-rolling Stevie, waggling a can of beer at them.

'Have a great time!' Dad had over-enunciated, Maggie lipreading him, above his exuberant double thumbs-up. Steve took a swig of his beer and saluted them with the can.

'Well,' Mum had cried as the limo rounded the corner of Charlotte Road and they were on their way. 'Would you look at the pair of us?'

'I know!'

Mum was wearing a navy dress with a keyhole neck that tied into a little bow and a very smart pair of navy slip-on jewelled slippers. Maggie was braving a silky jumpsuit with sheer sleeves – very Lauren Hutton and probably not her at all, but the lady at C&A had said the emerald green would look amazing with her colouring. She had on the highest heels she had ever worn in her life, too – gold platform sandals.

'Knockout,' Ed had said, when she'd first shown him. She hadn't seen him for three days; he had been up in London rehearsing for what he rather understatedly called 'a turn' at tonight's performance, a skit from an Oscar Wilde play and a sketch with Morecambe and Wise, playing his character Vaughn Petit from the current big hit: a romantic-comedy television series, *Meet Me on Primrose Hill.*

Ed was currently London's darling. He was fresh from appearing at the Coliseum in *The Importance of Being Earnest*, as Algernon Moncrieff. He'd stayed in a flat in Bayswater for two weeks while the play was on, and the fourth time Maggie had been to London was when she and Janey had gone up on the train to watch him in the play two weeks ago on opening night. She had sat and cried happy tears in row six as Ed had been so bloody good as Algernon – the charming, idle, decorative dandy. There had been rave reviews, of course. Dozens of them. Ed was flying high.

'There's even champagne,' Mum said, gesturing excitedly to the bottle in a side pocket of the leather back seat.

'Let's crack it open, then,' said Maggie. She poured a good measure into two plastic champagne flutes and they toasted each other, laughing, as the bubbles went up their noses.

'Are we still picking up Ed's mum from Westcliff?' asked Sandra.

'Oh, sorry, I forgot to tell you,' Maggie said. 'She's not coming now. She's got the flu. She's ever so sorry about it. She said she'll watch it on telly tonight.'

'Oh, that's such a shame! She'll miss all the excitement, poor love.' Sandra sipped her champagne and gave a huge, contented sigh. 'And this limousine. Goodness, I never travelled up to the Palladium in anything as grand as this,' she said. 'When I moved to Southend with your dad, after we got married, I used to go on the train and Mary Hegarty, a fellow Tiller Girl, would get on at the next stop, in Rayleigh, and we'd travel up together. I'd have a little carry case with my dance shoes in it.'

'It sounds amazing, Mum,' Maggie said, but the guilt was already gripping her, like she knew it would. Guilt would be on her heels all night, rasping at her with long, cold fingers, tripping her up, toppling her. She took a big gulp of her champagne.

'Oh, being a Tiller Girl was always amazing!' cried Sandra. 'And the Palladium was the icing on the cake. Six times I danced there. I'll never forget it. You look guilty,' she said quickly, glancing at Maggie with concern. 'Please don't feel guilty, Maggie.'

'I don't feel guilty,' said Maggie, 'I'm fine.' She plastered on her most convincing smile.

'Good,' said Sandra happily. 'And don't overdo the champagne. You've got work in the morning.'

'I know, I know.' It was Monday night. Tomorrow, Maggie would get up at 7 a.m., as she always did, and walk to the *Gazette*.

'How's it all going, love?'

'Great.' Maggie balanced her champagne flute on her lap. 'There's been some nice stories on the Where Are they Now?s recently. Last week someone wrote in to ask if I could help him find his desperately missed colleagues from a photo of the carnival in '71, and I found them, all of them – via several phone calls and the electoral role – and they're all booking a reunion caravan holiday in Camber Sands.'

'Well, that's wonderful!' said Sandra. She was proud of her daughter working at the *Gazette*. She told all her friends about it. And about her daughter's famous boyfriend.

'And I tracked down someone's daughter,' Maggie continued. 'She'd been in a photo of a prizegiving at the town hall in 1969, and her father, who had lost touch, called me, and I found her working in Whitstable. He cried when I called and told him, with her permission, of course.'

'All the lost and lonely people,' said Sandra, smiling at her daughter. 'You've done some good things there, Maggie.'

'Have I?' Maggie felt she was ready to move on from Where Are They Now? after three years, but Damian wasn't offering anything else, not yet, and they *were* a big hit, every week. *All the lost and the lonely people,* she thought. It seemed those people would always reach out to those who were lost and lonely, too. Maggie looked out of the window of the limousine and sipped her champagne and thought that people's stories could truly be poignant and sad and happy, all at once.

The traffic when they got to London was awful, but Maggie enjoyed seeing the red double decker buses, and the Thames, and Sandra marvelled at the tall, beautiful buildings. When they finally swept into Argyll Street, the chauffeur helped Sandra into her wheelchair, and she looked elated as she gazed up at the façade of the Palladium.

'Just as I remember it,' she whispered, and the glow from the teardrop lights of its majestic portico lit up her face, and Maggie could only mirror her smile. She knew the reason she was doing so well at the *Gazette* was because of her mum. She knew, because she'd cut her mother's dancing career short, that she needed to make hers in journalism big and bright and serious.

A young woman waiting on the steps in a headset checked their names off on a clipboard. 'Maggie Martin and Sandra Martin, guests of Ed Cavanagh, yes, here you are.'

She gave them a ticket each. 'Backstage pass' was printed on them. 'Have a wonderful night,' the young woman said, and she pointed out the ramp, which Maggie pushed Sandra up with the assistance of a gentleman with a huge bow tie. There was a lift to the stalls, and they headed for the bar where they ordered gin and tonics and talked in low voices about how glamorous everyone looked.

'Oh, *no*, darling, you look *heavenly!*'

A posh, husky voice behind them, belonging to a beautiful woman in a long, shiny tent of a sapphire dress – all fluffy with feathers at the neckline – admonished her equally beautiful posh friend, who was in a baby-doll bulb of red Lurex. They both had huge backcombed hair, chests you could serve cheese boards on and extended gold-tipped cigarettes they puffed on elegantly.

'Oh, *stop!*' cried the friend, her voice public-school loud. 'I'm only one hairpin away from looking an absolute fright!' She reminded Maggie of Janey, putting herself down all the time. Janey would have scoffed; this woman was Margo Leadbetter glamorous. 'Tell me,' she bellowed, 'who are you looking forward to seeing *most* tonight?'

'Oh, definitely Ed Cavanagh,' husked the woman in sapphire. 'He's so *sexy* in *Primrose*, isn't he? I wonder if he's single? Do you think we should hang around backstage for him? See if I can take him home with me tonight?' She laughed croakily.

Maggie looked at Sandra, who raised her eyebrows in mock horror. Maggie pulled a comic 'yikes' face.

'Well, you could try,' foghorned her friend, with a wink of her left eye, heavy eyelashes bristling below blue eyeshadow like a garden broom. 'I certainly wouldn't say no. He can shin up my drainpipe any day of the week.'

Ed played a cheeky and charismatic roofer in the show who first encounters his love interest, Linda, whilst working on her grandad's semi-detached house. Ed's tool belt was currently setting hearts aflutter across the nation.

Both women tittered throatily. The cheese board trays wobbled. *Throwaway lines*, thought Maggie, *just idle chit-chat*, but *she* was a little thrown. Women could be serious in pursuing a famous man, she thought, especially one as handsome as Ed. These weren't just giggling girls on a doorstep, clutching headshots to sign, but real grown-up women wanting a bigger piece of him. Wanting to take him away.

Mother and daughter drank their gin and tonics. It was announced over the tannoy that the performance would be starting in five minutes. Maggie found entrance C4 of the stalls and pushed Sandra carefully into her reserved space, taking the seat next to her. They had a brilliant view of the stage, with the Queen and Prince Philip directly opposite them in the Royal Box. There was a palpable frisson in the audience, expectant in all their finery. Mum had smoothed her dress over her knees.

'I feel like bloody Deborah Kerr,' she'd said merrily, referring to *An Affair to Remember*, Maggie knew. 'Without all the misery. Who needs Cary Grant when you're as happy as I am right now?' she'd added gracefully, and Maggie had leant down to kiss her cheek. 'Thanks for bringing me,' Sandra had said again, 'it's good to be back,' and that guilt had smoked through Maggie's body once more like a drop of ink in water, but she breathed past it with her best smile.

'Pleasure,' she said.

◆ ◆ ◆

The show had been a roaring success. All the acts had been brilliant. Maggie and Sandra had laughed, applauded, they had joined in with the national anthem, they had sung along to Rod Stewart crooning about being sexy while strutting in his leopard-print trousers. Ed and his *Importance of Being Earnest* co-stars had performed a witty and rousing scene from the play to rapturous applause. Ed was luminous and very, very funny, his comic timing exquisite. The hilarious sketch with Morecambe and Wise, in which roofer

Vaughn appeared on a 'roof', with Eric and Ernie as his fellow tradesmen, went down a storm, too.

Maggie roared and adored with the best of them. The non-famous girlfriend from back home, who Ed had talked to as she sat on a wall on their street, and had first kissed in a bingo hall. She was so very proud of him.

After the show, with their special passes, Maggie and Sandra were let into the green room, which was like nothing Maggie had ever seen before. The first things she noticed were huge bunches of flowers everywhere, both stuffed in vases or idling on occasional tables still in their ribboned wrapping. Then the hordes of glamorous people crammed into every inch of the room. More giant bouffant hairdos defying taste and gravity, more bosoms squished and cajoled into shiny dresses. Peeping painted toenails from the hems of floor-sweeping skirts. Men with smarmed-down hair and handlebar moustaches, and oversized bow ties and shiny shoes under bell-bottomed trousers. Gallons of colluding perfumes and aftershaves. The loud pop of champagne corks and the thrilled collision of over-full flutes.

Maggie was pushing Sandra carefully into the quietest corner of the room when there was a sudden whoop and a ripple of ripe applause, and in they came: the famous people, the performers, the *talent*, borne on an invisible wave of being *spectacular* and *chosen* and *adored*. Backs were slapped and hands were shaken and there was kissing, so much kissing – on cheeks, lips, the backs of hands, into the air – *mwah mwah*. At first, Maggie couldn't see him, but suddenly there he was, Ed Cavanagh, freshly changed into a suit and tie, and his curls all smart and combed down. Her heart leapt within her body and threatened to whoosh towards him, but look how many people there were before he got to her! How many air kisses and greetings, and lipstick on his cheeks and ruffles of that no-longer smooth hair. Until he was standing before her, her Ed, the man she loved, who so many other people loved, too. She had never loved him more.

'Maggie!' He put his arms all the way around her and kissed her softly on the lips. He smelt of hairspray and other women's perfume. 'Sandra!' he added, charming and ever-polite, pulling back and greeting Maggie's mum. 'How are you? Thanks for coming.'

'Wouldn't have missed it for the world,' said Sandra. 'It was wonderful.' They all beamed at each other; Maggie's eyes not able to leave Ed's lovely face. How glowing he looked, how alive, she thought. This was it for him, she thought. This was him really *living*. 'But I'm going to wheel myself to the other side of the room now, to get myself a drink, so you two can be alone.'

Ed and Maggie both protested, but Sandra had already turned her wheelchair and was waving to them over her shoulder and disappearing into the throng.

Ed placed his hand on Maggie's arm and looked at her with tender eyes.

'Alright?' he asked.

'Better than alright,' she replied.

'Was I good?'

'*So*, so good. Very, very funny, as well,' she added. 'Everyone loved you.'

'Did they?'

'Absolutely. The whole place was in stitches. They *adored* you, Ed.'

'And your mum? Did she enjoy it?'

'Very much so. Honestly. She's so happy she came.'

'I wish mine was here,' he said, 'and, well, also . . .' Ed shrugged, and then he paused, and an odd expression came into his eyes, and he suddenly looked like a lost little boy, gazing across the sea to the horizon and still wondering. Always wondering.

'And your *dad*?' she ventured. 'You never know, he might have been watching tonight. On telly. He might have seen you.'

Ed nodded, sudden tears flashing in his beautiful green eyes. He still talked about it sometimes, his dad's disappearance. *Islands of the Indian Ocean* was on a shelf inside their sideboard. Mémoire Island was occasionally pored over, a forefinger tracing its shores. She felt she should be able to help somehow, in her role at the *Gazette*, in being able to find Ed's father, but she couldn't – a few phone calls and a scroll of the electoral role could not conjure up the missing Neville Craddock, although she had tried.

'I don't know, I don't know,' Ed said, squeezing her hand tight. And all she could think of was that August evening when they had walked down to the seafront and searched for Rothmans cigarette butts, and a man who had gone out for a walk one evening and never come back.

'I love you,' she said, and it was the only thing to say in that moment, at that dazzling hour tinged with sadness.

'I love you, too.' Ed shook his curls as though shaking away all his bad thoughts and Maggie gently took one between her finger and thumb and tucked it back in with the others. 'Let's go and find your mum.'

Sandra was talking to a large man in a straining burgundy smoking jacket who was laughing his head off while Sandra beamed, her cheeks flushed.

'This is Alistair,' said Sandra. 'A very funny man who writes for the *Express*. He thinks you're marvellous.'

'Indeed, I do,' smiled Alistair. 'Indeed, I do. Can this *very funny man* take you out for lunch next week?'

'Sure,' said Ed easily. 'Why not?'

'Great! I'll call Rupert. Lovely to meet you, Sandra. See you next week, *superstar*.' Alistair tilted his head at Ed and coasted off into the crowd.

'You really were fantastic, Ed,' said Sandra, turning to him. 'Absolutely super.'

'Thanks, Sandra.' Ed looked so delighted, so happy. Like he would never get tired of hearing people saying he was great. 'How does the good old Palladium compare to when you were here?' he asked.

'It's the same,' said Sandra happily. 'Thank you for bringing me,' she said to Maggie.

'All thanks should go to Ed,' said Maggie, guilty again, but plastering on a big smile. 'This is all because of him.'

'I'm your humble servant,' said Ed, with a mock bow, but he couldn't have looked *less* like anybody's servant.

'Oh, how was the Queen?' asked Sandra.

'Yes! The line-up! How was she?' Maggie cried.

'Terrifying, but lovely.' Ed grinned. 'She told me never to forget my roots.'

'Did she?'

'No,' he laughed. 'Not that I will. But she asked me how I found it, being new to it all. Showbiz. Performing at the London Palladium.'

'And what did you say?'

'I said it was the best night of my life.'

There was a record player in the corner of the room, and someone must have opened it and put a record on. It was 'Fly Me to the Moon', and Ed grabbed Maggie at her waist and spun her around and around, and then he took one of her hands, and one of Sandra's, and they danced, the three of them, in a makeshift circle, and Maggie knew this was a perfect, perfect night, never to be repeated. Dancing in the green room of the London Palladium, to 'Fly Me to the Moon', with two people she loved dearly. And she knew it was the time of her life, too.

Maggie felt a gentle tap on her shoulder.

'Maggie! Ed!' It was Rupert – in a flared burgundy suit with a matching waistcoat. Skinnier than a cigarillo. Smile wider than a coat hanger. 'Ready for that photo with the *Mail*?' he asked.

'Ready as I'll ever be,' said Ed happily, and he was pulled away. Swept into the adoring crowd and his future. He had been ready for this all his life, Maggie thought, the path rolled out before him smooth and easy. All he had to do was follow it.

'Be right back,' Ed called over his shoulder.

Chapter Fifteen

12 A.M., ON THE ISLAND

The stars in the black sky were the brightest Maggie had ever seen. She gazed up at them, amazed. They were so different to the shy celestials that slouched over the grey rooftops of London, hidden by dense cloud. The twinkling diamonds in the Mémoire heavens seemed far more dazzling than the ones that dimly lit her grey existence back home.

'Would you like to walk along the beach?' asked Ed. 'It'll be far from romantic, if that's what you're worried about. It'll be pitch black and there'll be sand flies.'

They were in the doorway of Olly's. The stars had halted Maggie in her steps. She looked down from them to Ed's face.

'Oh,' she said. She had a headache. She needed to lie down. She needed to get away from Ed and the dangerous seduction of incomplete memory.

'There's not really sand flies . . .' Ed said. Maggie knew it wouldn't be pitch black either, as the moon was big and round and mocking in the sky. 'But shall we?'

Maggie nodded. They headed down the beach, where the inky black sea looked warm and mysterious, and the tide softly encroached on the shore like ghost's fingers. Ed's boat was on the shore, sleepy water lapping against it: *slap, slap*. It was all quite beautiful. If they were a couple, they would have held hands while they walked. If they were friends, they would have linked arms. But they weren't anything; they were Ed and Maggie, who had once loved each other, but both life and time had taken them apart and not put them back together again.

Maggie looked up at the moon bathing the island in a milky light, touching the tops of the trees and whispering over the surface of the sea. She looked down at her feet, walking in the sand. Neither of them mentioned the dance. The drink. The things that had and *hadn't* been said tonight.

'What would you be doing now in London?' he asked her eventually.

'Now, this minute?' She checked her watch. 'Five past midnight?'

'It's five past eight in London,' he said. 'What would you be doing?'

'I'd be making myself a cup of coffee,' she said. 'Flicking through the *Evening Standard*. Staring out of my window.'

'Tell me about your home.'

She glanced at the moon. The same moon that would be hanging over London, looking down on all the lonely people. 'It's a flat in London – it's small, it's clean, it has a really nice bathroom. It's close to the Tube.'

'Did Graham ever live there with you?'

'Yes, for a little while.'

'Why did it fizzle out?'

Perhaps it was easier to talk now, with the moon and the stars and the sea to focus on, and not each other's faces. 'We liked each other a lot,' she said. 'He was an academic – Political Science. There was a lot of respect between us, maybe too much. It was all polite reciprocation and no fire.'

'Fire can burn.'

'Well, yes, I know that.'

'I'm sorry it didn't work out. Are you lonely?' he asked.

'No,' she lied. 'I do have . . . someone.'

'You do?' He turned to her, and she saw his face, lit by the moonlight, although its expression was hard to glean.

She nodded. 'I currently have a . . . boyfriend. Of sorts. He's also a journalist. A war reporter, so he's away a lot. He's sweet and kind. And he makes the best baklava. He's half Turkish. He stays with me in my little flat in London when he's in the country. We have a nice time together.'

'A war reporter, how earnest.'

'Don't take the piss!'

'No, I'm not. He sounds . . . great. And so does the baklava. But he must be *serious*, I imagine.'

'More serious than you?' She looked at Ed quizzically.

'Yes. Isn't everyone? I've spent my whole life making a living from messing around.'

'Well, yes, he is. He *is* serious. But he can be fun sometimes. *We* have fun.'

'And are you in love with him?' The blankness of the night sea was reflected in his eyes.

'That's none of your business.'

'No.' Ed put his hands in his pockets. 'Of course not. But it sounds a nice life. Simple. Not too glitzy.'

'It was never the glitz I objected to.'

'Whatever you say, my friend.'

She shook her head angrily, but Ed didn't see it as his head was down, looking at the dark sand as they walked along it. They may have danced at Olly's, his hand at the small of her back, but he was right: it was only a temporary ceasefire. This was the real dance they did together. The dance they had been in for so long, the pair of them, every step of it painful.

Eventually, she said, 'No, I'm not in love with him.' Of course she wasn't. She had avoided all shades of love for a long time. 'But it's . . . nice. Really very nice.'

She'd only known love *once*, and that had been with Ed. She wouldn't tell him she had washed up, at sixty-one, on to a remote Indian Ocean island with no real sense of having a place in this world. To be without love, after all, when once the promise of it had seemed so iridescent and so certain.

'What would *you* be doing?' she asked. 'What time is it in LA?'

'Two in the afternoon?' He looked up. 'I'd be filming or sitting on my terrace having a cup of tea. Maybe having a swim.'

'*The Swimmer*.' Maggie smiled. 'Where's Alexia in this picture?'

He pulled a face. 'She isn't. Well, she won't be.'

'Oh?'

'We're . . . getting a divorce. We're over. That's not why I'm here, by the way. You can put your pencil away . . .'

'I won't put anything in the profile you don't want me to,' she lied again.

'Good.' He was snappy, his silver eyebrows knitted into an intimidating scarf no one would want to wear.

'But you're leaving her? Or is it the other way round?'

'None of your business.'

'Touché.' She deserved that, but still she threw at him, 'Another wife you're not in love with.'

'Cutting.'

'Bang to rights.'

'We separated a while ago actually. She moved out. The press don't know.'

'Well, then, I shan't tell them.'

'Good.'

'Did you phone Alexia from Doha airport before or after you mailed that postcard to me?'

Ed stopped walking. She stopped, too. The sand was cool beneath her toes. '*After*. I'd had a few beers.'

She glanced at him but could read nothing more in his face. So that was his explanation, was it? 'Fair enough.'

'And here you are. The reporter. So good at her job.'

'Like you're so good at yours.'

'Yep.'

It seemed neither of them had anything more they could add, or answers they were willing to provide. Ed started walking again. Maggie fell into step on the soft sand and turned to look at the sea. The moon hung above them, and she thought that it wasn't the stuff of anyone's dreams, that moon, neither bathing them in romantic light nor milkily witnessing the secrets of their hearts. It was just a big grey rock.

Moonlight was overrated.

Chapter Sixteen

12 A.M., 6 OCTOBER 1979

Ed was in the hall, on the telephone. He was sitting on the bottom stair, the curl of the telephone cord wrapped round his index finger as he took The Call. He was mostly smiling. Occasionally, a look of concern flickered over his face, then disappeared. Frequently, he said, 'Thank you, thank you.' Sometimes, he asked a question. Twice, he laughed. Once, he said, 'This is really unbelievable!'

Maggie was in her pyjamas. The silky green ones Ed had bought her last Christmas. It was the very end to what had been an idyllic day. They'd spent much of it on their Southend doorstep doing all the things tourists flocked to the town for. They had been down to Peter Pan's Playground and had been on the attractions: the go-carts, the Ferris wheel, the rollercoaster. They had eaten chips from newspaper and had Rossi ice creams – double cones with flakes in. They'd walked along the promenade and stared at the moving pirate waxwork. No one had bothered them, despite Ed's national superstar status. Yes, some teenage girls had stared. Yes, an old bloke had peered at him when they stepped into their carriage on the rollercoaster and had shouted over from his, 'Oi!

Are you famous?' but Ed had simply called back 'No!' and pulled his woolly hat further down on his head.

They'd wandered into the arcades and played shove ha'penny, and the 2p slot machines, and took their chances with the claw, failing to pick up a teddy bear. They had loitered at the entrances, debating laughingly between painted metal horses, or aeroplanes, or a fire engine to ride on. They'd gazed – fascinated – at the chipped plaster head of the fortune teller woman in the glass box, not daring to have a go. They banged the side of the gobstopper machine when their 5p got stuck. And they had returned again and again to the woman in the change booth with the thick red fingernails, enjoying the clanging, colourful rush of the arcade, the neon-lit faces, the heady diamond-patterned carpet.

They had done it all a thousand times before, but they didn't know today was the last day they would spend like this in Southend.

The Call had been waited up for, with a lot of yawning and a great deal of anticipation. Ed had watched television in the sitting room; Maggie worked at the dining-room table in her green pyjamas, as she knew her work would keep her awake. A Where Are They Now? puzzle was occupying her, a puzzle that had taken up most of her time for the past couple of weeks. She had the photo in front of her.

Maggie had come across it in one of the grey filing cabinets, a photograph of four women at the Stanley Chase Working Men's Club, the one her dad went to, all holding small glasses of wine and cheers-ing at the camera. The familiar bar could be seen in the background. After the photo had gone out in the *Gazette*, asking Where Are They Now?, two of the women had come forward. They had both worked at the local biscuit factory in 1968, when the photo had been taken, and had written in to supply the names of the other women – Pat and Maureen. Maggie had found Maureen in one phone call, but Pat Mint, a woman with an astonishing barnet of brown beehive and thin lips of chalky coral pink in the original photo, was proving harder to track down. Maureen had hooted with laughter on the phone about her.

'Oh, Pat was a scream!' Maureen had exclaimed. 'Always gadding about, always with a different man in tow. I'd love to know what she's doing now. If she's still local. Well, she went to Spain sometime in the early seventies, but I presume she came back. I hope you can find her.'

Tonight, Maggie was close to finding Pat Mint. She was working on a photocopy of the electoral roll and tomorrow she would make a few more phone calls.

'How are you getting on?' Ed had asked, from the sofa.

'Yeah, good, thanks. How are you feeling?'

'Nervous, on edge, excited.'

'I bet!'

Ed had told her about The Call when they were on the Ferris wheel, as she'd been gazing across the dirty water to Canvey Island.

'I'm receiving a phone call tonight,' he'd said, overly formally, and she had looked back from the sludgy horizon. 'From America. Rupert has set it up. Sandy Stein from Fox is calling me.'

'From America? Oh, Ed, that's so exciting!'

Things had been set in motion at Ed's lunch with Alistair Edwards of the *Daily Express*, who knew someone, who knew someone else, who knew someone else in America. Things had snowballed until there was a very *big* snowball in existence. Ed was going to be on an American TV show called *The Millers and the Smiths*, working with Warren Beatty and Jacqueline Bisset, no less. It was a new drama about a corporate American family – half English, half American – in which Ed was to be the English cousin who turns up and takes a job in the mailroom, trundling his trolley to all corners of the building to very cute and eventually dramatic results. Ed was off. Ed had a ticket to ride. Ed was going to America.

America . . . It was inevitable it would come calling. In the past ten months Ed had ridden high on the success of *Primrose* and had appeared in Britain's most highly rated drama – *A Bloom of Shattered Dreams*. He had been constantly in newspapers and magazines, including the front cover of the *Radio Times*, and there had been talk about moving to London, to be closer to all that work, and travelling home to Southend on the weekends, but then the snowball: this offer from America.

So, yes, tonight, one of the big American producers would be calling Ed in person to congratulate him and welcome him on board. Just a little courtesy call that would change his whole life. That was all.

As she stood in the doorway, Ed ended the call with, 'Bye, bye, thank you, bye,' in that terribly English way of never actually putting the phone down – Sandy Stein had probably hung up long ago – and Maggie found she was holding her breath.

'Well?' she said.

'Nice man.' Ed beamed. 'I think he's going to be really great to work with. And he said he was thrilled to have me join the cast.'

'Ed!' Maggie squealed and launched herself at him, throwing her arms around his neck. 'America! America!' she cried. 'You're going to America!'

Ed spoke into her hair, a huge grin on his face. 'He confirmed it will be a four-month shoot, starting on the fifteenth of January. I have to go out there two weeks before.'

'That's great,' said Maggie, pulling back from him so she could look at his face. 'This is amazing, Ed!'

'And you'll come out, in a couple of months' time? Or maybe a month, if you can swing it. To see me?'

'Of course, I will!' Maggie squeezed him tight again. 'Just you try to stop me! Where's that bottle of fizz we bought – the Babycham?'

Ed fetched the bottle from the fridge and Maggie reached into the sideboard and pulled two champagne flutes from the back of the shelf.

'Cheers!' Maggie said, when they were sitting side by side on their sofa. 'Hollywood *star*. You're going to go all the way.'

Ed's cheeks were flushed. He was buoyant, beaming. 'Cheers!' He clinked his glass against hers. 'And you'll be alright, while I'm gone?' he asked. 'In this house? You won't be too lonely?'

'Of course not!' Maggie took a big gulp of her Babycham. 'It's not like you haven't been away for work before. And how can I be lonely when I'll be having Janey round every night, and you phoning me from America?'

'I *will* phone you,' Ed promised. 'I'll phone you all the time. And soon you'll be coming out to be with me.'

'All that sunshine,' said Maggie happily. 'I can't wait. Congratulations, Ed. You deserve this so much, you really do. This is the best day of our lives, isn't it? The best day ever?'

'The best day ever,' agreed Ed, and they sat on their sofa and they drank their fizz and the future awaited, shiny and gold, for Ed and Maggie.

Chapter Seventeen

Maggie lay in her little single bed in her bungalow, listening to the sound of the sea and ignoring the whispers of her heart. Playing back the walk here with Ed, and everything they'd said and not said. The barbs they'd nicked each other with because of who they had become, and how far it was from what they had been.

'Mind your step.'

'Oh, thank you.'

As they'd continued along the shore, the moonlight a languid bulb above them, Ed had helped Maggie over a spiky piece of driftwood washed up on the beach like a giant stick insect.

'We need to head up to the path now,' he'd said, and they'd turned from the infinite blackness of the sea and walked up the beach to the indistinct mass of waiting jungle at its backshore. They turned right on to the scrubby path, and the moonlight was immediately concealed, so Ed pulled out a little torch from his shorts' pocket.

'I'd be lost without it on this island,' he said.

They walked, following the flickering beam of the torch as it danced on the forest floor. There was rustling in the rainforest above them, a warm shiver of night breeze ruffling the stillness of the leaves, which overlapped each other like silent hands.

'Are you happy here?' she asked him, her voice hushed now they were cocooned in the jungle, under the dark, rippling canopy over their heads.

'Shouldn't you be saving this for the interview?'

'This is something I just want to ask you, off the record.' His happiness didn't fit with the angle of her exposé piece. Her cautionary tale of his life. Her take on how it could only be a *man* who could pull a stunt like this, absconding from Hollywood and expecting to be welcomed back with open arms, months later . . . She had her pre-planned list of questions, but this was not one of them. 'Are you happy in your shack?'

'Yes,' he said. 'I didn't think I would be.'

'After your little stunt . . .'

'Ah, we've upgraded from a "flounce" to a "stunt", have we? Nice.' He smiled sarcastically at her, then the smile disappeared. 'I thought I would find it tough, this simple existence, but it has been . . . surprising. Stripping my life bare. I bet you never thought I'd have it in me.'

'I am surprised,' she said. 'A little,' she qualified, not wishing to boost his ego in any way.

He laughed. 'I can fish and lie in the sun on the beach and drink my rum and Cokes in Olly's and people-watch without people watching *me*. I can kick back, relax, not worry, be happy.'

'So, you *are* happy here?'

'Happy?' he scoffed. 'Who wouldn't be happy *here*? I'd say look around you, but it's dark . . .' He grinned in the shadows. 'You know what I mean. The sand, the blue skies, the sunshine – what's not to love?'

'You have all of that back in LA.'

'All the things you never wanted.' Maggie didn't say anything. She could hear a creature in the undergrowth, a shuffling of some animal. A snuffling. 'But here I have peace. So, yeah, I'm happy enough. For now.'

'And you came here because of your dad,' she risked saying.

'Please don't talk about my dad.'

She could feel the wall going up. Thick. Metallic. Impenetrable. When Ed was younger, he'd had a vulnerability you could see on his face but in Maggie's eyes, Hollywood had wiped it from him. Now that vulnerability was only to be found in his screen smile, and she'd known that for a very long time.

'But *Mémoire*,' she pressed, rapping her knuckles on that wall. 'This was the island in his book. The one he liked the most. Surely that's why you came here. Surely that's why—'

'I don't want to talk about my dad with you.' Ed's face, and the subject, was closed. 'And I won't be talking about my dad in our interview.'

'Sorry,' she said, quite reluctantly, and she hated that she sounded so pathetic.

'You're always sorry,' he snapped.

And you're always an arse, she thought.

They walked in silence, in this intimate space, but Maggie had never felt further from him. *Fine,* she thought. *No Dad.* But this would not be just a fluff profile piece, skimming the surface like a seabird skirting out to sea. She would be digging deep into just how badly Hollywood fame had screwed with Ed's life. Showing his loyal fans who he really was.

'*Supernova*'s going digital,' she said after a while, a little masochistically. 'That's why my editor wants you for its big scoop.'

'Is that so?'

'Yes. We have to make a splash, and you're a pretty good one.'

'I don't owe anything to *Supernova*—'

'No, but I do.'

'Ah, yes.' He nodded in the green of the torchlight. 'You're retiring. I'm your swansong. Your big hurrah.'

'It will be my last piece, yes.'

'Well, good luck. Career first, that's Maggie Martin.'

'That's not true. Eloise comes first with me.'

'Of course. The saintly mother and daughter duo. Maggie Martin, the perfect parent in every way.'

'That's not fair. We both had the same opportunities to be good parents, only you screwed it up.'

He laughed bitterly. 'Because you wouldn't bring your precious daughter to LA, and I made my poor son suffer there every day. The money, the houses, the weather . . . *poor kid* . . . I know exactly how you see it.'

'Come on,' she said. 'You must know that you weren't the dad you could have been to Michael. You must have known . . .'

'So bloody perfect!' Ed retaliated. He almost tripped over a tree vine but managed to stay upright. 'It's who you've always been and it's really bloody irritating!'

'And you've always been Ed Cavanagh,' she retorted angrily. 'Even when you were *Edward Craddock*, Ed Cavanagh was right there waiting in the wings. Hollywood star. Arsehole. Dazzled by the bright lights. Seduced by fame and glory.'

He looked pained. The torchlight gave his face flickering shadows. 'But you could have made it better. You could have made everything better if you'd only shared it with me!'

'What, and saved your kid? Come on, I could never have made up for not having his *own father* there to love and support him.'

'Ouch.' Ed's face was thunderous. He shook his head. 'You never gave Ed Cavanagh a chance.'

'*You* let me down.'

There was an angry silence. It throbbed between them and steeped into the dark foliage of their canopied tunnel.

'We're almost there,' she said finally, her voice still seething. 'I think I can see the bungalows.'

There was the ancient sprinkler, switched off and abandoned for the night. The terrace of the first bungalow softly lit up. And at Marguerite, a small hurricane lamp had been lit outside, casting an amber glow on a gecko, static as a plasticine model on the door frame. Maggie hurried up to the doorway.

'So, this is me,' she said tersely.

'This is you,' Ed echoed from somewhere behind her.

'Goodnight.'

'Goodnight. 7 a.m. for the tour, remember?'

'7 a.m.,' she confirmed, opening the door.

He hesitated. 'I never wanted it to be like this between us, Maggie,' he said, his voice low. 'Considering how we once were.'

'Neither did I, Ed,' Maggie replied. 'I really didn't. But I don't know how *not* to be like this.' Because of all that had happened. Because of all that hadn't. Because of how wide the ocean had been between them, and the magnitude of some of the things they had done.

Ed sighed. 'We have tomorrow to get through. The interview, a few photos. Let's try to make the best of it, shall we?'

'We can do that.' She turned her head and attempted a weak smile.

'We can be civil, friendly . . . friends?'

'Another ceasefire.'

'All weapons laid down.'

'Okay.'

'Good.' Ed held her gaze for just a little too long. She had to look away.

'Goodnight, then, Maggie,' he said.

'Goodnight, then, Ed,' she said to the door.

And at 1 a.m., in the single bed with the white sheet, Maggie tried and failed to fall asleep, all of their words ringing in her ears. *A few more hours*, she thought. The morning, the tour, the interview, and then the journey home . . . all were to be endured tomorrow, laid out on a map that curled at the edges and wouldn't lie flat, like all the other maps she and Ed had tried to plot a course on.

They had met, time and time again, but each time the chimes of fate had rung hollow.

Each time, they weren't meant to be.

Chapter Eighteen

1 A.M., 1 JANUARY 1982

Maggie had missed midnight and the ringing in of 1982 to replace 1981. She had missed the kissing, the Auld Lang Syne-ing, the chimes of Big Ben on the television in the corner and the fireworks let off outside to enthusiastic whoops and elongated aahs. She had, in fact, missed most of the party. But she had promised the mayor she would make it and, knowing his annual End of Southend Pier New Year's Eve party would go on until at least 3 a.m., she was in a taxi hurtling towards the seafront – in a blue dress, faux fur coat, strappy sandals over tights – dog tired and already wishing she was in her nightie and her bed.

She had changed hurriedly in the loos at Southend train station, not having time to nip home. She had thrown her interviewing 'uniform' of navy trousers and slate grey silky blouse into a C&A carrier bag and replaced it with the blue dress she had bought there last week. She had rolled on the tights, buckled the straps of her sandals and sorted her hair into a fit state. From the back seat of the taxi, she could hear the echo of a distant firework above the low skyline of the buildings as the driver turned the radio down.

His heater wasn't working, and Maggie had her faux fur coat pulled closely around her.

'Pier train running all night, then?' the driver asked her. 'What do I have to do to get myself an invite to the mayor's shindig one of these years?' he chuckled.

Maggie laughed. 'In my case, work for the *Gazette*,' she said. 'I could always try to sneak you in?' The driver was a jolly chap and she'd been to enough of these mayoral New Year's Eve parties – four, to be precise – to know that everyone would be roaring drunk by now and certainly wouldn't notice.

'Nah.' He smiled. 'You're alright. I have the missus and a bottle of red wine waiting for me when I get home.'

'Good for you.' Maggie smiled back.

Maggie was invited to the mayor's New Year's Eve party as a senior reporter at the *Gazette*. She had been there for six years now and, two years ago, had finally graduated from the Where Are They Now?s to profiles of former sons and daughters of Southend, who had found fame once upon a time but were faded now and hidden somewhere within the town, or in places far away. Maggie had come belatedly from interviewing Selena Dole – who had once been a screen starlet, of Diana Dors ilk – now in her fifties and living in Nottingham. The train from Nottingham to King's Cross had been delayed, stopping for a full hour on a dark track somewhere outside Watford, then the Tube had been painfully slow. Maggie had only just made the last train to Southend from Fenchurch Street.

'Be lucky,' the driver said as he dropped her off at the mouth of the pier. 'Enjoy yourself!'

'Thank you,' she said. 'Enjoy the wine.'

Walking in shoes that were way too high, Maggie made her way to the entrance of the pier train station, past the fish and chip kiosk where her mother used to work. She knew the pier train, covering the mile to the café at the end, was running on the ten past. She showed her gold ticket to the bored-looking man at the station entrance and sat down in one of the cold carriages, shivering a little. A group of youths were by the closed Rossi's ice cream kiosk, stamping their feet on the cold ground and drawing exaggeratedly from cigarettes.

'I can't relate to today's young people,' Selena Dole had said during their interview. 'It feels like they're on another planet. The legwarmers, the headphones. Cliff Richard with a giant radio on his shoulder . . .'

Selena had been quite a character. Her tiny flat had been covered in old photographs of her in glamorous poses – skipping up beaches, laughing in the arcades at Southend, posing in a bumper car – but she let Maggie take a photograph of her by the window with the new Minolta camera Maggie had bought for work. She took her own photographs for the *Gazette* now (budget cuts) and she was pretty good at it for a twenty-four-year-old rookie, even if she said so herself.

Maggie looked through the grubby train window out at the black night, unable to tell where the sky ended and the sea began.

'Come on,' she demanded of her stationary carriage. 'Hurry up.' She was cold; she wanted to get going. At the periphery of the blackness, she was aware of the party at the end of the pier waiting with warmth and lights and love.

'*Happy New Year.*'

Maggie jumped, startled at the man's voice, and her carrier bag of work clothes fell to the floor. He stood in the doorway smiling at her. Familiar curls, grown a little longer. Eyes warm and curious. Eyes that millions of people in America and Britain and *who knows where* had seen full of laughter and tears, anger and sadness, writ large on the small screen.

'Oh, my goodness, it's you!' she exclaimed. 'What on earth are you doing here?' Shaking, she retrieved her bag, set it in her lap and pulled the drawstring so tight she would struggle to get it open later when he was gone.

'May I come in?' he said formally, like he was knocking on a front door and asking to come in for tea and, indeed, he did a whimsical little knock on the frame of the carriage door and smiled his lopsided smile.

'If you like,' she said, trying to keep her voice from wavering. 'I'm going to a party.'

He walked into the carriage and sat on the little bench opposite her. He was wearing jeans, boots and a hooded overcoat. His eyes were as green as she remembered them. She crossed one leg over the other, clamped them down to stop them from trembling – her hands cocooning the bag on her lap.

'I know,' he said. 'I phoned the *Gazette*. Asked them where you were. I've been hanging around for you since five o'clock. Totally incognito,' he said, pulling the hood of his coat up over his head and Maggie would have laughed if she wasn't totally blindsided at the sight of him. 'I've had four lots of fish and chips. I don't suppose your mum still works at that one?' he said, pointing to the old blue and white kiosk.

'No, she doesn't. She retired. So, the *Gazette* told you about my interview with Selena Dole?' she asked him. 'The trains were awful,' she added, unfathomably, 'that's why I was so late.'

'Janey told me. Selena Dole made a few appearances at the working men's club my dad used to go, too. She had a terrible singing voice, the times he took me in there – sweet woman, though.'

'You spoke to Janey?' What an odd and astonishing thing it was, talking like this with Ed after two whole years. Chatting about Selena Dole and his dad's working men's club like no time had passed at all. She noted all the small ways in which Ed had changed. The little crease at the top of his nose, between his eyebrows, she was sure hadn't been there before. The suntan, obviously.

The smarter clothes, definitely. He was more expensive-looking. He didn't seem quite real. Well, he wasn't a real person any more, was he? He was a huge TV star.

'I got through to some bloke first. He said, "Oh, Janey will know!" and put me through to her. I didn't know she worked at the *Gazette* now.'

'She works in Accounts,' said Maggie absently. She noticed Ed's black scarf looked very soft and very warm – was it cashmere? She was still shaking, and her nerves and her disquiet were a betrayal of the life she had now, the one she had constructed for herself, brick by brick, from a design she knew would make her happy and she was, wasn't she? She had everything she'd ever wanted.

'It was very easy getting information out of Janey,' continued Ed. How *relaxed* he looked, marvelled Maggie. With his legs stretched out and his cashmere scarf and his *hood*. She guessed Hollywood and mammoth success did that to a man. 'About the interview and the party. She'd make a terrible criminal.' Maggie couldn't help but smile, as that was true. Janey was a champion blurter. She'd also hung on to a ridiculous romantic notion about Maggie and Ed for far too long. That they were soulmates or something equally silly, meant to be together, when time and circumstance had clearly proven that wrong. 'She said she wasn't going to the party, and she seemed a bit pissed.'

'Pissed as in drunk? Or pissed *off*?' offered Maggie quickly, widening her eyes in amusement. 'You've gone all American.'

'I've been there quite a while,' Ed said, his gaze steady on her.

'You have.' Maggie looked down again. Some days she succeeded in not thinking about him. Some days she was able to forget.

It had happened slowly, their falling apart. Ed had flown to Los Angeles on the 8.05 flight from Heathrow on the morning of 6 January 1980, and he'd phoned Maggie every day. He'd told her cheerfully about the apartment that had been rented for him, about the production meetings, the cast members he had started going out for drinks with. She'd talked about her days at the *Gazette*, what she'd had for dinner, funny things Janey had told her. They whispered that they loved each other, that they missed each other. They discussed, with great excitement, Maggie's forthcoming trip out to LA. Her flight, booked for 3 March, the week off work ringed on the calendar. Maggie had started shopping for new summer clothes. She had bought a bikini, some sunglasses, telling Ed she'd got Marmite and tea bags already packed.

In the middle of February, Sandra became unwell. Maggie's mother had a small stroke and had to go into hospital. Malcolm was hopeless; he couldn't cope at home with the laundry and the supermarket and the cooking, so Maggie had to take over, going round there every day after work, then heading to the hospital to visit Sandra. They needed her. She felt she couldn't leave them both so soon. She put her flight back to the beginning of April, rebooked the time off work.

Sandra took a long time to recover. Maggie couldn't fly to America at the beginning of April. Damian became very grumpy about moving her holiday dates again. He needed her, too. And Maggie needed her career. Maggie explained on the telephone to Ed that she couldn't come, that it was impossible. Ed said he missed her and would wait for her. He couldn't phone her every night now because she wasn't there. She was at her parents' house, and it was difficult to talk, or she was at the hospital. Ed had said, 'I'm sorry we never get to speak to each other any more.'

'Me too,' Maggie had replied, trying not to cry.

Ed was busy; shooting had started. The schedule ran over, and four months turned into five, then six. Ed's show came out in the States and was a huge success. When Ed did get hold of Maggie, he no longer asked her when she was coming out. He no longer talked about coming back. Maggie told her mum, in the hospital, that the two of them were trying to make it work, that Ed was still telephoning from America. But one day, the phone stopped ringing. And the next day, Maggie saw a photograph of Ed in the *Daily Mirror* with his arm around an actress, a bottle of whiskey dangling from his free hand. And Alistair Edwards reported in the *Daily Express* that a second series of *The Millers and the Smiths* had been commissioned and Ed had signed a new contract. Maggie wrote a letter to Ed and told him it was over. He didn't reply.

Maggie fiddled with the string of the carrier bag on her lap. 'Anyway, it's journalists only,' she said.

'No dodgy actors allowed, then?'

'No.'

Wouldn't the mayor just love it if Ed Cavanagh walked into the party, she thought. Ed was reported about a lot in the national papers: his success, his famous girlfriends, his Emmy win a year ago. And, as Southend's favourite son, he was always in the *Gazette*, occasionally accompanied by a photo of his mum, grinning over a cutting from *People* magazine, or *Variety*, at her kitchen table. Ed was still in *The Millers and the Smiths.* He was no longer in the mailroom but one of the swanky offices at the top of the building. His character remained the handsome British fish out of water, but one who was swimming in all sorts of delicious tides, including an affair with somebody he shouldn't be having an affair with. He was amazing in it.

'Why are you here?' she asked him again.

'I'm over for a couple of weeks. To see Mum. She's had appendicitis.'

'Oh. I'm so sorry to hear that.'

'She'll be okay. How's your mum now, health-wise?'

'Good, thanks,' said Maggie. 'She's doing really well at the moment.' Sandra was better, but had reluctantly given up work, and spent her days doing 'thoroughly boring things' (she said) like housework, cooking and crosswords.

'You keep going with your career!' she'd made Maggie promise, over a tricky fourteen down. 'You make sure you're absolutely marvellous!' And Maggie had promised.

'That's great,' said Ed. 'I'm glad she's okay.'

Small talk, Maggie thought, when being this close to him was bringing back every bittersweet hour they had ever spent together.

'You look great,' he said.

She pulled self-consciously at the seam on the toe of her tights, peeping out through her sandal. 'So do you.'

The doors of the carriage finally bumped shut and the train started to rumble and creak, before giving a long, slow exhalation of breath and trundling slowly up the track.

'So that's what you're doing now, at the *Gazette*?' Ed asked as the lights of Southend began to fall away and the black blankness of sea filled the left-side window of the carriage. 'Celebrity interviews?'

'Sort of,' she said. 'I hunt down and interview faded starlets, old singers and the odd TV personality, and do nice little profiles. There seems to be a real appetite for it at the moment – nostalgia for the forties, fifties and sixties – maybe because the eighties is all plastic and neon and yuppies. I suppose I'm just tapping into that.'

'You write so wonderfully.'

'Do I? What, you mean my old stuff?' He had read most of her Where Are They Now?s, back in the day.

'No, the new stuff. Mum sends me clippings. Well, she has been doing . . . And the mayor must rate you . . .'

'Oh. Well, I guess so.' She wasn't sure she liked the thought of Ed reading her words, and wondered why he did. 'It's New Year's Eve,' she added, looking at him curiously. 'Well, New Year's Day now. Haven't you got anything better to do?'

'The hospital kicked me out at five. And my old mates all seem to have had babies and are at home tonight.'

'Even Freddie Taylor?' she asked, looking at Ed's neat Hollywood fingernails, buffed and nicely shaped. He probably had a *woman* do them for him.

'*Especially* Freddie Taylor – he's got three. You're married,' Ed said, staring at the ring on Maggie's left hand.

'Did you think I wouldn't be?' Her glibness belied her sadness when she looked at him.

'No. I would have been surprised if you weren't. Who *wouldn't* want to marry you?'

She smiled gently. She remembered when they thought they'd been so cool, in their little house, eschewing the old-fashioned ties of marriage, thinking they were utterly modern, when wasn't marriage just what she needed, eventually?

Maggie had married Ray Bridgeman four months ago. He worked in the print room at the *Gazette*. He had very dark straight hair that flopped over his forehead, statement sideburns and nice eyes. They had first met in the corridor outside the newsroom in late 1980. She had been carrying a pile of box files and he had let her pass him.

'After you,' was all he had said, but something about the way he'd said it had made her smile. And she'd turned back, as she went into the newsroom, and he'd turned back at the same moment and erupted into a small explosion of delighted laughter, like he couldn't believe she was in the world.

A couple of days later, they had bumped into each other in the pub opposite the *Gazette* at lunchtime, queuing for a jacket potato and a pale ale. There had been an instant crackle between them, a teasing sparring, the promise of endless snarky, sexy banter if they got together and they did, soon afterwards. *Why not?* Maggie had thought. It had been almost eleven months since Ed had gone;

what better time to launch herself head-first into a new relationship in the hopes of forgetting about him once and for all? Maggie and Ray became a very quick item, the talk of the *Gazette*. The newspaper power couple, said tongue in cheek, of course, as neither of them were very powerful, but they were happy together.

Ray liked dancing. He liked going to soul nights down at the Kursaal, taking Maggie with him, where he wore a navy slim-fitting suit and a deadly serious expression. He did a Mod dance she found rather amusing, particularly when a small crowd gathered around him. He loved noir detective novels, where the girls on the covers all looked like Veronica Lake and there was always the shadow of a gun from an outstretched arm, assailant unknown. And he made her laugh. Ray had a sense of humour based on bad joke telling and physical comedy. He wasn't conventionally good-looking, but when he smiled, his face lit up like a torch, and on their wedding day, eight months after they day they'd met, he had said to her, 'I'm so glad you're mine, Mrs Bridgeman. This is the best day of my life.'

'Where do you live?' Ed asked her. He turned up the collar of his coat.

'Richmond Road.'

'Nice. Do you have children?'

'We've only been married a few months.' ('We'll just practise, for the moment,' Ray said. And he particularly liked to practise on a Saturday night after dancing at the Kursaal.)

'The honeymoon period.'

'I suppose. Do you think you'll marry Lacey Mae?'

Ed shrugged. 'I still don't believe in marriage, so probably not.'

Maggie knew all about Lacey Mae Stephenson, a petite blonde soap actress whom Ed had been dating for about six months. Lacey Mae was a fitness guru and actress, according to the *Daily Mail*. Maggie had pretended to glance casually at her photo, which turned into a long ten minutes perusing every inch of her, until Lacey Mae was just a collection of tiny grey dots.

There'd been a few women in the last year. All beautiful, all with lovely teeth. None with wild red hair. Sometimes she told people she had once gone out with Ed Cavanagh and sometimes she didn't. She'd told Ray, and Ray had said, 'Well, good for him,' on his success, and 'Well, that would never have worked out, would it?' But if Ed came on the telly, Ray got up and switched it to a different channel.

And now Ed was back, not far from where they had searched for clues of Neville Craddock's disappearance; not far from where they had walked hand in hand, many times, or where they had gathered with others in 1976, when the end of the pier went up in flames and people on the stony beaches either side had stood and stared.

'So, how is it,' she asked, 'the showbiz world?' She found it hard to imagine these days: the studio lots, and the scripts, and the whizzing around on carts. The sunshine and the lunches with producers, and the fans at the gates, and being whisked everywhere in sleek black cars.

'It's great,' said Ed. 'It's manic and busy and bewildering and amazing. What's he like, your husband? Is he anything like me?'

The train was chuntering into the little station at the end of the pier. *Too quick*, Maggie thought. *Not enough time.*

'Who's anything like *you*? He's nice. He's just an ordinary guy.'

'*I'm* just an ordinary guy.'

'Oh, come on! Why *are* you here, Ed? You've visited your mum and now you've come to visit me, for old time's sake. You're feeling nostalgic?'

The train had stopped. The door slid open, and Maggie stepped off on to the wooden platform, the cold night air a welcome relief.

Ed stepped out, too, and reached for her arm. 'Don't go in yet, I want to talk to you.'

'You've *been* talking to me.'

'I want to talk some more.'

'About what?' She was cross now. And confused. He was standing too close to her.

'About how much I miss you.'

'I'm married, Ed.'

'I know. Are you happy, though?'

'Yes, I am. You think I can't be happy without you?'

'No.'

She laughed. Derisive. 'You stopped calling me. You started seeing other women.'

'I didn't want to. I waited for you. I waited for you to come out and see me, but you never came.'

'I couldn't! You know that. And come on! You've been having the time of your life! All those adoring women, all that fun!'

'Maybe it's all not so much fun without *you*.'

'No. No.' She was angry now. 'You can't do this to me, Ed. It's too late. I'm married. It didn't work out for us. It's been two years. It's fine, Ed. I'm *fine*. It's all worked out for the best, hasn't it?'

'Has it?' She took his hand off her arm. She needed to get away from him. Into the party. Back to her new life. She couldn't trust herself not to say she still loved him, that she had never stopped. 'I've missed you,' he said again. 'I miss your face. I miss the time we spent together. I miss a lot of things.'

'Well, *hard luck*!' she shouted. 'You wouldn't wait for me when my mum was ill. You got seduced by all that Hollywood stuff and you love it – you love it! I'm married, Ed. Married. You can't just come back here and start saying all these things. It's not *fair*.'

She could hear music. Olivia Newton-John, who wanted to get physical with someone. She could see the cascading disco lights inside the café. The smoky shadows of people dancing. Outside, there was a man standing against the wall, swaying drunkenly. She took a step back from Ed, lowered her voice. 'I've made a whole other life. We were just kids when we were together. Well, not much more than kids. I need to go in. I need to go into the party.'

'I need you,' said Ed. 'Things were simple with you. Fun. Nice.'

'Simple . . .' mused Maggie. 'Is that what I was? The good little English girl waiting at home, safe and dependable? The person who isn't famous always gets left behind,' she added. 'Don't you realise that? It was always going to happen. I was blind to think it wouldn't.'

'Not always.'

'Yes, *always.*'

Ed tried to take her hand. 'Dance with me!' he pleaded. 'We never danced, did we? It's something we never did. We played bingo, we ran down the steps to the seafront, we went on the Ferris wheel, and we *loved* each other, but we never danced.'

'Careful!'

The man from the wall was staggering towards them, a worse-for-wear look of recognition on his face as he held Ed in his drunken sights. Ed pulled Maggie around the side of the wooden-slatted café, where it was near-dark, the music thumping in the planks beneath their feet.

'We *did* dance,' Maggie whispered, her heart thumping, 'don't you remember? We danced in the green room of the London Palladium,' and then she wished she hadn't said that, because saying that aloud implied she set store by it, that it meant something to her. When it didn't. None of it meant anything to her. She was married to Ray.

'Yes, I remember,' Ed said brusquely, his eyes flashing in what borrowed light there was from the café, and his arms on her coat, at her waist, and she wondered what it would feel like if he were to slip them inside it and touch the slippery satin of her dress with his fingertips. 'But it was too brief. Everything about me and you was too brief. There are lots of things we never got to do,' he said, 'and lots of things that never got said. I feel as though I never got to know all your secrets.'

'I've never had any secrets,' said Maggie, but she had one now, she thought. Something she couldn't tell him. 'Go home, Ed. Go home to America. I'm not your missing person. I'm not anyone to you now.'

Ed looked sad. *Missing person*. She shouldn't have said that. 'My mum came out to LA,' he said. 'Last year. She complained every single day. That it was too hot, too bright. She missed being at home. My dad would have loved it. The blue skies, the beaches, the palm trees. He would have got such a kick out of it, me being there – the whole TV thing, I reckon.'

'I can imagine.' She felt sad for him, too. 'Didn't he always say you were going places?'

'He did. You know, sometimes . . .' Ed shook his head. 'Sometimes, I get so angry about it, that he's not around. Sometimes I don't know what to do with how I feel. Maybe that's why I couldn't wait for you. Maybe that's why . . .' He sighed. Attempted a smile. 'I really can't come in with you, to the party?'

'My husband is in there, Ed. My Ray. He's waiting for me.'

'I still love you.' Ed looked seventeen again, his eyes beseeching. 'I think you might be the best person I'm ever going to meet in my entire life.'

'Don't be stupid.' Maggie tried to step away from him, but tripped, a heel apprehended between two planks, and Ed caught her in an awkward hug, her silly C&A bag still in her hand, and they both collapsed into resistant heart-breaking smiles. Maggie buried her face into the collar of his coat, breathing him in. His warmth. His smell. Then she forced herself to pull away from him.

'Goodbye, Ed.'

'Can I write to you?' he entreated, opening his arms as if to catch her again, but she succeeded in stepping away this time and he let them fall to his sides. 'What number Richmond Road is it?'

'No, you can't write to me. Go back to America. Go back to Lacey Mae. *Please*, Ed.'

Maggie turned from him and started walking to the door of the café. She looked back at him, just once, when she got to the doorway, and his hands were in his pockets and he looked so lost and so alone, in his coat and his hood, when wasn't he one of the least lonely people in the world? Ed took one hand from a pocket and gave her a solitary wave and she gave a sad little wave back, for wasn't *she* about as sad as she had ever been, tonight, despite her new, attentive husband waiting inside for her, ready to show her off?

'Goodbye, Ed,' she whispered.

Chapter Nineteen

2 A.M., ON THE ISLAND

Maggie couldn't sleep. She got out of bed in her thin cotton nightie and closed the gauzy curtains at the window, then opened them again slightly, so she could see the pearlescent moon which looked down on this half of the world.

The last few hours . . . she needed to absorb them. To adjust to seeing Ed and being with him again. His boat on the shore, the bar, the dance they'd had, the memories of all that had gone before that were being scooped up like handfuls of sand in her mind, and sifted through, before falling softly back to the beach. His anger and hers, roaring in and out like the sea. The power they still had to hurt each other.

She slipped back into bed. She had purposely not imagined Ed Cavanagh, the man, when she had said 'yes' to Simone, and on the whole of the long journey here. She had only thought of Ed Cavanagh, the star, recently resurrected in the stratosphere. An entity, a commodity, the subject of her take-down piece on him. But she should have known that Ed, *her* Ed, would be waiting here for her and all that might portend. He was flesh and blood. He was the past and memory, and loss and regret.

A woman's face came to her as she finally drifted into sleep, the thin curtains fluttering at the window. The beehive hair, the chalky lipstick. The chubby fingers on the stem of a stubby wine glass. Pat Mint, the woman in the photo. The woman she had searched for in a Where Are They Now? in 1979, and then found. Pat Mint was the secret Maggie was already keeping when Ed turned up in the train carriage on Southend Pier, on New Year's Eve 1982.

◆ ◆ ◆

Pat Mint had phoned Maggie on a Friday night in early December, almost a year after Ed had left for America. What Maggie remembered most about Pat's voice was that it had a clear bell of a ring to it, like there was always laughter there.

'Hello?'

'Hello,' Pat had trilled.

'Who is this?' Maggie had just got home from a date with Ray. Their third, in fact, which had ended with a chaste kiss on her front doorstep and a less than chaste squeeze of her bum, and she had been ascending the stairs with a beaker of water.

'My name's Pat Mint,' said the woman. 'I found your home number in the phone book. I believe you've been looking for me.'

Maggie sat on the bottom stair. 'Yes,' she said, 'I have. Well, I *was*. Some time ago.'

'I got your letter, a long while after you sent it.' Pat Mint laughed. 'Last week, in fact. Sorry about that.'

Maggie had posted it in the autumn of 1979, along with a clipping of the Where Are They Now? from the *Gazette*, the photo of Pat and friends in the bar of the working men's club and the plea underneath for any of the women to get in touch. 'No problem,' she said. 'How have you only just got it?'

'I've been in Gibraltar for the past few years,' said Pat. 'I married a man in the army. The letter had gone to my dad's house, where I used to live, and it was caught up in some old papers I found in the house clearance after he died,' she added. 'I was surprised when I opened it, but I remembered Sally and Roisin, my old workmates. And Maureen, of course. That was a great night, the night that photo was taken. *1968!* She laughed. 'We got quite bevvied. I lost my house keys down a drain.'

Maggie smiled. Sally had been right – Pat was full of spark and mischief.

'So, I just called Maureen straight up. Well, I called her mum and she passed me on. We chatted for quite a while about the good old days . . . the social club. We always had a laugh in that place. It was particularly packed that night as it was after the footie . . .' Maggie could hear the smile in her voice, imagined her wearing that same chalky coral lipstick. 'Everyone we knew was in there, or people we always saw around. And, well, there's something else you might find interesting about that photo . . . something worth mentioning, at least . . .' Pat paused for obvious effect, while Maggie waited. 'Ed Cavanagh's dad is in that photo.'

'What?' said Maggie, leaning forward.

'Yes,' said Pat, sounding excited, 'he's in the background – in profile, you can't see all of his face. He's turning to talk to someone behind him.'

'Hold on,' said Maggie. She had that photo somewhere. The clipping. She had a scrapbook of all her old Where Are They Now?s in a drawer in the hall table. She hurriedly found the scrapbook and flicked to the right page, with the clipping and the original photo. Yes, in the far background was a man with dark hair, face partially obscured, sitting at a table and twisting his body to the edges of the photo. One of his hands was up to his face – white shirt cuff, bottle green jumper sleeve.

'I see him,' Maggie said, back at the phone. 'So that's Neville?' She wouldn't necessarily have recognised him, not from the obscured face and her minimal knowledge of his appearance; photos she had seen printed in the *Gazette* at the time of his disappearance, and a couple in an album Ed had once shown her.

'Oh, yes. Neville Craddock. Father of Ed Craddock, now Ed Cavanagh. He always wore that green jumper. I'm telling *you*, so maybe you can do something, about what I know. What I *saw*. I wouldn't have bothered phoning you after all this time, but . . . well, I'll tell you what happened, and you can see what you think.' Maggie could hear Pat taking a deep breath. 'So, when I was chatting to Maureen on the telephone, I said that's Neville Craddock in the photo, and she hadn't noticed, because he's right in the background, you see, but I never forget a face. I used to find him ever so dishy . . . and she said, oh, didn't I know? He went missing in the early seventies, Valentine's night 1971, she thought it was, that it was quite a big deal, all over the papers. And I said, no, well, I don't read the newspapers for starters – bloody rags – and I'd left by then. I was in Spain before I lived in Gibraltar – that's where I met my bloke in the first place – and then she said, well, you know Neville Craddock is Ed Cavanagh's dad, don't you, the TV star? And I said, well, how the hell was I to know *that*? I don't follow Ed Cavanagh, particularly. I knew he was from Southend, but he's got a different name for god's sake, and, well, to tell you the truth, I was quite disturbed, when I remembered what I remembered, as the upshot is that I *saw* him on Valentine's night in 1971. Neville Craddock. I saw him.'

'You saw him that night?' Maggie leant further forward. 'You said you were in Spain.'

'I went the next *day*,' said Pat. 'I had no idea Neville Craddock was a missing person until last week. I went to the police last Thursday about it, actually, about what I'd seen, but they did

163

bugger all. Took a statement and then told me to sod off, basically. Well, it had been nine years. Case closed, they said. They weren't interested.' Maggie could almost hear Pat shrugging. 'I thought maybe you could do something. Seeing as you're a journalist and everything. I thought the least I could do was tell you. Tell you what I saw that night. If you want to hear.'

'Yes, I do,' said Maggie. She had grabbed a pen and a piece of paper when she'd fetched the clipping. 'Please tell me what you saw.'

Pat took another deep breath and what sounded like a slug of coffee.

'The night I saw him, I was out. I'd been drinking in one of the pubs on the seafront and was snogging a man I shouldn't have been snogging – Valentine's night, desperate singles, you can imagine . . . and I was excited, you see, as I was flying to Torremolinos the next day, on holiday, but actually I ended up working in a bar on the strip. I met my Wayne there. I married him and moved to Gibraltar. Married, divorced, lots of fighting in between, and now I'm back. That's my sad story.' She laughed her musical laugh. 'Anyway, that night. There weren't many people around down at the pier – there wouldn't be at that time, about midnight and in the cold, like it was – but Neville Craddock *was*, and I remember it so well because I saw him arguing with someone. A man in a suit – a grey suit, no tie, some sort of badge or brooch on the lapel, a medal? – strange to see a man in a suit at that time of night, or maybe he was a Mod, you know, with a target badge on or something?'

'What were they arguing about?' Maggie asked.

'I don't know. I wasn't close enough. But the man in the suit was sort of barking. His face was all screwed up and he looked . . . feral. The man I was snogging obviously thought it all seemed a bit dodgy, too, and he pulled me under an awning of one of those gift shops, and when we emerged, which was about fifteen minutes later – say no more' – Pat did a startling coarse giggle – 'they were gone. Of course, I didn't think any more of it, until I spoke to Maureen. As I say, I never forget a face. And then I went to the police, but blah, blah, according to them, I was drunk, I was unreliable. No one else had seen anything or seen this other man. So . . .' Pat paused again for dramatic effect. 'Can you do anything with this information?' she asked Maggie. 'I only want to help in some way. *Shame*, Neville going missing like that.'

'I'm not sure I can,' Maggie said, 'if you've already gone to the police. But that is really interesting. Thank you for telling me.'

'Could you do a little write-up?' asked Pat. 'In the *Gazette*, mention my name?'

Maggie imagined this would please the gossipy Pat Mint no end. 'I don't think so,' she said. 'As you say, it's been nine years. Not enough local interest,' she added carefully. 'I think we probably have to leave it there.'

'Well, never mind,' Pat had said, clearly disappointed. 'I do love a good mystery.'

'Me too,' said Maggie, 'but I'm glad you've managed to catch up with Maureen again.'

'Yeah,' said Pat. '*Maureen the Merry!* Me, too.'

And they had said goodbye and Maggie had put down the phone, but of course Pat couldn't possibly know that Ed Cavanagh meant something to Maggie – would always mean something to Maggie – and that finding out what had happened to people was a near-obsession for her, so no, she wouldn't be leaving it there at all.

Chapter Twenty

2 A.M., 21 JULY 1982

The letter that had been waiting for Maggie all day and most of the night – the one with the American postmark – was flattened between Delia Smith's *Complete Illustrated Cookery Course* and *The Taste of France,* a heavy hardback Ray had optimistically bought her at Christmas, and she had never cooked from.

Maggie had spotted the letter on the mat that morning, the blue and red chevron of an airmail envelope as recognisable as the lilt of the handwriting on the address, and she had quickly snatched it up, her heart pounding, before Ray came downstairs for his tea and toast. She'd hurried to the kitchen and swiftly slipped the letter somewhere he would never look, amongst her heavy stack of cookery books, and she finally unsealed it many hours later, long after he'd gone to bed.

The day had been interminable while the letter waited. There had been the walk to the *Gazette*, in the slanting morning rain. The hours at her desk, in the hubbub of the newsroom, researching more once-famous sons or daughters of Southend. Making phone calls, arranging interviews. The loud relief of Friday lunch in the pub with colleagues – the overdone jacket potato and the wilted lettuce, the pints of beer and the warm gin and tonics. The sleepy afternoon punctuated by a leaning Victoria sponge brought in by Janey for her manager's birthday, swilled down with large mugs of tea. Then walking home from the *Gazette*, part of the way with Janey complaining hilariously about her fat thighs, until she turned off for Rover Street and home to her husband Brian and their twin girls. The second half with Ray, ambling out of The Rose and Crown on Hender Street (he had left the printing room after a 'mild dispute' and now worked at the brewery), meeting Maggie with a shouted 'Hey!' as she rounded the corner.

She had made Ray's dinner, scrutinising a recipe for coq au vin he'd torn from a magazine and frowning over missing ingredients she'd forgotten to buy. She arranged her efforts on a plate, and added a parsley garnish, like they had in the illustration, then watched with trepidation as Ray hoovered it up. She had cleared away after dinner, served Ray a dessert of tinned fruit cocktail and evaporated milk in front of the telly. Laughed when Ray laughed at *Are You Being Served?* and *Till Death Us Do Part*. Batted off his occasionally snarky comments (how startingly quickly the crisp tennis rally of banter between them had become a dull thunk of a desiccated shuttlecock on a broken bat) about her housekeeping, her job, her everything.

They had gone up to bed, where Maggie had attempted to read *The House of the Spirits* but got moaned at for having the bedside light on. Ray heaved all the covers over to his side before settling into a deep sleep and a rhythmic snore. Maggie knew he wouldn't wake now, not even if a burglar entered their bedroom and played a bugle at the end of their bed, so finally, quietly, she eased back what covers she'd been left with and tiptoed downstairs to the kitchen, and the dresser, where she fumbled for the letter between the two cookery books, and sat at the kitchen table under the single cloche ceiling light to read.

Dear Maggie,

Hello! I found out which number Richmond Road from the Gazette. *I'm afraid I called them and put on a fake voice and pretended I had a coal delivery for you. I'm sorry for the subterfuge – you'll probably put it down to TV star arrogance or something, and I'm sure you'll tell me off for it in one way or another. But I wanted to get in touch with you. I wanted to write to you. I know you said 'no', but maybe TV stars also don't take no for an answer. I can't, I don't think, when it comes to you.*

I hope life is treating you well. I hope your job is going great guns, that you're happy. I hope you enjoyed the party on the pier. I won't apologise for turning up, Maggie, as it was so good to see you and, as you know, I was in the area. You looked beautiful. I hope you don't mind me saying so.

I've started filming a new show, while The Millers and the Smiths *takes a short break.* Saloon, *it's called. It's a good cast and crew and brilliant fun playing the gun-slinging 'youngest sheriff in the county' – there are a lot of laughs on set, particularly about my American accent, I fear! No, I am getting the hang of it. I have a good voice coach. We're shooting out in the desert, near Palm Springs. It's a joy, really. I'm enjoying myself immensely. It's nice to tell someone about it, who isn't in the business. Someone who'll be as amazed by the whole thing as I am. Me, a cowboy, Maggie! It's pretty hilarious, don't you reckon? I think they're pleased with me, so far. Some days I pinch myself that I'm here, you know, doing this job that's the most fun in the world. The Californian sun shining above me with that certainty it will shine every day.*

You may have read some things about me in recent months, the playboy stuff again. You might have seen me in the English press, falling out of nightclubs, a girl on each arm. I must admit that since Lacey and I split I have been going out a lot, drowning my sorrows and looking for love in all the wrong places. So, the playboy thing . . . I don't know, I don't have any justification for it, but I want to tell you that it doesn't make me happy. That's what I want you to know. It really doesn't. I don't want you to think badly of me, Maggie.

I also think that if you were here with me, well, my life would be different, but you can't wish for something you can't have, can you? I've been playing a lot of The Carpenters recently, Maggie, fool that I am . . . and feeling sad. Wallowing in it, you know. I miss you. Sorry, I'm crossing that out . . . But sometimes the memories of you and me just come crowding in and I don't know what to do with them all. So I put on The Carpenters and I wallow.

I know you probably won't reply. I do hope you're happy, Maggie. I think of you often. Those memories, eh? There are so many of them, all those hours I spent with you, Mags. I'm going to write to you again if you don't mind. Sometimes the sunshine is just too bright here and I crave grey skies and the kind of wind that slices you in two – and yes, that painful pebble beach. Remember that night we lay on it, on that blanket? I'll never forget that. Sometimes I just crave you. Yes, I've had a drink or two. Yes, I'm feeling morose, with my glass of Jack Daniels by my side. I may read this back in the morning and not send it, but I think I will. I think I just really want to write to you, Maggie. Because it's the next best thing to talking to you and we can't do that.

Okay, well, I'm going to put my glad rags on again now and go out on the town with the crew. We're going to a little bar in a dusty town, and I may be practising my accent.

I can't wait to be with you again, Maggie May, even if it's just in my dreams.

Yours,
Ed xx

◆ ◆ ◆

Maggie sat and read the letter over and over, one ear primed for the telltale creak of the kitchen door opening. She wiped a fallen tear from Ed's smudged signature and blotted it in the palm of her hand. She noted it all: the easy bravado, the melancholy, the Jack Daniels sentimentality, the arrogance of sending this letter, unbidden, and his complete ignorance of the ramifications such a letter would have with Ray, if discovered – while the kitchen clock ticked, and she knew she would sit here for as long as she could get away with.

She had so much to tell Ed that she couldn't. Funny things, like the discovery of an escaped pot-bellied pig on Southend sea-front this summer, snuffling inside a lady's beach bag for corned beef sandwiches, that had made the front page of the *Gazette*. A blazing hot day last week that would surely rival LA, when the children of Richmond Road came out to pick at the melted tarmac, reminding Maggie of a day in the summer holidays when a young man had sauntered down the street with his mates, with the sun behind them – like they were on the cover of an album. The phone call from a woman called Pat Mint, who held a hazy, long-forgotten memory of a man at a table in a working men's club. A man who had walked out of his house one night and never come back.

She folded the letter carefully and smoothed down the tabs to make it an envelope again, before tucking it back into bed between Delia and *The Taste of France*. She would read it again, she knew, but she would not reply. She would not tell Ed about the swift but incremental failure of her marriage, like the puncture of a tyre with a sharp, deadly stone in it. She would not tell him she was miserable, that some nights she cried softly as Ray snored beside her. That she was beginning to be scared of him. Of the way he talked to her. Of the way he controlled. She would not tell Ed that he was in her dreams, too, every night, and she couldn't wait to escape to them, as Ray took not only all the covers but tiny pieces of her, as the months went on and the dark nights of married life never lightened.

She wanted to leave Ray, but she was frightened. She'd wanted to make this work. She didn't want to admit she had made a mistake. And sometimes he joked that if she ever left him, he would kill her.

Chapter Twenty-One

3 A.M., ON THE ISLAND

Maggie tossed and turned in her island bed. She heard voices, the muted rumble of a man's voice, the high register of a woman's – in French – from the bungalow behind. She heard the twitch of a bird at the window, feather against glass. She drifted to and from sleep as images floated in and out of her mind.

She saw Ed's letters, his slanted handwriting, the way he wrote the 'd' of his name with a curved tail, making it a musical note. She saw him in the doorway of a train carriage on a pier, in an expensive hooded coat. She saw him as a cowboy, reaching into his leather holster, a heroic curled smile on his face. His face then became Ray's, mocking and snarly, then someone else's – a man in a grey suit, his features angry and blurred. *The* man in the grey suit, from Pat Mint's phone call in late 1980, which had sparked an obsessive quest for the truth.

Maggie had been armed only with a description. She didn't have a photograph. She didn't have a name. She didn't have a clue where to begin asking after a man in a grey suit who had once – and only possibly – argued with another man on the end of the pier on Valentine's night almost ten years before. She knew the search was pointless before it had even begun, and that she would sound like a fool, asking strangers who worked on the pier if they had seen the man she was looking for.

But she asked anyway – for Ed and for Neville and for Pat Mint. She asked food vendors and plastic windmill sellers and candyfloss makers and the man at the ticket kiosk for the pier train. She asked at Rossi's ice creams and at the little kiosk that sold buckets and spades, and at the fortune tellers, although they were telling the future, of course, and not the past. Then she headed right from the pier, and asked the man who operated the Ferris wheel in Peter Pan's Playground, and the woman who gave out the chafing hessian mats on the helter-skelter.

She asked the crazy question, 'Did you see a man in a grey suit walking around the pier on Valentine's Day, 1971?' She said the man may have been a Mod, or someone who'd been in the military, and she felt even more foolish because when Neville Craddock had argued with the man who looked like he was barking, all these places would have been closed. The people she asked looked at her as though she was crazy, which she was. No wonder the police had sent Pat Mint away with a 'case closed', as that's what it was.

The next day, though, Maggie popped out at lunchtime, eschewing the pub and the baked potatoes. She asked at the all-night greasy spoon opposite the pier. She asked at the seafront pubs. She was still crazy.

Maybe *someone* had seen him.

They hadn't.

On the third day, she decided she could no longer go out there and ask. No one knew of a canine-sounding man in a suit with a metal badge on the lapel from so long ago. Everyone knew she was a strange woman trailing the streets of Southend with an impossible mission. But on the way home from work that day, a man in a grey suit came out of the newsagent's she used to work at on Russell Street with a newspaper under his arm.

'Evening,' the bus driver said to her. Grey suit, white shirt, no tie, metal name badge on his lapel.

'Evening,' Maggie replied.

The next morning, she told the newsroom she had an appointment with a faded star at a house in the town centre, but instead walked to the bus depot on London Road and asked to speak to the supervisor.

'What can I help you with, Miss?' the supervisor asked, stamping his authority on her as he sat in a wooden chair, knees apart. He blew smoke at her from the cigarette stuck in the middle of his florid face.

'I work for the *Gazette*,' she said, standing – as there was nowhere for her to sit – and flashing her lanyard at him in retaliation, a poor shield against all that smoke. 'I'm investigating a story. Could I please see your records of who worked shifts on 14 February 1971?'

The supervisor didn't answer. He looked her up and down, his flabby lips moist. She kept her nerve, riding the misogynistic silence, until he eventually raised a bushy eyebrow. '1971, Miss?' he queried. 'That's a long time ago.'

'It is,' she said. 'But it's for a very important historical story.'

He narrowed his eyes at her through the smoke. 'Hmm,' he said. 'Well, I suppose I *could*. Are you willing to butter me up?'

'Butter you up, Mr *Jackson*?' She read the badge on his straining lapel. 'There will be no *buttering*, I'm afraid.'

He looked disappointed. 'Will I get a credit?' he asked meatily. 'Will my part get mentioned?'

She didn't want to *think* about his part. 'Certainly. I might even come back and take your photo. It depends.'

'You're very *pretty* for a reporter.'

'Is that relevant?'

'I suppose not.' He did not blink. 'But it always helps. Righto,' he said, 'I reckon I can help you out.' He heaved himself dramatically from his chair and walked, whistling, over to a metal cupboard at the back of the room. Wrenching one of the doors open, he ran a fat finger down a long stack of ledger books on a crooked shelf, then shunted one free.

'Here you are,' he said. 'January to April 1971, all the shifts. Help yourself. I'm off to the little boys' room.' He hoicked the waistband of his trousers over his stomach and was off.

Maggie sat gingerly on the edge of the lascivious Mr Jackson's desk and turned eagerly to February 1971, and the day of the fourteenth, and the shifts scribbled in pencil on narrow-ruled paper. There were two shifts. 7 a.m. to 3 p.m., and 3 p.m. to 11 p.m. She focused on the afternoon-to-late shift, reckoning it unlikely a bus driver finishing at 3 p.m. would still be in his uniform at midnight. There had been three men on it that day: Larry Graham, Ted Young and Bob Sinclair. She scribbled their names and addresses down in her notebook. Three men wearing that grey suit on *that* day, finishing an hour before *that* time. It was a start.

'All done?' Mr Jackson was back, staring at her legs – his shirt untucked.

'All done.' She hopped down off his desk.

'And you'll be back to take that photograph of me, maybe?'

'Yes, hopefully I'll be back.'

'Do I get a hug?'

'What?'

He laughed, his rosy face wobbling. 'Only joking, Miss. Off you go.'

And he watched her chest walk out of the room.

Chapter Twenty-Two

3 A.M., 17 MARCH 1983

Dear Maggie,

Thank you for your last letter. I'm kidding, I know you haven't replied to me. I mean, I have been checking my mail for the past seven months . . . ! It's okay, I understand. You're married. We both have busy lives. There's not the time for writing to lost loves. Yet, here I am.

What have you been up to? I hope you're still at Richmond Road, so this letter finds you. I've been thinking about you again recently. I've been wondering what you've been up to. Are you still at the Gazette? *How are your parents?*

You may have seen a picture of me on page 6 of the Sun *last Sunday, coming out of La Spaga with Sally Field. I'm deluded and hopeful enough to wonder if you saw it, if you looked at the picture and saw through it, to me. Could you see my heart Maggie, under all that Lala Land stuff? I like to think you could see me, Maggie, but who knows — you probably didn't even buy the paper.*

Sorry, maudlin in the second paragraph, that's no good. I don't mean to be. I actually have a lovely piece of news to impart in this letter, so don't worry, I'm not going to start banging on about The Carpenters or gazing at my own navel for half an hour . . . or saying that I miss you (even though I do, still). I've got a couple of months off between projects, so I'll have a little more time on my hands and I'm going to need it, too. There's going to be something else in the papers very soon. About me. Indulge me in letting me talk about it, Maggie? This is a difficult one. I wanted you to be the third person in the world to know.

I'm going to be a dad!

She's an actress, the baby's mother. Her name is Veronica Gray. I did a talk at an acting class in West Hollywood and she asked me a lot of questions and afterwards we went to get a coffee. She's smart, talented. I hope she gets a break in this industry. We dated for a couple of months then she had to go out of town for a job — Vegas — and we didn't see each other again until now. She hung around for me outside the studio and told me she was pregnant — well, she didn't need to tell me, it was pretty obvious, she only has a month to go — and the kid is mine. Maggie, I know it's not the best circumstances, and we don't want to be together — well, I offered, to do the right thing, you know, but she turned me down — but she really wants this child and I'm happy about it, I really am. I want to be a great dad. The best, I hope. I'm going to see the baby

*whenever I have a day off, I'm going to be fully involved
in his or her life.*

*That's my news. I just wanted to share it with you. I hope
you're happy, too. I hope there's something every day that
makes you smile. I'll let you know how it goes, I promise.
I just want to be in touch with you, share a little part of
my life with you, even if you can't do the same. I hope
you're well, there in the grey of Southend. I hope you're
doing well, Maggie May. I'll write to you again when the
baby is here and tell you all about it.*

*I bloody miss you (broken my promise, oops) and nobody
here says 'bloody' and I miss that, too.*

*Yours,
Ed xx*

◆ ◆ ◆

Maggie smoothed her hand over the thin paper of the letter on
her lap. She smiled at the thought of Ed's son or daughter, coming
soon, shiny and new. Their eyes, their curls, their wriggling arms
and legs. *Ed's baby.* She brushed away tears at the thought of him
creating a baby with someone, a shared forever, something trea-
sured and perfect.

She was in the downstairs cloakroom, the door locked. If Ray
came downstairs, she could say she had felt ill – tummy trouble. If
he knocked on the door, she could quickly slip the letter – discovered amongst a pile of post this morning and hastily dropped into
the back of the cereal cupboard – behind the toilet cistern. There
was only silence beyond the cloakroom door, so she read the letter

again. What a surprise for Ed, she thought. A shock at first, she imagined, before all the happiness. And he would have to weather the press intrusion on it: a baby out of wedlock, prime celebrity gossip. Talk both sides of the Atlantic. No doubt the *Gazette* would do something, too. Maybe half a page, maybe a full. There'd be the usual trotting out of all those snippets of information about Ed. Where he had lived in Southend. What happened to his dad. How he got his first break in *The Dumb Waiter*. The newsroom had never put in print that one of their staff reporters was an ex-girlfriend of Ed Cavanagh (was Craddock), famed Southend son – because she had begged them not to – but there could always be a first time.

Ray would hate that, Maggie thought. He had a real thing about it now, when once he had brushed it off, her having been with Ed Cavanagh. Shacking up with him. *Shagging* him, as Ray put it. He liked it less and less, the more famous Ed Cavanagh got, and Ed was in an advert, now, shown often in between shows like *Charlie's Angels*, sipping a Mateus Rose on a transatlantic flight. Ray had once thrown a slipper at the television when it had appeared, clocking a smiling Ed on the nose. Another time, he had come home late from the brewery to discover Maggie watching *The Millers and the Smiths*, the sound turned down, staring at Ed's face. He had kicked the television off the table, where it had landed with a dull crunch on the carpet. Then he had kicked the wall, and the gaping craggy crater of it was still there, just left of the sideboard.

It wasn't just Ed he was jealous of. Ray met Maggie from work now, blank-faced, straight from the door of the *Gazette* – there were no more hilarious ambling walks home with Janey. He had recently tussled a man in the pub who had dared engage her in a couple of words while Ray was queuing for a pint ('tussling' was how he had put it; Maggie saw it as Ray punching the poor man in the side and snarling at him to 'Fuck off!'). He wanted to know who she went for lunch with – was it with any men and who were they? Maggie found herself struggling in a flimsy tissue of lies for a while, particularly as she had recently been going for lunch every day with her mate Dave Diller, crime reporter, which soon became untenable. Instead, she began to surround herself with female colleagues only, limiting her contact with men in the newsroom. She wasn't so 'threatening' to Ray, then. Not so 'full of herself'. He hated her for thinking she was intellectually superior to him – and accused her of choosing him in the first place so she would always be the 'cleverer' one.

There was a bump from upstairs and the sound of rushing feet on the stairs. Maggie shoved the letter behind the cistern and opened the cloakroom door.

'What are you doing?' Ray stood in front of the doorway in pyjama bottoms. Angry.

'Tummy trouble,' she said, a tired smile on her face. 'Sorry. I couldn't sleep. I thought I'd better come downstairs. Sorry to wake you.'

'The bloody birds woke me up. Are you coming back up?'

'Of course.'

'I doubt I'll get back to sleep now,' he said, scratching at his bare chest with his thumb. 'Maybe we can make love now we're both awake.' He grinned. 'Would you like that? If you're feeling up to it.'

'Of course. I'm alright now.'

'Good girl,' he muttered, winking at her, his words blunt and jagged spears, but it was Ed's words that were in her heart as she made her way upstairs to their bedroom, Ray bearing up behind her. Ed's words filled her with light as the darkness awaited her. *A baby!* she thought. *A baby.*

Thank goodness she hadn't had one with Ray.

Chapter Twenty-Three

4 A.M., ON THE ISLAND

Maggie dozed off again, bathed in the now eau de Nil light from the bungalow window. She began to dream of Michael, Ed's son. She dreamt of him as a baby, although she had only ever seen one photo of him, which had been printed in both the *Sunday Mirror* and the *Gazette* – wearing a bonnet the colour of a quail's egg. She dreamt of his face, closed and angry, at a wedding scene with his wife and his father. She dreamt she saw him walk up to a postbox in Eagle Rock, Los Angeles, and post a letter.

A bird rehearsed its line from the dawn chorus, outside the window, and Maggie dreamt about fathers and sons.

The denouement of Maggie's search for the man in the grey suit – the pre-denouement, in fact – was entered into by a chance remark. Maggie had been on the sofa at Charlotte Road, watching *The Waltons*, and stirring a cup of tea for both herself and Malcolm, as her mum was out at a whist drive with one of her friends. It was after work, and time in her calm, quiet parents' house was trailing as beautifully as the flocked flowers down the new wallpaper. She'd been remembering her date last night, with Ray. How they had gone to the pictures to see *Scanners*, and Ray had put his arm around her shoulder in the back row and had wrenched her right into him, so she had watched the entire film from his left armpit.

Dad came in from the kitchen with a big tin of biscuits.

'Where did you get those from?' Maggie asked.

'One of the neighbours, Jerry,' said Dad, his Beatles hair floppy and grey and on the brink of being sorted with a box of Just for Men she had seen on the bathroom windowsill. She had to remember to talk him out of that.

'Jerry? Who's Jerry?'

'You know Jerry. Married to Denise. Number forty-seven. The bus driver. He won these in a raffle and didn't want them. Gave them to Mum.'

Maggie set down the teaspoon on the coffee table. 'Denise's husband is a bus driver?' She had a vague recollection from her childhood of a man in a navy dressing gown, putting out the bins on a Friday morning. A man with a crew cut and a snarly expression, who looked like he was furious at the bins for some reason. He slammed them, sometimes kicked them, while Denise twitched the lilac curtains.

'Yeah.'

'Does he work lates?' Maggie knew he didn't, or at least he hadn't on 14 February 1971. He was not one of the drivers who had worked the last shift of the evening and whose names she had written in her notebook. She had checked them all out. Larry, Bob and Ted. None of them had been on Southend Pier on the night of Valentine's Day 1971.

'God knows why you're asking, but no – he knocks off every day about three, then goes straight to The White Horse, has done for years. Belligerent bugger, really. Best avoided. Something not right in their marriage, I think. Do you want one?' Dad sat in his armchair and attempted to open the biscuit tin on his lap.

'Let me do that, Dad,' Maggie said, taking it off him. 'Something not right . . . ?' she prompted. 'With Denise and Jerry?'

'She's flighty, Denise,' said Dad, holding out his hand for a biscuit while Maggie prised open the lid of the tin. 'A bit too friendly with some of the regulars at the social club. Not that I've even seen anything . . . recently. And he's just a weird character altogether, a strange loner, drinks alone, but apparently he has pen pals at Chelmsford prison, criminals he writes to, as a hobby. *Very* strange. Aren't you having one?'

'No, thanks, Dad.'

'Don't blame you. Fig rolls, ugh.' He grimaced as he popped one in his mouth. 'Work of the devil.'

While Dad turned to *The Waltons*, Maggie rummaged in her bag for the photo of Pat Mint, Maureen and the other two women, Neville Craddock's face in the background. Ever since Pat's call, she had carried that photo in her bag like a talisman. She studied it now, every speck of it, every inch of it. Pat's hair, the number of glasses on the table, the handbag . . . the handbag. She had never questioned it. All along she had imagined it to be Pat's, or Maureen's, or one of the other two women's – or had not thought about it at all – but now she peered at it closely. It was big and it was dark red, the colour of blood, and it resembled a doctor's bag, and if she looked very carefully, there was a hand resting on it, at the edge of the table, and there was something languid about the curve of the masculine fingers, resting on that bag like that – almost intimate. And the hand became a white cuff and a triangle of bottle green.

Maggie had seen that handbag before.

'Dad,' she said. 'I need to pop out, just down to the newsagent's. I need to get some . . . crisps,' she said, already out the door. 'I'll be back shortly.'

She marched up Charlotte Road in her navy skirt and white work blouse, tucking it in as she walked and brushing off biscuit crumbs from her skirt, and knocked on the door of number forty-seven.

'Hello?' Denise was in a house coat, her white-blonde hair, usually a motorcycle helmet of stiffness, separated around big pink curlers. 'Oh, it's you, Maggie,' she said. 'Everything alright with your mum?'

'Yes, she's fine,' said Maggie. 'Can I come in? I'm here in a professional capacity.'

'Er . . . alright,' said Denise, looking bemused. She opened the door wider and let Maggie into the hall. Its wallpaper was a garish print of giant red peonies on a black background; the console table was littered with post and Mills & Boon paperbacks. 'Do you want to come into the sitting room?'

'Thank you,' said Maggie. She followed Denise into a room with a dusky pink carpet, bowls of dusty pot pourri everywhere, and an ornate fireplace where fake black coals lazily glowed. A gold sunburst clock marked the hour over the mantelpiece; the lilac net curtains were fully drawn. Denise wedged herself in a huge floral armchair, offering Maggie the matching sofa. Her nails were painted bright apricot and she had stained lips that looked like they had been painted raspberry red yesterday, but not attended to today.

The scene was set. Maggie felt vaguely sick.

'Was there something going on between you and Neville Craddock?' asked Maggie, getting straight to the point. Denise immediately went red in the face, so her cheeks and her mouth merged into the same shade, and her apricot-painted toes, in fleecy mule slippers, visibly curled.

'Don't be stupid! This is a wild accusation if I've ever heard one!' Denise cried, flapping at her face with both hands like a trapped pigeon. 'Of course not!'

'Did your husband *think* something was going on between you?'

'No! What on earth gives you that idea? Are you mad?'

Maggie reached into her bag for her notebook and pen, trying to appear professional, but she was inclined to agree with Denise. This *was* all rather mad, and preposterously concocted from a series of evidence that was so flimsy as to be non-existent. (A handbag! A man in a grey suit, seen by a drunk reveller! An arguing man with a face like a dog! The certain curve of a set of fingers!) Had Denise not gone quite so red, or looked quite so nervous, or had not done all the classic things that liars do – which Maggie had learnt from Dave Diller in the newsroom (the avoiding of eye contact, the finger-scratching at the edge of a pink ear, the nervous cough) – Maggie would have made her excuses and fled, taking her notebook and pen and her professional misconduct with her.

But the denial was vehement and laid on thick and Denise carried on making it for a further three minutes. Eventually, Maggie had heard enough. She scribbled on her notepad, 'This is not going to work', and she said, 'Well, thanks so much for your valuable time, Denise. I seem to have exhausted all my enquiries here. If you'd be so good as to see me out . . .' And within seconds she was back out on the street again, having got nowhere.

Maggie went to the police anyway. She spoke to a detective called Marsons. She told him about Pat Mint and what she'd seen at the end of the pier. She told him Jerry Sullivan was a bus driver who finished at three and often went straight to the pub. About the handbag, and Denise and the possible affair with Neville Craddock. Marsons sighed and wrote a brief report. He allowed her to give in a handwritten statement she had penned on lined paper at home (knowing there was insufficient evidence for an official statement to be taken), and although he added it to the file – holding it disapprovingly by one corner – she suspected he'd remove it, after she'd gone, and throw it in the bin.

She was ushered out with a dismissive, 'Thank you very much, Madam, we'll look into it,' and a curt, patronising smile, followed by the chuckled mutter of, 'A bloody handbag . . .' Then, as she stepped over the threshold, he said, 'Don't you work at the *Gazette*? There's a *Maggie Martin* there, isn't there?'

'Yes,' she said, shamefaced, and she'd felt like a sub-standard private detective, there on the pavement outside the police station. A hack. She had failed in the search for Ed's father. She had not been able to retrieve the missing ghost of Neville Craddock and return him to his son. She had failed *Ed*, who was about to be a father himself. She was just a hack who should stick to looking for the missing people who were easy to find.

Chapter Twenty-Four

4 A.M., 3 MAY 1983

Dear Maggie,

Hope you are well. I'm starting to feel like a very bad penny, the one you see on the ground that's all black and green and you don't want to pick it up. I get that you can't reply to me. I know these letters are being sent over the Atlantic with no guarantee of reply, but I do want to keep writing to you. I hope they're not causing you any difficulty?

I wanted to let you know something. I've seen him. I've seen my boy. And he is amazing! I went over to Veronica's house in Eagle Rock and he was in a pram at the bottom of the garden under a cherry blossom tree. As I walked towards it, my heart was soaring, soaring right up to the sky, and I was so excited. I'd imagined having a child, but not like this, I don't know what I'd imagined, really – but to walk towards that pram in the beautiful garden, knowing he was inside, was just the best thing ever. His name is Michael and he's the most beautiful baby boy in the world! I'm going to visit him as often as I can. He's going to know I am a devoted dad. I'm going to be the very best I can be.

It feels so good to tell you this. You might see my grinning mug in a newspaper sometime soon and the grin on my face will be because of him.

I do hope you're okay, Maggie? I have other news. I'm going up for a part in a film. The film is called A Sunny Day in the Valley. *I hope you can be happy for me. I have to go for an audition on Friday. It's unlikely I'll get it as Michael J. Fox is up for it too, but I will do my best and see what happens.*

Maybe I'll write again to tell you the outcome? I don't know now, Maggie, I don't know what I'm doing here, sending these letters. I feel I might be just sending them into the ether. Take care of yourself, won't you?

Bye for now, Maggie May.

Yours,
Ed xx

Maggie reread every line of the letter, in her mind, as she lay on the kitchen floor, staring at the edge along the bottom of the fridge and thinking she must clean it. How could she have missed that sticky line of jam, or was it ketchup . . . ? She needed to scrub the whole fridge, really. Ray would complain about it if she didn't do it soon.

Ed's baby, she thought. Michael Gray-Cavanagh. A kicking baby boy in a pram at the end of a sunny Californian garden. How lovely, she thought. How lovely for Ed. All those sunny days together with his boy. She was jealous, she realised. Jealous of his happiness, and of him being able to love something so precious. An unconditional love, when her own had so many conditions they were wrapping around her throat like an anaconda, strangling her.

She put out her hand and felt the sticky warmth of the blood coming out of her head, looked at her fingers and thought it could well be the same as the sticky stuff on the fridge. It had started with nothing, really. The row. A strained weekend had led to her making a roast dinner for Ray on a Monday night – all the trimmings – but overdone potatoes had left him incandescent.

'I thought you'd like it,' Maggie had stuttered. 'A roast.' She'd wondered how she had come to this, sweating over a roast dinner on a Monday night, like a Stepford Wife, to please a man who could never be appeased.

'Who would be stupid enough to do a Sunday roast on a *Monday*?' Ray had scoffed cruelly. 'And fucked it right up in the process! Or are you feeling guilty about something?' he had demanded, looming over his loaded plate and the offending potatoes. 'Have you done something you shouldn't?'

'No, of course not.' But talking about feeling guilty *made* her feel guilty.

'Have you been chatting to any men at the bloody *Gazette*? Did you have lunch with anyone today?'

'No, no, of course I haven't.' She had risked a lunch with Dave. They had sat at the back of the pub with a ploughman's. He had demonstrated how a pickpocket was able to get someone's watch off without them having a clue.

Ray launched off his chair and had her up from the table, her arm twisted behind her back, suddenly, painfully. 'Who is it? Who have you been flirting with?'

'No one, no one.' The pain was excruciating. Ray let go of her arm and while she was shaking it, wincing, he grabbed her by the shoulders and thrust her back from him, holding her at arm's length, like she was a flopping mannequin. And then he punched her in the face.

The floor was cold. Ray had long walked away. She could hear the television blaring in the next room: J.R. was berating Sue Ellen and sending her to the sanatorium again. At the sink, the tap was dripping. Maggie didn't want to move. She didn't want to rise up from the floor and go next door and sit down with Ray on the sofa and watch television. She didn't want to stand up, after a while, and fetch his washing from the clothes horse upstairs. Put away his pants and socks. Iron his shirt for tomorrow. Brush her teeth later and get into bed beside him. But she didn't know how *not* to. Not any more.

So, she continued to lie on the kitchen floor and think about Ed's letter. She imagined herself in that sunny LA garden, with a swing seat, maybe, and a kidney-shaped swimming pool that glistened turquoise in the sun, and the pram at the bottom of the garden with Ed's beautiful baby in it. She imagined the immaculate lawn and the sunshine and the wriggling, kicking baby and Ed's happy, happy face. And she imagined she was happy, too, just for a moment, because she had forgotten what happiness felt like.

Chapter Twenty-Five

5 A.M., ON THE ISLAND

Maggie checked the time. It was still only 5.03 a.m. She sat up, a headache pulsing at the back of her skull – it had hardly been a stellar night's sleep – then slipped out of bed to the bathroom and quickly showered. Afterwards, she pulled on a pair of navy shorts and a loose white cotton shirt. Dragged her hair into a ponytail, applied a little make-up, and opened the bungalow door to the fresh morning air and a man holding a bushy broom.

'Hello?'

'*Bonjour*,' said the man. The hand on the pole of his broom was as wrinkled as a crumpled piece of parchment.

'Are you Pa Zayan?' she asked, then, raking her brain for O-level French, '*Êtes-vous* Pa Zayan?'

'*Oui*,' said the man and he said something to her she didn't understand at all. But he was smiling at her, and gesticulating with the broom, and she noticed a collected pile of fallen tropical leaves in the corner of the veranda. *Quiet sweeping*, she thought; she hadn't heard a sound.

'*Merci,*' she said. 'Thank you. Your . . . bungalow . . .' she ventured – heaven knows what 'bungalow' was in French – '*Votre maison?*' That would have to do. '*C'est très jolie.*'

He nodded, looking pleased.

'*Merci pour la bibliothèque,*' she continued. (Oh – that was 'library'.) '*Le livre,*' she corrected herself. The book. On the bedside table. It had been a battered copy of Jilly Cooper's *Riders*, which had made her smile.

Pa Zayan nodded again. '*De rien,*' he said ('you're welcome'), then he said something she couldn't understand, '*J'espère que vous trouverez ce que vous cherchez en Mémoire,*' before tucking the broom under his arm and walking off, all bony limbs and bonhomie, in the direction of the path to the beach. It was only after he had disappeared from sight that some kind of ancient secondary school recall made Maggie realise what he'd said: 'I hope you find what you're looking for on Mémoire.'

She wasn't sure she would, she thought, admiring her neat veranda, but it was nice of him to say so. She may as well grab her bag and everything she needed and start the day now, she reasoned, as early as it was. She would walk down to the beach, take in the view. Fill her lungs with fresh morning air. Start thinking about the local colour – those brushstrokes of a piece. At home, it was usually the artwork above the head of the faded starlet as she sat on the sofa, the arrangement of sleeping cats. Or the leafy walk the cast member of a once-loved soap took daily down to his greenhouse and his tomatoes. Here, she already had the words for just the right shade of blue in the sky outside Ed's chalet and for the smell of the bougainvillea that pervaded this island. She knew how she would describe Ed's physical appearance and the sound of his voice, a little gravelly now with age. The background stuff was all she had, so far. The profile of Ed and his symbiotic relationship with a toxic Hollywood would follow.

The scrubby path was dappled in muted light, the canopy overhead a rinsed-clean crochet filigree of palm leaves that dripped lightly on her as she walked. She followed it until she saw the gap in the foliage, the bent branches of the palms forming an arch. Through the arch, the deserted beach awaited, stretching down to the sea like a canvas, only etched on here and there by straggles of driftwood and a lone crane stretching its long legs in the shallows of the shore. Maggie headed right, the horizon an indistinct spirit level on her left, the sky above her a beautiful, gloomy duck egg blue.

She breathed deeply as she walked, savouring the sweet, salty air. She passed the place where her boat had come in, Amine waiting for her, and imagined herself clambering into it this afternoon, her time on the island over. She passed Olly's, shuttered up.

And then she saw him.

Ed was further up the beach, down by the shoreline, where his skiff lolled in the water. In pale pink shorts and a white t-shirt, his back was to her as he sat cross-legged in the sand sorting through his fishing stuff, the sail and the mast beside him.

She spoke first. 'Morning,' she said, a little nervously, as she walked towards him.

'Morning.' He laid another fishing hook flat in his tin and looked up at her. 'You're up early. How did you sleep?'

'Not great.' She felt awkward this morning, after all the fire and ice of last night. 'A couple of hours. How about you?'

'Patchy.' He grimaced. She had dreamt of ghosts; she wondered what he had dreamt of. 'All ready for the tour at seven? I see you've brought your camera.'

'Of course. I hope you're ready for your close-up, Mr Cavanagh.'

'Of course,' he echoed, then they both lapsed into silence. It would be tricky and uncomfortable, going on this island tour with him today, she thought. It would be something to be borne, as would doing her interview with him. Then she could pack up her memories – as shifting as the streaks of cloud drifting across the horizon – and her camera, and escape.

He placed another fishing hook carefully in his pail. 'I'm about to go fishing,' he said. 'Just a quick trip. Do you want to come with me?'

'Would you like me to?'

Ed sighed. 'I've just asked you, haven't I?'

She looked out across the pale opal water, shimmering in the early morning light. A primrose-yellow sun was low in the sky. A bird looped towards the horizon. The atmosphere between them may be as strained as a line stretched on a hook, but the morning was beautiful. 'Well, I'm up now,' she replied. 'So, yes, I'd like to.'

'Great! Help me grab the mast, then, would you?' he said, standing up and brushing sand off his shorts. 'Make yourself useful.'

'Okay,' said the newly appointed understudy, with an uncertain smile.

Ed bent and hoisted up one end of the pole from the sand, and Maggie lifted the other. Together they carried it to the skiff and Maggie followed directions to help Ed fasten it to the boat.

'Now fetch the pail and the bait tin,' he said, 'and I'll have those in the stern.'

'Yes, skipper!'

'No need to be insubordinate,' Ed quipped, and she couldn't help but laugh. 'Twelve more hours on the island, Mags,' he said, once all the equipment was stowed correctly on the skiff and it was ready to set sail.

'Twelve little hours,' she agreed, and she hoped she could survive them.

Ed started the engine and they set off gently under skies streaked with lilac and amber and in the fine spray of a scoping sea mist, the water a muted pearly aqua and not yet a true blue. Maggie licked her top lip and tasted the tang of the salt. She was sitting on the side bench, her feet on the flat bottom of the boat, looking out across the water. Ed was in the square stern, operating the tiller, a fisherman's cap squashed on to his silver curls.

'All you need is the beard and you'll look like Captain Birds Eye!' she called over to him, wondering if he would remember the reference.

'Leave me alone, I'm driving,' he retorted, demonstrating that he did.

She had the urge to stick her tongue out at him, and he looked as surprised when she did as she'd felt doing it.

They skimmed across the water, the sun rising in a haze slowly above them, the horizon a wavering line. Maggie used her hand to make a visor and took in her view, three-hundred and sixty degrees of it, not wanting to miss a thing: the sea, the jewel of the island receding behind them, the reticent ship's captain – and his funny hat. It was gorgeous, it really was, the loamy sea and the mottled sky and the mist.

When the boat reached water the colour of spearmint, Ed started reeling off to her all the different types of fish in these waters – the butterfish, the sardine, the Indian mackerel, the clown fish and the purple sea perch. Then he jumped over to the engine and the boat puttered to a stop, the waves gently lapping at its sides.

'And now we fish,' he said. He clambered to sit on the bench next to her and opened his bait tin. 'Shrimp,' he said. They were big ones, not like the tiny little frozen prawns you got in English supermarkets, she thought. A whole box packed full of them.

'You remove part of the shell,' Ed explained, 'so the scent is stronger.' She watched as he picked up a shrimp, plucked off pieces of its shell, which he threw into the water, and, taking a hook, spiked it through the plump body.

'Like so,' he said, showing her, 'so the tail dangles and the mackerel can't resist.'

He expertly worked his way through the bait tin, working quickly until all the shrimp baits were on their hooks. She noticed the ring finger of his left hand, no ring now, and no tan line either. The skin was uniform, with no traces of his marriage remaining, not like they had for her for about two decades.

'I'm impressed,' Maggie observed. 'You look like you've been doing this for a long time.'

'I have.'

She took a couple of photos of him baiting the hooks. She wondered if he'd turned his head to show her his best side.

'Oh,' she said, 'you mean fishing with your dad at the end of Southend Pier?' She shouldn't be mentioning Neville but she knew all his emotions surrounding his dad, how they had shaped Ed, coloured him, over the years. How she had played her own part in them.

'And with Michael at the end of Santa Monica Pier. When he was a kid.' Ed hooked another shrimp. She held out a hand to touch the end of the shrimp's tail and Ed's finger accidentally brushed against hers as he worked. She placed her hand back in her lap. 'And at Huntingdon Flats. I've never stopped fishing. I go most weekends back in LA.'

'Oh, right.' Maggie was surprised. 'And do you catch fish every day here?'

'Yes. I catch quite a few. Watch.'

Grabbing a ball of fishing twine from a box under the bench, Ed threaded it through the eye in each fishing hook and used the flat of its shank to attach it to each rod, winding the twine around the rod several times to make it tight, and securing the hook with a knot.

'Clinch knot,' he said. She watched, then, as Ed lined up the rods along the side of the boat and cast five or six lines into the water. 'And now we wait.'

He sat back on the bench, stretching his legs out in the bottom of the boat. His left foot nearly touched her right, but she surreptitiously moved hers an inch away.

'What do you do while you wait?' she asked.

'Listen to the radio, think about my life.'

'What kind of things do you think about?'

'Regrets,' muttered Ed. 'Excuse me.' He leaned across to grab the old radio that was lying on its side on the bench opposite. He fiddled with the knob until some old swing tune came on, something you might hear in a black and white Hollywood musical.

'This is nice,' she commented. She wondered if it reminded him of the same night, many years ago, when his star of fame and success was high in the London sky. Ed didn't answer. He had his eyes closed, his face to the haze of the sun. She closed her eyes, too, let the sound of the violins and the piano swing through her, accompanied by the lapping of the water and the distant cry of a bird. *What am I doing here, out on the Indian Ocean with a man I used to love?* she wondered. *What has brought me to this place?*

'Here we go!'

She started and opened her eyes to see Ed leap across the boat.

'I think we got a bite!'

He grabbed a rod in the middle of his row and yanked on it, flicking the line and the fish caught on the end of it into the air. The fish was struggling, twitching and spinning. Ed reeled it in, elated.

'Fishing makes you really happy,' she observed.

'Yes,' he replied. There was another bite, then another, until, within ten minutes or so, Ed had six large flapping fish of various hues and sizes in his pail.

'Enough for Olly's?' she asked.

'None for Olly's,' he replied. 'Not this trip.' And one by one he carefully removed the hook from the mouth of each fish and gently lopped it back into the water. 'This trip was just for fun. Have you enjoyed it?'

'Yes,' she replied. 'I really have.' The sun in his eyes, he looked at her for a moment too long, until she had to glance away.

◆　◆　◆

When the skiff slid back on to the shore, the sun was beginning to truly ripen and the skies were clearing. Ed hopped off the boat into the shallows. Baptiste, who was waiting on the beach, stepped forward to help Maggie out.

'*Salut!*' said Baptist, showing his jolly, snaggly teeth. '*Ça va?*' He smelled of chewing gum and cardamon.

'Good morning,' Maggie replied, taking his large warm hand.

'You're early, my friend.' Ed wasn't wearing a watch, so Maggie glanced at hers. It was approaching six.

'I thought we could meet for breakfast,' replied Baptiste, gesturing with his moustache to the cloudy Tupperware box and the rolled-up towel he was holding. 'I knew you would be fishing. And Maggie is here too,' he said, looking delighted at the sight of them together. 'Don't worry, I will give you plenty of time on your own today,' he added. 'I'm sure you two have lots to talk about.'

'We really don't,' trilled Maggie flippantly. 'But thank you. I'm happy to have breakfast and start the tour early.'

'Yes, why not just get going?' said Ed in equally jolly tones. 'We can eat whatever's in that box on the go. Let me just stow my mast and my sail. Can you help me, please, Baptiste?'

Maggie waited on the sand while Ed and Baptiste took the boat paraphernalia to Ed's shack.

'Wakey, wakey,' said Ed, on their return.

'Oh, sorry, I must have fallen asleep for a couple of minutes.' Maggie sat up, blinking.

'You have sand in your hair.'

'Do I?'

'Yes.'

She patted at her hair until all the sand dislodged itself and returned to the beach.

'There,' Ed said. 'Pretty, again.'

'Ha, ha,' Maggie retorted.

Baptiste was standing with his cap in his hand. 'Let me take you to my car.'

'Oh, the tour is by car?' Maggie queried.

'Yes.' Baptiste nodded. 'Although the island is only twelve miles in diameter, the tour is best on wheels.'

He led them along a dense, leafy trail behind Olly's which opened into a small clearing where a battered old car – off-white with a rust trim – was sagging like a defeated slug on worn, mismatched tyres. It had one windscreen wiper, an amateur-looking registration plate latched on with string and an optimistic 'go faster' stripe down one side.

'Very nice,' said Maggie.

'Baptiste's pride and joy,' Ed remarked, giving the car an affectionate slap on the rump.

Inside, the car smelt of coconut. An air freshener in the shape of one hung from the rear-view mirror, along with a string of rosary beads. There was a box of tissues in a rigid gilt case on the shelf behind the back seat, covered in dark grey terry towelling.

'The air-con is broken,' said Baptiste, once Ed and Maggie were in the back, both seated by the windows with a safe space between them. 'Well, it works a little but it's noisy and it smells like mackerel. Better to have the windows open.' He cranked his down and Ed and Maggie did the same. Then Baptiste placed his cap on the passenger seat and turned and handed his box back to them.

'Here is your breakfast,' he said happily, and he turned the key in the ignition and indicated left, with a rhythmic click-clock, to pull out of the clearing.

Chapter Twenty-Six

5 A.M., 4 SEPTEMBER 1983

Maggie was not sure she'd ever seen a 5 a.m. Southend before. It was dark, but only around the edges. At the centre of the horizon a deep blush was forming over the gas works, on the barren island in the distance. A solitary boat – Soviet, gunmetal grey – sat suspended and purposeless in the grey swamp of the Thames. The shutters were down; the streets were empty. The seagulls were lone and looping, crying their sorry cry over the roof of the Palace Hotel; a street cleaner shuffled along the promenade, dragging a trolley with a mop and a brush sticking out the top. And somebody's dog, escaped, ran joyously past Maggie and down on to the wet pebbled beach, where it hurtled into the loaming.

Maggie had not been able to sleep. Alone in the bed, there had been too much sheet, too many pillows, too much space, not enough warmth. The house on Richmond Road, cold for so long, felt like it wanted to kick her out – like she didn't belong there if Ray didn't, and he had been gone for three days now. She'd got up, restless, and had paced the landing until she had crept downstairs to get her coat. As she'd quietly let herself out of the front door – coat over pyjamas, feet slipped into white Adidas trainers – she'd felt as though she'd been letting herself out of her *life,* and panicked, rummaging in her bag for the keys she'd only just dropped into it, making sure she could get back in.

The streets were cool but not cold this early September morning. She walked briskly at first, then didn't see the point; she was in no hurry. It was a Sunday. She could be out all day, and no one would know or care. Ray – at his mate's house, sleeping the peaceful sleep of someone who didn't care what they had destroyed, followed by a matey bacon sandwich at the kitchen table – certainly wouldn't. He would have the untroubled breakfast of a man who had ruined so many of theirs and had once thrown bacon at the wall where it slid on to the top of Maggie's head – because *she* had been thrown there first. And she didn't want to knock on her parents' door, or ring at Stevie's flat.

'Morning.' A man with a different dog greeted her as she passed the pirate-themed moving waxwork, not switched on yet, the open mouth of the prone captive pirate gaping at a motionless cutlass. Maggie nodded at the man and smiled weakly at the dog. She passed the mouth of the pier. The entrance to Peter Pan's Playground. The slopes. She headed listlessly towards Westcliff and then she saw them, on the pavement.

She shouldn't have been surprised to see him. She had read all about it, in the *Gazette,* back in August, before the paper had even gone to press that week, that Ed Cavanagh was coming to Southend to film. She'd registered the news with no more than a flicker. She'd had no mental ability to be affected, other than to give a sad nod of the head, and feel a muffled pang somewhere deep within her chest. In August, there had been so much energy required just to hold herself together. To put one foot in front of the other. The daily wrestle to get Ray to leave. The fog of fear, and the scream of nightly arguments. She had read the report about Ed and his filming impartially, almost wholly detached from it, like Ed Cavanagh was just a name in print and not a memory.

Ed hadn't looked *her* up. Why would he? As far as he knew, she was happily married. So happily married, she didn't reply to letters. But there he was, on that pavement, big puffer jacket on, being powdered on the chin by a young girl and surrounded by assistant directors, runners and sound people, plus a small crowd of civilians. Rubberneckers in cagoules, early morning risers, joggers and open-mouthed dog walkers. *Echo Beach* was the name of the new TV series, as the *Gazette* had reported, and Ed was playing the 'handsome son of an American astronaut, who comes to a British seaside town to search for the BBC secretary his late father fell in love with during the British TV coverage of the moon landings'. The lead role. A huge part. Reading about it, Maggie had wondered, through her fog, if Ed himself had suggested Southend as a location, so he could see his mum. But apart from that, she had wondered next to nothing, felt next to nothing.

Maggie immediately turned around. She started walking back the way she had come.

'Maggie!'

She heard running footsteps on the pavement behind her and quickened hers.

'Maggie?'

A hand touched the sleeve of her coat. She turned round and he was standing there: twenty-nine years old, blue jeans, big grey coat and black trainers. Green eyes concerned at the sight of her, because she was someone to be concerned about now, wasn't she? She was one of the haunted people wandering the streets at 5 a.m. on September mornings, looking for something that couldn't be found.

'It's really you,' he said. 'How are you?'

'I'm fine,' said Maggie and her heart was beating a little faster in its tarnished cage and she didn't know if it was because she was seeing him, after all this time – looking so well and so surprisingly *Ed* – or if it was the shame of being discovered on the streets like this, her coat thrown over her pyjamas and the cold failure of her marriage written all over her face.

'It's good to see you. I was hoping to . . . somehow, and here you are.' He looked eager, excited. She stared back blankly at him. Chilled, silent. 'You're out walking early,' he said. 'Where are you going?'

'Nowhere. Well, I was going to the shops. How are you?' she asked stiltedly.

'I'm fine. Which shops?' he asked. 'None are open yet.'

'The corner shop, to get some milk. It opens really early.' The shame flooded every inch of her, liquid, freezing. The guilt that her marriage had gone wrong, that *she'd* got it wrong, that she had been bullied and belittled and thrown against walls. It had all been her fault, hadn't she been told that often enough? She was too stupid, too untrustworthy, too much of a terrible cook, too catastrophic a homemaker, too superior, too clever, too fucking useless. And now she was numb, so very, very numb. Even with Ed in front of her on the pavement, here in Southend.

'The corner shop? Isn't there one nearer to Richmond Road?'

'No.'

'Are you okay?' Ed was still holding on to her arm, concerned.

Maggie tried to pull herself together. She attempted to zip herself up like an anorak, stiff and rigid and unbreakable. 'I'm fine,' she repeated.

'You're in your pyjamas, Maggie. What's going on?'

'Nothing . . . really. I'm just out walking. Go back to your . . . crew.'

They both glanced up the pavement where the crew was staring anxiously at Ed, one woman looking at her watch and a man stepping out into the road, his arm raised. Maggie imagined he might produce a whistle from his pocket, to summon back their leading man.

'You never replied to any of my letters,' said Ed. 'I thought you might, maybe. Just once. I hoped you might.'

'No.'

'Is everything okay, really?' he pressed. 'With you? With life?'

She had clung to the hope of things turning out differently for far too long. She had believed in marriage, that it could give her what she needed. But the morning Ray had slammed her against the kitchen wall, for no reason, and then threw bacon at her, was the day it had to end. The day she had felt numb enough, and destroyed enough, and broken enough, to begin to peel him off her life like a dirty plaster.

They were calling Ed, now – the crew – impatient for him to get back on his mark (Ed had once told Maggie all about those): an orange neon cross taped on the pavement.

'Everything's wonderful.' The guilt and shame were numbing her body like she had slipped through a crack on an icy lake and now, face up and floating, she could only see the world through fractured glass. 'How's Michael?' she asked politely.

'He's great, thanks.' Ed was puzzled and concerned, but she couldn't help him.

'Good. Great. Look, I should go. I need to go. *You* need to go.'

'I'll call for you. I'll call round to your house. When I finish filming tonight, it might be quite late, but I'll call round . . . if . . .'

'No, please don't,' she begged him, and the zip was slowly coming down, threatening to expose her deadened centre, and she couldn't let it, so she tried to wrench it back up. 'Don't come round,' she said brightly. 'I won't be in. Ray and I are going out to dinner tonight. It's our anniversary.'

Oh, the lie was as shiny as a sheet of metal and just as impenetrable. He hadn't considered Ray anyway, had he, Ed? Not really, if he thought he was just going to breeze on round later tonight . . . Maybe Hollywood stars really *did* just do what they wanted.

'Oh, right, okay then, I'll leave you. So . . . enjoy your walk and your . . . dinner.' Ed shoved his hands in his pockets. Raised his eyebrows in resigned confusion. 'I still think you're being a bit strange but if you're telling me you're okay—'

'You don't know me any more,' said Maggie. 'How would you know what I was supposed to be like?'

'Okay, I'm going.' He was backing away from her, trotting, signalling to the crew he was coming. 'Take care, Maggie.'

'Hope the series is a big success,' muttered Maggie robotically, and she turned and walked in the direction she had come in, her footsteps plodding dully on the pavement. She would go home eventually, maybe in a couple of hours, maybe three, back to the house that was no longer a home. She would go home and try to forget she'd bumped into Ed Cavanagh this morning, for what did it matter? What did anything matter? Until then, she would trail the early morning streets of Southend, her coat over her pyjamas, and try to walk off her ghosts.

Chapter Twenty-Seven

6 A.M., ON THE ISLAND

Baptiste's car rocked from side to side up a dusty dirt track, the rosary beads and the air freshener swinging, the rainforest either side of them thick and lush. Maggie spotted a parakeet with a coral pink face, spying on them from a branch. She put her hand through the open window and waved her fingers gently in the warm air.

The track wound its way to the centre of the island, Baptiste told them. 'To the old plantation house,' he added.

'Fantastic.'

'You'll like it,' Ed said, and it was the first time he'd looked at her since they'd got into the car. She glanced back at him, then turned to her open window, and the soft breeze, and the deep secrets of the rainforest.

'Are you happy for me to put some music on?' Baptiste asked, catching Maggie's eye in the rear-view mirror.

'Of course.'

'Are you taking requests?' Ed asked.

'No, my friend,' said Baptiste, and he reached into the glove box and rummaged for a cassette, opening it one-handed on his lap and snapping it into the car's ancient tape deck.

Maggie recognised the track that was halfway through at once. 'Please Mr Postman' by The Carpenters.

'Jaunty,' said Ed. 'You can't beat a bit of The Carpenters.' His face, as she looked at it quizzically, was giving nothing away. *Does he remember the first time?* she wondered. *In my single bed? Does he remember the letters he wrote to me from California?*

All three listened to the rest of the song, Karen Carpenter stopping the postman to repeatedly ask him to look in his bag for any letters from her love, as Baptiste's old banger of a car bounced up the track. Ed had started to hum, Maggie realised, with surprise. And Baptiste's head was wiggling appreciatively to the music.

'The seventies were the best,' Baptiste concluded, as the track finished. 'All the seventies music was very good.'

'I agree,' said Ed. 'It was brilliant. Tell me, Baptiste' – and Ed, astoundingly, suddenly decided to wink at her – 'did you ever hear of a band called Wired Tomb?'

'Wired "too"? No, I don't know it . . .' Baptiste looked confused in the rear-view mirror.

Ed laughed, so Maggie said, 'It was the name of Ed's terrible seventies band. He could play the guitar like a fish rides a bicycle.'

Baptiste's face broke into laughter, his eyes screwed up with mirth. 'You knew each other in the seventies?' he asked.

'Yes, we did,' said Maggie, looking at Ed and fearing he might randomly wink at her again. 'We were neighbours, first of all. Well, opposite ends of the street, but close enough.'

'And then you dated?'

'Yes,' said Ed and Maggie in unison, and she couldn't help but glance down at his wrist, where she had once placed the transfer of the star and wetted it with the sponge.

'But you didn't get married?'

'Er . . . no, we didn't get married,' Maggie muttered. A look passed between her and Ed, on the back seat. 'Well, not to each other.'

'I know Mr Ed he has married two times. How about you, Maggie?' said Baptiste. She concentrated on his curious eyes in the mirror.

'Just the once,' she said, overly lightly.

'So, it was never a suggestion for the two of you?'

Ed leant through the gap between the two front seats, placing his tanned hand on the left-hand headrest. 'You're not usually so full of questions, Bap,' he said jovially. 'Baptiste and I have a very alpha relationship,' he explained, turning to Maggie. 'We talk about fishing, and incoming storm clouds, and how to fix a rudder on a boat, but now he wants to talk about emotions and stuff? *Mon ami*'s getting *personal* . . .'

'Sometimes the time is right to get personal,' said Baptiste solemnly. 'Sometimes the time is right to talk, before the time runs out.'

'Well,' Ed shrugged, 'I guess you could say the time ran out for Maggie and me. On several occasions.'

He turned away again. 'Please Mr Postman' had finished now and 'Hurting Each Other' had swept on. *Very apt*, thought Maggie.

Karen Carpenter's clear, sweet voice swelled around the car and the car bumped up the track, which narrowed suddenly, and there they were, at the bottom of a yellow-earthed slope that wound up to a quite breathtaking old French colonial plantation house. Pale lilac in colour, it was a faded and flaking single-storey *grande dame*, perched on stilts. Its stately windows were crusted and shuttered, two dovecotes punctuated its disintegrating pitched roof, and its foundations were overgrown with grasses and ferns that licked their way up to its pretty wraparound veranda.

'It's beautiful!' Maggie exclaimed.

'The Lilas Plantation House was first built by the Dubain family, who lived here for many generations. In 1976, when the island gained independence, a local family, the Payets, bought the Lilas and it finally became a place of great pride for Mémoire.' Baptiste got out of the car and opened the door for Maggie and Ed. 'The house is now in a state of disrepair, but the ghost of its former beauty remains, as you will see.'

'Thank you,' said Maggie. 'It's so pretty. It's like if Miss Havisham was a house.'

Baptiste led them to the steps of the veranda. 'Be careful,' he said. 'They are old and creaky.'

'Just like me,' said Ed.

'And me,' agreed Maggie.

They shared a quick smile and walked up the steps, which did indeed creak, and the safety of the safety rail was not certain, decided Maggie, but she couldn't wait to see inside this fine relic of another age.

The slatted front door was ajar, and Baptiste nudged it open with his hand, spilling light into the interior: a dilapidated, open-plan space with an entrance hall and three, possibly four, flanking reception rooms marked out by fretwork pillars and nodded on by low beams and long-silent ceiling fans. The interior shutters, their patinas patchy and whitewashed, were falling off their hinges.

'Wow!' said Maggie, looking around. 'Absolutely stunning.'

'Isn't it?' said Ed, wandering around too, the soles of his plim-solls making a faint echo on the bleached wooden floorboards. 'It's haunted,' he added, 'if you're of the persuasion.'

'Oh, yes,' she said, moving over to a window and running her finger along the edge of its worn shutter. 'I do believe in ghosts.' She was thinking of her Where Are They Now?s, back in the early days, how people long absent from life could stay caught in those sometimes-awkward photographs, in Damian's grey filing cabinet – forever saying 'cheese' – and held in the memories of those they had left behind. She was also thinking of Ray, whose ghost had walked the lino-ed hall and the carpeted landing of their little terraced house long after he had packed up and left, his disapproving voice soaked into the plasterboard of the party walls.

Then she thought of Ed's father. She risked a glance at Ed, but he was over by the whitewashed fireplace, studying the grain of the simple mantelpiece.

'Shall we visit the bedrooms now?' Baptiste asked.

'Yes, please,' Maggie replied.

The bedrooms – four of them – all bleached wood floors and shabby beamed ceilings – ran along the rear of the house. They were all empty except for an old, rickety dressing table in one, and an elaborately fashioned child's white rocking horse – now almost piebald where its paint had flaked off – in another.

'I gave Michael one like that once,' Ed said, looking dejected. 'What good it did me.'

'I'm sorry,' she said, not daring to say anything else.

Baptiste led them through the rooms with an outstretched grubby sleeve, pointing out all the features of the pretty colonial architecture and the ramshackle picture windows peering over a lush, completely overgrown lawn beyond them.

'Let's go outside now,' he said, when the bedrooms – and the still-graceful, functioning bathroom – had all been considered. 'There's a spectacular view.'

He was right. The overgrown lawn sloped down to a tropical valley studded with bougainvillea and beyond that, in the distance, was the sea – a shining ribbon of azure blue with the early sun already glancing dazzlingly off it.

'Magnificent,' she said, putting her sunglasses on and, to Ed, 'I can see why you love it here.'

'It's a beautiful island,' Ed agreed, his face alight at the sight of it, and she could see why he'd chosen Mémoire for his escape, his father's favourite picture book island. She could understand why Neville Craddock, in his sitting room in Charlotte Road,

Southend-on-Sea, may have traced his finger over its curves in his book. It was idyllic here.

'I'll leave you for a moment,' said Baptiste. 'I have to go to the car. You may walk to the pergola,' he added, gesturing to the ruins of a white wooden arch to the right of the lawn. 'It's where all the plantation's marriages have taken place.'

Maggie and Ed walked through the long thick grass to the pergola, the house's rear elevation graceful behind them – and even more faded than its front.

'I wonder how much money it would take to bring the plantation house back to life?' Maggie pondered, as they stood under its arch.

'Thousands, I expect,' said Ed.

'*You* have lots of money,' she teased.

Ed shook his head, kicking at a tuft of knotted grass with the toe of his tennis shoe as he walked. 'Not here, I don't.' He patted at his wallet in the back pocket of his shorts. 'Just a few local notes and a completely redundant American Express card.'

'Well, I didn't think you had it all with you, stuffed under your mattress!' She thought of Ed's Bob Marley single bed, in his shack. How he was choosing to live. 'But you have access to money, surely?' She thought of the avocado telephone by the ladies' room in Olly's, and wondered if he'd ever used it. 'You could do anything you liked, including turning the plantation house into a hotel.'

'And make this island a tourist destination?' Ed shook his head again. 'Hold horrible weddings here? I think this place should be left well alone.'

'Like you?'

Ed didn't answer. He ran his finger down the wooden frame of the wedding arch. She wondered about his own 'horrible weddings'. The women he had promised to love – but hadn't. Pamela Bruelle, in the mid-nineties – the brunette heiress he had a short-lived,

212

tempestuous marriage to. Alexia Bailey – the actress and fitness darling he had recently extricated himself from. Had they been weddings to remember? (With Pamela Bruelle, it had certainly been a *divorce* to remember – it had made the papers for weeks.)

'No, no horrible weddings,' she finally said. She thought about *hers* for too long, as they stood in silence. A tiny bird landed on the apex of the pergola and stared at them, twitching its green and gold tail feathers.

'What really happened with Ray?' Ed asked. He didn't take his eyes off the horizon.

'Oh,' she said. On her wedding day to Ray there had been laughter, and soft kisses, and confetti in her hair and hope, lots of it. Lots of unfounded hope.

'You don't have to say anything.' Ed's voice was surprisingly kind. 'Forget that *I* did.'

The little bird twitched its tail and took off. Before them was only the old wedding arch and the valley and wide blue sea.

'Ray was abusive,' Maggie said, and as the words came out of her, she didn't know why they were – perhaps it was the kindness in Ed's voice, the rush of inescapable memory – but she could not stop them. 'He was not who he made himself out to be when I first met him. I believe he was on his best behaviour before we got married, and then we were married, and he let the mask slip. It was . . . awful. Cruelty, violence – well, that was the culmination. It started in all the little things – the put-downs, the complaints, the undermining – that said, "Look how I tricked you!" At first his cruelty was so subtle it was almost like it was what marriage was supposed to be. But I knew it wasn't, and things got worse very quickly. He hit me, sometimes for some imagined slight, sometimes for no reason at all. This was . . . well, it was all the time you were writing to me.'

'Those jolly letters from California,' said Ed, and perhaps he was thinking of Michael, and of the pram in the sunny Los Angeles garden, but then his eyes narrowed in the bright sunshine, and he shook his head angrily. 'I'm so, so sorry, Maggie. So sorry. I had no idea. So, all that time I was writing to you were going through *that* – with that *bastard*! – and then when I saw you that morning, on the seafront, with the crew . . .'

'I was a wreck. A literal shipwreck. Ray had finally left, and I was dragging my body round the streets, trying to breathe life back into myself . . .'

Ed stepped forward. He placed his hand gently on the crook of her elbow. She simultaneously wanted to flinch and gasp. 'That bastard,' he repeated. 'Why didn't you tell me? Why didn't you say something?'

'I couldn't.' Maggie shook her head. 'I was numb. I was broken. I just couldn't.'

'Bloody hell, Mags! I can't believe I'm only just hearing about this *now*.' Ed looked furious, distraught. 'I was trying so hard to be happy for you – because *you* were happy.'

'It doesn't matter now.' Maggie looked down at the grass. This confession, this spilling of old emotion . . . She felt foolish, exposed. She had laid out a map of her heart for him to trace his finger over and she wasn't sure she wanted it there. 'Let's go back to the car. Let's find Baptiste,' she said. 'Let's move on. *Please*, Ed.'

'Alright,' said Ed finally, and he looked a little lost, standing in the too-tall grass in his shorts and his white t-shirt, the old wedding arch and the sea behind him, and then he smiled at her sadly. 'Okay, let's move on.'

Chapter Twenty-Eight

6 A.M., 4 SEPTEMBER 1983

At 6 a.m., Maggie was still walking the streets of Southend. At 6.30 a.m., she was almost at Old Leigh, but she kept on going. In that grey, silent hour, as the town woke up around her, she tried to walk off the fear and the loneliness and the shame and the guilt, but each step just took her closer to going home, where it was all still waiting for her.

When she arrived home, she took down every photo of Ray in the house. Gathered up every towel that smelled of his aftershave and threw them in the bin. Put on the stereo system in the dining room – Neil Diamond, track six – and cranked up the volume so when Neil Diamond started singing 'Love on the Rocks' – his voice husky and thunderously, satisfyingly loud – she let it soak into her miserable skin and fill the shape of the hole where her heart should be. She didn't know that as she boiled the kettle afterwards, Ed Cavanagh would be approaching her front door, ready to ring the bell, the drawstring of his coat hood pulled so tightly his eyes were huge in his face.

'Surprise!' he said. 'We wrapped early. Problem with sound. We'll pick up again this afternoon. I wasn't sure you'd be in . . . but here you are.'

'Here I am.' She looked a state. Her hair was windswept and frizzy. Her face was free of make-up. He looked utterly beautiful in his coat with the hood – an escaped curl peeping out from under the navy nylon. She wanted to crumple at his feet. She wanted to cry and cry. To tell him she loved him, she still loved him. But she was locked too tightly inside herself.

'Well, are you going to let me in? I remembered your address,' he said, as she opened the door to him and tried to smooth down her wayward hair. 'And Sam drove me here.' He gestured to a little red Fiat parked on the other side of the road. 'He's the second assistant director.'

'He can't park there,' said Maggie. 'Mrs Avery will be out with her bins in a minute.'

Ed laughed. His face, she thought. His lovely face the whole world adored. 'Sam will be alright,' shrugged Ed, 'he can always move along a bit.'

'Would you like a cup of tea?' she said, as Ed followed her into the kitchen. She was conscious she was wearing her oldest, most unflattering pair of jeans and a very unfortunate sweater. Ed took off his coat to reveal an attractive pair of black cords and a pale blue striped shirt. Yes, he looked *exactly* like a handsome astronaut's son, she thought.

'Yes, please. I've been enjoying a good old British cuppa while I've been here. They don't have builder's tea in LA.'

Maggie took two mugs from the cupboard and reached for the tea caddy. She was terrified Ray was going to appear at the kitchen window, hands up against the glass.

'Why do you keep glancing at the window?'

'I don't know.'

'Where's Ray? Is he not here?'

'No, he's away today, actually. On business. Back tonight,' she added, remembering her lie.

'With the brewery?' Ed pulled an incredulous face.

'We can't all be Hollywood royalty, Ed,' said Maggie. 'It's only Maidenhead,' she added, to the lie, 'but, hey . . .'

Ed leant against the worktop. Picked up a folded tea towel and put it down again. 'It's a nice house.'

'It must seem like an absolute flea pit to you,' she said, 'after your Beverly Hills mansion.'

'Not at all. I like it. It's very *you*.'

She shrugged, looking at the all the nice things in the kitchen Ray had 'allowed' her to have. 'Not my domain,' he'd always said. *That was benevolent of him.*

'Look, it's just really great to see you, Maggie,' said Ed. 'I wasn't expecting to, while I was here. I would never have come knocking if we hadn't bumped into each other on the street. After . . . well, you not replying to any of my letters . . . I thought you didn't want anything more to do with me.'

I love you. She shrugged again. Plunged a tea bag up and down in boiling water. 'How's the filming going?' she asked. 'What's it like being back?'

He looked at her in some confusion.

Avoiding questions, she was good at that. Her parents, asking where Ray was when she came to visit them on her own. Janey, asking why she didn't come out in the evenings any more, even though Ray had gone. Why Ray still seemed to be controlling her.

'Well, great, so far,' he said. 'We have three days of exteriors, then it's back to LA for studio. It's called *Echo Beach* – you know, after the Martha and the Muffins song?'

'Yes, I know, that's a great title.' She handed a mug to Ed and took the other one, leaning awkwardly against the sink and feeling strange.

'And being back . . . well, it's been nice to see Mum.'

Maggie nodded. 'Is she well?'

'Yes, thanks. How are your mum and dad?' asked Ed.

'Good, thanks.'

'And Stevie?'

'Amazingly, working in a bank and being quite good at it.' Ed grinned. 'How's Michael?'

Ed took a sip of his tea. 'Gorgeous,' he said, his face lighting up. 'He's nearly five months now. I've been seeing him every Sunday. Going over to his mother's house and playing with him in the garden.'

Maggie nodded. She took a gulp of her tea, trying not to think about fathers and sons, and Neville Craddock; what she had found out and what she hadn't. The dead end of it all. 'That's wonderful,' she said.

'It is,' agreed Ed. 'Why did you never reply to my letters?'

Maggie couldn't look at him. She set her mug of tea down on the worktop. 'I couldn't, Ed, I was married. I *am* married,' she fudged, keeping up her lie. 'You shouldn't have sent them here.'

'Did you have to hide them?'

'Well, I didn't exactly read them out to Ray . . .'

'Is he really away on business with the brewery?'

'Well, of course he is. We're going out for dinner tonight. Our anniversary, remember? Why are you asking that?'

'Just a feeling,' said Ed, looking at her curiously, the kitchen window reflected in his eyes. 'Just the way you are.'

'I'm alright,' said Maggie. 'Actually, you need to go,' she added, picking up her mug again and clattering it noisily into the washing-up bowl in the sink. 'I'm not feeling that great.'

She held her hand out for his mug and he gave it to her reluctantly, then she turned back to the sink. Was there any universe, she wondered, in which she could tell him, right now, that she loved him, straight from her heart to his? If there was such a place, she imagined it to be a little like one of the desert islands in Ed's old coffee table book, the one that had belonged to Neville. A tropical place of beauty and peace where the beaches were as endless as hope and truth. A place where dreams soared like birds of paradise, and she could be free. *Mémoire*, wasn't that the name of Neville's favourite?

She was not in that place. She was in her kitchen, where she had not so long ago lain on the cold floor and looked at the sticky line of jam on the fridge. Where Ray had told her she was useless, again and again and again. Where breakfasts had slid down the wall and hearts had been sucked dry. She didn't believe she could ever be free.

'I don't believe you, but okay,' said Ed, from behind her. 'Thank you for the tea.'

She heard him walk out of the kitchen. She suddenly couldn't bear not saying goodbye to him, so she trailed up the hall behind him like a lost little girl.

'Don't be a stranger,' he said at the door, but his slight grimace confirmed they already were.

'We don't live in each other's worlds any more,' she said, and it came out in a whisper.

'That's a very sad thing,' replied Ed, his eyes fixed on her face.

'It is.' She felt the tears threaten, but she wouldn't let them come. She could hear the clatter of Mrs Avery's bins. 'I'm just a bit under the weather,' she added, unconvincingly.

I love you, she thought. *I love you.*

'I hope you feel better soon . . . Oh, god, Maggie, I just don't know when I'm ever going to see you again,' he said, the words rushing from his mouth, and his face crumpling a little, and when he said those words, her heart folded in on itself, like an origami butterfly.

'It doesn't matter,' she said. 'It really doesn't matter.'

He stared at her. 'Goodbye, Maggie May,' he said sadly, and he turned, and he was gone.

Chapter Twenty-Nine

Baptiste was standing outside the car waiting for Maggie and Ed as they walked back down the yellow-earthed slope from the plantation house in silence.

'Next we go to the tortoises,' Baptiste said. They set off back down the dusty track with a new tape in the cassette player: Billy Joel singing about being the Piano Man and playing people their memories. 'One hundred and twenty giant tortoises. They have been on the island for thousands of years.'

'I can't wait to see them,' said Maggie.

They drove slowly for ten minutes or so, rocking along rough roads inside the rainforest, where the sun was camouflaged and the air was hot and still. Billy Joel sang about honesty. Maggie and Ed ate some of the contents of Baptiste's Tupperware box: mango slices, pots of rice porridge – with tiny spoons – and boiled eggs.

After another ten minutes, the car spluttered to a halt on a very stony track.

'Petrol finally run out?' Ed enquired, leaning between the front seats. He hadn't said a word since they'd stood under the arch at Lilas House. Maggie felt guilty, like she'd had no right to burden him with the woes of her marriage from thirty-five years ago. She should have kept her mouth shut, kept her secrets. Why had he asked her? He shouldn't have asked her.

'No, plenty there,' replied Baptiste, checking the gauge on the antiquated dashboard. 'It must be something else.'

He took off his seatbelt and got out of the car, walked round to the front and lifted up the bonnet. Ed also climbed out and went and stood next to Baptiste, scratching his head. Maggie was hot without the breeze through a moving window, so got out of the back, too.

'It's the ignition cables,' said Baptiste finally. And he leant through the open passenger window to the glove box and pulled out a small bottle of WD40. 'This will fix the problem.'

Ed and Maggie shrugged at each other. They watched as Baptiste sprayed some oil on some incomprehensible part inside the engine and then he closed the hood and they all clambered back into the car.

Baptiste started the engine, but the car would not budge. The motor was turning over and over, but the tyres could not move, as they were skidding on loose stones.

'*Mon dieu!*' he exclaimed. 'Mr Ed, you and I will need to push.'

Maggie was instructed to get into the front seat and start the ignition. The engine rumbled into life, but the car again would not budge, the tyres still skidding. Ed and Baptiste got behind the car and started to push it, their hands on the boot.

'*Un, deux, trois!*' cried Baptiste.

The car did not move. They tried again. Maggie could see them both in the rear-view mirror, pushing heroically against the boot of the car, the strain showing on their faces. On the third try, with a massive grunt from Ed and a rousing war cry from Baptiste, the car suddenly released itself from its abortive stone-skittering and started trundling forward. Jubilant, Maggie put the old car in first gear and let it pick up a little speed, away from the worst of the stones, but when she looked in the rear-view mirror, she could only see Baptiste and not Ed. She stopped the car on a smoother portion of the track and got out.

Ed was scrambling upright, examining his knee.

'I went down on that final push,' he muttered. 'Stupid old fool!' His knee was bleeding a little and had tiny stones embedded in it.

'Hold on,' Maggie said. 'I have water and tissues in my bag.'

She dived on to the back seat and retrieved her tote bag, delving past Michael's letter and her rolled-up swimming costume to pull out a small bottle of water and a packet of tissues. She soaked one in some water and dabbed at Ed's knee, gently excavating the stones and wiping off the blood.

'Well, this is a reverse of old times,' he said, almost warmly, as he looked down at her dabbing away tenderly at his knee.

'Indeed it is,' she retorted. *Sitting on the wall. The low afternoon sun and the album-cover boy in the rainbow t-shirt . . .*

'It feels rather nice, having you tend to me,' he teased.

'Does it now?'

'Yes.' She looked up at him and caught his eye. He winked at her again. What was he doing? Didn't they hate one another? 'Well, there you are, then,' she said brightly. 'All done. You'll live to fight another day.'

'Thank you.'

'Well done, my friend,' said Baptiste, patting Ed on the back. 'Teamwork is dream work.'

Ed laughed. He slapped Baptiste good-naturedly on the shoulder, and the two men grinned at each other. *They're true friends,* thought Maggie. She was sure Ed never had any in Hollywood.

They got back in the car, Baptiste driving ultra-carefully, and they drove for a further fifteen minutes.

'Here we are,' said Baptiste finally. They had stopped at a grassy clearing. He pointed through the windscreen ahead of them, and Maggie gasped.

'Oh, my goodness!' she cried. 'Just look at them!'

At the funnelled end of the clearing, in a shallow muddy crater edged with tall, fretted grass and a bank of low trees, were a dozen or so tortoises the size of shopping trolleys – roaming, lumbering with slow, curved limbs and nodding heads or nibbling on the leaves of fruit trees.

'Wow!' Maggie got out of the car. 'This is truly incredible. Thank you, Baptiste!'

Ed got out of the car, too. His face lit up at the sight of the tortoises like they were old friends.

Baptiste was positively beaming. He held his white cap in his hand, and he said, 'Of the two hundred and twenty tortoises here on Mémoire, most grow in size to weigh one hundred and fifty to two hundred kilos. They reach maturity when they are thirty years old and they can live to one hundred and twenty-five years old. Last year, Biba, our oldest ever female, sadly died. She had lived for one hundred and twenty-two years.'

'Goodness, how would you even know?' asked Maggie.

'They are all tagged,' explained Baptiste, 'from birth. We have two tortoise specialists on the island who monitor them.'

'But no tourists come here to see them?' asked Maggie. They were walking towards these amazing creatures. She grinned at the cumbersome, magnificent sight of them and marvelled at how they completely ignored the three humans as they went about their business.

'We don't have as many tortoises as Aldabra, and we are too remote,' said Baptiste, the too-short trousers of his white suit flapping through the long grass. 'The tourists go *there*. Our tortoises are just for Mémoire.'

'Aldabra?'

'Another island. Closer to the Seychelles.'

'I see. Well, they are absolutely gorgeous!'

Ed walked over to one of the larger tortoises, chewing on a leaf at the base of a fruit tree. He immediately started petting it, patting it on the head and calling it 'boy'. Maggie stared at him, amused.

'How do you know which ones are male – and which ones are female?' Maggie asked Baptiste.

'Underneath,' explained Baptiste. 'Females have a flat under-carriage – males are lightly concave. It's so they can fit on nicely when they mount for procreation.'

'A perfect system,' she commented.

'Yes, it works for them,' said Baptiste, and Maggie realised she was blushing. Ed was laughing, his hands on his hips.

They lingered for a while, following the tortoises around, watching, fascinated, as they nibbled at grass and plucked cutely at lemons with their toothless snatchy mouths. Maggie fell in love with Mimi, a young female of a mere forty-five years, who had the crinkliest castle-battlement feet and the prettiest eyes. She knelt next to Mimi and stroked her wrinkled neck, smiling with delight at how soft it felt.

'You can feed them,' said Baptiste. 'Just collect some leaves and they will eat right out of your hand.'

Maggie and Ed gently tore some leaves from a fruit free and held them in their palms for the tortoises to nibble at. Maggie found herself glancing at Ed periodically. It was the most relaxed she had seen him so far on the island.

'Are you going to take some photos?' Ed asked.

Maggie nodded. She started snapping away, getting some lovely shots of the creatures in action and inaction. Ed knelt down to the tortoise he had called 'boy' and stroked the top of its head.

Maggie laughed, saying the shot was far too cute, and – lying – said she was going to use it for the profile.

'Showing people you can be fun, after all?' she teased.

'I'm always fun with tortoises,' he said. 'Some humans, not so much.'

She raised her eyebrows at him. They stayed for about forty minutes, feeding and following the tortoises around. Talking to them, running their fingertips over their hard but silky shells. Maggie took several more photos. She caught Ed staring at her as she chatted and cooed to Marie, who was chewing on a leaf very seriously. Maggie gave him a curious glance, and he looked away.

'Let us go now,' said Baptiste eventually, blocking the sun from where Ed and Maggie were crouching on the grass, talking animated nonsense to the largest of the males called Pierre. Baptiste put his cap back on.

'Bye, Pierre,' said Maggie, standing up.

'Bye, Pierre,' echoed Ed. 'Well, what did you think?' he asked her, when they were back in the car. 'You liked our not-so-little friends?'

'Very much,' replied Maggie. She noticed he said 'our', like he really belonged to Mémoire. Like he was part of the island. And she wondered if he was ever going home, back to real life. She could see why he would claim the island as his own. Claim it was *home*. It was wonderful here. It did give you a chance to breathe. In some kind of magical, alternative universe, wouldn't it be lovely to stay here forever and just *be*?

'Cute, aren't they?' Ed said, and he grinned at her, and Maggie grinned back at him, blushing a little, as Baptiste's eyes watched them in the rear-view mirror. She thought, yes, sometimes she and Ed could still have fun together, and just when they least expected it.

Chapter Thirty

7 A.M., 14 JUNE 1991

The light hesitated at the sash window. Maggie blinked and readjusted her eyes. This was a *very* posh bedroom, Maggie thought to herself. There weren't just 'curtains', they were *drapes* – heavy and flanked by sweeping pelmets and bordello-ruched blackout blinds and huge fluffy tie-backs like giant cornettoes. There was gold wallpaper, which may have been *actual* gold, a painting of an old master on the wall in a thick gilt frame, an empty champagne bottle and a half-full glass on Maggie's antique bedside table. Maggie suspected it was a very warm day already, judging by the yellow-gold of the early morning sun, but she couldn't really tell, as the room's rather incongruous air-con was very effective and she was under a duvet and a posh wool blanket.

Next to her, the movie star lay sleeping, his curls flicked on to the pillow, his bare chest rising and falling where the silk edging of the blanket stopped, his arm flopped over the top of the covers. Maggie found it hard to suppress an enormous grin.

Yesterday had been a rather ordinary day, as ordinary as it could be for a thirty-four-year-old journalist who wrote glamorous profile pieces for a glossy lifestyle magazine called *Actually!*. One who spent her days and nights doing what her dad called 'gallivanting' around London in pencil skirts and heels, her red straightened hair cut to an arresting shoulder length and a Mac 'Spice' lipstick always in the Birkin she had treated herself to.

Packed full, it was, Maggie's London life. It was kitten heels skittering down steep steps into late night bars. It was ice chinking at the bottom of tall glasses of vodka, lime and soda. It was sushi and sashimi and scooting along dark wood corridors to touch up lipstick in restaurant bathrooms. And it was taxi doors slamming in the street at three o'clock in the morning and bags flung down in the hall of her tiny flat in the old, picturesque part of Battersea, in the shadow of the power station, where she never ate at home, as she did breakfasts and lunches and dinners and drinks *out*. Always out.

'Morning, love,' the doorman to her building had said to her, yesterday morning – as he did every morning – and she had felt young and bright and – quite frankly – *sassy*, as she strode up the street to Vauxhall station. She was a woman who had escaped her past. ('Ray who?' she would have answered, should anyone ask her, but nobody would, as nobody knew, because she was *reinvented*, wasn't she?) She was a single woman with freedom, and with money and with ambition.

Yesterday morning she'd had breakfast at the Wolseley – croissants and black coffee – and a light lunch of cod fillets and Chardonnay with Simone at Fish One. Simone had brought a packet of Marlborough Lights and her usual brand of irreverence.

Maggie had met Simone on her very first day at *Actually!*, in the office's tiny kitchen. Simone Blanc – features assistant – had been failing to microwave a miso soup and telling the misbehaving microwave to 'fuck off'. Maggie had interrupted with a tuna salad and the 'miraculous power' (according to a grateful Simone) of knowing how to turn the microwave from 'Defrost' to 'Cook'.

Maggie had found Simone rather miraculous herself. She was wearing the highest pair of heels Maggie had ever seen, causing her to navigate the kitchen by hanging off the worktops. She had an arresting black bob and the smallest, poutiest mouth, plus a husky cigarette laugh that often erupted into a good-natured cough.

Yesterday, Simone and Maggie went out for dinner, too – a wonderful Thai restaurant that did amazing cocktails – and Maggie had then gone on to meet aristocratic Harriet Green – the twenty-something girl who did the publicity for *Actually!* – in the lobby of the St Martin's Lane Hotel, at 11 p.m., for a party she and Harriet had been invited to on the fifteenth floor. They ordered Moscow mules, they slouched at the bar, people watching the roped-off VIP area behind them. It was a showbiz party for visiting Hong Kong businessman and socialite Wilbur Tang, who they could see wearing an elaborately embroidered Chinese frock coat and engulfed by a small crowd of people by a floor-to-ceiling window overlooking the glittering London skyline.

'Reports are . . .' said Harriet, her blonde high ponytail swinging and immaculate in a jewel-coloured satin shirt, black cigarette pants and high studded heels with silver tips. She leant in to Maggie and whispered in her ear. '. . . that Ed Cavanagh's in the VIP area. Bloody movie stars,' she added, her eyes wide with excitement.

Maggie tried to swallow a mouthful of her Moscow mule without spluttering it out.

'*Really?*' she managed to stammer. 'How do you know that?'

'Tog told me while you were in the loo.' Tog Trinder was *Actually!*'s marketing director, also present. He was doing the rounds in a velvet lounge suit and a permanent cigarette. 'Ed Cavanagh's in London for a junket to promote *West Point*,' continued Harriet. 'Eight magnums of champagne have gone in there already, apparently.' Harriet pointed over to the dark, roped-off area sentried by a huge man in black suit and an earpiece, behind which was a palpable buzz of exclusivity and a rarefied frisson of 'You're not coming in.'

'Blimey,' said Maggie. She swiftly knocked back half of her Moscow mule.

Ed Cavanagh was now a movie star. *A Sunny Day in the Valley* ended up being in pre-production for a reported six years, but when it had finally come out was the surprise hit of 1989, winning awards at the Venice and Cannes film festivals. Ed's role as genial and ultimately triumphant factory boss, Harrison Edge, had also been highly acclaimed. He'd had two more huge movies out in the past couple of years, ones that had earnt millions at the box office. There were billboards with Ed Cavanagh's face on. Adverts on the Tube staring at Maggie as she got off at Marble Arch. Ed was thirty-seven years old and at the top of his game.

Maggie was over him. He was just a face on a wall. She would turn away, or shrug at him, comically. Once, she uncharitably gave him the middle finger, when she walked past a billboard on Gray's Inn Road, drunk on Grey Goose vodka. Yet her heart was racing. Ed was just *there*, behind that velvet rope. But he was no longer Ed, was he? He was bigger than his own being. He was *huge*, and people had billions invested in him.

'Do you want to try to get in?' Harriet asked.

'Get in?' stammered Maggie.

'I can get us in.' Harriet's blonde ponytail swung like a helicopter blade. She rummaged in her enormous bag. 'Tog gave me a couple of passes – I think he fancies me.'

'Oh, right.' Maggie was terrified. 'And what do we do when we get in there? Just hover around, looking stupid?'

'No, we sit ourselves at a table and we get ourselves a drink and we look like we've every right to be there. Which we have,' Harriet added, waggling the lanyards under Maggie's nose.

'I don't know if I want to do that.'

'Come on, it'll be a laugh,' pleaded Harriet.

'No, no, I don't think so.' Maggie knew she sounded panicked, but Harriet started to drag her there anyway, pulling on the sheer sleeve of her Clements Ribeiro shift dress.

'No, I *know* him!' Maggie burst out. 'Ed Cavanagh. I went out with him when I was eighteen.'

'*What?*' Harriet stopped pulling and looked astounded. 'Really?'

'Yes.'

'Then we're *definitely* going in there!' cried Harriet, grabbing Maggie's hand instead. 'Come on.' She marched them up to the bouncer swaggering near the velvet rope. Harriet flashed the lanyards Tog had given her. And a winning smile. *He* unsmilingly lifted the rope.

The VIP area was a dark, low-ceilinged womb, with softly flickering stubby candles on white Perspex tables. It was hard to make out anyone's faces, thank goodness. Harriet and Maggie sat at the only vacant table – tiny, low to the ground – on Moroccan leather pouffes. There was champagne on ice in the middle of the table, chilled bottles of vodka, a carafe of cranberry juice, some fancy-looking nuts and four empty glasses. Harriet immediately made them a triple vodka and cranberry each, stirring the drinks with a silver swizzle stick.

'Well, where is he?' she asked, flicking that ponytail.

'I daren't look,' said Maggie. She kept her head down. She started attacking her drink.

'Oh, I think that's him,' said Harriet excitedly. 'God, he looks goooooood.'

'I'm not looking,' said Maggie.

'Well, *he* is,' said Harriet. 'I think he's spotted you, actually. He keeps glancing over.'

'Oh, god.'

'Oh, watch out!' shrieked Harriet. 'One of his "people" *incoming . . .*'

Maggie found the bottom of her glass suddenly fascinating, each cube of ice a work of art.

'Maggie?' There was a man standing at their table. Expensive shoes.

'Yes?' Maggie heard Harriet say.

'Ed Cavanagh is requesting you both at his table. Would you like to follow me?'

'No,' said Maggie. 'Hello, Rupert,' she added, looking up at the tall, rangy man with his expensive suit hanging off him like a flag. She'd recognise that Essex accent anywhere. *Ed's agent.*

'Hello, Maggie,' Rupert said. 'How are you?'

'Very well, thanks. How are you?'

'Great. And "No"? Really?'

'Yes, what are you *thinking*?' Harriet protested.

'No, thank you, Rupert, we're alright where we are,' said Maggie. 'Thanks, anyway. Nice to see you again.'

'As you wish,' said Rupert. 'Nice to see you, too, Maggie.' And he turned and walked away.

'You bloody idiot!' snapped Harriet. 'What on earth? Why can't we go over?'

'I can't,' muttered Maggie. 'I just can't, sorry.'

'Bloody hell,' rumbled Harriet, her cut-glass vowels grinding against each other. She swizzled her drink furiously. Maggie drained the rest of hers, poured herself a generous refill, and sipped at it morosely until she became aware of a pair of legs close to her right thigh. Shaking, she slowly raised her head, though she really, *really* didn't want to – and this time Ed Cavanagh himself was standing there.

'Why don't you come over to my table, Maggie?' he asked, his eyes shining. He was wearing a silky black shirt, a little unbuttoned.

Dark trousers. Expensive shoes. His hair was gelled into sleek satin curls. He looked like an actual god, she thought – a god here on earth, and at this party.

'I'm alright here,' she muttered. 'I've just come for a quiet drink.' There were a million eyes on him in the VIP area, pretending they weren't.

'What about your friend?'

'What about Harriet?'

Harriet looked completely dumbstruck. She was kicking Maggie furiously under the table.

'Would *she* like to come over?'

'Well, of course I bloody well would!' Harriet cried.

'*Maggie?*' repeated Ed.

Harriet kicked Maggie's shins again. Those metal-tipped pointed toes really hurt.

'Okay, just for one drink,' Maggie said, and she stood up, and there he was, looking into her eyes and she into his, and the last time she had seen him he had been in her front porch, looking sad and a little confused, and she had wept buckets once she had closed the door on him. Cried and wailed for three hours. Cried for him and cried for her marriage, and for herself.

She picked up her bag and the three of them walked over to a table at the back of the VIP area, those million eyes on stalks. She could do this, she thought – her legs threatening to fail her – she could totally do this. She was the new 1990s Maggie. *London* Maggie. She was a whole different person to the tragic figure he had last encountered on Southend seafront, that early Sunday morning, and then in her kitchen of the little house on Richmond Road (dejected, windblown, sad and wearing a tragic jumper). Now she was glossy and high-heeled and sassy and stylish. Now she had *got this*. Okay, let him see the new her, she thought. Let him see how she had turned out. She was no movie star, but her life was pretty amazing, too.

Ed's table was glass-to-glass with a chaos of bottles and champagne flutes and tumblers, full and empty. Ed gestured to two of the seven or eight people gathered around it to shunt up on the leather pouffes so Maggie and Harriet could sit down, Ed at Maggie's right. Harriet got immediately commandeered by a handsome producer type who started talking to her about her ponytail, and the man to Maggie's left, a smiling fellow with a thick head of side-parted dark hair and a putty-coloured polo shirt, thrust out his hand to her.

'Hi, I'm Reece,' he said, in a gregarious American accent. 'Ed's manager. Good to meet you.'

'I'm Maggie,' she said.

He stood up. 'Off to the bar.' He grinned. 'Enjoy the night.'

'Thank you,' said Maggie. She stared into the space he'd moved from, fearing both the man to her right and her own beating heart. She wished she'd brought her drink with her or had something to do with her hands. Knitting. Macrame. Cat's cradle . . .

'It's good to see you,' said Ed.

'You, too,' she said, voice pin sharp, trying to keep composed.

'I like the hair.'

'Thanks. I like yours.'

Ed laughed and ran a hand self-consciously through those immaculate curls. 'Drink?'

'Yes, please.'

'Vodka and cranberry okay?'

'Perfect.'

He poured them both a drink then he smiled at her, slow and sweet. 'What are you doing here?' he asked.

'What are *you* doing here?' she cheekily retorted. 'No, I know actually. *West Point*. Interviews in plush hotel rooms and a couple of press conferences. And I'm here because I work for a magazine called *Actually!*.'

'Yes, I'm aware of *Actually!*, actually,' Ed said.

'Oh, good, right.' Maggie tried to look anywhere but into his eyes. She noticed a very beautiful, twenty-something girl staring adoringly at Ed from across the table. Maggie lasered over her best sassy look.

'You haven't been assigned to interview me for it yet – are you avoiding me?'

'I mostly do home-grown people. Soap stars. You're a bit too major league for *Actually!*.'

'*I'm* home-grown.' Ed the god looked anything but.

'Oh, come on! You grew out of England a long time ago. How's the big fuck-off mansion in Mulholland Drive?'

'It's . . . big,' he admitted. He had new crinkles at the corner of his eyes, she realised. She liked them. 'Do you still live in Southend?'

'No, I live in Battersea.'

'Oh, nice. A good life, then?'

'Not bad,' she said. 'So, how is it,' she asked, 'being in the movies?'

'It's fun.' He nodded. 'It's a lot of fun.'

'How's Riva?' She was pleased at how unconcerned she sounded.

'Great, thanks. Single. Like me.'

'Oh. You split up.' Ed and Riva had been a Hollywood power couple for the past seven months. Maggie had read all about them, and their holidays to Mexico, in a Sunday supplement. She also knew that Riva had been an anomaly; Ed was a serial dater and one of Hollywood's most eligible bachelors, with a reputation for absolutely no interest in marriage.

'Yeah, we split up. I'm single,' he repeated. 'That big fuck-off house is going on the market. Don't tell anyone.' He grinned. 'We haven't announced it yet. You?'

'No, I don't have anything to announce,' she joked. 'But I *am* seeing someone. Casually.'

'So, you're not married any more?' He checked out her bare left hand.

'God, no! No, very lucky escape.' She remembered the lies she had told him in her kitchen.

'A lucky escape? What happened?'

'Incompatibility,' she said quickly. She still wasn't ready to tell Ed the truth of the abuse. She hadn't told anybody, although she had long attempted to scrub the guilt and shame from her and leave it all behind. She'd even told her parents, long after the fact, that she and Ray had drifted apart, like a couple of boats, and not that daily life had been Battleships, with her losing each and every encounter.

'You didn't look okay,' he said, 'when I last saw you. I didn't believe any of that stuff about Ray, you know. The dinner, the brewery trip.'

'You remember?' She was surprised.

'I remember everything,' he said softly. 'Are you okay now?'

'Well, what do you think? How do I look?' She sat back, crossed her legs in her silky dress. Boy, was it easy to flirt with Ed Cavanagh. He was utterly transcendent.

'You look pretty good,' he agreed.

She leant forward again. 'I was in a bad place,' she said. 'That's all. Last time I saw you. And now I'm in a very good one.'

It had taken a long time. It had taken a year to clear out the house on Richmond Road and get it sold, then Maggie had moved into a little rented flat just up from the bus station and she had, for a while, only gone to work and come home again, not seeing anyone but her parents, and not doing anything but her interviews and her writing. But Janey had not given up. Janey, who had kept calling her every single night, who had knocked on her back door every Friday night with a mug of tea, or a piece of cake, or a bottle of gin. And eventually Maggie had started stepping outside the little flat and going places again. *Living* again. And then she had seen a job advert for a writer for *Actually!* in the *Telegraph* and she had applied, thinking she wouldn't get it, and could she leave Southend, and her mum and dad? But they practically put her on the train to go for the interview themselves and she was ready, ready for a new adventure away from her hometown, at last, and she was loving it.

'Who are you seeing?' asked Ed. 'Casually? Anyone I know?'

'I don't date famous people any more.'

'Probably wise. A lot of them aren't very nice.'

Maggie grinned. 'I'm seeing someone called Lance. He's an investment banker.'

She had met him in a bar at Charing Cross. She liked him enough. He was nice, and he looked and smelled nice. The sex was good. She couldn't see a future with him, but she was very careful about that kind of thing now, and she imagined she was a stopgap for Lance until he found someone he actually wanted to fall in love with, too.

'He sounds awful,' said Ed. 'You can basically consider yourself single, I reckon.'

'Are you asking me out?' Maggie spoke with a bravado she didn't feel. Her leg was shaking under the table.

Ed threw his head back and laughed. 'Well, I don't know,' he said. 'Where would you like to go?'

'I'm okay here,' she said. It felt good, sitting here with Ed. It felt great as the New Maggie. She didn't need to dwell on the fact she still loved him.

'How's your son?' she asked him.

Ed nodded. 'He's good,' he said. 'Great, actually. He's eight.'

'Wow.'

'You haven't got any children?'

'God, no!' she laughed. She was so thankful she hadn't had them with Ray; she hadn't really thought about them since. And she loved her life.

A song came on, out there in the part where the normal people were. The non-VIPs. It was a new dance track, about giving someone 'devotion'.

'I guess you're not allowed to dance,' she said.

'What makes you say that?'

'Well, you can't come out from behind the velvet rope, can you? It's too dangerous.'

'Dangerous how?' His green eyes were dancing, mesmerising her.

'Well, you'll have people clamouring, trying to touch you. How much are you insured for?' she asked.

He laughed. 'I have no idea.'

'I bet those curls are insured for a million dollars.'

'I can risk the curls. Let's go and dance.' He stood up. His bodyguard, the tall man who'd been standing behind them the whole time, made to move, too.

'Mr Cavanagh . . .'

'It's okay, Bob,' said Ed. 'We're just going to take a turn on the dancefloor. You can stand down.'

'The studio won't let me *stand down*,' said Bob. 'I'm going to shadow you.'

'Oh, if you must. Come on, then. By the way,' Ed said to Maggie, as they moved away from the table, Bob behind, 'there's no paparazzi here tonight, so no photos. You don't have to be worried.'

'Who said I was worried? It's not me who's more famous than the Queen.'

Ed laughed. He put his hand on the small of Maggie's back as they slipped out of the VIP area and headed for the dancefloor. All eyes were still on them. Harriet's, back at the table, were boggling.

The dancefloor was virtually empty. Maybe everyone was too cool to dance, thought Maggie. Ed certainly wasn't. He practically threw himself on the dancefloor and started to move, so she threw herself next to him, and moved with him. They'd only ever danced a comedy waltz at the London Palladium; this was quite different. Ed was a good dancer. She couldn't stop smiling. And he was grinning, too, as they shook and shuffled and spun. A circle of awe soon formed around them. People staring, whispers, no doubt, of 'There's Ed Cavanagh,' and 'Who's he with?' Beyond the circle was Bob, his eyes never leaving his charge.

Maggie was trying so hard to be in the moment, and not all the other moments they had shared and the many moments they had missed. This could only be *now*, she thought. This night. Where sheer simple luck had brought them in front of each other again. Relish every second, she told herself. Make this night forever. But mostly she thought, this was fun. This was a whole lot of fun.

'Where are you staying?' Ed asked her, voice raised above the music.

'What do you mean, where am I staying?' she half-shouted back. 'I'm staying in my flat. Where I live. Where are *you* staying?'

'Surrey. In a house they've rented for me.'

'Oh, *fancy!*'

'It's where Marilyn Monroe lived when she came to England to shoot *The Prince and the Showgirl*. It's very pretty. My manager knows the owner. It's . . . quiet. And I have a script to learn.'

'It sounds lovely.'

'Would you come back there with me?'

'What for?'

His eyes flashed. His smile was intoxicating. 'Because I don't want to say goodbye to you, after this. After the party. I want longer. I want more time.'

'Will I fit in?' she asked, pretending to think about it. 'I'm no Marilyn Monroe.'

'You'll fit in as well as me. We're just a couple of ratty kids from Southend, remember.'

'I don't think *you* are!' Maggie scoffed. 'You big Hollywood star, you!'

'On the outside.' Ed moved closer to her, snaked his arms around her waist. He smelt gorgeous. 'On the inside I'm just a boy you used to know. Come to Surrey with me,' he whispered in her ear.

'Words I never thought I'd hear . . .'

He laughed. 'Oh god, you still make me laugh more than anyone else in the world,' he said. Last time she'd seen him, she had been a ghost of herself, walking around. Now she was alive. Life was sizzling through her, like battery fluid, charged and potent. 'Lance won't care?'

'*I* don't care.'

'And do you need to tell Harriet?'

'Yes, I'll tell Harriet.' They swayed together, in time to the music. One of Ed's immaculate curls flopped down on to his right eyebrow. She smoothed it back. 'Let's keep it light, hey?' she said.

'We can do light,' Ed replied. 'If that's what you want.'

'Yes, please.'

She could do this. She could go to a house in Surrey and spend the night with Ed Cavanagh. She could have her fill of him, drink him in, then say goodbye. Tonight, she could be strong and in control and a night with Ed could just mean that: a night. A fun night. It didn't matter about tomorrow. It didn't matter about yesterday.

This night was so serendipitous it had to be drunk from, right to the bottom of the glass.

'When do you want to go?' he asked.

'Now?'

He nodded, took her hand, and they went back to the VIP area, and the table – Bob in their wake. Maggie told Harriet she was going, and who she was going with. Harriet looked absolutely delighted and was given strict instructions not to tell the press.

'Oh, ya, of course not,' Harriet drawled. 'How wonderful,' she said. 'Sweethearts reunited,' she said. 'Ed fucking Cavanagh,' she exclaimed, shaking her head. '*Amazing.*'

'Well, I don't know,' said Maggie, but she was thrilled; the new Maggie, utterly thrilled. She felt like her heart had been lit up in neon and was ricocheting like a pinball around her body.

Ed told Rupert, who told somebody else. Maggie saw the Chinese whispers swiftly going round amongst his 'people'. A plan was being hatched, for how to get them out of here without alerting the paparazzi, who were no doubt waiting outside. Walkie-talkies were spoken into. Watches were peered at under black cuffs. It seemed to be quite a military operation.

'Are we going through the kitchens?' Maggie asked Ed as they stood by the table, waiting for the plan to be executed.

'No,' Ed laughed, 'we're not going through the kitchens. Bob is going to take you through the fire exit and I'm going to go down in the lift with Reece.'

'How exciting.'

'*You're* exciting,' said Ed, and he leant his face down to hers, a little, and she thought he might kiss her, or she might kiss him, and the moment crackled between them – like ice or fire – and she shivered a little in her silky dress and then he whispered in her ear, 'And now I don't know you,' and, with a wink, he walked away from her as though she had been a waitress offering him a drink, and Bob was approaching on her right and taking her arm and calling her 'ma'am', and he was pushing at the door of the fire exit, and she was being led down dim-lit grey concrete steps and through a laundry room and an area with stacked tables and chairs (a *bit* like the kitchens, she thought) and out the back of the hotel and to the door of a black minivan that was sliding open and Ed was waiting there, grinning at her, and he held out his hand and the door shut and they were off, rushing through the streets of London.

And here they now were, in Ed's plush, gilded room, at Parkside House, Englefield Green, Surrey, where Marilyn Monroe and Arthur Miller had once stayed. When they had arrived last night, Maggie had gazed up at the pretty wisteria frontage and the shuttered windows in awe. She had crunched on the gravel drive satisfyingly in her heels. And she had walked hand in hand with Ed up the sweeping staircase from the hall.

Maggie no longer suppressed her giant grin but let it break on to her face like a tidal wave, as the movie star she was staring at, under that posh blanket, opened one sleepy eye, whispered, 'Good morning,' and pulled her back on top of him.

Chapter Thirty-One

8 A.M., ON THE ISLAND

Ed had a scar on his hand, a tiny one. It was at the base of his thumb, a short horizontal line, like a hyphen; the sunlight from the open car window was picking it out. He'd had it since before she knew him, Maggie remembered. A childhood accident with his dad's razor, left out on the bathroom sink one morning. She didn't want him to catch her staring at it, so she looked away, out of the window, and held out her fingers to snaggle the tail of a passing fern.

'The lagoon is up here on the right,' said Baptiste.

'Yes, my friend.' Ed nodded.

Baptiste indicated right and turned clumsily on to a sloping, crusty track. His old car bumped down the slope, past terraces of palm trees leaning like giraffes to a water hole. Baptiste stopped the car, with a crunch of the gearstick, at a thicket of dense tropical shrubs.

'We walk from here,' he said, pulling a bulging raffia bag from under the passenger seat and looping it over his wrist. He also grabbed the rolled-up towel he'd held on the beach earlier.

'Careful,' Ed said to Maggie. 'It's a bit spiky.'

There was a narrow path through the thicket. Ed grabbed a stick from the ground and began to thwack at protruding leaves and branches.

'You love a stick,' Maggie couldn't help but say.

Ed smiled like a child, happily beating his way along the path; Baptiste assisted by using his hat as an ineffectual scythe. And there, suddenly, laid out before them like a melted boiled sweet, was the lagoon, shimmering in the virgin sunshine of the morning. There was a small, pretty waterfall at the far end, and, at the other, a brace of weeping tropical bushes genuflecting into the water. Maggie snapped a couple of photographs of it.

'It looks like something from a movie,' she said. 'I think it even beats the lagoon in *Waikiki*, Ed.' *Waikiki* was a nineties movie where Ed had played a former drunk struggling to get sober while living on Waikiki beach and working as a pimp. It sounded unsavoury but it was actually a sweet, poignant film, and audiences and critics had adored it.

'This one's real, at least,' he said.

'The lagoon in Waikiki wasn't real?'

'Only partly.' He shrugged. 'That's showbiz, folks!'

'Are you two going to take a dip?' asked Baptiste. He had led them to a small grassy slope up from the weeping bushes and was laying his threadbare towel out on the grass.

'Will it be cold?' Maggie asked with a frown. 'It's still so early.'

Baptiste plonked himself down on the towel and took off his hat. 'Nothing is cold on Mémoire,' he said.

'The lagoon will be like bath water,' agreed Ed. 'Did you pack your swimming costume?'

'Well, yes,' said Maggie. She had her Speedo costume, with the 'boy legs'. It was rolled inside a clear plastic bag on top of Michael's letter. 'Where would I get changed?'

'There's a large bush over there,' suggested Ed.

'Okay. Fantastic.' She was not thrilled about appearing in front of Ed, or Baptiste, or *anyone* in a swimming costume. She got changed in a soft breeze and a fluster of embarrassment and emerged from behind the bush with her towel wrapped around her waist and her hair tucked into a hasty bun. Ed was already in a pair of yellow swimming trunks with palm trees on, the skin on his shoulders and torso as tanned as a hazelnut shell.

'Alright?' he said, and he sounded like a teenager again.

'Yes,' she said, but she was mortified at the thought of dropping the towel and immersing her sixty-one-year-old body in the water. As if reading her mind, Ed patted his stomach. 'Not quite the buff young things we once were, are we? Despite the personal trainer and the macro diet,' he added with a laugh.

'Not quite,' she agreed, 'though I'm not a Hollywood star, so I don't have those. I have a *very* occasional Joe Wicks exertion and an extensive Dairy Milk habit.' She considered if Ed remembered what Dairy Milk was. 'You were quite buff in *The Swimmer*, though,' she added. 'Did you have to train much for that part?'

'Yeah. Not quite Burt Lancaster, but I tried my best . . . You saw that movie?'

'Yes,' Maggie replied shyly. She looked down at her feet. She'd gone to see the remake of *The Swimmer* one Sunday afternoon on her own, having told herself for weeks she wasn't going to. She'd been pleased there was a woman in the row in front of her, noisy and distracting with a family-size packet of crisps, but still she had felt strange afterwards, like she'd been visiting with spirits. 'You were excellent.'

'Thank you,' said Ed, and when she looked up, he was down the slope and plopping into the water, launching into a comical doggy paddle, and she remembered, with a smile, that once upon a time, long before all the extensive coaching of *The Swimmer*, that this was the only stroke he could do.

'Turn around!' she demanded now.

Ed pivoted his canine form one hundred and eighty degrees and paddled off in the other direction. Maggie draped her towel over a bush and stepped gingerly down the bank. Conscious of her thighs, her upper arms, her bum, her face, her elbows, she moved into the water. It was warm; it was like a caress. She lunged forward, ungraceful, and sighed with relief as the water engulfed her. *Bath water*. Gorgeous. She turned on to her back, faced the sky, where the sun soothed and the periwinkle sky calmed. Maybe it didn't matter any more, all of that body stuff, here in the water. She was floating; she was free.

'Don't you dare think about splashing me!' she called out, her eyes closed.

'I wouldn't dream of it!' Ed called back, from somewhere beyond.

They lolled around like manatees. Happy seals. *Is this what Ed dreamt of for his father?* she wondered. A lagoon like this on a tropical island, Neville's face turned towards the sun and all his worries ebbing away? Ed was on his back now, his feet at right angles, toes to the sky. He didn't look like a Hollywood star. He looked like a man floating on his back in a tropical lagoon.

'This is heaven,' she uttered eventually.

'Paradise,' Ed agreed.

Maggie opened her eyes and attempted her once-beloved breaststroke – a couple of lengths. She enjoyed the feeling of her hands slicing through the water, her legs frogging under its surface. She and Ed soon found themselves over by the waterfall, lounging in the lagoon's bubbling depths.

'You two look good together!' Baptiste called over. He was still sitting on his towel on the bank of the lagoon, his cap perched on giant bent knees. Maggie pretended she hadn't heard him. 'How long was Ed your boyfriend for?' he called to her.

'Five years,' she called back reluctantly.

Ed was half-perched on a rock and letting water cascade over an outstretched foot. 'Five and a *half* years,' he corrected, from behind her.

'That's a lot of hours,' Baptiste projected from the bank. 'Shame there was not more, *non?*'

Neither Maggie nor Ed had an answer for this. She sneaked a look at him over her shoulder, his foot under the waterfall, his face impassive. She decided to swim another couple of lengths, then circumnavigate the lagoon. When she was almost back at the spot where she had entered the water, Ed was clambering up the slope to get out.

'Baptiste is making noises for us to move on to the next step of the tour,' he said to her, over his shoulder. 'In ten minutes or so.'

'I don't think I ever want to get out,' Maggie replied, but she did, Ed offering his hand so she could manage the slope. Baptiste had laid another thin towel out on the bank, from his raffia bag, and Ed flopped onto it. Maggie remained standing, self-consciously letting the sun dry the droplets of water on her skin.

'Alexia has a costume like that,' observed Ed, squinting at her.

'I doubt it.' Maggie grabbed her towel from where she'd left it on the bush and held it up against her. 'Hers will be from Versace or somewhere glitzy. Mine is from M&S.'

'I like M&S.' Ed's eyes were closed as he stretched out on his towel.

Maggie shook her head at him, tucked her towel around her and gingerly sat down on a prickly patch of grass a little away from him.

'I'm going to the car,' said Baptiste. 'See you in ten minutes.'

'Okay,' Ed and Maggie said in unison. She watched as Baptiste disappeared into the line of bushes.

Ed, next to her, scratched softly at his shoulder. 'Do you think you'll always hate my life?'

Maggie looked at him. His eyes were fixed upon her. 'Meaning?'

'The glitz. You've always despised it.'

'I don't *live* in your life.'

'I know. But you hate it all the same. Hollywood and all that means.'

'It wouldn't be for me,' she admitted, although she thought of her little flat on the grey London street. The rain at the window. The occasional boyfriend, who she didn't love.

'You were never willing to give it a try.' It was a statement and not a question.

'No.' She'd had her reasons.

'Even though lots of it could be far from how you've imagined?'

She pictured him fishing every weekend at Huntingdon Flats, wherever that was. Sipping tea on his terrace before going for a swim. But she said, 'Which parts? The parties, the boozing and the women?'

'You like parties,' he proffered. 'The boozing, it never gets out of hand these days . . . And the women . . . Shall I tell you about the women, off the record?'

She looked at him and he looked back at her, shading his eyes with his hand. 'If you *want* to say something about them,' she said, a little nervously. This was one of the subjects on her agenda for the interview.

'The women were a distraction.' He didn't take his eyes from hers. 'I treated them well, I tried to make them as happy as they deserved, but I couldn't love them, unfortunately. Yes, I was a giant arse, much of the time. But all those lovely women stopped me thinking too much about my life.'

'Not loving them is not treating them well,' Maggie said. 'I just think I ought to point that out.'

'Fairs dos,' he said.

'Why didn't you want to think about your life?'

'Because it wasn't what I wanted it to be. Because . . . I wasn't happy.'

Maggie felt uncomfortable. She lay on her back on the towel and closed her eyes. 'And why weren't you happy?'

Ed sighed. He didn't reply. Maggie didn't hear anything else for a few moments except for the crickets chirping in the grass and the soft rustle of the bushes in the breeze behind them.

'What about Delphine?' she asked him, opening her eyes. 'Here on the island.'

'What about her?'

'You've been sleeping with her, haven't you?'

Ed looked incredulous. 'What? No! She's young enough to be my daughter.'

'Oh, sorry, maybe she just likes you, then,' said Maggie. 'Maybe I got that wrong.'

'Were you jealous?' Ed examined her quizzically.

'No, of course I bloody wasn't!'

There was another long silence. Maggie closed her eyes again. Eventually, Ed said, 'How *is* M&S these days? Do they still do those nice shortbreads?'

'Uh-huh.'

'Which M&S do you go to? Marble Arch?'

She opened one eye. Turned her head to look at him. 'No, the one at Clapham,' she responded, both mildly amused and relieved to be back on safer ground. 'Are you feeling nostalgic for the UK?'

'Maybe.'

'I don't suppose you've seen inside a department store or a supermarket in years.'

'Not really. It's difficult going into places. I have approximately three seconds before someone's face does something weird.'

She opened the other eye. 'Like what?'

Ed turned to face her. 'Like eyes nearly popping out of someone's head, or a mouth dropping open ten inches . . . or there's a scream. I once had a woman shout, "Christ alive, Phyllis, it's that bloke from *Echo Wotsit!*" and fall into a dead faint!'

'Good lord, I hope she was okay.'

'Yeah. She landed on a pile of fur coats. It was at a party,' he explained.

'I'm guessing that last encounter was in the UK you're sometimes nostalgic for.'

'Yes,' Ed laughed, and she wondered when that was.

'It must be weird,' she admitted. 'Still, it's not a big deal, is it, not being able to go into Tesco's, or wherever in LA, and do a big shop? I bet a lot of people would be glad not to.'

'A "big shop",' Ed chuckled. 'I think I last heard that phrase in 1975.' He fell silent for a second. 'I miss the murk.'

'The *murk*?'

'Yeah. The murk of the UK. The grey skies. The rain. The moaning and the endless jabbering on about the weather. No one talks about the weather in LA as it's always the same. I miss Southend. The unique dreariness of the colour of the sea. The way you can't tell where the sea starts and the sky ends.'

'Nobody likes *murk*,' Maggie said, but it had always between them, hadn't it – that faded coastal town and the secrets of its murky sea. 'Next thing you'll be saying you miss pigeons and warm beer.' She closed her eyes again and enjoyed the deep orange haze of the sun on her eyelids.

'Well, sometimes I do. Sometimes I miss all sorts of things.' Ed was snapping off a blade of grass and rolling it between his fingers. Maggie dug her left heel into the soft earth. 'Ten minutes is up, I think,' he said. 'We need to go.'

'I could never have entertained Hollywood once I had Eloise,' Maggie blurted out. 'That was a big part of it. I couldn't have brought her to that life.'

'I know,' said Ed, staring at her. 'And I understand.'

◆ ◆ ◆

'Wet bums,' Maggie commented, as they got back into the car. Baptiste started the engine and soon they were bouncing back up the dirt track so speedily that Maggie had to hang on to a strap that was dangling from the ceiling. She was worried about her head hitting the roof, and more worried about bouncing into Ed.

'Sorry,' said Baptiste from the front seat, but he did not slow down. 'This is a rough road. But the trip is worth it, if we are to fit everything in.'

He reached in the glove box for another cassette and popped it in the stereo. 'Rocket Man' by Elton John filled the car.

'Oh, man, I love this song,' sighed Ed.

'Me, too,' said Maggie. Elton John's songs could make her cry. The memories they flashed into her mind. Her dad, cranking up the album *Goodbye Yellow Brick Road* and blasting it from open summer windows. 'Rocket Man', his favourite, that he used to play over and over, continually rewinding to the right part of the tape.

'It reminds me of your dad,' smiled Ed.

'Me, too,' replied Maggie.

'And mine. He liked this one, too. He used to play it on Sunday afternoons after we got back from fishing.'

'I didn't know that,' said Maggie quietly, and she lost herself to the song for a while, and to the memory of two fathers, one of whom she had never even met, but who she had tried to find.

'It also reminds me of the *murk*,' said Ed, after Elton had sung the part about raising children on Mars, and Maggie smiled.

Baptiste caught her eye in the rear-view mirror and turned and looked out of the window.

She could just about make out the sea – in a chink of space between the leaning rows of palms – shimmering like a sapphire in the far distance. A drift of white clouds temporarily bothering the perfect sky. And when she risked turning back towards Ed, her head full of all he had said at the lagoon, and Elton John, his eyes were waiting for her.

Chapter Thirty-Two

8 A.M., 15 JUNE 1991

Breakfast at Parkside House was quite the affair. It had been sent to their room and there was so *much* of it. They had croissants and jam and toast and a full English including baked beans, which Ed was thrilled about, and orange juice and coffee and tea *and* hot chocolate. They sat on upholstered velvet chairs butted up to a polished round table. They wore waffled white dressing gowns and the fluffy white slippers they'd found in the wardrobe. Maggie didn't have a hair band, so she'd piled her hair up on the top of her head and secured it with a sock.

It was Maggie and Ed's second morning in Surrey. Their first seemed a long time ago. Yesterday morning, they had eventually slept in until eleven o clock, exhausted from the party at the St Martin's Hotel and flying back here to fall within the sheets. Ed had suggested bagels and coffee to be sent to their room, after which Maggie had phoned Simone from the phone in the en suite bathroom.

'Oh, *Pretty Woman*,' Simone had quipped, on hearing where Maggie was.

'Less of the prostitute references,' Maggie had countered, whispering indignantly. 'He's hardly paying me to be here for the week. And it's a *house*, not a hotel.'

'No, but *still*. Is there a grand piano?'

'Well, actually, yes,' Maggie had hissed. 'But we've been nowhere near it.'

'How long *are* you going to be there for?'

'I don't know. I don't know anything. We'll see how the morning goes. As long as I show my face in the office at some point, I don't think anyone will care.'

'Especially when you tell them you're banging a Hollywood star.'

'Well, I won't be telling them that, obviously . . . And who says we've been *banging*?'

'Oh, come on, Maggie! You've hardly been knotting the sheets together and weaving baskets out of them!'

Maggie had laughed and hung up, then had got back into bed for more bagels and another round of basket-weaving. Later, about two o'clock, she came out of the shower to find Ed sitting on the bed, strumming on a guitar.

'What?' Maggie started. 'Where did that come from?'

'I brought it with me. Have guitar, will travel . . .'

'You still play?' She sat down on the bed next to him, her towel wrapped around her body and tucked in at her chest.

'Badly, but yes.' And he strummed a few bars of a tune she recognised.

'"Maggie May",' she said softly.

'I'm still trying to master it. You remember?'

'Of course I do. Pub garden. Transfers. Wired Tomb . . .'

'Terrible guitar player . . .'

'Eyeliner . . .' She laughed as his fingers tucked under the top of her towel and stroked her skin. 'And just look at you now,' she said. 'Hollywood bad boy, confirmed bachelor . . .'

'Not quite so confirmed now,' he replied, gazing at her. 'I found something,' he added, leaning across the bed and opening the drawer of one of the bedside tables. 'I wonder if it was Marilyn's.'

There was a silver bangle in his hand, with a tiny blue butterfly at its centre.

'Probably not,' she said. 'But it's pretty.'

Ed dropped it gently into her palm. 'It would look nice on you.'

'We should hand it in. Someone somewhere might be missing it.'

'Or they might not.' Ed smiled. 'Try it on. We can ask the housekeeper if anyone's left it behind or has been asking about it. If not, it's yours.'

She slipped it on to her wrist. It *was* very pretty.

'It does look great on you,' he said, seduction in his voice, 'but it would look even better if something else came off. If that's alright with you.' He tucked his thumb under the front of her towel, just below her breastbone. Melted her with green eyes.

'Oh, yeah?'

'Yeah.' Without taking his eyes from her, he slowly undid the tuck and she let her towel fall behind her to the bed.

◆　◆　◆

At 1 p.m., Ed was picked up by his driver to go back into London, to the Dorchester, to do a series of press interviews. The car dropped Maggie at Battersea, where she picked up some clothes, then she headed to her office and wrote up a feature on a soap star who was now a pub owner in the Pennines. Just after five, Ed and his driver were waiting for her on the pavement outside the building.

'So, this is how movie stars live every day,' Maggie had commented, sliding on to the soft black leather of the back seat.

'Not *every* day,' Ed had replied happily. 'Some days we have to show up and pretend to be other people.'

'Oh yeah,' she teased. 'That.'

'And *you're* hardly down the mines.'

'No, I know. I love my work.' She felt safe on the subject of work with Ed, now she was no longer looking for missing people but doing her fluff pieces on soap stars. The memory of her little secret was in less danger of creeping forward, the image of herself – cringeworthy amateur sleuth, sitting in Denise Sullivan's kitschy living room, and hapless hack opposite a cynical DC Banks at the police station – more easily banished.

'Do you miss your missing people?' he asked, smart and deliciously handsome in his jeans and blazer on the back seat.

'No,' she said. She didn't. But she couldn't forget them. She could never quite shake the feeling that Neville's hand had been on Denise's handbag, and that Jerry the angry bus driver had found something out about them. Particles of memory attached to these characters and how things may have played out between them were always in danger of accosting her.

'There's something I have to go to later tonight. Will you come with me?'

'What is it?' She reached for his hand, to anchor him to her, and circled the little scar at the base of his thumb with her finger.

'It's a party. A London movie producer's party.'

'Back into London again?'

'We'll take the helicopter.'

'Oh, the *helicopter* . . .'

'Stop it! Will you come with me?'

'You've twisted my arm,' she said. 'I'll come. How will you explain me?'

'*Explain* you? You'll be there as my date, my plus one.'

'Your date . . . Won't it just be easier to say I'm a journalist?'

'You think I'd be ashamed to have you as my date?'

'No. But, there will be . . . questions.' She shrugged. 'If you don't mind questions, then I'll come.'

'I don't mind questions. Questions come with the job. Do you need to touch base with your investment banker?'

'I don't think *he'd* like to join us.'

Ed smiled. 'No, I mean, do you have plans to cancel with him or anything?'

'No plans,' she said truthfully. 'Private party, so no paps again?' she asked.

'No paps.'

'Okay,' she agreed. 'I'll be your date.' But by the time they left Parkside House at 9 p.m., Ed had taken a call from his press officer, and Maggie was no longer a plus one, or a date, but a journalist who was part of an entourage.

'Sorry,' Ed had said as he'd shrugged on his jacket. 'It seems I'm not in charge. I forget that sometimes.'

'That's okay,' Maggie had replied as they walked out of their suite on to the landing. 'I can be a journalist in an *entourage*.'

'The prettiest entourage member ever.'

'Well, I doubt that's true.'

He caught her hand in his. His 'people' were waiting for him down in the hall. 'How are you feeling?' he asked her. 'How are you feeling about this? About us?'

'About *this*? I'm happy to be here,' she said, making it sound as though she was at a work awayday.

'That's all?'

'You don't want me to be happy?'

'Of course I do. I just . . . well, seeing you again. The serendipity of it. I don't know . . .'

'Let's just go to the party,' said Maggie. 'We can deal with serendipity later.'

◆ ◆ ◆

The party was in a white stucco four-storey building two streets behind Harley Street. Everything was huge: huge house, huge fireplaces, huge personalities draped in expensive suits and expensive jewellery. Huge egos, undoubtedly. The 'entourage' settled themselves in the main reception room, on red velvet armchairs or standing, champagne flutes in hand, with outsiders welcomed in and out like a choreographed dance.

Ed was charming, gracious, the centre of it all. He flashed Maggie a smile now and then and asked her if she was alright. She nodded. Of course she was. She was at a swanky movie producer's party, and she'd flown here by helicopter! But she wanted to go and sit on his lap. She wanted to rush him outside and snog him against a wall. She was a 'journalist', though, so she played her part like he played his. She had to be one of his many 'people': the bodyguard; the two solicitous PR women; Rupert; Ed's manager, Reece; and Cordelia, Ed's stylist.

Canapes were brought round. Drinks were constantly served. Maggie got embroiled in a conversation with a playwright who insisted he was better than Pinter. (She remembered Ed's shoes in *The Dumb Waiter*. The matches. The newspaper.) She suppressed a yawn and stole a look at Ed who was laughing genially at some terrible duffer's old jokes. It was 10.30 p.m.

'Ladies and gentlemen.' A man dressed like a butler was standing at the far double doors of the room, calling everyone to attention. 'If you'd like to make your way outside on to the terrace for tonight's entertainment . . . ?'

The gathered funnelled out, under a swelling murmur of excitement, and found themselves ushered on to a large terrace – descended from each end by a sweeping set of curved rococo stairways – and a central marble square chequered like an enormous draughts board.

'Ladies and gentlemen,' the butler man announced again. 'May we pray have silence for Terrence Bartholomew and Sindy Augustus . . .'

A couple came running, hand in hand, up the right-hand stairway, and Maggie's first thought was *Fred Astaire and Ginger Rogers*. The man had gelled-down, side-parted hair. Dark trousers and black-and-white spats. A white shirt and white double-breasted waistcoat. The woman, her hair in elegant 1930s rolls, was swathed in a scalloped confection of a dress: a pale blue sweetheart bodice and a mille feuille skirt of shimmering, ribbon-edged layers and layers. They swept, as she ran to the centre of the chequered marble square, like film running through an old-fashioned movie camera.

The crackle of a gramophone record about to play came over hidden loudspeakers, and Maggie recognised the opening bars of 'Let's Face the Music and Dance'. 'Fred and Ginger' danced majestically, swooping and turning, kicking up their heels in tandem, and pirouetting each other around the floor. They waltzed, they swayed and sashayed, they tap-danced, mirroring each other's moves exactly. It was magnificent. It was old-school Hollywood glamour, a hark back to the world of the Follies and Busby Berkeley and black and white movies, where hearts could be healed by a turn on the dancefloor, and love salved with a brush of lips on a waiting cheek.

'Amazing, aren't they?' Ed was standing next to her, his face bathed in the moonlight, his eyes luminous. He looked transcendent, she thought, in his smart tuxedo and his slicked-back curls:

not of this world. Even the moon above, wisped across by a nonchalant strip of cloud, looked fondly down upon him, acknowledging how special he was.

Maggie held his gaze, drank in those luminous green eyes.

'You're one of them,' she said softly. 'Fred and Ginger and Robert and Paul and Dustin and Meryl. You're one of them. One of the greats.'

'I'm not,' whispered Ed, shaking his head. 'I'm really not.'

'You *are*. You're part of the dynasty. Hollywood, the heritage, the legends. You'll always be remembered.'

'I'll be remembered for a little while, sure, but nothing lasts forever.'

'*You'll* last forever,' she insisted. 'You will.'

'It doesn't mean that much to me.' He looked directly into her eyes. He was beautiful.

'Why not? Don't you want to be remembered?'

He spoke sadly. 'That's not why I was happy to become famous. It was . . . well, it was so my dad would always be able to find me. So, wherever he was in the world, he would know where I'd be. Isn't that ridiculous?'

'That's not ridiculous.' The moonlight was highlighting the curve of his top lip, the heavens were blessing the velvet of his cheeks. She loved him.

'But he's *not* going to find me, and I'm not going to find him.'

'Oh, Ed,' she sighed. 'Wherever you are in the world, *I'll* always come and find you, I promise.'

'So you'll remember me?' he asked her gently, and he took her hand.

'Yes,' she whispered. 'I'll always remember you.' But here was one of the PR girls sidling over, all sleek hair and Calvin Klein perfume, and she was dragging Ed to talk to Don Heller, the producer whose party it was, and Ed released his hand, and he was gone, waving goodbye to her over his protesting shoulder, and Maggie was left alone.

◆ ◆ ◆

'Sorry,' said Ed. It was an hour later. The entourage was back in the house; Maggie had had two more glasses of champagne and a brace of miniature hamburgers.

'That's okay,' said Maggie. She was leaning against the mantelpiece, amusing herself by examining the family photographs of extremely wealthy people.

'Would you like to get out of here?'

'Are you allowed?' She returned a photo of a bunch of bundled-up, grinning people on the ski slopes to its rightful place.

'Yes. There's a plan, if you're willing. I thought we'd go walking in Regent's Park.'

'Won't it be closed?'

'I can have it opened.'

She nodded. 'Of course. Bob coming with us?'

'No. I'm sending Bob home. It'll just be us.'

'Wow. Mr Cavanagh can move mountains.'

It was a blissfully warm night. The stars were out, clear above the trees and the majesty of the buildings. After they were dropped off and told they'd be picked up in an hour, Ed took Maggie's hand, and they walked through the darkened park. They spoke quietly about the night and the dancers, who had got changed into jeans and t-shirts and joined the partygoers. Terrence, the male dancer, had turned out to be quite an excellent raconteur, with tales of Monaco and Budapest and Blackpool, and Ed and Maggie had joined his laughing audience until Maggie could see from the look on Ed's face he was thrilled for someone else to be in the spotlight – just for a little while.

'What *are* those?' asked Maggie as they passed a green hut, just beyond the cast iron railings, a little like a scout hut. 'I've always wondered.'

'Doesn't the line of cabs alongside give it away?' teased Ed.

Maggie looked clueless.

'They're taxi huts,' said Ed. 'Shelters for the drivers. Grade II listed they are, now, with their upkeep paid for by the Cabmen's Shelter Fund. Cabbies pop into them before or after their shifts for a cup of tea and a bacon butty.'

'I never knew that,' said Maggie. 'I always thought they were public loos. How do *you* know so much about them?' she asked.

'My grandad used to be a London cab driver, who operated out of Bayswater. He taught me a lot of things. Shall we go in? I'm starving.'

'Don't you have to be a cabbie?'

'I'll use the celebrity card. Besides, there's *Grandad*. He might hold some sway.'

'Alright, then,' said Maggie. She didn't mind what she did or where she went, on this second miraculous night with Ed. Her heart was soaring up into the moonlit sky just being with him.

It was warm inside, heat coming from a three-bar electric fire. Two cabbies were sitting opposite each other at a wedged-in U-shaped bench, beyond which was a serving hatch where a woman in a hairnet was barely visible behind the steam of hot tea in huge china mugs and the fug of salty smoke from a huge pan of frying bacon.

'Well, look at you two,' she chirped, as Maggie and Ed stepped inside. 'You don't look like cabbies. Oh lord, you're joking, aren't you?' She held her spatula aloft in surprise, fat dripping on to the floor. 'Aren't you *Ed Cavanagh*?'

'Sorry,' said Ed, looking sheepishly delicious. 'I'm afraid I am.'

'Bleedin' 'eck,' said the woman. She went white, then red. 'What on earth are you doing in here? Don't tell me my bacon butty reputation has reached as far as bloody Hollywood?'

'Indeed, it has,' said Ed cordially. 'This is my good friend, Maggie. Can we please come in for a cup of tea and a bacon sarnie? My grandfather used to be a London cabbie,' he added, with a quick wink. 'Perhaps you've heard of him? Reg Craddock, F9261?'

'*Old Reg?* Of course I bloody haven't! Blimey.' The woman took a breath. Fanned herself with a grabbed paper napkin. 'What do you say, gentlemen? Shall we let them in?'

One of the cabbies looked up and said, 'S'alright with me, Sylvia, as long as you're not expecting me to go all posh.' The other didn't look up from his paper.

'Course not, you just be yourself, 'arry. Okay, then,' she said to Ed and Maggie, 'but this must be kept a secret within these four walls,' she said sternly. 'No one can know we let a couple of civvies in.'

Ed smiled. 'Mum's the word,' he said, touching his nose, and he and Maggie made themselves comfortable side by side at the Formica bench, the cabbie who had spoken shoving up to make room for them.

'They've been going since 1875,' Ed said to Maggie. 'These shelters.'

'That's right,' said Sylvia. She brought over two steaming hot mugs of tea and two bacon sandwiches and plonked them on the bench in front of them. 'Never thought I'd be servin' a bona fide movie star, in 'ere,' she said. 'I'm tickled pink, truth be known.'

'Sylvia,' said Ed, 'it's an absolute pleasure. And this is a beautiful cup of tea, my love.' Sylvia blushed and bustled back to the kitchen. 'The perfect end to a perfect night,' Ed declared, munching on his sandwich, 'depending on what happens back at Parkside.' He raised his left eyebrow.

'You sure you want me to go back there with you again tonight?' Maggie took a bite of her sandwich, the ketchup oozing out.

'Don't you want to?'

'Well, of course I do. But I wonder about . . . the point . . . ?' She looked at him through the steam of her tea, suddenly feeling a little sad, a little breathless.

'The *point*?' queried Ed. 'The point is I've missed you,' he said, 'and . . . well, we can make all sorts of plans, if you like. For us. If you want to . . .'

'Well, let's see,' said Maggie, now studiously stirring her tea.

'Don't you want to? We're both free, aren't we? Kind of?'

'Kind of, yes. But I'm scared.'

'Of?'

'I don't want to say.'

'*Please* say.'

The cabbie shuffled his newspaper. Maggie lowered her voice.

'Okay, I'm scared of losing you. I'm scared of losing you again. I just want to enjoy this, this time together. The parties, these bacon sandwiches, this tea. I'm frightened if we make plans, they will get broken. That we always get broken.'

'We won't always get broken,' said Ed, serious.

'I don't know. I can't talk about it now. We can't talk about it *here*.' She glanced at the other, silent cabbie but he refused to look her way.

'But maybe we could talk about it tomorrow?'

'Maybe tomorrow. Let's see how the rest of the night goes.'

And now, at Parkside, at eight o'clock in the morning, after their indulgent room service breakfast and with soft summer rain tapping at the huge windows, Maggie placed her bone china cup and saucer of hot chocolate back on the polished table and reached her hand between the 'v' of Ed's dressing gown – to feel his warm heart. 'Thank you,' she said.

'What for?'

'For this,' she said. 'For London. For these hours.' They had been picked up from Regent's Park at 2 a.m. and swept out of London, her head on his shoulder. They had made love for half the night again. Over and over, the sheets tangling, the air-con rumbling.

'You make it sound like the end,' Ed said, frowning. 'It doesn't have to be. Come out with me again tonight, Maggie.'

'*Again?* Are you sure?'

'Yes. I leave tomorrow. Let's go out again tonight, stay *here* again tonight, and love each other a third time. I love you,' he said simply. 'I mean, I still do. I always have. Bumping into you like this . . .'

'Stop,' she said, 'just stop.' She was London Maggie. She was her own woman, a success, she was independent. She couldn't put her heart on the line like this again. Not like she had when they were young, before Ray had trampled all over it. And Ray had said she was the bad one, that she was at fault, that *she* had turned the relationship sour . . . what if that was true?

'I don't want to stop,' Ed pleaded, clutching her hand with his, warm and familiar. 'I want to acknowledge what we have. I want to make those plans—'

'Oh, Ed . . .'

'—plans to continue this. To carry on seeing each other. Plans to bridge the ocean between us and make this work. Wouldn't you like that? Don't you think we could make it work?' He squeezed her hand. He looked right into her eyes, her soul.

'I don't know, Ed. You're a big movie star, I'm just *me*. I'm happy at the moment. Really happy here in London. I don't know. I'm scared.'

'It's just you and me, Mags. Don't you think we could try? Don't you want to? Look, Michael's coming here today, later. He's been at Windsor with the nanny, having a great time staying in a fun little cottage on the lake at Virginia Water. I thought he'd be bored staying here, with me in and out for work. But he's coming this afternoon to be with me, and you can meet him, and—'

'Michael's been here the whole time?'

'Yes.'

'You never said. I asked after him that first night and you didn't say he was here!' She was bemused and a little cross.

'I suppose I just wanted you all to myself. And I didn't want to put you off. That my kid was here with me. You laughed when I asked you if you had any.' This was true. She hadn't exactly been enthusiastic about children. 'And he's been having a great time. He really has.' She nodded, her head down. She had read the newspapers. And the magazines. She'd read things about Ed and Michael's relationship. 'You'll love him, you really will.'

'That's not the issue.'

'We can do this, you know? We can make this happen. We have to, Maggie.'

She wanted to, she really did. She had let Ed go before, when he first went to America. She had *sent* him away from Richmond Road – the morning she had bumped into him down on the sea-front – devastating her for a long time when she was already used up and numb. And now here he was, right in front of her, giving her another chance. Shouldn't she take it? Shouldn't she take every golden moment offered to her when each moment with him brought her such happiness? Yes, their worlds were far apart, but worlds collided sometimes, didn't they, and yet kept turning?

'Okay,' she said. They could make plans. She could meet Michael. Didn't they deserve to be happy?

'Good,' said Ed, folding her into his arms. '*Good*, Maggie May. We're going to be so happy, you and me, I promise you.'

Chapter Thirty-Three

Baptiste stopped the car. He flung open his door, leapt out and started stomping his right leg on the ground.

'You okay, my friend?' Ed called through the driver's side window.

'Cramp,' huffed Baptiste. 'It is an affliction. A curse.' He hurled his shoe to the earth and grabbed his toes, wiggling them frantically.

'Can I help?' Ed asked.

'No, no, my friend. I'll be fine in a moment.'

Ed got out of the car and hurried round to Baptiste's side. Ed patted him helpfully on the shoulder while Baptiste stomped.

Finally, Baptiste exhaled, and stretched out his leg, wincing slightly.

'It is okay now,' Baptiste said. 'But it hurts a little.'

'Will you be okay to drive?'

'*Bien sûr*. I'll be okay.' He made to open his door, but he winced again – rather dramatically – and Ed placed his hand on Baptiste's arm.

'Don't you worry, my friend,' Ed reassured, as Maggie looked on through the window. 'You take the passenger seat. I can drive.'

He helped a mildly protesting Baptiste around to the other side of the car, put his seatbelt on for him, then walked back around to the driver's seat.

'You can *drive?*' Maggie was flabbergasted from the back seat.

'Of course I can bloody well drive!' retorted Ed, starting the engine. He crunched the car into first gear, and it lurched forward.

'When did you learn to drive?'

'Yonks ago.'

'But you always have drivers.'

'Not always. I have a truck,' he said, rumbling up the track at low speed, then ramming the gearstick into second when the engine started to strain. 'I learned how to drive it. And thank goodness I learnt stick shift, too, or I wouldn't have a hope in this old banger.'

The car, finally in fourth gear, settled into a comfortable grumble. And Maggie, who had learnt to drive when Eloise was small, for the school run, play dates, taking Eloise to Southend to visit her grandparents, said, 'I had no idea.'

'You never asked me.'

'Do you know where you're going?'

'Baptiste, where are we going?' asked Ed.

'Straight ahead and turn right at the fork,' said Baptiste. He took off his hat and placed it in his lap.

'That's where we're going, then,' said Ed.

'I'm quite impressed with your driving,' Maggie ventured, quite amused, too.

'Thanks,' said Ed sarcastically, but she caught his eye in the mirror and he looked all twinkly, like he was thoroughly enjoying himself.

'What's the actual destination, Bap?' Ed asked. 'I think my tour ended with the tortoises.'

'To the promontory,' Baptiste replied. 'Keep heading right and I'll show you where to stop.'

The sun was secure now in the sky, the island's grasshoppers fully awake and performing noisily in the undergrowth as Ed rolled the car to a halt by a small sandy clearing, the coconut air freshener swinging gently from the rear-view mirror.

'Bicycles,' Baptiste said. Ed wrenched on the crusty-sounding handbrake and switched off the engine. 'Here, you go on bicycles.'

'Oh, god, really?' Maggie was concerned.

'Yes, you will be cycling to the end of the promontory,' said Baptiste, turning his head to look through the gap in the headrests. He beamed, showing all his jagged teeth. 'Where you can see dolphins.'

'I like dolphins, but I haven't been on a bike since I was fifteen,' she protested. 'Don't tell me, Ed, you cycle around your Hollywood estate every morning in full Lycra,' she joked.

'No, I don't,' he countered. 'I haven't been on a bike in years either. But I suspect we'll be fine. After all, it's like . . .'

'Riding a bike?' Maggie offered, and Ed laughed. They got out of the car and Baptiste led them around the back of a falling-down straw shack to the right of the clearing, and to the ricketiest bikes Maggie had ever seen. She dubiously prodded the tyres and squeezed the brakes on one of the handlebars.

'Full working order,' confirmed Baptiste proudly. 'I serviced these machines myself only last week.'

'Fabulous,' said Maggie. She was still terrified.

'It'll be great,' Ed responded, but Maggie wondered about his insurance policy, and thought it was a good job his agent, Rupert, or his manager, Reece, weren't here, as they'd have kittens.

They walked their bikes to the path Baptiste pointed out to them, a path that at first seemed stony but was actually made from thousands of tiny seashell fragments. From the start of it, they could see the promontory stretching into the distance, a long finger of land fringed by golden sand, which nudged at the twinkling blue sea.

'On you get, then,' said Ed.

Maggie pulled a face. She mounted the bike unsteadily, then planted both feet firmly back on the ground. Ed got on his bike and set off up the path, wobbling from side to side.

'Oh, for goodness' sake,' she muttered to herself, launching off, too, the handlebars and her legs shaking. 'I'm not sure riding a bike is "just like riding a bike", after all,' she called to him as they tottered behind each other along the seashell path.

'No,' Ed called back. 'It seems a whole new set of skills are required.' He went into a bigger wobble and had to stop and put his foot down, before hobbling off again.

'You need a stunt man.'

'I'm not sure any of my guys could handle this particular instrument of destruction,' he muttered, then swore at the bike as one of his pedals got stuck and he had to whack it with his foot.

They were laughing so hard when they reached the end of the path that it took them a few seconds to realise just how spectacular the scenery was. They were at the tip of the golden finger of sand and rock, brilliant blue water wrapped all around it, tiny crests of wind-whipped waves studding the smooth of the blue.

'Wow,' said Maggie.

'This is really something, isn't it?' said Ed.

They dismounted their rusty steeds, setting them carefully at the edge of the path, and made their way down some makeshift steps, hewn out of the craggy rock, to the narrow beach below. It was desolate. Beautiful. There was a fallen tree trunk on the sand, bleached tie-dye grey and white by the sun. They sat on the tree trunk, side saddle, the sky sapphire-velvet above them.

'Look!' cried Maggie. 'I can see dolphins! Three of them!' They both stood up and looked out across the water. There were

271

three slick, cavorting dolphins out in the middle of the blue-green expanse, their snouts bobbing out of the soft waves they were creating, their bodies dancing and twisting. 'They're so beautiful!' she exclaimed.

'Aren't they?' Ed agreed. 'They're spinner dolphins – one of three different species around the island.'

'Well, they're certainly living up to their name.'

They watched as the dolphins frolicked, spinning around each other then, one by one, dived back below the surface of the water and disappeared. Maggie and Ed sat back on the fallen tree trunk.

'It's just so damn peaceful,' mused Ed, after a few minutes. 'This island. LA is just nuts, sometimes. The traffic, the chaos, the ambition of everyone, waiting on tables, waiting in traffic, waiting for that big break . . .'

She looked at him. 'We could start the interview now, if you like,' she said, thinking he was going in the right direction for what she had planned.

'Not yet.' He turned to glance at her. 'I said two o'clock, remember?'

She wouldn't apologise. She had to try to remember why she was here. But she felt a little sorry. 'You love it, though,' she said, instead. 'LA.' She didn't want to make him angry again, too much was at stake. It was the same reason she still hadn't given him Michael's letter.

'Yes, I do.' He didn't look angry. He looked thoughtful. He hesitated, then he said, 'I'd love it more, if I had people in my life that I loved, to *really* share it with.'

She wasn't sure if she really wanted to say this, but she did anyway. 'Do you mean a woman, or do you mean Michael?'

'I mean both. When did you last see him?' he asked her.

She took a moment, then she said, 'A while ago, when he came to London for another play.'

'Another play . . .'

She could feel the letter almost smouldering in her tote bag. The knowledge she had a relationship – semi-professional, bordering on friendship – with his son, since bumping into him at a London theatre in 2002, quite accidentally, when Ed *didn't* have a relationship with him, fired up her guilt. Should she simply take the letter out of her bag and give it to him? Watch as he opened and read it, whatever it contained?

'How was he?'

'He was good.'

'Great. How's his book coming along?'

She almost winced but she couldn't give herself away. 'I don't know,' she said truthfully, willing him to change the subject. There were unsubstantiated rumours that Michael was writing a tell-all book about his relationship with his father. 'I don't know if he's even writing one.'

'I feel . . .' he said, looking downcast. 'I feel if he was, I probably deserve it. I feel I would have every word coming to me.'

The letter continued to burn and so did her guilt.

'I'm sorry,' she said.

'What are you sorry for? It's my own fault.' Ed shrugged miserably. 'I neglected him as a child, berated him as a teenager – for being sensitive about the paparazzi, for not being grateful enough for the life I paid for. I let him down constantly, never doing what I'd said I'd do. I introduced him to a never-ending succession of "lady friends" . . .' He pulled a face. 'So, I've got what's coming to me,' he repeated. He picked up a twig from the sand and flung it down the beach. 'So, how *is* London these days?' he asked. She had got her wish, him changing the subject, but she was not sure she wanted that now. 'Apart from the Marks and Spencer's?'

'Can't we carry on talking about Michael?'

'No. Let's move on. How's London?'

'London is good,' she replied hesitantly. She didn't want to move on, now they were getting somewhere, but she took up the baton. 'It's also mad, although I live a more sedate version of it these days. No booze, not many nights out. Wrapped up under a blanket most nights, watching the world go by from my window.'

'Occasionally entertaining a war reporter.' They turned to look at each other.

'You sound a little jealous,' she teased, as she didn't expect he was at all.

'Of course I am.' He smiled. 'I love London.'

Maggie held her hand out to a passing butterfly, a soft yellow flutter of a thing, lost on the beach. 'Actually, I feel I'm too old to live in London now,' she admitted. 'It's too cold, too grey. I'm not sure it's still the place for me . . .' She focused on a soaring seabird, gliding as high as the sun. 'I've seen you in London,' she added quickly. 'Or rather, I've seen you on telly, on *The One Show*, *Graham Norton* . . . You even made the *Ten O'clock News*, once. Opening something or other. And didn't you rock up to London Fashion Week one time?'

'Yes, I had the joy of being front row at Stella McCartney, pretending I knew what on earth was going on.' He picked at a flaking piece of grey bark, rubbed it between his fingers, then let it fall to the sand.

'You didn't look me up.'

Ed glanced at her curiously. 'No, I didn't,' he said. 'Would you have liked me to?'

'I don't know . . .' She felt vulnerable. She knew there were traces of sadness in her voice she couldn't disguise. 'Why would you, with all that anger in the middle of the thing that used to be *us*? With both your father and your son – huge rocks wedged between us? I wonder if—' She started, but there was a sudden shout from the sea. A movement above the surface of the water.

'*Bonjour!*'

There was a man on a flimsy-looking kayak, no more than a couple of planks of wood strapped together, it seemed to Maggie. And the man's oar, no more than the branch of a tree, was being waved in the air.

'Oh, it's Pa Zayan,' she said, standing up. She waved back at him. '*Bonjour, monsieur!*' she called across the water to him. He kept waving as they watched him paddle contentedly past them and disappear from view around the bill of the promontory.

'He's quite the character,' said Ed, as Maggie sat back down. 'A real Robinson Crusoe.' And the mood between them shifted, once again. Maggie wished she could capture the thread, the feeling, of what they'd been starting to talk about, but like a butterfly, it had fluttered out of reach, and Ed seemed happy to let it. 'Sometimes he just lives on the beach, making fires, the lot. When I first arrived, he was very good to me. I slept on the beach by his campfire, on a rolled-up mat and, after LA, it was absolute bliss. To have all that space, suddenly, all that air.' Ed looked wistful. 'It was like I could breathe again. I soon needed some home comforts, though,' he added. 'I needed a *cupboard*, so I found the shack.'

'And now you have access to a bike,' she added. 'If only you could learn how to ride one.'

Ed laughed. Looking out to the sparkling sea, Maggie remembered how she had taught Eloise to ride a bike, one summer. Lance was out of the country and Eloise had asked for a bike for her birthday and so Maggie had taught her, in Regent's Park, and it had taken ten or maybe fifteen or maybe twenty goes, with Maggie yelling, 'That's it, now *pedal*!' at her, until Eloise had managed to execute the perfect alchemy of launching and pedalling and she was off, she was flying. Afterwards they got an ice cream from a kiosk and Eloise walked the bike and they wandered past the green hut where the cabbies took their break and drank tea and ate bacon sandwiches, and Maggie had looked at Eloise wistfully and thought, she was worth it, she was *so* worth it.

'What *happened* with you and Michael?' She kept her eyes on the horizon, so she didn't have to look at his face. She needed to ask him. She wanted to pick up the thread. 'After you saw each other in California in 2003? What happened with him?'

'He didn't tell you?' Ed continued to face forward, too, but she was aware of a slight breeze playing with one of his soft curls, lifting it up and setting it down again.

'We don't talk about you,' she said. It was only partly true.

'Nothing happened. Things stayed the same. We didn't speak – we haven't spoken. Not for years. Then I went to the wedding.'

She nodded.

'I went cheque in hand. Everyone could see how that went down, with me being escorted off the premises. So since then, I haven't tried to give him money. Instead, I've been donating to the community theatre Michael is the founder of in Eagle Rock. Anonymously, although the manager there is reportedly very indiscreet . . .'

'So, he may know?'

'He may do.' Ed nodded, then looked sad. 'I've lavished him with money all his life and I've finally realised that's the last thing he needs from me, personally. But I hope the donations to the theatre will mean something, to *something* that means a lot to him. And recently I . . .'

'Recently you . . . ?'

'I sent him another olive branch before I travelled here. I don't know if he got it. I heard nothing.' She nodded at him, but he seemed unwilling to offer any more information. 'I just want . . .' he started. 'I just want . . .'

'What is it you want?' Should she risk giving him the letter? she thought. Was now the time? But Ed suddenly stood up.

'I want to cycle back now,' he said, his face closing down like a high-street shutter.

'Okay.' Maggie got up slowly, too. 'If you're sure. We—'

'I'm sure.'

Ed started walking up the rocky steps to the seashell path, Maggie following. Ed hoisted up his bike and got on it; Maggie did the same. They wobbled back up the path in uneasy tandem.

The past is not an island, she thought, separate and remote and only reached by two planes and three boats, but a road that wound its way through people's lives and was difficult to navigate, as it hurt too much. And the man in front of her was not an island, either, she realised, but a series of them, still to be discovered.

Chapter Thirty-Four

9 A.M., 16 JUNE 1991

The newspaper that came with their third Surrey breakfast had Ed and Maggie in it. Page six. The page lay open, by a plate of almond croissants. Their photo, black and white, staring at them as they sipped morosely on freshly squeezed orange juice. In the photo, Ed was dashing out of a back entrance of a restaurant, one hand up to his face. Maggie had her head ducked into his shoulder. It was raining. A street lamp in the corner of the photograph picked out the scratchy, cinematic slant of it on their faces.

Yesterday morning, their second – after the producer's party at the big house behind Harley Street – had started well. They had finished their full English breakfast, with all the extras, and made their 'plans'. They were to carry on seeing each other – long distance at first, and then look at a more permanent solution in a few months' time, with Maggie hopefully relocating to LA and either writing remotely for *Actually!*, or looking for a new job.

They had tumbled back into bed for a while, and then had gone out walking in Windsor Great Park, which bordered the village. Ed had been in disguise, a hat pulled low over his head. Bob had followed six feet behind – they'd had to call him, inevitably. They purposely took a quiet route and enjoyed the warm breeze and the sunlight dappling through the trees, but after a while, people started to leave their eyes on Ed for just a few seconds too long. A lady walking a dog did a double take and began to approach, but Ed and Maggie managed to head her off. A man walking towards them actually shouted, 'Hey! It's him! It's him, isn't it?', looking round for apparent confirmation, then had run right up to Ed and said, in his face, 'Oh my god, it is you, isn't it, mate? I'm a big fan, mate, a really big fan. Can I shake you by the hand?'

'Of course,' Ed said, but Maggie could tell he didn't really want to, and the man did more than shake him by the hand; he bruised up against him, slapping him rather violently on the shoulder, as though he were angry with him, and it all happened rather quickly. Bob was suddenly there, manhandling him, and the man started shouting, 'Who do you think you are? Billy Big Nuts Hollywood Star? Aren't you from shitty Southend or something? Why don't you go back there? Why don't you stop going out if you don't like meeting the "little people"? *Wanker!* before running off.

'I guess it's time to go back to the house,' Ed had sighed.

'I'm sorry,' Maggie had said, feeling the day had already taken a dark turn.

'It's not your fault. It's an occupational hazard. Listen, I used to work in a ladies' shoe shop. It's all good.' He glanced at his watch. 'Michael should be there now anyway,' he said. 'Let's go.'

Michael was waiting in the drawing room downstairs, the one with the grand piano. His nanny was with him, a brisk-looking woman in a grey trouser suit and trainers who perched on the edge of a Chesterfield chair, her knees and feet clamped primly together.

'Michael!' declared Ed, holding his arms out wide to the boy with a grand flourish, but Michael wandered over slowly to them, looking shy.

Maggie had seen the headlines about Ed and Michael. She'd read an interview with Veronica Gray, saying Ed was not a very good father. That he was never around, away for months filming, that he put women before his son, that his son hated the paparazzi and the constant press intrusion. That Ed might buy Michael extravagant presents like rocking horses and remote-controlled cars, but he was never there for his son. It wasn't a secret.

'Hello, Daddy,' said Michael, and Ed drew his son to him and gave him a big squeeze. Michael's blond hair flopped over Ed's arm.

'I've missed you. How was the cottage?' Ed pulled back from Michael and studied his face. 'Was it good fun? Did you go fishing every day?'

'Yes, Dad,' said Michael, his face solemn. 'It was fun. But *you* didn't come fishing with us. You said you would!'

'Well, no, because I couldn't. I've been working, I haven't had time.' Maggie thought of the two mornings they had spent together in bed. Walking in the park this morning, the party in London. 'You understand, don't you, Michael?'

Michael nodded. Ed looked quite crestfallen. 'I've really been looking forward to seeing you *today*,' he said. 'And we're flying back to America together tomorrow, aren't we? We're going to get a McDonald's at the airport, and we're going to watch a silly movie on the plane. I thought you'd be bored, hanging around here. I thought you'd have more fun at the cottage with Jane.' He stroked Michael's arm in its stiff blazer, vaguely. 'And we did those three sightseeing days in London, didn't we, at the beginning of the trip? Three heavily scheduled days,' he said to Maggie, and she felt she ought to be giving him a thumbs-up. 'It was exhausting, wasn't it, son? But you got all those nice things from Hamley's. All those teddies.'

Maggie thought Michael a little too old for teddies. The boy nodded morosely, Jane smiling encouragingly behind him. 'Tell your father about the heron we saw yesterday,' she said.

'It was really big,' said Michael robotically.

'He seems a bit tired.' Ed frowned at Jane. 'Hey, Michael, this is Maggie.' He beckoned Maggie over. 'Say hello.'

'Hi, Michael.' She held her hand out to him and he shook it formally. 'Pleased to meet you.'

'Pleased to meet you, too, Maggie.' He barely looked at her. 'Your bracelet is cold.'

'Oh, sorry.' The little silver bangle with the blue butterfly was dangling on to the boy's wrist from hers. She drew her hand away.

'Are you my dad's new friend?'

'No, I'm his old friend.' Maggie made an attempt at a laugh.

'Oh. I liked Riva,' said the boy. 'Although sometimes she was pretty rude to me.'

'The precociousness of youth,' Ed quipped. He checked his watch. 'Right, well, I think it's nearly lunch time,' he said. 'Michael eats early,' he explained to Maggie. 'Time to go into the kitchens with Jane and get yourself fed. It's all been arranged. Chef's waiting for you.'

Maggie had never seen Ed so awkward, so stilted. His son made him uncomfortable. They were both uncomfortable in each other's presence. They were like a king and a prince only ever brought together for state occasions.

'I guess I got it wrong,' said Ed, after Michael and Jane had gone. He plomped down dejectedly on to one of the sofas. 'I guess Michael wanted to go fishing with me and just hang out. Maybe the Tower of London and Madame Tussauds just didn't cut it.' His head was in his hands, his face wan. 'I thought he'd be bored hanging around here. I thought . . .'

He looked wretched. Maggie felt sorry for him. 'Don't worry, I'm sure you can make it up to him when you get back to LA. Or on the plane . . .' But she wondered if he would. She wondered if it was too late. She was glad she didn't have children.

'It kills me,' he said ruefully. 'It kills me that I wanted to be a good father so badly, because mine disappeared, but it turns out I have no idea how to be a father at all.' He lifted his head and looked up at her. 'Let's go out for dinner tonight, somewhere quiet?' he pleaded.

'What about Michael?'

'We can go after he's gone to bed. I'll play Scrabble or something with him, whatever he wants, and you and I can go out about nine.'

'Okay,' she said, squashing down guilty feelings about Michael, and Ed's father. 'That sounds nice.'

They went to a Japanese restaurant in Windsor. They ordered sake and sashimi and sukiyaki and a cute plate of what looked like savoury Battenberg squares. They positioned themselves in a dark corner, she in a charcoal silk slip dress, he in a navy shirt and jeans. Ed had clearly tried hard to be smiling and attentive, but he was distracted, bending low over his food and barely making eye contact. Her pager buzzed and it was Lance, wanting her to call him. She switched it off.

'I feel like I'm going to the guillotine in the morning,' said Ed, over green tea at the end of the meal. 'I'm not ready to say goodbye to you again. Come with me, Maggie. Come with me, tomorrow.'

'I can't come *tomorrow*,' replied Maggie carefully, setting down her cup. 'That's way too quick. We said long distance, for a while. I have my job, my flat – I can't just ditch it all.'

'You could! You could just ditch it all and get on a plane with me tomorrow! You won't need any of that any more. Come live with me! Share my life!'

'No, Ed.' She shook her head. 'I like my job. I like my flat. I'm not running out on both, just like that. And you're flying with Michael, it's all planned. You're getting a McDonald's. You're going to watch the film together . . .'

'But you'll come? Soon? Promise me?'

'Yes, I'll come. You know I will.' She had been seduced by him, in London and Surrey. She would go anywhere to be with him, despite the tiny niggles she would ignore, she *had* to ignore. The three-ring circus of his life: The downsides of that – not the helicopter or the fancy parties, but the ever-present entourage, and the people on the street who thought they owned a piece of him. His relationship with his son.

'We still love each other,' Ed said confidently. And suddenly he was back in movie star mode. Steady green eyes, wide smile, adjusting his tie. 'We're going to make this work.'

'We're going to make this work.'

They stayed there so long that by the time they came out, it was pitch black and raining. A flash had gone off, then another. Ed had put an arm up in front of Maggie's face.

'They've found me,' he said. 'Quick,' he'd entreated. 'The car's just here.'

The door of the sleek BMW had slid open, and they'd jumped inside.

'Oops,' she'd said, on the back seat, shaking the raindrops from her hair.

'Oops,' he'd echoed. 'But does it matter?'

'Not really,' she'd replied, but the next morning their picture in the newspaper looked up at them as they nibbled on almond croissants in their room at Parkside House, and she had felt exposed, like she'd been caught doing something wrong in the dark summer rain. And Ed was leaving for the airport in an hour with Michael, to go home to LA, and that made her feel exposed and lonely, too, but she would follow, she would follow.

She would follow him to the ends of the earth.

Chapter Thirty-Five

The two cyclists parked their bikes back behind the shack. Baptiste was waiting for them by the car.

'Did you enjoy?' he asked.

'I'm not sure *enjoy* is the right word . . .' Maggie replied, and she wasn't just talking about the bikes.

'We now go to the next stop,' said Baptiste. 'To the cemetery.'

'The cemetery?' Ed was still out of puff from cycling back up the path. 'Are you trying to finish me off?'

'No, my friend,' responded Baptiste. 'We are going there because it is beautiful.'

◆ ◆ ◆

Ed was driving again. The shaky old car was on a rumbling road snaking through the centre of the island, thick tropical foliage on either side, the sun poking through where it could. Maggie had finished eating a few more of the mango pieces. Baptiste was whistling along to Neil Diamond's 'Sweet Caroline'. When the song finished, he opened the glove box, rummaged in it for a few seconds, and handed a photograph back to Maggie.

'This is my wife, Cecile,' he said, with a toothy smile. 'When we had time, we used to go every week to visit the tortoises together. Her favourite was Barat, who was over one hundred and twelve years old.'

'You've never mentioned a wife,' said Ed, looking confused suddenly in the rear-view mirror. 'Why have you never told me about your wife?' He had hardly spoken since they had got back into the car.

'She doesn't live with me any more,' Baptiste replied. 'But every Friday she would bring a basket of fresh mango. For the tortoises. They love fresh mango.'

'She's beautiful,' said Maggie, looking at the woman in the photo. Smiling, and with her hair pulled back from her face, she was standing on the beach at dusk, in a red top with lace cuffs and a white sarong. Had they split up? she wondered. Were they divorced? Maggie held up the picture to Ed, who looked over his shoulder.

'She's lovely,' he agreed. 'How did you meet her?'

'She was not from Mémoire, but from La Digue. I met her when I used to work as a mechanic on that island. She worked at the little café next door, in the wooden shack. Every day I would see her filling the urn with tea and making the breadfruit chips. And each lunchtime she would walk past with her friend to go to the wharf, and I knew, from the first time I saw her pouring the tea, and every time I watched her walk by, that I loved her.'

'Love at first sight,' Maggie commented. 'How romantic!' Ed glanced at her in the mirror. 'Keep your eyes on the road!' she fired at him, a little too playfully.

'Yes,' continued Baptiste. 'One lunchtime, when she and her friend passed by, she asked me what I was looking at and

I whispered, because I was shy, "The most beautiful girl on La Digue." And she said she hadn't heard me, so I came to the door of the garage, and I looked in her wonderful eyes and I said those words again, that she was the most beautiful girl on La Digue.

"'What am I supposed to do with that information?" she asked me, for she was a smart girl, my Cecile, and I said, "Do with it what you will, but I hope you decide on something that will last a lifetime because that's how long I would like to spend with you."' Baptiste laughed, his eyes shining. 'The next day she brought me baked bananas in coconut milk and lemongrass tea. And the next day she brought me ginger ale and caramelised pineapple. And on the third day, I took her some flowers from my mother's garden, and I asked her to walk with me on the beach, when we had both finished work. From that day, we were inseparable.'

He smiled proudly. He straightened the neck of his jacket and righted his cap.

'That's a wonderful love story,' said Maggie, and she thought of how she and Ed had first met, at the wall, and she wondered how a beginning could have nothing whatsoever to do with an end. 'Do you have any children?' she asked Baptiste.

'No, we never did. Do you, Maggie?' he replied.

'Yes, I have a daughter. Her name is Eloise.' She wondered if Ed had told Baptiste about Michael. They seemed such good friends in many ways, but it appeared they had not shared all their secrets.

'*Merveilleux*,' said Baptiste. 'That is a beautiful name.'

'Thank you.'

'What does she do, your daughter?'

'She's a research scientist,' said Maggie. 'She works on finding cures for diseases.' The thought of Eloise in her lab coat, poring over Petri dishes through a microscope and concentrating on saving the world, made her smile.

'*Fantastique*.'

287

Maggie handed the photo back to Baptiste and he placed it carefully in the glove box. The foliage rolling either side of them cleaved, and Maggie could glimpse the sea again, sparkling like a jewel in the distance. Ed steered the car expertly to the right and parked it at the base of a softly sloping hill sprinkled with wildflowers.

The scent of wild vanilla hit Maggie as she stepped out of the car. The hill rose prettily to the sky like a scoop of ice cream.

'I may need some help up the hill,' said Baptiste. 'My leg, it's still not so good.'

'Well, we could go up and take a look, while you wait here,' said Ed. 'If you'd like?'

Maggie wasn't sure she wanted to be alone with Ed at the top of the hill.

'No, I need to go up.' Baptiste shook his head. 'Help me, please.'

He held out both his arms like he was about to about the execute the butterfly stroke. Ed and Maggie glanced at each other, shrugged, then hooked themselves under Baptiste, either side, so he could lean on their shoulders.

'Come on then, old boy,' Ed grunted.

The threesome lumbered their way up a winding, crumbly path, here and there assisted by a stack of chalky steps. It was hot now, the sun beating down. Grasshoppers were in the bushes, strumming away, and there were yellow and white butterflies flitting around. Baptiste was a big old unit and very weighty on Maggie's shoulder, his steps heavy and faltering. Her bag kept nearly falling off her other shoulder.

'I'm clearly not as young as I used to be,' puffed Ed, about halfway up.

'Neither am I,' huffed Maggie. They flicked their eyes to each other across Baptiste's mighty chest, Ed raised his eyebrows, and they both found themselves falling into an easy smile at this comical scenario.

'I am sorry.' The huge plank between them grinned his gratitude.

'Don't you worry, my friend,' said Ed. 'We'll get you up there.' They heaved themselves up the hill for a few more minutes, navigating the crumbly path and the chalky steps, Ed and Maggie working together to keep Baptiste upright and not plummeting to the ground below.

'Take my hand,' said Ed, holding his free one flat against Baptiste's chest. 'It will help us to ballast him.'

Maggie gave him her hand and he clasped it, holding it tight, so they formed a bridge across Baptise, providing the ship's hull of their three combined bodies with more stability.

'Better?' Ed asked her.

'Ridiculous, but better.'

Ed's hand was surprisingly unsweaty. And familiar and strange. Maggie ignored how it made her feel. She ignored the warmth of electricity it sent shooting into hers. They trudged on and finally made it to the top of the hill. Maggie gasped.

Stretching down to the sea below them was the prettiest cemetery Maggie could have ever imagined. It was grassy – bright green, lush grass – and haphazardly terraced, hotch-potched with pristine white graves: smooth ledgers in staccato rows, with headstones arched and turreted and carved and adorned with photographs of once-loved ones, like miniature churches. There were red and pink and orange flowers placed on the stones or woven amongst them by nature. It was peaceful. It was picturesque. It was like nowhere Maggie had ever seen.

'Perfect!' Ed declared, catching his breath. 'Just perfect!'

He and Maggie let go of each other's hands. They released their charge. Baptiste flopped to the ground and gave an almighty sigh. Maggie and Ed shook out their punished arms.

'On a day like today, you can see right across to Praslin – look!' Ed pointed. 'And you can see your bungalow, too, Maggie.'

Maggie looked and yes, to the right, down the hill, was the little sandy rudder of land, and the handful of bungalows, including Bungalow Marguerite.

'So, we've come full circle,' she said.

'Lovely, isn't it?' Baptiste, from his seated position with his dodgy leg stretched out before him, gazed out over the sea, where a lone boat on the horizon loped and bobbed and a kestrel transcended the sky. 'I do believe it's the nicest place on the island,' he added, taking off his cap and placing it against his chest. 'And my wife is here.'

Chapter Thirty-Six

10 A.M., 9 AUGUST 2003

Ed's face was tender, full of worry and care. His green eyes were soft and warm, the light from the window reflected in them. His smile was hesitant but gentle, his upper body turned towards her and a hand, light upon his arm, uncertain whether it had a place there.

'What is love but this?' he said, and a thousand eyes filled with tears and a million hearts soared. Maggie shifted in her seat and took another great big bite of her double caramel Magnum ice cream. She didn't like being so near to the screen, but she couldn't deny that Ed Cavanagh, this close up, was incredible. The movie was *Professor Clarke*. Ed and his love interest, Gemma Gleason, were standing by his study window on a frosty January day. It was the final scene. The beautiful final scene.

Professor Clarke had been a big hit. It was a cross between *Dead Poets Society* and *Educating Rita* and was the story of a lonely but inspirational professor in New England, and his working-class cleaner – shy and rough around the edges, but with a thirst to learn – which ends in a school tragedy. Ed Cavanagh's wardrobe was Autumnal Academic: he wore cabled knitwear and soft cords, worn at the elbow, in shades of brown and orange; tweedy moss-green blazers and polished Oxford brogues. His curls had been left to grow longer for the role. They were unrulily sexy and constantly in his eyes.

His eyes – Maggie couldn't imagine anyone wouldn't fall for those eyes. The soft self-deprecating smile. The genius of everything Professor Clarke knew. His widower status, his beginning-to-be-faded handsomeness. There had even been an awkward sex scene that started with Ed in an emerald-green towelling dressing gown, removed to reveal a smattering of forty-something chest hair, which was terribly endearing. The lumbering, the self-consciousness was lyrical movie gold. Oh, the heart strings were being pulled here. It was a movie with all the right ingredients. The plot points could be ticked off one by one, the denouement, inevitable and satisfying. Maggie took another bite of her Magnum, and she knew she was not alone. Whatever she was feeling, thousands – no, millions – had felt it, too, for Ed Cavanagh.

The last time she had seen Ed in person had been in 1991. She hadn't realised it would be such a big deal. Being on page six of the *Sun*, and page twelve of the *Guardian*. She hadn't known that Lance would phone Parkside House ten minutes after Ed and Michael had left for the airport, although she wouldn't take the call. She hadn't known that Riva Jones, over in Hollywood, would be photographed tight-mouthed and stoic at a West Hollywood nightspot ('Riva drowns sorrows after Ed's London betrayal! Who's that girl?' shouted the headlines). That Riva would 'welcome' Ed back to their lovely Beverly Hills home after a three-week stand-off (the intensity of that period in the spotlight earning her a role on *Days of Our Lives*), without anyone knowing she and Ed had even split up. And Maggie hadn't known that all the time she had been in Surrey with Ed Cavanagh, she had been eight weeks pregnant.

It wasn't like it was in books or films. She hadn't thrown up in a plant pot at work, or suddenly wondered why mince tasted like mints, or watched Simone raising a knowing eyebrow over dinner when her friend said she didn't fancy the dover sole. She had been in the local supermarket in Battersea, wandering down the aisles, the day after Ed had gone back to LA, planning how to fend off Lance, who kept calling her, and how to shut up the newspapers, who were also badgering her, when, drifting towards the paracetamol, she'd noticed the boxes of tampons and realised she hadn't had a period for a while.

She went through the dates in her mind, by the panty liners. She was on the pill, so she couldn't be, could she? But she bought a pregnancy test and went home and did the test and she was pregnant. She had a three-second fantasy it was Ed's, but quickly got real; she was pregnant with Lance's baby, on the very unlucky chance of being so, and a private scan three days later confirmed she was eight weeks along.

'Finally!' Lance had exclaimed when she'd phoned him at his office. 'I thought you were never going to return my calls!'

When she'd told him her news, he went quiet for a few moments, before giving a reaction that was almost as big a surprise as the pregnancy. He'd always wanted a kid someday, he was willing to marry her, he would do the whole kit and caboodle. She had told him that wouldn't be necessary – he didn't love her, did he? – and he admitted he didn't, although he'd really liked having her as his girlfriend (which was another surprise), but when she told him she wanted to go it alone he settled for fully supporting her financially and emotionally, and he would see his kid every weekend.

And then he'd asked about Ed, but Maggie had said it was a storm in a teacup, that it was nothing, that he had gone.

The biggest surprise of all was that four seconds after finding out she was pregnant, Maggie had decided to keep the baby. She'd spent most of her thirties trying *not* to get pregnant but now she was, there was strangely and wonderfully no question of her not doing this. It felt a necessity, suddenly. A baby. And for her to become a mother. Some primal hormonal need had kicked in. She wanted to continue with this pregnancy. She wanted this baby.

She kitted out her flat with baby paraphernalia. She stopped drinking. She read *What to Expect When You're Expecting*. She researched. She *prepared*. And when the baby came – her perfect, tiny, bleating, screwed-up scrunch of a thing, blinking at her with dark navy-blue eyes – *Eloise* – she was more than ready for her life to be turned upside down, although it wasn't like that. It was . . . blissful. Maggie settled into milky, baby-powdered heaven. A year of maternity leave when she had only left the flat to go on cute walks with Eloise in the sling, or to the mother and baby group in the little church up the road. Visits to Southend where she and her mum and dad ambled up the promenade with the pram and, later, took Eloise as a toddler to the beach. And then, later still, Maggie took her to the trampolines and the helter-skelter, and to the arcades with the 2p machines. Lance saw her every weekend, as he'd said he would, except when he was away, and Maggie never faulted him as a dad. And Eloise had proved to be the love of her life.

But, of course, after *five* seconds of knowing she was pregnant, Maggie knew her plans with Ed were over. She loved him, but she couldn't move to LA and take Lance's excited involvement away from him. She didn't want to bring up a baby there. She didn't want to rely on Ed's support, his money. And, as ashamed as she was to admit it to herself, she didn't like how he was as a father, and she wanted to be the very best mother. Hadn't her own mother sacrificed everything for her? Well, she would do the same. She would lose Ed, and cry over him often at night, as her baby kicked inside her, but she would not and could not go to him.

Many years had passed since then. Eloise was now eleven years old. The movie, *Professor Clarke*, was not new, either. Maggie had seen it many times, but she still sighed as the credits rolled, tears in her eyes; a sigh that made the woman in the seat in front turn and look at her, but Maggie *did* feel alone. Alone enough that when the stewardess moved along the aisle with her cart, offering more iced waters and Magnums, Maggie wondered – when the plane eventually landed in California – if she might dare, despite everything, to get in touch with him.

Chapter Thirty-Seven

11 A.M., ON THE ISLAND

Ed and Maggie had helped Baptiste to one of the higher slopes of the cemetery, where he had gathered a small bouquet of wildflowers from the hillside and knelt clumsily in the sand to place them at a pure white, very pretty headstone.

Cecile's grave.

'How awful. I wonder when his wife died,' Maggie said finally. They had stepped away to give Baptiste some privacy, on to a small ridge of grass behind a leaning, gnarly tree – the wide blue-green of the Indian Ocean below giving them a spectacular view. They had waited here for some time, for Baptiste to execute his slow and careful tending of his wife's grave.

'I have no idea,' said Ed. They had sat down on the tufty grass, then, waiting patiently, had gradually stretched back to recline on it, and Ed had nodded off for a while, his hands crossed behind his head. Maggie had stared at his sleeping face, boyish in repose, and had felt an unexpected tenderness in her heart for him, a poignancy she had to look out to the horizon to dispel. When he'd woken up, he had run his hand through his hair, the silver curls dispersing then springing back together. 'I can't believe he never told me about her.'

'I'm so sad for him.'

They watched as Baptiste swept the stone of Cecile's grave with the flat of his hand for the umpteenth time, his suit straining at his knees. He adjusted the flowers in their little stone vase. He gently touched the edge of his wife's photograph on the headstone. Then he stood up, brushing down his trouser legs, and started making his way gingerly back up the terraced slope to them.

'You okay there, fella?' Ed called down to him, looking a little alarmed. 'The leg okay?'

'Yes, my friend,' Baptiste called up. 'Kneeling seems to have released something.'

'I'm so sorry, Baptiste,' said Maggie, when he reached them. She and Ed stood up.

'Me, too,' echoed Ed. 'You never told me.'

'It makes me too sad,' Baptiste replied, a wan smile on his face. 'But today I want to.'

The three of them stood and looked down over the hillside and beyond, to the expanse of the sea. The horizon was indistinct, the sea darker at its far reaches, a rich teal.

A soft breeze ruffled Maggie's hair. Ed shaded his eyes with his hand. Baptiste was holding his cap to his chest in silent salute. What an odd tableau they made, she thought. The movie star, the journalist and the chauffeur. Standing on a hilltop here on this island. One who had lived on Mémoire all his life and had buried his wife here. Another who had made it his temporary home, in a bid to escape Hollywood. The third, who had been displaced from her London flat with its books and its seventies record collection, for an increasingly uncertain mission, and who had not belonged to anywhere or anyone, apart from Eloise, for a long time.

'Cecile liked many things,' said Baptiste. 'She liked stories about sailors and pilots, and sunrises over the beach, and breadfruit chips and pretty clothes. She liked cars,' he added. He didn't take his eyes from the horizon. 'She had a book when she was a little girl, from America – a picture book about a schoolgirl who gets driven around the island of Manhattan in her father's big car. She was thrilled when my cousin started sending pieces of the Toyota over. She would stand and watch me as I built the car and bring me hot tea and breadfruit, just like in the early days. She would talk to me and ask me questions.'

'That's a lovely memory,' said Maggie.

'Yes.' Baptiste nodded. 'But the car took a long time to build, and then she got sick, and I had to stop building it to take care of her. And so she never got to see it finished, or ride around in it on the island like she wanted to. The last trip she made was on bicycle, and it was here to this cemetery, and we sat at the top and looked down, just like this, and she said, "If I have to be anywhere that's not with you, then I'm glad I'm going to be here."'

'Oh, Baptiste,' said Maggie.

'Sorry, my friend,' echoed Ed, sadly. Maggie was sure he had tears in his eyes.

Baptiste smiled shyly. 'It was God's will,' he said, 'that she would go missing from my life, but not my heart. I still see her in the breeze of the mango grove.' Maggie nodded, tears in her eyes, too. 'I held on to my wife until the very end,' he continued, 'and she held on, too, because we wanted to be together and we did not want to waste an hour or even a second.'

Baptiste turned to face them. 'Don't waste a second,' he said, searching their faces. 'Live each hour, live it to the full. If you have love, hold on to it very tight, like a baby bird in your pocket. Feed it, nurture it, keep it safe. Don't let it fly away. We all have to fly away from each other in the end – in the *very* end – but until then, let love be a baby bird in your pocket. Hold it tight, my friends.'

Maggie didn't dare look at Ed. She realised she was holding her breath, here at the top of this hill with its beautiful cemetery. Where love didn't quite last forever but was commemorated so beautifully by those who loved on.

'Love is "hello" and "goodbye" and "good morning" and "goodnight",' added Baptiste, returning to the horizon again. 'Love is both the beginning of the day and the end.'

'Not if you lose it,' said Ed, and the tone of his voice was so unsettling Maggie's heart jolted. She looked at him and his face was stern. 'Then, love is just goodbye and not at the end of the day, either. It's more like halfway through. Like a needle coming off a record.' He was angry, his words sharp blades cutting into the sunshine and the blue. 'Sorry. I'm very sorry about your wife,' he repeated to Baptiste. 'Shall we get going now?' he added quickly. 'What's the next place on the tour?'

'This was the final stop,' said Baptiste. 'There are no more places to go. Now it is time for the two of you to talk.'

Chapter Thirty-Eight

11 A.M., 12 AUGUST 2003

Maggie had been in San Francisco for three days before she'd called Ed. She'd been over the Golden Gate Bridge, she'd crossed the water to Alcatraz, she'd wandered down the astounding floral bends of Lombard Street. She had also interviewed Davinia Regine, former actress of melodrama *The Coleman Saga*, who now lived in Bodega Bay, where Hitchcock's *The Birds* had been filmed. Davinia lived in a wooden two-storey house that toppled right over the craggy rocks of the ocean, and where she kept ten bright parakeets who didn't stop talking. The light at the house – a peachy pink in the early morning when Maggie had been there yesterday – was perfect for the photos Maggie had shot of her.

Maggie now worked for *Supernova* magazine, an international film publication, where she profiled once-feted actors and actresses who had faded from public view but were now living interesting lives far from the madding crowd. Some needed a lot of tracking down. Some, like Davinia, were easy to find via a couple of phone calls and an internet search. Maggie had interviewed Davinia out on her terrace, then captured her with her new camera: draped across a pink chaise longue in the sitting room, with the blue and charcoal bay streaking behind her; down on the beach in a big cape; and perched on the edge of her wooden hot tub in an apricot mu mu and a bout of joie de vivre.

'Go for what you want!' Davinia had declared spiritedly, just before that last photo had been taken. 'That's my motto!' And she had said it again when Maggie had left to return to her guest house behind the Golden Gate Bridge. 'Go for what you want in life!' she had cried, brandishing a mid-morning Cosmopolitan. 'It's the only way!'

Maggie had thought about that enthused declaration as she'd set down the receiver of the telephone in her guest room yesterday afternoon. She'd been talking to Eloise, in Majorca with Lance for half the summer holidays. Eloise had been swimming every day and pony-trekking, she'd told her. 'I've been having an *immense* time!' Eloise had said. 'And Dad's taking me to the waterpark tomorrow!' Maggie was pleased. Lance was a great dad who always made sure his daughter had the best of everything, including his time.

Maggie had fingered the cord of the phone for a while after their call, thinking about Eloise, and about Lance, and about pony-trekking, and about going for what you wanted in life, then she'd grabbed her handbag from the desk and flicked through her small red address book to the Cs.

Ed had answered on the fifth ring.

They had exchanged home telephone numbers in London, back in 1991, before the Japanese restaurant and the camera flashes and page six and Eloise. Maggie had never called him, but she'd written to him when she'd found out she was having a baby – a letter, via his agent, that she hoped he would get, saying she was pregnant with Lance's child and although she and Lance wouldn't be staying together, she was staying in London to have her baby. Ed had replied, also in a letter, saying he was gutted, and he was sorry, that he loved her, and he'd wanted to make it work, but he understood. And Maggie understood he would return to his life as a confirmed bachelor.

For most of these years, there had been no one in her life but Eloise. She had raised her daughter; she had continued to work at *Actually!* and now *Supernova*. She had tried to forget about Ed Cavanagh, who had got back together temporarily with Riva, and then surprised the world by marrying someone called Pamela Bruelle on a ranch in Palm Springs in 1995, moving her into his beloved Mulholland Drive pad.

In 1996, when Eloise was four, Lance had tried to start up a renewed and proper relationship with Maggie, having clearly exhausted all other possibilities and decided he was finally ready to settle down, but Maggie had said no. There was only Eloise. No men. No complications. No drama. Just the Eloise Years. But since the turn of the millennium, Maggie had dated half-heartedly, and only because Simone had made her.

And now she had seen Ed in a movie on a plane.

'Hello,' she'd said, and she was surprised he had answered, as the call was a long shot after all this time (although she knew he had never moved from Mulholland), and he could have been doing any number of other things. Shooting a TV show – he was still a star, but the huge movies had dried up for him now as he neared his fifties, and he had gone back to television. *Professor Clarke* was his last massive celluloid hit. Or learning lines at home, out by his big swimming pool. Or napping after a big Hollywood night. Or not answering his phone because he was Ed Cavanagh, and he didn't have to.

'It's Maggie. Maggie Martin.'

'Hello, Maggie Martin.'

The warmth and familiarity with which he spoke to her threw her. 'I'm in town,' she said, which wasn't true but sounded like something someone might say in a movie, then she added quickly,

'Well, not in town, exactly, but I'm in California. I've been work-ing in San Francisco, and I'm taking a few days' holiday to drive down the coast. I'll be in Monterey tomorrow, and I wondered if, possibly, you could swing some time off and come and meet me?'

She waited, praying he couldn't hear her rapid breathing, and focused on the dark red expanse of the Golden Gate Bridge through her picture window. It was a rare day, free of San Franciscan mist. The Californian sun was bright, the pacific Hockney blue. There was definitely a 'why not?' feeling to the afternoon. A 'maybe' ele-ment to the hour and the light coming in from the window. There was a soft eternity before Ed spoke.

'Let me make a couple of calls,' he said, and the line went dead, and she wondered if this was how it was now, for people like Ed Cavanagh: their communication edited right down, their time so precious and so micro-managed they would hang up without even saying goodbye. She went to the window, convinced he wouldn't be calling back. Maybe he was calling Rupert, his agent, to alert him to a *botherer* – or the Californian police. She did some of her unpacking. She straightened the cheerful counterpane on the bed. She read the hotel brochure about spa packages for the third time. Then Ed called back.

'I can swing it,' he'd said. 'I can be in Monterey at 11 a.m. tomorrow morning. Meet you at the Old Monterey café.'

'Great,' she'd said, 'see you then,' and she'd hung up on him as quickly as he had on her, to stop him changing his mind.

◆ ◆ ◆

The café was cool and light and homespun. It had yellow oak cabi-nets and a burbling coffee machine. Old school Coke bottles lined up on the counter. Haphazard pictures and local artifacts scattered over the walls. A young couple at the table next to the one Maggie

303

sat nervously waiting at were clearly on a first date as they were awkwardly asking what the other did for a living.

Maggie had driven down the Pacific Coast Highway in a rented VW Beetle – playing Elton John, crying to 'Rocket Man' (because she always did), sing-shouting to every word of 'I Guess That's Why They Call It the Blues', and warbling along to 'Philadelphia Freedom' – the sun in her eyes, the sea, to her right, magnificently and dramatically crashing on to deserted beaches and rocky out-crops. She stopped every so often to step out of the Beetle and walk to the edge of the highway and breathe in the view, distracting her-self from the fact she was about to meet up with a man she hadn't seen for twelve years.

The boy at the next table was losing interest, she could tell. He was pretending he desperately needed to look at something on his phone. She'd been there, on dates with uninterested people, or uninterested herself, realising within the first five minutes this was a no-go. She had done it all in the last few years. Speed dating, internet dating, dating in the dark, mixers, blind dates. Searching, searching, but never finding. No one had got to her.

Oh god, but here he was, coming through the open door in jeans and a button-down shirt, Timberlands and a navy beanie hat, pulled down over his curls. The teenager working behind the counter did a vague double take but returned to fiddling with the espresso machine. Maggie stood up, feeling shy, feeling incred-ibly silly.

'You came,' she said, and she walked the three endless steps over to him and kissed Ed on the cheek as he engulfed her in a half-hug, nuzzling his face into her neck when he might not have quite meant to. 'How did you get here?'

He extracted his face. 'Private plane,' Ed muttered, as though he were embarrassed about it, but she knew he wasn't, as he loved all this stuff, the treats he could afford with all his well-invested wealth. The papers said so. 'Then I got a car.'

'How long have you got?' she asked.

'Three nights,' he said.

'Right.' He had an agitated air to him, she thought. He tugged at the rim of the beanie it was way too warm for. Tucked an escaped and greying curl behind his ear. She suddenly felt surprisingly calm. 'Were you shocked to hear from me?'

'Of course I was.'

'And I was shocked you were able to drop everything and come. Amazed, actually.'

When Eloise was born, Ed had sent gifts from America – a blanket, a soft rabbit, a silver rattle. He had phoned Maggie once, when she was seven months pregnant, a muted and poignant call when he said he was happy for her, and he understood why she had to change their plans and stay in London and he said he was happy enough with Riva, as happy as he could be. He was certainly going to give it a go. Like he had with Pamela in 1995. A three-year marriage he had talked about in the press as entering with 'gusto and an open heart'. But recently Ed Cavanagh had been getting a reputation again for being a rolling stone that gathered no moss. He had announced happily in recent months, to those who were still interested, that he was 'resolutely single', with 'no plans for love, not now, maybe not ever'.

'What did you think I would do?' he said, looking at her quiz-zically. 'It's *you*, Maggie.'

He pulled his chair back with a bit of a clatter and it nearly fell over. He fidgeted with the edge of the menu, worrying at its corner with his finger and thumb.

'So, what have you been up to?' she asked.

He grinned, his lips and his teeth and his mouth lovely. There was another escaped curl sticking out from the hem of his beanie.

She had the urge to tuck it back in, but she kept her hands on the table.

'Same old, same old,' he said, and now she grinned, too, as nothing Ed ever did was *same old, same old*, surely? 'How about you?'

'I've just come from interviewing Davinia Regine,' said Maggie. 'She lives in Bodega Bay.'

'Oh, I remember Davinia. How was she?'

'Charming,' said Maggie. 'Brave. Inspiring. She inspired me to call you, actually.'

'Oh, really?'

'Yes, she told me to go for it, so I thought I would.'

'And why did you want to?'

He gave a bashful smile. He flicked at the corner of the menu. It had been so long, she thought. When they had clung on to each other in the night. When they had walked through Regent's Park and smiled at each other over bacon butties in the green cabbies' shelter. She suddenly felt foolish. She was forty-six. Was he disappointed? Was he counting every new wrinkle at the corner of her eyes?

'Let's just call this a whim,' she said.

He laughed and she blushed. He put down the menu. 'So, work's good?' he asked.

'Yes.'

'And how's motherhood?'

'Lovely.'

'Well, it suits you.'

'Am I glowing?' she teased, with a smile. 'I think that's supposed to be at the beginning, not when your kid's a lanky pre-teen.'

'You've always been glowing. Does she have red hair?' asked Ed.

'Yes, red hair. She's beautiful. Would you like to see a picture?'

'Yes, please.'

Maggie took a photograph from her bag and showed him Eloise ice-skating at Somerset House, last Christmas.

'You're right,' he said. 'She *is* beautiful. I'm so pleased for you.'

She was aware Michael was not in Ed's life. It was common knowledge in the press that they were properly estranged, and to her knowledge, too. She didn't dare mention Ed's son to him. She believed *she* had seen him more recently than Ed had – in London. Last year, in fact. It was all quite astonishing, really. How it had happened. How she had bumped into Michael.

'Thank you. How's it all going on *Echo Drive*?' *Echo Drive* was the sequel to *Echo Beach*. In it, Tim O'Shea, the astronaut's son – who had fallen disastrously in love with the BBC secretary's daughter in her faded seaside town – had returned to the States middle-aged and charmingly grumpy. He had then started a new career as a charmingly grumpy middle-aged private detective in San Diego, and was having all sorts of adventures. It wasn't quite hitting the rating heights of *Echo Beach*, but it had done well enough for a second series to be commissioned – not that Maggie was following Ed's career.

'The second season has just wrapped,' Ed replied. 'They're in post-production, that's why I've been able to sneak a few days off. I go in to do some voice stuff for it when I get back. Have you been watching it, *Echo Drive*?' He pulled at his escaped curl, letting it spring back.

'Of course.' She watched it every Thursday night with Eloise. She didn't tell her daughter she once used to date the main character. 'Are you enjoying it? Is it fun?'

'A blast.'

'Fantastic. You always have a blast.'

'I do. I'm very lucky.'

'And do you miss the movies? Or is that a question for your therapist?'

He laughed. 'I don't have one. And no, it's fine to ask me that question. I had a good run. I'm still working. As long as I'm acting, and I'm working, then I'm happy. That's all us actors want to do – work.'

She wondered if he was thinking about Michael. Michael was an actor, too, a theatre actor, doing pretty well for his young age and without relying on his father for contacts, apparently. The surprising evening she'd met him, last year, in the green room of the Old Red Lion Theatre where she'd arranged to see Phillip P. Masterson (a veteran actor she'd once profiled, but who'd made somewhat of a comeback), she almost hadn't gone after an exceptionally busy day and the temptation of an early night. She'd rallied, because she liked Phillip, an irascible old raconteur, who'd invited her to come and see him in a play, and there *Michael* had been, in the programme, on stage, and in the green room.

'This is Michael,' Phillip had said, introducing them. 'He's here on a summer programme. Wasn't he excellent in the part of my young agent? This is Maggie Martin, a writer.'

'Journalist,' corrected Maggie. 'You were fantastic in the play,' she said to Michael. She remembered Ed in *The Dumb Waiter*.

'You're the one who finds the missing people?' Michael replied, shaking her hand like he'd done all those years before. 'The lost and the forgotten. I think I've read some of your work online.'

'You have?' Maggie was surprised. She also wondered how much Ed had ever told Michael about his grandfather, missing person Neville Craddock, then she remembered he would have read about it in the press, over the years. 'I'm amazed! And you might be amazed that we've actually met before,' she told him, as she could see no reason not to. 'I met you in Surrey once. I knew your father.'

Michael smiled wryly, a lopsided smile. 'Not another of my dad's many girlfriends?'

Maggie's heart had given a little start. 'I'm afraid so. Remember the bracelet?' she asked him. She was wearing the same silver bangle with the little blue butterfly. She wore it a lot – and gave it a little jangle.

'No,' he said. 'I don't remember you. But it's really nice to meet you – again – Maggie.'

It felt treacherous of her, but they got on well, chatting there in the green room, and if she were honest with herself, she was curious about Ed's son, now nineteen and with the same curls and the same smile as his father. Michael asked if she'd consider doing some press for him, to raise his profile, and she agreed. They exchanged email addresses. Two weeks later, Maggie did the little piece for him, freelance, and got it into the *Evening Standard* under a pseudonym. And now Michael sometimes wrote to her, keeping her abreast of his career, in case she wanted to write about him again.

'Shall we order?' Ed said.

'Of course.'

They ordered pancakes with maple syrup, and muffins, and coffee. Ed surprised her by barely touching any of his.

'Oh,' she said. 'Are you not hungry?'

'No, it's not that,' he said.

'Are you thinking you shouldn't have come?'

'No, of course not.' His eyes were steady on hers but there was a flicker of disquiet at their edges.

'You can always call back the car, and the plane, and go home.'

'No.' His eyes dropped to the table.

'Come on. What is it?'

'The thing is . . .' He rubbed at his head, before looking up and flashing her an enigmatic, lopsided smile.

'*Ed?*' Alarm bells were going off. Sirens. There was a fire truck outside revving its engines.

'The thing is . . .' he said. 'Well, the thing is, I'm getting married again next week.'

'What?' Maggie's hand froze at her glass of orange juice. 'What about you being "a rolling stone that gathers no moss"?'

Ed looked slightly confused. 'Well, it's all been a big secret,' he said. 'I met her on the set of *Echo*. We've kept things really private. I . . . well, I cancelled my bachelor trip to come here. I was supposed to be going to Palm Springs to play golf.'

'You're not making sense!' Maggie cried. 'You're getting *married?*'

'Yes.'

'Who to?'

'Alexia Bailey.'

'Right. Bloody hell, Ed,' Maggie scoffed. 'How did you manage that? You're still quite attractive and all that, but she's, like, *twenty!*'

Everyone knew who Alexia Bailey was – a willowy twenty-five-year-old up-and-coming actress who'd starred in last year's surprise indie hit at the Sundance Festival, *Indiana Falls*. She had perfect blonde hair, a teeny tiny gym body and a quirky fashion sense, and she obviously thought she'd take her chances with a Hollywood legend with his best days behind him and millions in the bank.

'She likes me,' Ed shrugged, 'and I like her.'

'*Like?*' queried Maggie. 'What about *love?*'

'I don't do "love".'

'This is ridiculous! Did you tell anyone you were coming to meet me? Is she going to find out?'

'I don't think the press will . . .'

'Unless you get spotted.'

'I won't get spotted. No one knows I'm here. And I'm really not that famous any more.'

'You're more famous than anyone else in here.'

Ed looked around him. The girl behind the counter gave him a shy smile.

'She,' said Maggie, '*she* could tell them.'

'Nah,' said Ed, 'I don't think she will. I'll talk to her on the way out.'

Maggie shook her head. 'I think you need to call your pilot and go back!' she exclaimed. 'Go on your stag do, or bucks thing, whatever they call it here. Go and play golf in Palm Springs!'

Ed shook his head. 'No, no,' he said. 'I don't want to. Your call came at the right time, Maggie.'

'Well, what on earth does that mean?'

'You called me at *exactly* the right time. When I'm having . . . doubts, about the whole thing. When I heard your voice, it was as though I was dreaming. You're right, she's twenty-five, I'm forty-nine, it's not love. This could be a huge mistake.'

'Right.' Maggie was *furious*. She placed both hands on her lap and pressed down, trying to contain her anger. 'You're using me then,' she said. 'Using me as a little escape. Some soul-searching time. I don't want any part of this. This is not right.'

'Please,' Ed pleaded, his hands face up on the table. 'Let's just have this time. Three nights, that's what we could have. Three nights. You wanted to see me, didn't you? You called me. Stolen hours, isn't that all we've ever had?'

'I'm not sleeping with you.' What had possessed her to call him? Really, what had it been? Curiosity, nostalgia, hope, reflection, proximity . . . 'You're a prat, Ed.'

'*Prat*.' Ed gave her a droll smile. 'I haven't heard that word in a long time.'

'Well, get used to it again, as it's what you are!' she spluttered. 'I'm stunned, Ed, I don't know what I was thinking, or expecting, but not *this*. Poor Alexia,' she added. 'Poor girl, and all this time – however long it's been – she thought you were being sincere.'

'Please, Maggie,' Ed implored, one hand now gripping the edge of the table, like he was hanging on for dear life. 'Please let me just hole up with you for a few days, figure this out. I won't try to sleep with you, I won't get near you, I promise. Yes, I have run away. Yes, I don't know what I'm doing. But I want to "not know what I'm doing" with *you*. Please, Maggie.'

'It's all gone to your head, Ed,' said Maggie, shaking hers. 'You always said it wouldn't, but it has. The Hollywood drama and the gloss and the throwaway nature of it all. It's got to you. I think it did a really long time ago.'

He took her hand across the table, and she flinched at its firm, tender and familiar touch. His eyes were beseeching. 'It's still me in here, I promise. It's still Ed Craddock, that boy you met on Charlotte Road. Please just give me this time.'

'I don't know.'

'You called me,' said Ed. 'You called me, and I came. Doesn't that mean something?'

'It means you're an idiot and so am I.' She exhaled, long and slow. Why *had* she called him? She saw no future with him, because she was sure there was no room in Ed Cavanagh's life for a Maggie Martin. She saw no future with him because she had her own life, and so did Eloise – happy in England with her school and her friends and her father. And Maggie wasn't on a booty call. She'd called Ed because she'd been compelled to. Because they were in the same country. And she wanted to see him. 'Okay, this is just a holiday,' she said. 'A holiday from our lives. We'll catch up, we'll see some sights, and then we'll go back, okay? You need to go back and sort your life out, Ed.'

'Yes, boss,' Ed said, his green eyes shining.

'And I repeat, I'm *not* sleeping with you.'

'Understood. God, it's good to see you, Maggie,' he said, and he took off his beanie and ruffled his hair and she was already, probably, going back on her word.

Chapter Thirty-Nine

'We've already talked. Lots of times,' Maggie told Baptiste sadly, from that spot on the hill above the cemetery. 'I don't think there's anything more for Ed and I to say.'

She stared down at her feet. They had still not done any kind of interview. They had started conversations, but not finished them. They were done here, like they had been many times before.

'I will return to the car,' Baptist said. 'I have a fence behind one of the bungalows I must fix. I will be back soon.' And to Maggie's surprise, he set off jauntily down the slope.

'What about your leg?' Ed called after him.

'There's nothing wrong with my leg, my friend!' Baptiste called back over his shoulder, as he began to clop down the hill. 'I just wanted to shake things up here a little.'

'Madman,' Ed muttered, shaking his head. He looked angry, but his eyes were still glistening. The sadness from Baptiste's story was written across his face.

They watched in silence as Baptiste made his way down the winding, tumbling slopes of the hillside and to the car. When he had finally lumbered into the driving seat, and had driven away,

Ed said dryly, 'I nearly put my back out lugging that big lummox up this hill, you know.'

'Me, too.' Maggie sat back down on the ridge of grass, leaning back on her elbows. Ed turned away from her, staring out to the sparkling sea for a long time, his hands in his pockets.

'That's so sad, about Baptiste's wife.' He finally turned to her; his face morose. 'Tragic. I can't get that image out of my mind, of him kneeling at her graveside and tending it so carefully. The love and the care.' He sighed. He was silent again for a few moments. 'I do have something to say,' he began, eventually, 'and it's an awfully indulgent thing to say, and pretty maudlin, so bear with me, but I don't think there's anyone who would come to tend to *my* grave on a hillside. No one to refresh my flowers, give me a little sweep. Nobody . . .'

'Don't be silly,' Maggie protested. 'There'd be lots of people—'

'Who? My housekeeper? My driver? My agent? Some *fan* who never knew me?' He scotched his finger against his forehead, like he was trying to disturb the contents in his head. 'Here's something *else* to talk about. Here's something to shock to you.' He took a deep breath and exhaled slowly. 'I'm lonely. There. Is that the kind of thing Bap wants me to say?'

'I don't know.' Maggie was taken aback. Ed looked so distressed; his brows knitted together. His eyes full of pain.

'Well, I am. I'm lonely. I'm *lonely*, goddam it!' He sat down next to her. 'I'm lonely here and I was lonely back home.'

The look on his face was making her heart break. 'Tell me,' she said gently. 'Tell me about it.' And, for the first time on the island, she wasn't thinking about the interview at all.

He put his elbows on his knees and his chin on clenched fists. 'Here? I only have Baptiste, and he's always off fixing something or other, and we're friends, yes, but we don't tell each other everything – as we found out. We don't really *know* each other. It's just been a lovely island fling.' Ed attempted to raise a smile, and Maggie remembered her mistake about Delphine. 'And of course, I have the sea, and the fish, but, still, I'm on my own most of the time.'

'And in LA?'

He sighed again. 'LA . . . Alexia and I lived separate lives for a long time before I left. She'd moved out, we just kept it a secret. And even when we were together, it was all pretty empty. My life there is empty. Yes, I have my fishing and my other hobbies and my house and my truck. I have my career. I have lots of things. I have everything I could ever want for in this world, but not the things that I need, the one thing the humblest person can find in a shack selling tea, or in a mechanic's garage, or out on the street, just like that. Friendship, love, company.' He plucked out a blade of grass from the earth, rubbed it between his finger and thumb, and smiled sadly at her. 'I've lost everything, Maggie. I've *been* so lost. I don't have anyone special in my life, I don't have any friends. I don't have my son. *My son* . . .' Ed's face crumpled, and his voice wavered. He closed his eyes. 'I lost my son,' he said, in barely a whisper. 'I came here to . . .' He sighed again, rubbed a hand over his chin, briefly closed his eyes, then spoke quickly. 'I lost him a long time ago and there's no certainty I'll ever get him back.'

Maggie's heart started to beat in double-time. She had Michael's letter in her bag. She was terrified of making things worse, increasing Ed's pain, but she had to give it to him sometime. She had to give it to him before she left.

'I'm sorry,' was all she could offer. A 'sorry', and the regrets of her own heart. So many of them.

'No, *I'm* sorry!' Ed cried, wretched. 'I've screwed things up. I'm a complete mess. While you're totally together. Look at you! You have your daughter, you're about to retire, you have some hot Turkish man in your bed . . .'

Maggie shook her head. 'No. *No,*' she said, and it was time for her to talk, too. To share her pain, like he had shared his. 'I'm lonely, too,' she whispered. 'In my little flat with my blankets and my books, on my little London street. Eloise is all grown up and living her own life. I have friends, yes, but everyone's so busy. I do my interviews and go to the office, but when I come home, I'm on my own most of the time – apart from when my boyfriend comes over who doesn't really love me and I don't love him, and it all seems so pointless . . .' She trailed off, but then she picked up the trail as she had to walk it. She wanted to reach him, suddenly, to let him know. She owed that much to him. 'Sometimes I don't know who I am any more, or where I'm going. I'm about to retire, because of the age I am, and it's expected, and I keep getting told how excited I should be about it, but I'm not sure I want to, because what exactly is waiting for me?' She drank in his face, his curls, his mouth. She needed him to know. 'I'm not sure anything is except grey days and sad nights, where something's always missing. I'm frightened, Ed, if you want the honest truth,' she said. 'I'm frightened of not filling my days with the job that I love, and I'm frightened of spending the rest of my life alone.'

Ed hadn't taken his eyes from her. They were full of warmth and sadness and empathy. 'We're a couple of lonely old fools,' he said finally, and, just for a second, she thought there was something more in the way he looked at her.

'Absolutely,' she agreed. 'Absolutely.' And then she added, 'I don't know if any happiness is waiting for me, not real happiness, like I've experienced in the past.' She couldn't look at him, but then she did. 'It's the uncertainty that wears you down,' she said. 'About the future. The not knowing if this is *it*. Is this where I'm going? Is this where I'm going to end up?'

'And about the past, too,' he said, and he suddenly looked like he was far away. 'It's the not knowing.'

He focused on her again and she was drowning in his green eyes, crinkled at their edges by the sun and the passing years, but still so familiar to her. She could feel her pulse drumming in her veins, trying to imagine what he would say or do next. They had both unfolded a worn corner of their heart's map to each other. Now, they could either unfold a further piece, letting each other trace their finger along their borders, or tuck that corner back in.

'You said once,' she ventured, 'that you were happy about becoming famous so your dad would know where to find you.'

'We weren't supposed to be talking about my dad.'

'I'm feeling brave.' She smiled. She wanted him to lay out the worn map of his heart, so she could lay out hers. 'Do you still feel that about fame? That it keeps you visible?'

'Is this the interview?'

'No. But I want to know. Do you like to be seen? Do you want people to always know where to find you?'

Ed looked at her. 'Honestly?' he said. 'Yes. Recently I have felt like I might disappear without fame. That it is holding me up. Filling in my blank spaces. Maybe it always has. I don't want to blame the man I am, the man I have been, on my past – as what kind of man would that make me? – but I wonder how much it affected me, my dad disappearing, then being thrust into fame and wealth. How angry it made me. How lost . . .' He shook his head. 'But now I've come here, yes, I'm lonely, but I don't need it, that validation. Particularly from strangers. I just need it from those I love.'

Maggie nodded. 'I understand.' She had just asked one of her pre-planned questions, but it had not been the answer she'd been expecting.

'Your career was about your mum, wasn't it?'

'Yes,' she replied. 'It has been. For me, too, of course – I've loved every minute of it, but hers was cut short because of me and I felt I had to do something really big and brilliant to honour her. To really do her proud.'

'I see that now,' said Ed. 'And I'm sure you really did make her proud.'

Maggie nodded. 'I think I did. Families, eh?' She shrugged. They both fell silent for a while, the sea a sparkling jewel laid out majestically before them. The sky a rich, cloudless blue.

'Michael . . .' Ed finally said. 'The olive branch that I sent him . . .'

'Yes?'

'It was an old photo album, full of photos of Michael as a baby and toddler.'

'Your photo album?'

'Yes, I've always had it. Right from the start. There was a picture of him in a pram at the bottom of his mother's garden in Eagle Rock, when he was first born.' Maggie nodded; she remembered Ed's jubilant description of that, years ago. 'Me holding him. One of him digging in the sand on Ventura Beach when he was a toddler, covered in the stuff. Us fishing together, at the end of Santa Monica Pier.' He smiled wistfully. 'There were a few of those, all Polaroid photographs. I got a *real* fisherman to take one of both of us, and Michael went all shy. He was wearing a red t-shirt and squinting into sun, his hair in his eyes. I always loved those photos of us fishing. And there were others, up until Michael was about five, when things were still good between us. When he wasn't old enough to realise what an arsehole I was.'

'Ed . . .'

'I left it on his doorstep in Eagle Rock, with a little note . . . before I came here. It was my message in a bottle. I hope he received it. And well, Maggie, I need to tell you that . . .'

Maggie had been listening intently, her nerve endings standing to attention. 'Oh, Ed,' she said, her voice trembling. 'I have a message in a bottle from *Michael*.'

And she turned and reached into her bag.

Chapter Forty

They arrived at a restaurant called Verbena, in Big Sur, just in time for lunch. Maggie had read about Verbena in her California guidebook on the plane over (when not watching Ed's movies) and told Ed about it on the way down there, as they'd enjoyed the VW Beetle's sound system and he'd sung along to Elton John too. Elevated above the coast, Verbena was a two-storey open-air café and restaurant with spectacular views, a relaxed vibe and amazing food, so the guidebook had said. Maggie parked the Beetle in the dusty car park out front and Ed had looked at her and remarked, 'Nice driving, Maggie. Anyone would think you'd been cruising the Pacific Coast Highway for years.'

'Sign me up as your next stunt driver,' quipped Maggie. 'If you allow women.'

'I'd sign you up as anything,' Ed replied.

She ignored his flirtatious tone. Yesterday, they had stayed in the café in Monterey for another two hours, drinking coffee and tearing a shared muffin into tiny pieces. They had walked down to the beach and watched the waves crash on to the shore from a striped blanket that Ed had bought from a little shop. He'd tried to sit a little too close to her and had made a joke about *From Here to Eternity* and Maggie had said, 'Not likely, buster! Keep your distance.' Then they'd laughed as Ed had leapt from the blanket, rolled up his trouser legs and cavorted in the surf like a ridiculous pony.

'Eat your heart out, Burt Lancaster!' he had cried.

Later, they'd booked into a small hotel room, twin beds, Ed jokingly asking Maggie if he wanted her to measure the distance between them, to make sure it was enough, and they ordered clam chowder, which they ate in dressing gowns. They had watched a little telly. They had sipped whiskey toddies and hadn't touched each other, the thick black curtains shut against the world but not thick enough to drown out the sound of the big waves crashing noisily on to the beach all night, or the voice in Maggie's head that asked her what on earth they were doing.

'Wow,' Maggie said now, as they walked up the steps to the raised red resin floor of the Verbena, laid out with a dozen tables and chairs. 'Look at this!'

The morning mist clinging to the coast had lifted. A solitary bird was stationary on the railing, nonchalantly overlooking the plunge of rocks and trees to the sea. Ed and Maggie took a table next to the railing and ordered eggs Benedict from a cute serving station under a thatched roof.

Their young waiter – hipster goatee and batik trousers – brought them their coffee.

'Hey, man,' he said, as he set a steaming mug of coffee down before Ed. 'I don't want to bug you, but didn't you use to be that movie star, Ed Cavanagh?'

'Yes, I did,' said Ed with a knowing smile, pulling down the rim of his beanie.

'And now you're in that detective show? In San Diego. *Echo* something?'

'*Echo Drive.*'

'That's it! Man, my mom loves that show!'

'Great! A lot of the moms do.'

'You just on a little vacation here at Big Sur?'

'That's right.'

'Well, that's great. Thanks for dropping by Verbena.'

'It's wonderful,' said Ed. 'Thank you.'

The waiter nodded and loped off. Some music started playing – pan pipes doing Nirvana. They smiled at each other.

'Cute,' said Maggie.

'Kitsch,' agreed Ed.

'Told you you'd be recognised. Are you worried?'

'Not really.'

'Any more thoughts about what you're going to do about the whole marriage thing?'

'Not yet.'

They'd avoided talking about it yesterday afternoon on the beach, and last night in the hotel. But it was always there. The reason Ed was here.

'Why did you call me?' he asked her. He laid down his knife and fork. A cloud moved across the searing sun and hovered for a while before continuing on its way.

She shrugged. 'I acted on impulse. I watched one of your movies on the plane and you wore some really nice jumpers.'

He laughed.

'Why did *you* come?' she asked.

'I wanted to see you. I was so surprised to get your call, but at the same time it felt so natural to hear your voice. And it's been a long time,' he added. 'I just wanted to see you.'

'And what do you *think* of me?' she risked asking. 'These days?'

'What do I *think* of you?' He looked surprised. 'I still like you,' he said, a gentle smile playing on his lips. 'I think I'll always like you.'

'I'm not sure it's enough.'

'Why not?'

'Let me count the ways.' She counted off points on her fingers. 'You're getting married. You live in another country. You're a movie star. You've got a terrible singing voice . . .'

Ed laughed. 'You couldn't ever see yourself living in another country?'

'Not this one,' she replied, not that she would ever move Eloise away from Lance, anyway.

'Why not?'

'Mostly, because I wouldn't subject my daughter to it. Not California. Not Los Angeles.'

'Oh.' The mood suddenly shifted. 'You think it's a life I've *subjected* my son to?'

'That's different,' she replied. 'I just wouldn't choose to.' He stared at her. 'It's too much, your life. Too much glitz, too much glamour.' She wanted to add, 'And not good for a kid,' but the mood was already shaky.

'What are we doing here, Mags?' he asked, a little downcast. 'What do you think about *me*?'

'*Everyone* thinks the same about you. You're Ed Cavanagh.'

'What about the *real* me?' he asked quietly. 'What about him? The man that's sitting in a restaurant in Big Sur with you—'

'Everything okay with your food?' Their waiter was back at their table.

'Great, thanks,' they replied in unison.

'Great! Hey, there's a man outside. Says he's arranged to meet you here, Mr Cavanagh. I don't know if he's just a crank, or what you want me to do . . .'

'No, it's fine,' said Ed. 'I *am* meeting him. It's my son. Can you tell him I'll be down in five minutes?'

'Sure.'

'*Michael* is here?' Maggie was flabbergasted.

'Sorry, I really didn't think he'd show up, that's why I didn't tell you. He's in a little play in San Francisco. I phoned him this morning and he's driven down the coast.' He looked excited. 'Shall we go downstairs?' They hadn't finished their food, but Maggie could see Ed was itching to go.

'Well, *I* don't need to see him,' she blustered. 'I can just stay up here, let you guys get on with it . . .'

'No, no, come,' said Ed, leaving some cash on the table. 'I might need backup.'

They walked down the steps to the car park, Ed buoyant, Maggie reluctant; her heart hammering with her secret. She had no idea what she was going to say or do.

Michael was standing by an old model sports car in shorts, t-shirt and a red baseball cap, talking to someone on his mobile phone.

'Yes, yes,' he was saying. 'Three weeks of rehearsal and then Press Night on the Thursday.' He clocked Ed and Maggie, his eyes widening in surprise. 'Gotta go, pal,' he said. 'I'll call you back tonight. Dad,' he said coldly, walking towards them across the sandy gravel. 'And *Maggie*, what the hell are you doing here?' he asked her, his voice warmer, but surprised, as he approached her for a hug.

Maggie hugged him back, cringing and terrified. What on earth was Ed going to say about her knowing the grown-up Michael?

'What's going on?' Ed looked incredibly confused.

'We met accidentally, at a play in London,' Maggie explained quickly. 'I did a little write-up on Michael for the *Evening Standard*. We've stayed in contact.'

'In contact, how?' Ed was frowning, his eyes glowering at her. 'Email contact.'

'Right. How nice. And did you remember Maggie from Surrey?' Ed asked Michael, mock-genially.

'No. Hey, how about, "How are you, son? Good to see you"?'

'It *is* good to see you,' said Ed tersely, but glancing furiously at Maggie. 'Thank you for driving here.' He painted a smile back on his face for Michael. 'Do you want to go upstairs and get a coffee?'

'No, I'm good,' said Michael. 'I only came to get the money.'

'But this morning on the phone you said you wanted to catch up, that we could chat, have a drink . . .' Ed was no longer angry but crestfallen.

'I lied,' Michael snapped. 'It seems I'm really good at saying I'll do things that I don't have any intention of doing, just like you. Do you have a cheque for me?'

'That's all you came for? I could have posted that to you.'

'It's a beautiful part of the state.' Michael shrugged nonchalantly.

'You wanted to torture me.'

'Hey, well, if the shoe fits.' Michael held out his hand, as though for the cheque.

Maggie wanted to shrink away, slink back up to the café, hide in the Beetle – anything. She was seeing the famed Ed and Michael Gray-Cavanagh estrangement at close quarters, and it was not pleasant.

'What does that mean?' Ed snarled. 'I'm not sure Maggie wants to hear all this.'

'No, I don't,' she agreed. It was hot. The sun was in her eyes from a winking beam between two of the mighty trees huddled together at the edge of the car park, and she wanted to get out of here, but Michael was twenty years old and as mad as hell, apparently.

'There was another stupid article about us last night in the *LA Times*,' Michael snapped. 'By some disgusting hack who appears to be so much on your side, I wondered if you'd paid him. How "sources" say it's been blown out of all proportion, our relationship. That you were a good father, that you *never* let me down, or broke promise after promise, never doing what you'd say you'd do. Or overcompensated for the lack of time you spent with me by lavishing me with money and ridiculous gifts. That you *did* attempt to shield me from the paparazzi and not have cameras in my face every fucking minute when I *had* gone out with you anywhere. That the women – *all* those women – was an exaggeration, just a bit of harmless fun.' He raised his shoulders theatrically. 'No effect *whatsoever* on a sensitive little boy who had no clue how to handle any of it . . .' Michael took a breath. 'Who was the "source", Dad? Was it *you?*'

'No!' spluttered Ed. 'I don't know anything about that article! I promise you. It's probably just the usual made-up bullshit. A writer trying to make a name for themselves . . .'

'Whatever! It's not always made-up bullshit, though, is it, Dad? These articles, over the years. All those ones about you and me. They were all pretty much true.' He turned his baseball cap around with a laboured sigh. 'You can lavish me with more money now,' he said, holding out his hand again. 'Give me the goddam cheque!'

Maggie shrank backwards as Ed – furious – dug his wallet out of his inside jacket pocket, opened it and prised a folded chequebook from one of its compartments.

'Do you have a pen?' he asked Maggie.

She rummaged in her bag, stepping forward again to hand him a black biro.

Ed scribbled furiously on one of the cheques and handed it to Michael. Michael folded it and stuffed it in the back pocket of his shorts.

'I'd go to the ends of the earth for you, son.' Ed looked done in, and very, very sad.

'I doubt that very much.' Michael patted the pocket with the money in twice. 'You're very happy exactly where you are. Thanks for the *cash*, Dad. Nice to see you again, Maggie,' he added, giving her a swift kiss on the cheek, and he strode over to his car.

'I would give it all up for you!' Ed shouted, as Michael got into his sports car. 'Hollywood, fame, all of it! I'd travel to the ends of the earth, live in a shack, if it would prove how much you mean to me!'

'Like *your* dad did when he ran off to a desert island?' Michael mocked, his mouth curling into a snarl as he spat out the words.

'That was just a childish dream!' Ed looked lost, standing in the car park without his father or his son. 'And no, Michael, because I would always, always come back.'

Michael turned, framed in the door of the car he was about to disappear into and drive far away in. He rubbed at the top of his head, dispersing the curls. 'Goodbye, Dad,' he said, and slammed the door.

Chapter Forty-One

Bewildered, Ed stared at the letter in his hands, then ran his finger along its seal and tore it open. He pulled out a postcard and another piece of paper, which fluttered to the grass.

Ed held the postcard up to her. Written on it in scrolly handwriting was, 'Maybe we could talk?'

Maggie picked up the scrap of paper from the grass and held it up to Ed in return. It was a silky piece of paper, a small square, dated digitally at the top. It was the blurry monochrome of an ultrasound baby scan photo.

'What the . . .?' Ed looked utterly dumbfounded.

'I think Michael is trying to tell you something, Ed,' said Maggie, and they both broke into delighted smiles.

'A baby!' cried Ed, shaking his head in disbelief. 'I'm going to be a grandfather?'

'It looks that way!' Maggie exclaimed. 'Oh, Ed, this is amazing!'

Ed took the scan photo carefully from her and studied it intently, tracing his finger over the shape of the baby. 'I can't believe this!' He shook his head. 'A baby, a baby. And Michael sent this to me. He wants me to have it. He wants to talk.'

'Wow.' Maggie smiled, tears in her eyes. 'That photo album must have really worked some magic. What did you say in your note?'

Ed hesitated. 'I said I was sorry. I said something like, "I would do anything to get back to where we once were". I told him how excited I'd been when he was born. How I'd wanted to be the best father, but I'd got it badly wrong. How proud I was of him. I said I wanted the opportunity to prove I can do what I say I'm going to do . . .'

Maggie thought of the letters he had once written to her about Michael's arrival into the world. His excitement. 'It was obviously a very heartfelt note,' she said. She gave him a warm smile, thrilled at his excitement. 'And then there was the pregnancy – I wonder if Leoni had any hand in sending you this scan, too,' she added. She remembered the photo she had seen in the newspaper from Michael's wedding. Leoni's hand on a dejected Ed's arm.

'Maybe,' Ed said. 'She *was* kind to me. And I know she's very close to her own father . . .'

'And maybe that theatre manager blabbed to Michael about the donations.'

'Perhaps he did . . . Oh, Maggie!' He shook his head again in disbelief and looked out across the water. The tiny crests of waves, glistening in the bright sunlight, winked back at him. 'He might be able to forgive me. He might be able to have me back in his life.' His voice seemed far away. 'He knows what I've done for him. He knows . . .'

'About the donations?'

Ed looked wistfully out to the horizon. He spoke to the ocean and not to her. 'He knows I gave up Hollywood and came to live in a shack.'

And he rubbed the curls at the top of his head just the way she had seen his son once do.

Forgotten images arrived, unannounced, in Maggie's head. A red baseball cap. A sports car. Snatches of words from long ago drifted to her, too. Words shouted in a Californian car park from a desperate father to his angry son. 'I'd give Hollywood up for you! I'd journey to the ends of the earth!' or words to that effect.

She remembered.

'You came to Mémoire for Michael,' she said slowly. 'That's what you've done, isn't it? You left Hollywood and came here, to live in a shack. To show him you could leave it behind, that life. Because you had once told him you could, and he didn't believe you. Because you finally wanted to do something you *said* you'd do.'

Ed turned to look at her and nodded. He had once made a despairing kind of promise to Michael outside the Verbena restaurant in Big Sur, and now he had despaired enough of his life to fulfil it. She could see that. 'Yes,' he said, but his eyes looked a little sad, a little uncertain, 'that's what I've done. Thank you, Maggie. Thank you for bringing his letter to me.'

'You're welcome.' She could see that world opening out for Ed behind his eyes. The hope the contents of this envelope had brought him. The message that things weren't futile, or irrevocable, after all.

'Maggie . . .' Ed took her hand and looked into her eyes. She gazed back into his, those green eyes she had known so well and had loved for so long. 'Maggie. This means so much to me. Michael sending this. You bringing it to me.' He was still holding the scan printout. 'I never imagined things would play out like this. I never thought – I mean, I feel that, since you've been here, I've . . .' He faltered a little.

'Yes?' she asked him, her breath quickening, and she was almost lost in that moment, lost to him again. His eyes, his face, his smile. The Ed she had known and the Ed she had rediscovered here on this island, but she wasn't quite lost, not completely, as she knew it was not really hers, this miraculous moment at the top of a hill and looking down on a sea that now held such promise . . .

'Are you going to call him?' The question jolted, but this moment was Ed and Michael's. It wasn't hers and Ed's, even if she might want it to be.

Ed blinked. 'What do you mean? How can I call him? We're on a remote island in the middle of nowhere without Wi-Fi or a phone signal.'

'Olly's has that telephone.'

'Olly's has a *telephone*?'

'Yes, out the back, by the Ladies. I saw it last night. If it works . . .'

'Really? I can call him?'

'Do you have his number?'

'Yes, I know his number. I've always known it.' Ed leapt up; excited, agitated. 'He didn't even have to find out where I was!' he exclaimed, looking back to the shimmering horizon, the sun in his eyes. 'He sent me the letter anyway . . .'

Maggie's heart stilled in her chest. Something else was dawning on her like the early morning sun over the ocean.

'Your plan to come here?' she asked carefully. 'Why didn't you just call Michael, before you left, and tell him where you were going?'

'That wouldn't have worked.' Ed stood still. He answered her steadily, but he didn't quite meet her eye. 'He'd have thought I'd be back in a week, like everyone did. He wouldn't have cared.'

'Why didn't you tip someone off in the press, so they would find you and report your whereabouts – so Michael would *know*?' Her pulse beat through her body while she waited for his answer.

'I didn't want to tip anyone off,' Ed replied, and now his eyes found hers and didn't stray. 'I wanted to be *found*. Can we go?'

She let him take her hand and she let herself be swept down the chalky steps and the wild vanilla slopes of the hill, the long and winding way down to ground level, but she knew the truth. She knew why Ed had sent the postcard to her, the *clue*, by slow ship across the seas.

He'd sent it so she would come for him, because she was the only one to know about Mémoire. He'd sent it so she would find him on the island, after three long months – long enough for the world to really start to wonder about him, and Michael, too. He sent it because he knew she wouldn't be able to resist the ultimate 'missing person' story. And once she was on the island, Ed had stalled for time with the tour; let her paint a picture of him, with the photos she had snapped of his simple life here, and the words she would write in the piece for *Supernova* that would let Michael know that his father had finally done what he'd said he would do.

When they arrived at the bottom of the hill Baptiste's car was rumbling to a standstill.

'Are you finished here?' he asked them, winding down his window.

'Yes,' said Ed, looking nervously at Maggie.

'*Yes,*' she agreed.

She climbed into the back seat of the car. Ed asked Baptiste to head to Olly's, his excitement undisguised. As they set off, the sun was high in the sky above them and the coconut air freshener swung back and forth like a ticking pendulum.

Chapter Forty-Two

1 P.M., 14 AUGUST 2003

Pismo Beach, halfway between Monterey and Los Angeles, was very pretty. The sky was a chalky grey-blue. The sea – a wide, clear expanse of it – was a pale slate green. They drove along the seafront, where people lounged in an outside restaurant, eating cracked crab with wooden forks. And past stalls selling surf t-shirts and fresh-water taffy, and the rickety-looking affair of the pier, spindly on a Kerplunk of wooden legs.

'Not a patch on Southend Pier,' remarked Ed, and Maggie smiled weakly at the man with the curls at the wheel of her Beetle, driving along the Pismo Beach esplanade and drumming on the steering wheel with his thumb as he sang 'Benny and the Jets'.

Maggie and Ed had spent the night before in a yellow guest house in Carmel. Accessed from the Pacific Coast Highway by a winding dirt track road and nestled among a gloam of huddling cedar trees, it had a cosy sitting room – squishy sofas, sheepskin throws, a little log burner with a pyramid of pale logs stacked next to it – and wooden decking out the back with two striped yellow sun loungers, overlooking the sea.

It also had a strained atmosphere as Ed was still angry with Maggie about Michael.

'I can't believe you didn't tell me you'd met him in London,' Ed had said, over half-eaten steaks and fully drunk glasses of red wine, sitting outside on the striped sun loungers. 'And wrote an article on him – and been in *email* correspondence with him!'

'I'm sorry,' she'd said, for the hundredth time. They were watching the sun set quite spectacularly over the ocean, in his-and-hers cable-knit cardigans they'd found in one of the wardrobes. 'I bumped into him, that's all that happened. He asked me to write a piece on him. The emailing has just been professional enquiry and small talk, really.'

'You could have said "no" when he asked you to write about him.'

'He's your son,' Maggie said simply. All she could think about was Ed's face when Michael gave her a hug in the car park. How shocked he was. 'I can keep saying that I'm sorry about it, I can keep saying that it happened by chance. Can't you see it as a good thing, maybe, that I'm in contact with him? That I know how he's doing?'

'The inside track? No, because I'm jealous,' admitted Ed. 'I'm jealous as all hell because you have a relationship with him, when I don't. You saw how bad it was today, you know how it is.'

'It *is* pretty bad.' She ran her finger around the edge of her huge wine glass. 'If I've made it worse, I'm sorry. I never meant to hurt you.'

Maggie thought of Eloise. Of her relationship with her own mother. She would do anything for her daughter, like her mum had done for her. But she found it easy. It had come easy to her, and so very hard to Ed.

They brokered an uneasy truce. They managed to limp on to other subjects. At midnight, they'd drained the remainder of a second bottle and retired to separate bedrooms, but a little while later Ed had come and stood in Maggie's doorway.

'Can I come and get in the other bed?' he asked, gesturing to the second of twin beds.

'Why, are you lonely?' she asked.

'I'm lonely without you. Can I?'

'Okay,' she replied, and he'd turned off the landing light and got into the bed, and this time, unlike last night, he'd stretched his arm out from under the blankets towards her, his fingers gently curved in the near-dark. She'd stretched out her own, to meet them, and they'd held hands across the space between them as the sea outside the little yellow house had rumbled its nightly roar and crashed on to the shore like it had all the days before them, and would continue to, all the days after they had gone.

The uneasy couple, still in a truce, found the hotel in Pismo Beach – the Pismo Club – two blocks back from the seafront and parked in the small adjacent car park. They dropped off their luggage and then got in the car again and drove to Avila Beach, which the bellboy had recommended to them as a smaller, even quainter place to visit, and they walked on the near-deserted beach up to a Russian doll miniature of Pismo's spindly pier.

'The beaches here!' exclaimed Maggie, looking around her. 'Can you imagine a beach like this in England? It would be *rammed*. There's just miles and miles of nothing here, untouched. It's amazing.'

'Far from those painful stones of Southend,' said Ed, and *damn*, she thought, all roads led back there, to that town, and always would with her and Ed, so she changed the subject and they talked about the cute weatherboard shops here at Avila Beach in ice cream, pastel shades. They explored them: cafés and gift shops and little places selling fudge, and the doorway to a tiny and overly pretty lawyer's office, probably the loveliest place in which the law has ever been followed.

They got an ice cream at a small artisan café and they sat outside it, on a low pistachio wall.

Ed's phone rang. He flicked it open and answered it.

'Yeah, yeah . . .' He stood up and turned his back to the breeze whipping freshly off the beach. 'Is it about my watch? Oh, okay . . . what a pain . . . okay, I'll call them when I can. Bye. Bye.'

'Who was that?' Maggie asked, when he'd slipped the phone into his pocket and sat down.

'That was Erica, Rupert's PA. The UK police have been trying to get hold of me, apparently. They called Reece's PA, Nancy, the temporary girl. I think it's about my watch that got stolen last time I was in London. It's been like Chinese whispers. They have a number for me to call, but I don't know why someone else at the agency can't deal with it. I've referred Erica back to *my* PA.'

'Oh yes, the little people can sort it out,' said Maggie teasingly. 'Was it a nice watch?'

'It was. You like teasing me,' he added, placing a gentle hand on her knee.

'I do,' she agreed.

'You're the only one to see through this crap.'

'I'm sure I'm not the *only* one . . .' And she knew he didn't see it as crap, this life. He loved it.

'I think you are. You look gorgeous by the way.'

'I'm windswept and a tiny bit sunburnt.'

'I think you're stunning.'

'This sounds dangerously like flirting. You're just having some time out, remember? We're just sitting on a wall . . .'

'Why did you call me?' he asked again.

'Haven't we already talked about this?'

'You said something about jumpers. You didn't give me a straight answer. Got one for me now?'

'I was curious,' she said.

'Always so curious, Maggie . . . it'll . . .'

'Be the death of me?'

'No, don't say that.'

'Well, it killed the *cat* . . .'

'No, I was going to say, it'll be a sad day when you're not.'

'I don't think so. I think it can get me into all sorts of trouble. When did you lose your watch?' she asked him, trying to change the subject. 'You were in London recently?'

He looked sheepish. 'A couple of months ago.'

'Ah, still no desire to look me up, then? Well, I feel slightly foolish,' she said flippantly, 'since I've just done *exactly* that with you!'

'You have Michael to meet up with in London.'

She pulled a stray wisp of hair off her face. 'Touché.'

'Alexia was with me,' he said. 'I'm sorry.'

'*Alexia*. Honestly, when I think about it, I'm pretty angry on her behalf,' she said, and she *was* angry, suddenly. 'You show up. You're getting married, you're *not* getting married . . . It's not good, Ed. You need to sort this out as soon as you get home. You owe her not to be messed around like this. Has fame screwed you up so badly you just trample all over people's feelings?'

'Whoa.'

'Yes, *whoa* . . .'

'You're right,' he said. 'I need to sort this out as soon as I get back.' And she still didn't know what he was going to do about anything. 'Fame . . .' he said. 'Fame's a funny thing.'

'Tell me. Tell me what's funny about it.'

Ed sighed. He looked across to the shoreline and the breaking waves. 'Fame can give you so many things but can never heal the holes in your heart. They're always there, the missing spaces, the unanswered questions. Fame can help you pretend they don't matter, but they always do. *That's* the funny thing about fame.'

'Your dad,' Maggie said simply.

'Yes, my dad. You know, something I never told you . . . I hired a private investigator, years ago, at the end of the eighties, actually. To have a dig around in Southend. See what they could find. They found nothing.'

'Really?' Guilt started pulsing through her. 'I'm so sorry.'

'Thank you,' Ed said sincerely. 'What was I expecting, really?' She nearly told him, right there and then, of her own detective work, of the man in the grey bus driver's suit, and the probable affair between Ed's dad and his neighbour, Denise, but she knew nothing for certain, and she didn't want to hurt him. 'It remains an unanswered question,' he added. 'And then there's you.'

'Me?'

He turned to her. His curls were being battered by the wind, and Maggie would have laughed at how they were tickling his face, if she hadn't felt so sad. '*You're* an unanswered question,' he said. 'Will we always have it, do you think? This . . . pull between us?'

'Sometimes I'm really afraid that we will,' she replied, and she wondered if it was enough for him, this stolen time. Or enough for her.

'And where are we going next?' he asked.

'On this little Californian road trip?' This melancholy little trip, going nowhere, and teetering on a very unstable path? Or did he mean something bigger? She should never have called Ed. She should have resisted. 'Venice Beach,' she replied, deciding to take his question literally. 'There's somewhere I've booked to stay before I fly out from LA. Do you want to come with me, or do you want to go home?'

He tucked a strand of red hair behind her ear. 'I want to come with you.'

Chapter Forty-Three

Baptiste parked in the clearing behind Olly's in a shower of dust. He had driven with great purpose, bumping along the tracks of the island exuberantly and bouncing his passengers off their seats. He had been absolutely delighted when Ed had told him about the baby scan.

'*Mon dieu*, it is a miracle, Mr Ed!' he had cried, raising his cap in salute. 'A baby and a new grandfather!'

'Come in with us!' Ed entreated him, as they all got out of the car. 'Come in and wait with Maggie while I make this call.'

'Who said I was coming in to wait?' Maggie asked, standing by the car.

Ed looked at her. 'What do you mean?' he asked sheepishly, but she knew he understood exactly what she was about to say.

'You used me,' she said. Anger and sadness pulsed around her body. 'You sent me that postcard so I would come and find you. So I would trail you around this island, taking cute photos of you outside your little shack and with your tortoises, and then write a piece that would let Michael know you had given up Hollywood for him. You planned it all, leaving him the photo album and then mailing me the postcard, by ship, so I wouldn't get it for, say, three months?' She nodded. 'Yes, three months was long enough, wasn't it, to prove you *meant* this to your son. And then have me turn up and tell the world all about it.'

'Used you?'

'Yes.'

Ed's face had clouded over. His eyes glinted at her. 'I could say you used *me*,' he countered. 'You were coming here to do an interview in order to launch a magazine. To get a big scoop. Go out with a bang on your retirement. To expose me. Write some kind of cautionary tale, I bet, how Hollywood has destroyed me.' His eyes had been flashing but now they softened. 'Does it matter, now, truly? After these past hours together? Does it matter now I've received Michael's letter?' His eyes searched hers. She had no idea what he was looking for.

'No,' she replied truthfully. 'No, none of it matters.'

'I need to phone my son.'

She let herself be ushered into Olly's, which was very quiet, just a couple of people relaxing over a late lunch. She found herself sitting down at a round raffia table by the bar.

'I'll be right back,' Ed said to Maggie. 'Please don't go anywhere,' he pleaded. 'Get yourselves a drink. *Please*. I'll be right back. Can I use my American Express card for the phone?' he asked Baptiste, about to dash up the little corridor to the Ladies.

Baptiste nodded.

Ed disappeared. Baptiste and Maggie looked at each other. Baptiste raised his right eyebrow a little and shook his head.

'What would you like to drink?' she asked him numbly.

'You are sad,' he replied.

'Sad?' She attempted a little laugh. 'No, do I look sad? Ed is about to reunite with his son. This is a marvellous moment.'

'I'm sorry things did not work out.' Baptiste took off his cap and laid it on the table.

'It doesn't matter.' She echoed Ed's words. 'I'd decided not to do the interview any more, anyway.' Baptiste was staring at her, an odd look on his face. Sorrowful, full of empathy, like he knew her, somehow, inside out. And maybe he did. Maybe it was written all over her face. She realised he had never known about the interview. She'd abandoned it somewhere at the top of a hill. 'Actually, I'm going to go,' she said, standing up. 'If you don't mind, Baptiste. My boat arrives in a few hours, and I need to pack.' There was nothing to pack; she hadn't been here long enough. 'Can you tell Ed that I'm sorry, but I couldn't wait?'

'I can tell him,' Baptiste replied.

'Thank you. And thank you for the tour. It was really lovely.'

'You are welcome, Maggie.'

On impulse, she bent down and gave him a kiss on his cheek. His moustache tickled the corner of her mouth. 'Goodbye, Baptiste,' she said, and he grabbed her hand for a moment and gave it a gentle squeeze before letting it go.

She walked out of Olly's, her bag over her shoulder and tears in her eyes. Her journey was over, like it had been so many times before. She should have known that the past doesn't forgive and forget. That the present can be a lonely place. And that the future wasn't a place you can sail to in a little boat, landing upon its shores and stepping out on to the sand, expecting it to be paradise.

Chapter Forty-Four

2 P.M., 15 AUGUST 2003

Venice Beach Boardwalk was mobbed. It was a shifting, roll-ing, criss-crossing mesh of rollerbladers and walkers and aimless wanderers and posturing men in muscle vests under a blistering Californian sun. To Maggie and Ed's right was a jumble of colour-ful stalls selling t-shirts and baseball hats and canvas art, plus a gaggle of medical marijuana dispensaries and tattoo shops. To their left were street art displays and the beach. Spirits and occasional tempers were high. A fight broke out amongst the scuffling crowd as they walked – two muscular women in neon sportswear – but was moved over to an alley between two shops, away from the gad-ding crowd.

'It's much warmer here,' Maggie commented.

'It's always warm in Los Angeles, baby,' Ed quipped. He was wearing his beanie again, despite the heat, and a pair of black Aviators. They both felt tired, despite an early night at Pismo Beach last night. They'd had dinner at the hotel, then retired to separate bedrooms, no twin beds. Maggie had pleaded a headache, which was true. She'd still had that melancholy feeling; she still hadn't felt great about what they were doing.

'How's the ice cream going down?' Ed asked her, as they walked past a huge floor display of street art.

'Good, thanks. Mint choc chip is always a winner.'

Ed was making fast work of butter pecan; he was almost down to the waffle cone already. He boyishly bit off the bottom and greedily sucked some ice cream through it.

'That's such a British thing to do,' she remarked.

Ed shrugged, licking a dollop of ice cream off his bottom lip. 'You can take the boy out of Southend . . .'

'You're nearly home,' she said, taking another crispy bite of her waffle cone. 'Los Angeles. You'll be home tomorrow.'

'And so will you. I feel a bit sad about that, Maggie, this being our last day.'

'Because you have to face the music?' she asked. 'With Alexia?'

'Because I have to face my *own* music.'

They stopped by the edge to the beach, a graffitied pillar just beyond them. Maggie was tempted to take a photo of it. She'd already taken a few, at the beach.

'What did we think would happen on this trip?' Ed asked.

'Nothing. Everything,' she said vaguely, staring at the pillar and taking in all the colours. She was beginning to detach from him now, from *this*. She had to. 'I don't know. But it doesn't matter, does it?'

'I think it does matter. Look at me, Maggie.' He took off his sunglasses and she turned to face him, dazzled by his eyes, his face, the whole of him she soon had to leave. 'I was awake half the night, deciding what I'd like to do with the rest of my life. Wondering how to get you into it. Wondering how we could ever make it work between us, and, well, as a start, I'm going to call Alexia as soon as I get home tomorrow and . . . Oh damn!'

Ed's phone was ringing again, in his pocket.

'Tamsin,' he said, pulling it out. 'My PA. I'd better take this. Sorry.'

Real life was clattering towards them, Maggie thought, ready to take them back. Ed rotated slightly from her, but she could hear every word.

'Hi, Tamsin. Yes, good thanks . . . Tomorrow, yes, yes . . . Yes, that's right . . . *Essex* police? . . . Okay, right, right . . . Erm, sorry, *what* did they say, exactly?'

There was quite a long silence. The bustle of Venice Beach passed around them. The sun scorched Maggie's face from the cerulean sky above. Ed tugged at the back of his beanie. 'Well, that's quite a shock,' he said. 'Are they sure? Well, yes . . . Okay, okay. Thanks, Tamsin. I'll call them now if you text me the number . . . Thank you . . . Thanks very much. Bye.'

When Ed turned back to Maggie, he was pale.

'What's going on?' she asked.

'The police have called. I need to call them back. It's not about my watch,' he said, shaking his head and looking bewildered. 'It's about my dad.'

She froze. Her heart stopped in her chest and then jolted to life, pounding in her ears and replacing all the happy, sunny sounds around them.

'Your *dad*?'

Ed's phone now lit up with a text. He clicked on the message, put the phone to his ear and keyed in a number. 'After all this time,' he muttered, 'all this *time*,' while Maggie, cold as ice in the Californian sunshine, stood rooted to the spot.

This time he stepped further away from her as he spoke. She couldn't hear what he was saying. When he had finished the call, he walked the few feet back to her and placed his hand, trembling, on her arm.

'They've found some evidence,' he said, his voice shaky. 'On Southend Pier. And they've put it together with a file they had from years ago. A statement from a woman saying she'd seen Dad arguing with someone at the end of the pier. Another statement, handwritten, not an official one, but it was in the file – God, I don't know, it was the seventies! – saying my dad had had an affair, that the mistress's husband may have had something to do with it. They've investigated. They've come to the conclusion . . . my dad was killed. That he was pushed in the sea at the end of Southend Pier.'

'Oh my god.' Maggie's heart was in her mouth, her ears, her head. It was threatening to explode out of her and land on the boardwalk.

'I'm to call them again later, when I'm back at the hotel.' He pushed off his beanie and rubbed frantically at the top of his head. 'What new evidence, Maggie? What *witness*? I just don't understand.'

'I need to tell you something,' she said, her words a strange buzzing coming out of her. Words that would condemn her. End their story. 'I need to tell you something.' The secret was out. What she'd done. The secret was out, and his dad was dead.

'*Tell* me something? What do *you* need to tell me?'

'I need to tell you,' she repeated. 'Please just let me say it, Ed.'

'You're scaring me.' His eyes were wild. 'What's wrong with you? You look awful.'

A roller-skating girl was suddenly there, about to crash into them. 'Sorry!' she chirped, all teeth and white-blonde hair, and she veered away.

'The person who went to see the police was me,' gabbled Maggie. 'It was me. The unofficial statement. This has happened because of me. It was years ago. I investigated, from a photo . . .'

'What on earth are you talking about?' Ed's voice was shattering. Venice Beach became a kaleidoscope, spinning, spinning around them.

Maggie tried again. 'There was a photo, for one of my Where Are They Now?s, at the *Gazette*. Your dad was in the background, and one of the women in it said they had seen him down at the pier, arguing with someone. And I investigated . . . and I told the police what I'd found . . . what I suspected.'

Ed looked dazed. 'What do you mean, you *investigated*?'

'I asked around. I . . . interviewed people.' She recalled smatterings of the awful twenty minutes with Denise Sullivan in her florid pink sitting room. 'I suspected that Denise Sullivan – who lived on our road – had been having an affair with your dad, and that her angry husband had something to do with Neville's disappearance.'

'And they think he's been *murdered*? I can't believe this, Maggie, that you never told me! This was my *dad*! Why have you never told me?'

'Because I didn't really find anything out!' she insisted. 'I went to the police, but they laughed me out of the station. I knew they wouldn't take a statement – it was so flimsy, it was just my *thoughts*, really – so I wrote them down on a piece of paper and they must have put it in the file. I don't know! I don't know how this happened!'

'You could have said something,' said Ed. He had stepped back from her. He was withdrawing from her, she knew. He had already gone. 'First Michael, and now this. *Secrets*. You should have told me.'

'I'm sorry.'

'You're *sorry*.' He took another step back. 'Sometimes that's just meaningless, Maggie.'

'I would never have done anything to hurt you. I didn't tell you because we weren't in touch for so long, and I didn't want to give you false hope of an answer when there was nothing concrete . . .'

'I need to go,' he said. And, just like that, he turned from her, and he disappeared, right into the crowd, leaving her standing there, alone, in the colourful kaleidoscope of Venice Beach, uncaring and unknowing. *Gone*. And, later that evening, she spotted his face in a different crowd. She saw him at LAX, at the airport, disappearing again into the first-class lounge, and home to Alexia who he married three weeks later, in a tux and a big smile, their happy photo in the *Daily Mail* featuring six cute 'bridesmaid' dogs in pink ribbons.

Ed turned, momentarily, in the doorway of the first-class lounge, when a man brushed past him, knocking his arm, and Maggie saw his wonderful face and he saw her wretched one, by Duty Free, and she said goodbye to him, once again, for they were one eternal goodbye, weren't they, she and Ed?

One forever goodbye.

Chapter Forty-Five

Her rucksack stood in the corner of the room, ready to go. She was sitting on the bed, having got changed into a black halter-neck top and a pair of white culottes, and flicking through the tiny photo album with the green leather cover she had pulled from the rucksack's front pocket.

The album had plastic sleeves, with the photographs tucked behind them. There was a photo of her and Ed on Southend seafront by the railings, looking swept to smithereens by an April wind. Another, in their little house on Brook Street, on the sofa, with their dinners on their laps, which Maggie's dad had taken. Three slightly different shots of the same moment in a nightclub, their arms around each other, 'red eyes' glowing demonically in their laughing faces. A photo of Ed, outside the Palladium, under the portico with the showbiz lights, standing next to Sandra, both smiling so widely they looked like they would burst. Then, a polaroid Ed's bodyguard, Bob, had taken of them in Windsor Great Park, in front of a huge oak tree, doing grinning thumbs-ups. California in 2003 . . . when she'd set up her camera on the table on the decking at the little yellow house in Carmel and snapped them on a sun lounger holding aloft glasses of red wine. Finally, the last in the album, a photograph of a smiling Ed at Venice Beach, in a coral pink t-shirt with a palm tree on it, endless white sand and a dazzling sea his backdrop.

She loved him. She'd loved him when she'd packed that little photo album, calling herself ridiculous for the nostalgia when she was coming to do her hatchet job on him. She'd loved him when she'd seen him sail to the shore on his little skiff, his hand at the mast. She'd loved him when he'd patted that tortoise and called him 'boy'. She'd loved him when he'd done doggy paddle in the lagoon, and when he'd opened Michael's letter and seen the scan of his grandchild.

She had loved Ed since she was fourteen years old. But she was a fool.

Maggie had come to the island to do an interview, launch a digital magazine and deliver a letter, but she had also come for *him*, drawn like a magnet, or a ship pulled on a long rope, across land and sea. And now she had fallen in love with him all over again, and it was a terrible, terrible mistake, as he didn't care about her. She was not his ship. She was not his reason.

She stood up. She needed to walk, and to think. She stepped off the veranda and headed up the path and into the tunnel of rainforest, enjoying the shade and the way it hid her for a little while, and then out on to the beach; breathing in deeply, breathing out hard. She walked and walked. Out on the water, bobbing along on his kayak, was Pa Zayan. He raised a hand to her, and she raised a sad one back. Down on the shoreline, she spotted the little boat that had brought her here – green hull, white sail – which was gently rocking in the frothy surf. Salou, in a red and white bucket hat, was on the deck, holding a rope. Amine was calf-deep in the shallows, examining something in the water.

'Miss Marty!' He clocked her and called over.

'You're early!' she shouted back.

'Hey!' cried Salou from the deck. 'Two hours, and then we take you home!'

She waved vaguely at him. *Home*. She didn't want to go. At home, nothing awaited her. No more love. No more adventure. No more Ed. There would be no more islands to find him on. No more times to see him bobbing out on the sea and have him come to shore. She should not have come looking for Ed Cavanagh. She should not have gone looking for things that were not hers to find.

She set off back to the bungalow. Her rucksack, ready to go. She would simply slip from this place and make her way home. There would be no goodbye. They had already had their last, after all.

Chapter Forty-Six

3 P.M., 5 DECEMBER 2003

Ed was standing at the end of Southend Pier, the cold December wind blasting around him. The collar of his coat was turned up. His woolly hat was pulled down low on his forehead. A tugboat, white and red, chugged disconsolately on the choppy horizon. A child, wrapped to the chin in padded coat and hat and scarf, shivered over an ice lolly as her mother cackled into a mobile phone, her head turned away and her hair whipping across her face.

Maggie was glad of the wind: its slicing and its numbing. She watched Ed, from behind a kiosk selling cockles and mussels, as he stood at the end of the pier and mourned his father. She watched him as he stood in the bracing wind, in his coat and his hat, and said goodbye.

It was quite the story, really, how the police had found out what had happened to Neville Craddock. The whole thing was reported in the *Gazette*. A young policeman, a local lad from Hadleigh, newly recruited to the force, was fishing off Southend Pier one Sunday morning on his weekend off, and, leaning over the edge to retrieve a hook he had dropped, he spotted something stuck in the wide grain of a horizontal plank of the pier. It was a gold chain with large links and a bar in the middle section, on which were engraved two initials: N.C. The policeman, hugely keen, as they often are at the beginning of their careers, read the *Southend Gazette* every week, to see which local crimes had been committed, and had recently read an article (lazy journalism as ever from the *Gazette*) called 'This Week Thirty-Two Years Ago' which described how a young father named Neville Craddock had walked out of his front door one February evening in 1971 and had never come back. Neville had been wearing a pale blue shirt and jeans. Neville had worn a chain with an initialled bar that was prone to falling off, but no one had ever found it.

When he'd returned to the station on Monday morning, the young policeman had asked for the file on Neville Craddock. It wasn't unearthed until July, as somehow it had been sent to another station and there had been a meandering flatfooted route, full of red tape, to get it back (implied with almost gleeful speculation by the *Gazette*). Once in his possession, the policeman was intrigued by a photograph and an informal statement, written on lined paper, by former *Gazette* reporter Maggie Martin, suggesting Neville's affair with a neighbour, Denise Sullivan, and Maggie's unfounded suspicions of the husband, Jerry Sullivan.

Still eager to make his mark, the young policeman took the necklace and made a visit to Mrs Sullivan and was surprised when, faced with a figure of authority (even if that figure of authority was, as she apparently commented, 'only about twelve years old') and her own guilt, clearly festering for so many years, an instant admission came gushing out of her. That, yes, she had been having an affair with Neville Craddock, and, through black tears of mascara and eyeliner, streaming down a chalky face, she told how her late husband had gone to the pub on Valentine's Day 1971, like he always did, and had arrived home at ten. He had left again about twenty past, after the discovery of Denise's affair with her

354

neighbour (she had told Jerry, she'd said, to get a reaction, as it was Valentine's Day, and her husband had not reacted to her in any way for twenty-five years).

Jerry had stormed out of the house, but had sworn blind, on his return, he'd been back to The White Horse to have 'one for the road'. And the young policeman was allowed to have a mooch around the house and the shed in the garden, where he found a grubby old Basildon Bond writing pad stuffed in an earthenware pot and, inside, in childish, angry writing, like a schoolboy forced to write a poem ten minutes before the bell goes, was Jerry Sullivan's letter, printed in reverse on a sheet of blotting paper, to an inmate at Chelmsford prison, dated 12 June 1971, revealing that he had 'done someone in'.

The article in the *Gazette* detailing this story – on page four, no less – told how a diver had gone beneath the pier at the pertinent spot but had found nothing. It concluded with a line of speculation about whether Ed Cavanagh would return to England on the day of the simple town memorial to Southend's lost son, Neville Craddock – a Sunday morning in early December – and whether he would bring a bodyguard with him.

Maggie had watched as a handful of locals had stood about, staring at Ed as he laid a wreath of purple flowers at the end of the windy pier, nudging each other, but they had then wandered away to the pub or the tea shop. She had watched as Ed, his hands entrenched in his long black wool coat pockets, like that coat was keeping him together, stepped right up to the wooden railing and looked out over the water.

'Ed!' she called now. She had watched and waited long enough.

He turned, his cheeks red from the cold. *'Maggie?'*

'Hello,' she said. 'I thought I'd come down.'

'From London? Why would you do that?' His voice was colder than the air between them.

'How was the memorial service?'

'It was nice. It was at the Sacred Heart.'

'That's good. How long are you over for?' She could make out the pier train, somewhere behind her, stuttering to a stop and the doors clunking open.

'Just the weekend.'

There was someone coming towards them, a woman walking up the pier with a white-blonde helmet hairdo, snakes of it flying free as it battled in vain against the wind. Chalky coral lipstick. A faux fur leopard-print coat flapping in the chill wind like she didn't care enough about herself to button it up.

It was Denise Sullivan.

'Hello,' Denise said, when she reached Ed. 'I've been waiting, over by the ghost train, where I could see the end of the pier. I've been waiting until it was quiet.'

'Hello, Denise,' Ed replied.

'I won't beat about the bush,' Denise continued, 'I just wanted to say something to you.' She smiled sadly, prised a straw of white hair from her lipstick and tucked it behind her ear. 'I loved your father. We met at the social club. Well, we'd seen each other around, as neighbours. When England won the World Cup in 1966 there was a street party and he poured some squash for me and I thought he was nice, but wasn't every other man who wasn't my husband?' She laughed a short, hollow laugh. 'And then I worked at the social club, and we got talking, sometimes, when he came to the bar. And I used to walk the dog in the evening, and he started walking, too.'

Ed nodded. Denise extracted another windblown strand of hair from her lipstick.

'We never slept with each other. We just kissed, down by the pier. In our eyes, at least, it wasn't sordid. It was lovely. But Jerry found out about the walks, and the kissing, and that I loved your dad – well, I told him, you probably know that – and he was angry, so angry, because he knew I didn't love *him* and he couldn't bear it, that I loved Neville when I hadn't ever even slept with him. But I never thought he'd *done* anything,' she protested, 'to your dad, although Jerry was a grumpy bastard, and he made my life hell after he found out. I'm afraid I'm one of those silly women who need to have a man in their life to look after, however awful they are.' She shook her head. 'But, anyway, I want you to know I believe your dad was happy when he was with me and don't they count for something, those moments of happiness? I hope they do.' Her voice became choked, her eyes full of tears. 'And I'm so sorry.'

'They do,' said Ed, taking one of Denise's gloved hands. 'I do believe those moments count for something,' he said, also glancing quickly at Maggie and her heart broke for a boy who had lost his dad and never found him again. And for Neville who went out for a walk one winter evening and never came back. And for her and Ed, for whom those moments were now gone forever.

'I'll leave you now,' said Denise. She hesitated. 'Would it be inappropriate to tell you I love you in *Echo Drive*?'

'It wouldn't be inappropriate at all,' Ed said, with a sad, lop-sided smile.

'Well, I do,' she said. 'You brighten up so many of our lives. And you have your father's eyes,' she said, and she turned, and she strode away, her blonde helmet buffeting, towards the early evening lights that were beginning to splutter on along the pier.

Neither Ed nor Maggie spoke for a few moments.

'I'm sorry that your vision of your dad somewhere on a desert island is gone because of me,' Maggie told him finally.

'Don't be. I told you, it was just a stupid fantasy, anyway.' He looked out across the water. He unfastened the top button of his coat and fastened it again. 'Goodbye, Maggie,' he said, and he began to walk away.

'You're going?' she called after him.

'Yes.' He stopped. Looked back over his shoulder. 'I'm going back to Hollywood. Back to my life.'

'Is there nothing more we can say?'

He shrugged. 'I don't think so, Mags. We have too many obstacles. Too many reasons not to be together. I don't think it was ever meant to work, you and me. I just don't think it was.'

There was so much she could say. So much she *wanted* to say. But her heart was like a clam in a shell and the shell was slowly closing. They had ruined it, what they'd had. Both of them. They had ruined it a long time ago and now it was truly over.

'Goodbye, Ed,' she said, and he walked away, without turning back now, and she knew that the love they'd once had was as far away as the grey-green horizon and the old tugboat bobbing upon it. She couldn't imagine a sky that wasn't grey, or a lonely heart that wasn't anchored to the cruel depths of the sea, and she wondered if the sun would ever shine on her again.

Chapter Forty-Seven

4 P.M., ON THE ISLAND

Maggie heard music, from outside the bungalow. Well, not music. The sound of a guitar being tuned up. A vague kind of jamming. At first, she ignored it. Maybe it was from one of the neighbouring bungalows. Maybe Pa Zayan was going in for a bit of impromptu afternoon busking. She tucked her photo album back in the front pocket of her rucksack and zipped it up. After she'd returned from her walk, she'd tortured herself by staring at it for another forty-five minutes, turning the pages slowly and lingering far too long over each photograph.

The twanging of the guitar didn't go away. Now the plucking of its strings, behind her bungalow door, became the near-melodic, lyrical introduction to a piece of music she instantly recognised.

She froze, standing by the rucksack in the corner of the room. Then she crossed the bungalow and opened the door. Ed was sitting on her veranda in his shorts and t-shirt. He had a guitar on his lap.

'Hi,' he said, over the intro to 'Maggie May'.

'*Hi,*' she replied coolly. 'You're wearing eyeliner.'

'It's tree bark.'

'Interesting. Where did you get the guitar?'

'My cupboard. In my shack.'

'What are you doing here?'

'Attempting to make amends.'

'And why would you want to do that?'

'Oh, Maggie,' he sighed. 'Would you just shut up and let me serenade you?'

He launched into the first verse of 'Maggie May', singing in his deep yet sweet tuneful voice and accompanying himself valiantly on the guitar. Apparently, he wanted her to wake up, he had something he wanted to tell her. It was coming into autumn, and he had to return to full-time education . . .

Ed alternated between looking at Maggie with earnest eyes ringed in bark, and down to the guitar to check he'd got the right string. He sang about the sun in the morning revealing the lines on Maggie's face. He shook his head at her, smiling, as if to say, 'No, not you . . .'

His voice was appealing; the guitar playing could use improvement. She stood in the doorway, listening to every word and wondering what was going on here. It had been a long time since he had last sung it to her, a very long time. She remembered the boy with the headband and the swagger and how he had made her feel. She remembered standing in that warm pub garden, on a summer's evening in 1972, and thinking he was amazing. Now here he was, back again in silver curls and the same terrible eyeliner, and he still couldn't play for toffee. But she felt the same, she still felt the same, and she had no idea what that meant for them.

Ed sang about wrecked beds and being kicked in the head. At the corner of her vision, Maggie saw Pa Zayan creeping forward from the bungalow behind and coming to stand at the corner of the veranda, out of Ed's eyeline. He looked quite bemused, but cheerfully tapped his foot in time to the music.

The familiar words of the song soaked into her, the conflicting lyrics of having a heart stolen but never wanting to see a person's face again. But Ed's smile, and the way he was looking at her, made a kind of wretched hope begin to flutter in her chest like the wings of hummingbirds.

Before she realised it, Ed was in the trilling, ascending and descending instrumental close of the song. He gave it his all on the guitar, his tongue between his teeth, for this bit was obviously tricky. Maggie remained in the doorway, her hand on the doorframe in an attempt to anchor her heart. Singing the last of the words with warbling gusto and a look in his eyes that made the blood flood through her veins, Ed trailed off the guitar to nothing, then placed his palm flat on the guitar and shot her a sheepish smile.

'The heart was willing, the musical prowess was weak,' he said.

'It was lovely,' she replied, uncertain.

'You liked it?' From the corner of her eye, Maggie saw Pa Zayan back away with a small bow and disappear to the other bungalow.

'Yes.'

'Good.' He didn't take his eyes from hers. 'I've tried to keep up the guitar, since I've been here. Make sure I don't get out of practice.'

'And was that what that was?' she asked, swallowing nervously. 'Another practice session?'

Ed's gaze remained steady. 'You're right,' he said, after a beat, 'I did send you that postcard so you would come to Mémoire and write a piece on me. So Michael would find out where I was.'

'And you were right about me,' she replied slowly. 'I came here to expose you. To write a damning story about how fame ruins people. I came to let people know you're not who they thought you were. That underneath you're someone else entirely.'

Ed nodded. 'So, I guess we're even,' he said.

Maggie smiled sadly. 'I guess we are.'

'But the thing is,' Ed continued, 'since you rocked up here, I haven't just been thinking about Michael.'

'And since I arrived here,' she echoed, her voice quiet, 'you're not who I thought you were, either. I feel I've really *seen* you.' It was true, she realised. Underneath he *was* someone else entirely. Wasn't he who he used to be?

They looked at each other for a moment, the seeds of apology and forgiveness beginning to be scattered gently between them. 'How *was* Michael?' she asked.

'Good. It was . . . tentative, you know. I'm not going to rush things. Push too hard, too soon. And I know I'm not going to make up for all those years overnight. But it was positive. I'm going to call him again. The baby's due to be born in two months and I'm really hoping we can make some plans.'

'That's fantastic, Ed, really fantastic.' She smoothed her hand down the rustic frame of the doorway.

Ed laid the guitar gently on the wooden slats. 'That rather shaky rendition of "Maggie May" was for our *past,*' he said tenderly, and his eyes were soft as they looked up to hers. 'To celebrate it. To honour it, for all its up and downs. But now I'd like to talk about our present and our future, Mags, if you'll let me.'

Her heart leapt, but she couldn't indulge it, not yet. 'I've been thinking, too,' she said hurriedly. 'But I'd like to talk about the past a little, first, if you'll let *me.*'

'Okay,' he said. He looked like a quizzical little boy, sitting there on the veranda with his guitar by his side.

She thought of their goodbye at the end of the pier, that moment on Venice Beach. How their ending was reached and how their anger, from many years ago, had brought them to this island.

'I'm so sorry,' she began. 'About Michael. That I hurt you by having a relationship with him. I know I could say it was no big deal, that we met by accident, and why not write a piece on him for the newspaper, why not keep up an email correspondence? But if I'm honest with myself, and you, I think there was more to it. I think it was because he's your son. Not only to help him, but so that I could stay connected to you, by being connected to him.' She dropped her eyes to the slats of the veranda.

'Maggie . . .' Ed shook his head. 'Maggie, it's fine. It took me a long time to realise it, but I used my anger about you and Michael as an all-too-handy deflection. If I was focused on being angry about *your* relationship with him, I could avoid focusing on my own . . . *My* relationship with him hurt me way more. All my mistakes. All the things I didn't do . . .'

'But it's okay now.'

'It's okay now.'

'And your dad,' she said hesitantly. 'Your dad.' A shadow of sadness crossed Ed's face, there on the sunlit veranda, but she continued. 'My investigation. What it led to. I'm so sorry about that, too, Ed. I'm so sorry.'

'Oh, Mags,' Ed sighed. The shadow lifted. 'It took me a long time to see that, as well. I was so cold to you about it. So unforgiving. So unforgiving to myself, too. And *angry*. So angry. But being here, on this island, being with you . . . I know now that what happened was a gift to me, as it was able to bring me closure.'

'Closure?'

'Yes, good old American therapy-speak. *Closure*. My dad had been killed. Not *proven*, but extremely likely. All those stupid dreams of mine that he was living on an island like this, Mémoire, lying on a beach with his face tilted to the sun, were finally irrevocably shattered. It was *huge*, what the police found out. But it was the not knowing, for all those years before, that had really destroyed me. What had happened to him? Had he wanted to leave us? Leave *me*? But he hadn't decided to leave. He was taken.' He smiled gently at her. 'So, in a way, you gave him back to me. You gave me closure. Please don't beat yourself up about it. I've got lots of other things in my past I don't feel good about. My bad behaviour, marrying women I didn't love . . . there's a list, really, we could go into, if we wanted to . . .'

'I forgive you for all those things,' Maggie said, and she felt that, in her heart. That she forgave him, and she forgave herself.

'And I forgive you.' The flowers of forgiveness opened their tiny petals wide, their tropical scent sweet filling the air between them and all around.

'I'd already decided to drop the interview. It doesn't matter to me now. Did Baptiste tell you?'

'No.' Ed smiled up at her. 'What he told me was that I was a Hollywood arse and I'd better come and find you before it was too late.' He stood up from the veranda and brushed down his shorts. 'Can we move on now?' he asked her, holding out his hand to take hers. 'Will you come down to the beach with me?'

Chapter Forty-Eight

The sky above them was poster-paint blue. The sun was rich and golden in the last few hours of its reign, toasting the honeyed sand. Ed's skiff was down on the shoreline, sleeping on the sand, lackadaisical waves tickling its underbelly. A simple red striped blanket was on the sand beyond its snout. And, on a wide expanse of sugar-spun beach and formed from what appeared to be a whole pailful of laid-out fishing hooks, was an enormous heart in the sand.

Ed looked giddy. He shrugged like an excited schoolboy. 'I wanted to show you my heart,' he said. 'What do you think?'

'I like your heart.' Hers was drumming in her chest, her pulse rushing to all her nerve endings. It had all the way from Bungalow Marguerite, along the canopied rainforest walk and down here to the beach. 'I like the way you serenade me with your terrible guitar, and I like your heart.'

They were already standing close to each other, but Ed stepped closer still.

'Good. Because *yours* was always what I wanted.' The sun was in his eyes and Maggie could see the flecks of green in his irises. 'Since you were a scrappy kid sitting on a wall, and I was a cocky teenager bowling down the street with my mates. Since you walked into a pub garden in 1971 with a box of glam rock transfers. Since you rocked up on this island, yesterday, a brighter light than the sun.'

'What's brought this on?'

'Realising I've been an absolute idiot. Realising what's been missing in my life, after all these years.' His face, in the dazzling sunlight, looked young again. Full of hope and promise and excitement. 'When I came to this island, I found my old self. And when I got my old self back, all I needed was you. But even before that . . .' He looked hesitant. 'Even before that I think I always wanted you to rescue me. Maybe *that's* why I sent you that postcard.' He ran a hand through his silver curls, looked into her eyes. 'Deep down.' He exhaled. 'Deep down, I *know* that's why I sent you the postcard.'

'Deep down that's why I hoped you'd sent it.' She stared at him for a moment. Then, she stepped even nearer to him, scooped a silver curl from the side of his face and tucked it back into the others. 'I've been wanting to do that for the longest time,' she said softly.

'I've been wanting to hold you.' He snaked his arms around her waist and pulled her in close to him. She could feel his heart beating in time behind the cotton of his t-shirt. She could feel his breath, soft on her cheek as he leant into her. He brushed his mouth against her ear.

'I've missed you,' she whispered, succumbing to his touch, her mouth dry but her senses roaring around her body, alive, alert. 'Thank heaven I found you again.'

'I've missed you, too,' he murmured, nuzzling his lips into her neck, sketching his hand up her back. 'We belong together, Maggie May. I love you. *I love you.* I've never stopped loving you.'

He kissed her now, softly on the lips, and then firmer and harder and with some abandon, and everything, everything surged through her body – all their history and their love. All the hours and the days they had ever spent in each other's arms. The Maggie and Ed they used to be, and the Maggie and Ed they were now, and could be. They kissed and kissed, wrapped in each other, standing on that beach, the sun beating steadily down on their backs and the soft waves of the Indian Ocean their subtle symphony.

'Oh god, can we sit down?' Ed murmured eventually. 'My knees are about to give way.'

Laughing, they lowered themselves on to the blanket, flanking their bodies close to one another. Holding each other tight. A tangle of heat and sand and hope and forgiveness and love. They kissed and kissed again. Maggie felt like she could kiss Ed forever, hold him forever, love him forever.

'I love you,' she whispered, between kisses. They were half-off the blanket now, their bodies pressed into the warm sand. 'I always have. I have loved you in all the moments I've ever spent with you, and every lonely hour I've been without you.'

'And I will love you in every moment we have left in this life,' Ed murmured. He gently pulled a strand of sandy hair back from her face and gazed into her eyes, long and deep. 'What do you reckon?' he asked. 'Are we ready to make space for each other? In our lives? I don't want to be lonely any more.'

'Neither do I. I want us to make space for each other,' she urged, tracing a finger down his forearm. 'I'm ready. Where do you think we should love each other?'

'It's written in fishing hooks.' He grinned, a lopsided grin. 'It has to be a beach, don't you think? Your place or mine?'

Her eyes widened. 'The English seaside or the Californian coast?' she mused. 'Decisions, decisions . . .' she said slowly. 'But I think I'm ready for a little bit of glitz in my life.'

'Really?'

'Yes.'

'Are you saying you'll come live with me?'

She nodded. And he laughed and held her more tightly than she had ever been held. They were tangled creatures in each other's arms, a film of sand coating them like a pair of sugar-dusted gingerbread men.

'Thank you. Thank you,' he whispered. 'But I don't want to go home just yet. Stay with me,' he urged. 'Share my shack and my single bed? At least for a few more weeks? Let's make plans. Let's love each other. We can even do the interview, if you like? How would *Supernova* like to hear about our decades-long love story? Bit of a scoop, wouldn't you say?'

She felt the island sun on her back and the joy in her heart, and she said, 'I'd say it was the biggest scoop of all,' before kissing him again.

Epilogue

April 2018

Three people were waiting for them at the barrier in the arrivals hall at Los Angeles Airport when they arrived, tired but excited, after their long flight. A tall man with dark curls, beaming from ear to ear. A woman with giant hoop earrings and an enormous smile. And a tiny baby in a pale pink sling, nestled to her mother's chest.

'Hello, Dad,' said the younger man, stepping forward.

'Hello, son,' said the father.

Maggie nodded at Ed, and they let go of each other's hands, held so tightly since they had left the island to make this journey. They exchanged a look full to the brim of love, for love was all they knew again, and love was all they hoped for.

Maggie had phoned Eloise from Doha airport. She'd told her of her plans and had made new ones with her daughter, to be carried out in the Californian sun, later in the year. It seemed there was much to look forward to – including a *non*-retirement, as Maggie had phoned Simone, too, and let her know she wasn't ready for her swan song, that she wanted to continue, from wherever she was. Simone had been as delighted at that news as she was at the love story between Ed Cavanagh and Maggie Martin, both formerly of

Southend in Essex, which would be launching the digital version of her magazine.

Ed opened his arms wide and Michael, his daughter-in-law and his brand-new granddaughter moved forward to let him envelop them in an enormous hug.

'Welcome home,' Maggie heard Michael murmur delightedly, from somewhere inside it.

Yes, welcome home, she whispered to herself, as she was invited to join them in their laughing, welcome embrace. *I know we're going to be really happy here.*

ACKNOWLEDGEMENTS

The Hours of You was huge fun to write. Who wouldn't want to spend their time on a beautiful desert island every day? And I really loved spending all those hours on the island of Mémoire with Maggie and Ed. But, as I was not the only one working hard on bringing this story to you, I have a few people to thank!

First, my editors at Lake Union, and the two fantastic Victoria's – Victoria Pepe and Victoria Oundjian – thank you both for your tremendous care, attention and support. I am so grateful to you both. Also, to Caroline Hogg, for your brilliant diligence and championship – your meticulousness is truly appreciated! I'd also like to thank the copyeditor, proofreaders, cover designer, marketing staff and everyone behind the scenes at Lake Union for this book's production.

Thank you, as always, to Diana Beaumont, my agent, a shining star and the best agent a writer could hope for. Thanks for choosing me!

Thank you to Mary Torjussen for taking this mad journey with me and being my virtual WhatsApp colleague each day, from our 'offices' on the Wirral and in the Essex countryside.

To Matthew and the children, thank you, once again, for putting up with me!

Lastly, to my readers. You are what keeps me sitting at my desk and putting in all the hours doing something I love. Thank you!

ABOUT THE AUTHOR

Fiona Collins grew up in an Essex village and, after stints in Hong Kong and London, returned to the Essex countryside where she lives with her husband and three children. She has a degree in Film and Literature and has had many former careers including TV presenting in Hong Kong, being a traffic and weather presenter for BBC local radio and as a film and TV extra.

Follow the Author on Amazon

If you enjoyed this book, follow Fiona Collins on Amazon to be notified when the author releases a new book!
To do this, please follow these instructions:

Desktop:

1) Search for the author's name on Amazon or in the Amazon App.
2) Click on the author's name to arrive on their Amazon page.
3) Click the 'Follow' button.

Mobile and Tablet:

1) Search for the author's name on Amazon or in the Amazon App.
2) Click on one of the author's books.
3) Click on the author's name to arrive on their Amazon page.
4) Click the 'Follow' button.

Kindle eReader and Kindle App:

If you enjoyed this book on a Kindle eReader or in the Kindle App, you will find the author 'Follow' button after the last page.